Obedient to Their Laws...

Private Brother Pyrrhos McKenzie spat, coughed, spat again. The fluid from his lungs seemed to be about half blood and half thick clear *something* that he didn't want to think about. Everyone else in the bunker was dead, he thought—Ken when the gas came, and Leontes with a bullet through the face in the last attack ...

The radio was squawking, but there was no time to listen to that. He stumbled two steps to the firing slit and collapsed over the gatling. The coughing went on a long time, but afterwards he felt a little better, and blinked his eyes clear while his hands fumbled ... He took up the slack on the spade grips, and the electric motor whined, spinning the barrels with blurring speed. His thumbs rested on the firing buttons on top of the grips.

God, there's a lot of them. Crawling towards him ... He depressed the muzzles, stroked the buttons. *Brrrrrrrt. Brrrrrrrt.* The recoil surged in his arms, and he coughed again; but rebels dropped, killed, sawn in half by the fire ... *Brrrrt.* They were shouting out there, or screaming, or something. Trying to crawl closer. *Brrrrrrrt.*

Leonidas. Megistias. Dieneces. The heroes of Thermopylae, he'd been a little bored learning that in school. *I suppose they didn't want to die either*, he thought with a sudden cold lucidity; his knees felt weaker, and the corners of his mouth were leaking. *Alpheus. Maro. Eurytus.*

Another burst. Another, swinging wide to cover the full arc of the bunker's semicircular firing slit ... More rebels down, others trying to crawl backward, some dragging their wounded.

Demaratus the lesser. Deonates—

GO TELL THE SPARTANS

GO TELL THE SPARTANS

JERRY POURNELLE
S. M. STIRLING

BAEN BOOKS

GO TELL THE SPARTANS

This is a work of fiction. All the characters and events portrayed in this book are fictional, and any resemblance to real people or incidents is purely coincidental.

A Baen Books Original

Baen Publishing Enterprises
P.O. Box 1403
Riverdale, NY 10471

ISBN: 0-671-72061-9

Cover art by Keith Parkinson

First Printing, June 1991

Printed in the United States of America

Distributed by Simon & Schuster
1230 Avenue of the Americas
New York, NY 10020

FOR THE THREE HUNDRED

Go tell the Spartans, passerby,
That here obedient to their laws we lie.

Distributed by Simon & Schuster
1230 Avenue of the Americas
New York, NY 10020.

PROLOGUE

The history of the 21st century was dominated by two developments, one technical and one social.

The technical development was, of course, the discovery of the Alderson Drive a decade after the century began. Faster-than-light travel released mankind from the prison of Earth, and the subsequent discovery of inhabitable planets made interstellar colonization well nigh inevitable; but the development of interstellar colonies threatened great social and political instability at a time when the international political system was peculiarly vulnerable. Whether through some hidden mechanism or a cruel coincidence, mankind's greatest technical achievements came at a time when the educational system of the United States was in collapse; at a time when scientists at Johns Hopkins and the California Institute of Technology were discovering the fundamental secrets of the universe, scarcely a mile from these institutions over a third of the population was unable to read and write, and another third was most charitably described as under-educated.

The key social development was the rise and fall of the U.S./U.S.S.R. CoDominium. Begun before the turn of the Millennium, the CoDominium was a natural outgrowth of the Cold War between the Superpowers. When the Cold War ended, the European nations once known in International Law as "Great Powers" retained some of the trappings of

1

international sovereignty, but had become client states of the U.S.; while the Soviet Union, shorn of its external empire, retained both its internal empire and great military power, including the world's largest land army, fleet, and inventory of nuclear warheads and delivery systems.

In the last decade of the 20th century both the United States and the Soviet Union experimented with foreign policies that left the rest of the world free to compete with the former Superpowers. It soon became clear, if not to the world's peoples, at least to political leaders of the U.S. and U.S.S.R., that the resulting disorder was worse than the Cold War had ever been. It was certainly more unpredictable, and thus more dangerous for the politicians, who had, under the Cold War, evolved systems to ensure their tenure of power and office. The political masters of the two nations did not at first openly state that it would be far better to divide the world into spheres of influence than to allow smaller powers to rise to prominence; but the former United Nations Security Council easily evolved into a structure which could not only keep the peace, but prevent any third party from challenging the principle of superpower supremacy. . . .

The 20th century social analyst and philosopher Herman Kahn would hardly have been surprised by this evolution. One of Kahn's speculations had been that the natural form of human government was empire, and the natural tendency of an empire was to expand, there being no natural limit to that expansion save running up against another empire of equal or greater strength.

There had been exceptions to that rule, the most notable being the United States of America, which, after the "manifest destiny" period of imperial expansion, attempted to settle into peaceful isolation. That repose was shattered by the latter half of the 20th century, when the United States was called upon to change its very nature, first to meet the threat of National Socialism, then of Soviet Imperialism. Kahn postulated in 1959 that in order to resist the Soviet Empire, the United States would be required to make such fundamental transformations of its republican structure as virtually to become an empire itself; and that having made the transformation, the end of the Cold War would not be sufficient to undo the change. He was, of course, not alone in that prediction, which proved largely to be true. Kahn did not live to see the CoDominium, but it would hardly have surprised him.

Of course no one predicted that the rapid development of faster-than-light space travel would rapidly follow the formation of the CoDominium. However, once the Alderson Drive was perfected, few disputed that there had to be some kind of universal government; and while few would, given free choice, have chosen the CoDominium for that role, there was a surprising consensus that the CoDominium was better than anarchy.

As the 21st century came to a close, it was obvious to most analysts that the CoDominium was doomed. There was widespread speculation on what would replace it. Astute observers looked to the CoDominium Fleet to provide the nucleus of stability around which a new order might be built, and they were not disappointed. What was surprising, though, was the role played by the Dual Monarchy of Sparta.

Sparta was not founded as an imperial power, and indeed its rulers explicitly rejected the notion of either ambitions or responsibilities extending beyond their own planetary system; yet when the CoDominium finally collapsed, no planetary nation was more important in building the new order.

As with any complex event, many factors were important in the transformation of Sparta from a nation founded by university professors seeking to establish the good society to the nucleus of what is formally called the Spartan Hegemony and which in all but name is the first interstellar empire; but analysts are universally agreed that much of the change can be traced to the will and intent of one man, Lysander I, Collins King of Sparta. It remains for us to examine how Lysander, originally very much in agreement with the Spartan Founders that the best policy for Sparta would be an armed neutrality on the Swiss model, came to embrace the necessity of empire.

—From the preface to *From Utopia to Imperium: A History of Sparta from Alexander I to the Accession of Lysander*, by Caldwell C. Whitlock, Ph.D. (University of Sparta Press, 2120).

CHAPTER ONE

Crofton's Essays and Lectures in Military History (2nd Edition)

Professor John Christian Falkenberg II:
Delivered at Sandhurst, August 22nd, 2087

In the last decades of the 20th century, many predicted that the battlefield of the future would be one of swift and annihilating violence, ruled by an elaborate technology. Instead, in one of history's many illustrations of the Law of Unintended Consequences, the 21st century saw military technology enter an era of stalemate. Cheap and accurate handheld missiles swept the air above the battlefield clear of manned aircraft; railguns, lasers and larger rockets did likewise for the upper atmosphere and near space.

The elaborate dance of countermeasures made many sophisticated electronic devices so much waste weight; tailored viruses made networks of linked computers a recipe for battlefield chaos. Paradoxically, many of the most sophisticated weapons could only be used against opponents who were virtually unarmed. By freezing technological research, the CoDominium preserved this situation like a fly in amber.

Beyond Earth, the rarity and patchy development of industry exaggerated these trends in the colony worlds. CoDominium Marine expeditionary forces often operated at the end of supply lines many months long, with shipping space too limited for heavy equipment, on thinly settled planets where a paddle-wheel steamboat might represent high technology. The Marines—and still more the independent mercenary companies—have been forced to become virtually self-sufficient. Troops travel scores of light-years by starship, then march to battle on their own feet, and their supplies may be carted by mules. Artillery is priceless but scarce, and tanks so rare a luxury that the intervention of half a dozen might well decide a campaign. Infantry and the weapons they carry on their backs; machine guns and mortars and light rockets, have come into their own once more. Apart from a few flourishes, body armor and passive nightsight goggles, the recent campaigns on Thurstone and Diego showed little that would have puzzled soldiers of the British Empire fighting the Boer War two centuries ago.

*   *   *

TANITH:

"Battalions, Attention!"

The noon sun of Tanith beat down unmercifully as Falkenberg's Mercenary Legion stood to parade in the great central square of the regiment's camp; the stabilized earth was a dun red-brown under the orange haze above. Behind the reviewing stand stood the Colonel's quarters; behind that the houses of the Company Officer's Line, then the wide street that separated them from Centurion's Row and the yellow rammed-earth barracks beyond. The jungle began just outside the dirt berm that surrounded the camp; a jungle that would reclaim the parade ground and all the huts in a single growing season once the hand of man was removed. The smell of that jungle filled the air, like spoiled bread and brewing beer and compost, heavy with life and rot. A thick gobbling roar boomed through the still muggy air, the cry of a Weems Beast in the swamps below the hill.

"Report!"

"First Battalion all present or accounted for, sir!"

"Second Battalion all present, sir!"

Men and women stood to rigid attention as the ritual continued. There had been a time when Peter

Owensford found it difficult not to laugh at the parade ceremonies, originally intended to show Queen Anne's Mustermasters that the colonels had in fact raised and equipped regiments that could pass muster; but he had learned better. In those days colonels owned their regiments as property. *And it's not much different now. . . .*

"Sound Officer's Call," the Adjutant ordered. Trumpet notes pealed, and the Legion's officers, accompanied by guidon bearers, trooped forward to the reviewing stand. This too was ritual, once designed to show that the officers were properly uniformed and equipped. *And I may be the only one here who knows that*, Owensford thought. *Except for Falkenberg.*

"Attention to orders!" Sergeant Major Calvin's voice sounded even more gravelly through the amplifier pickup in his collar. He read through routine orders. Then: "Captain Peter Owensford, front and center!"

And this is it. Peter marched out to face the Adjutant. Sweat trickled down his flanks under the blue and gold parade tunic, from his forehead beneath the white kepi with its neck-flap.

"Sir."

Captain Amos Fast returned Owensford's salute. "By order of the Regimental Council of the Legion, Captain Peter Owensford is hereby promoted to the rank of major and assigned command of Fifth Battalion."

Peter Owensford felt his stomach clench as he stepped forward another pace and saluted again. Colonel Falkenberg returned the salute and held out his hand. It was impossible to read his expression.

"Congratulations," Falkenberg said. A slight smile creased the thin line of Falkenberg's mouth below the neatly clipped mustache. Peter had long ago learned that it was a smile that could indicate anything. *But Oh, beware my Colonel, when my Colonel grows polite. . . .* Owensford took the proffered hand in his.

"Thank you, sir," he said. Captain Fast stepped forward with the new rank-tabs on a cloth-covered board. Owensford felt the regimental adjutant's fingers remove the Captain's pips from his shoulderboards, replace the five small company-grade stars of a senior captain with the single larger star of a major. It felt heavier, somehow . . . absurd.

"Congratulations, sir," Fast said, smiling as well.

It felt odd to outrank him; Fast had been with the Colonel back when the Legion was the 42nd CoDominium Marines. *Not that I really do. He's still Adjutant, whatever the pay grades. And Falkenberg's friend.*

Owensford swallowed and stepped back a precise two paces; saluted the Colonel, did a quarter-turn and repeated the gesture to the Legion's banner in the midst of the color-party, trumpeter and standard-bearer and honor guard. He swallowed again at the lump in his throat as he did a quick about-face. It was the sudden shout from the ranks ahead that surprised him into missing a half-step.

"*Fifth! Three cheers for Major Owensford!*"

"HIP-HIP *HOORAY!*"

The sound crashed back from the walls of the buildings surrounding the parade square, and Owensford felt the top of his ears reddening. When he found out who was responsible for this he'd—*do absolutely nothing.* He grinned to himself behind a poker face, taking up his position in front of the battalion. *His* battalion, now. Not as captain-in-command of a provisional unit, but *his.*

His responsibility. The weight on his epaulets turned crushing.

Sergeant Major Calvin's voice continued:

"Attention to orders. Fifth Battalion will be ready for transport to embarkation at 0900 hours tomorrow. Remainder of Regiment will continue preparations for departure as per schedule." There was a quiet flurry of activity around the command group.

"Regiment—"

The command echoed from the subordinate units:

"Battalion—"

"Company—"

"Ten' '*hut!*"

"Pass in Review!"

The pipe band struck up "Black Dougal's Lament." The color party followed them out into the cleared lane between the ranked troops and the Colonel, marching at the slow double longstep that the CoDominium Marines had inherited from the French Foreign Legion . . . and now Falkenberg's Mercenary Legion had inherited from *them*. How many of the forty-four hundred soldiers on this square had been with the Colonel in the 42nd, he wondered? Perhaps a thousand, the core of senior commanders and NCOs. A few specialists and technicians. And of course some long service privates who had been up and back down the ladder of rank a dozen times. Not Peter Owensford; he had been recruited out of the losing side on Thurstone, another planet the CoDominium had abandoned. Not Fuller, the Colonel's pilot. New men and old, the Regiment went on; the traditions remained, just as the Regiment remained. Would after the last trooper in it now was dead or retired—

Even after the Colonel was gone?

The color party had passed the Colonel, dipping the banner to the commander's salute, then turned at the far end of the parade ground to pass before the assembled battalions. It swung by in jaunty blue and gold, the campaign ribbons and medals fluttering from the crossbar, the gilt eagle flaring its wings above. Hadley, Thurstone, Makassar, Haven . . . Tanith as well, now.

Owensford came to attention and saluted the colors; behind him the noncom's voices rang out:

"*Pree*-sent *arms!*"

Five thousand boots lifted and crashed down, an earthquake sound. Owensford had heard people sneer at a soldier's readiness to die for pieces of cloth. *For symbols*, he thought. *For what they symbolize.*

"Battalion Commanders, retire your battalions."

* * *

SPARTA:

The moon Cythera had set, and the Spartan night was cool; it smelled of turned earth and growing things, the breeze blowing up from the fields below. Skida Thibodeau snapped down the face shield of her helmet, and the landscape sprang out in silvery brightness. The two-story adobe ranchhouse set in its lawn, barns, stables, outbuildings and bunkhouse; cultivated fields beyond, watered by the same stream that turned the turbine of the microhydro station. Very successful for a fairly new spread in the mountain and basin country of the upper Eurotas Valley. Shearing and holding pens for sheep and beefalo, although the vaqueros would be mostly out with the herds this time of year. Irrigated alfalfa, fields of wheat and New Washington cornplant, and a big vineyard just coming into bearing.

The owners had put up the extra bunkhouse for the laborers needed, hired right off the landing shuttles in Sparta City because they were cheap and a start-up ranch like this needed to watch the pennies. *A mistake*, Skida thought. And they had taken on a dozen guards, because things had gotten a little rough up here in the hills. She grinned beneath the face shield; that was an even worse mistake.

Trusting, she thought, reaching back for the signal lamp and looking at the chronometer on her left wrist.

0058, nearly time.

Very trusting they were here on Sparta, compared to someone who had grown up in the slums of Belize City, a country and a place forgotten and rotting in its Caribbean backwater. Even more trusting than the nuns at the Catholic orphanage who had taught her to read; she had been only nine when she realized there was nothing for her there. Runner for a gang at ten, mistress to the gang leader at twelve . . . the look on his face the day she shopped him to a rival was one of her happier memories. That deal had given her enough capital to skip to Mayopan on the border and set up on her own, running anything that needed moving—drugs, stolen antiquities from the Mayan cities, the few timber trees left in the cut-over jungle—while managing a hotel and cathouse in town.

0100. She pointed the narrow-beam lantern at the squat corner tower of the ranchhouse and clicked it twice. With the shield, she could see the figure who waved an arm there.

"Two-knife," she said to the man beside her. The big Mayan grunted and disappeared down the slope to ready the others. *Good man*, she thought. The only one who had stayed with her when Garcia sold her out and she ended up on a CoDo convict ship. Well worth the extra bribe money to get him onto Sparta with her.

Whump. The transmitter dish on the tower went over with a rending crash. No radio alarm to the Royal Spartan Mounted Police. *Whump*. The faint lights that shone through the windows went out as the transformer blew up in a spectacular shower of sparks. That would take out the electrified wire, searchlights and alarm.

Men boiled out of the guard barracks—to drop as muzzle flashes stabbed from behind; it had been more economical to buy only half of them. No need to use the mortar or the other fancy stuff.

"Follow me! *¡Vámonos, compadres!*" Skida shouted, rising and leaping down the slope with her rifle held across her chest.

Her followers rose behind her and flung themselves forward with a howl. *Fools*, she thought. All men were fools, and fought for foolish things. Words, words like *macho* or *honor* or *liberty*.

They were into the house grounds before rifle muzzles spat fire from the second-story windows. Some of the attackers fell, and others went to ground to return fire. Squads fanned out to their assigned targets, dark figures against darkness. Skida dove up the stairs to the veranda and rolled across to slap a stickymine against the boards of the main door, then rose to flatten herself against the wall beside it. Two-knife was on the other side; they waited while the plastique blew the door in with a flash and *crump,* then leaped through to land in a crouch. Her rifle and his light machine gun probed at the corners. The entrance chamber was empty; it was a big room, a hallway with stairs leading up. Pictures on the walls, books, couches and carpets and smell of cleanliness and wax under the sharp chemical stink of explosives.

Skida Thibodeau is no fool, she thought, motioning Two-knife toward the stairs. The firing was coming from the upper level; she covered him, ready to snap-shoot as he padded forward readying a grenade. *No fool who fights for words.*

Someday *she* was going to have a house even finer than this, and a good deal else besides. And it would all be nice and legal.

Because she would be making the laws.

*   *   *

TANITH:

"I still think I should be going with you, Colonel," Owensford said.

Falkenberg's office was hot. There was precious little air conditioning within the Legion's encampment: a few units for the hospital, another for essential equipment. The command center, because it might be important to think clearly and quickly without distractions. None for the Colonel's home, study or office.

The overhead fan stirred the wet air into languid motion, and Major Peter Owensford gratefully accepted the glass of gin and tonic proffered by Falkenberg's orderly. Ice tinkled; the sound was a little different with most of the familiar office furniture gone. All that remained was the field-desk, the elaborate carvings of battle scenes disguising highly functional electronics. Without the filing cabinets the fungus growing in the corners showed acid green and livid purple, with a wet sheen like the innards of a slaughtered beast.

"I'd like nothing better," Falkenberg said. "But the men will feel a lot better about going to New Washington, knowing the families are safe on Sparta. They trust you. One thing, Major. Nothing is ever as easy as it looks."

He looked up. "You're anticipating trouble?" The Colonel's face was as unreadable as ever, but Falkenberg did not waste words. Theoretically, the Fifth Battalion's mission was training Field Force regiments of regular troops for the embryonic Royal Spartan Army. There were said to be some bandits on Sparta, but not enough to be a real threat. "Any special reason for that, sir? I thought this was a training command. Troop exercises, staff colleges. Cakewalk."

Falkenberg shrugged. "No battle plan ever survives contact with the enemy. And don't kid yourself, Major. The Spartans have enemies, even if they're not telling us much about them."

"Has Rottermill—"

"Intelligence has nothing you don't know about," Falkenberg said. "But the Spartans aren't paying our prices without good reasons." He shrugged. "And maybe I'm suspicious over nothing. We do have a good reputation; hiring us to set up their national forces makes sense. Still, I have an odd feeling—pay attention to your hunches, Peter Owensford. Like as not, if you get a strong hunch, your subconscious is trying to tell you something."

"Yes—sir." *First names in the mess, except for the Colonel, but Major Savage calls him John Christian. I never heard anyone call him John. His wife must have—maybe not in public.* Peter had never met Grace Falkenberg, and none of the Colonel's oldest friends ever spoke of her.

Falkenberg touched a control in a drawer and the pearly gray surface of the desk blinked into a holographic relief map of Sparta's inhabited continent. "The latest word."

Owensford leaned forward to stare at the maps, hoping they'd tell him something he didn't already know. He'd memorized everything in the Legion's data base, and spent countless evenings with Prince Lysander. Not that it was so difficult spending time with the Prince. Lysander was a good lad, a bit naive, but he'd outgrow that. *And how does it feel to know that one day your word will be law to a whole planet?*

Sparta. A desirable planet. Gravity too high, day too short, but more comfortable than Tanith. One big serpentine-shaped major continent, three times the area of North America, and a scattering of islands ranging from the size of Australia down to flyspecks. The inhabited portions were around a major inland sea about the size of the Mediterranean, in the south. Originally slated as a CoDominium prison-planet, then leased out to a rather eccentric group of American political idealists on condition that they take in involuntary colonists swept up by BuReloc.

"Colonel, I am surprised at how much rebel activity there is," Owensford said. "It's much better run than the average autonomous planet these days. At least I get that impression from Prince Lysander."

Falkenberg sipped at his drink. "Problems of success." His finger tapped Sparta City, on a bay toward the eastern end of the Aegean Sea. "They've managed to keep the population of their capital down."

About two hundred fifty thousand, out of a total

three million. They had both seen planets where ninety percent of the people were crammed into ungovernable slum-settlements around the primary spaceport.

"But that means a lot of population in the outback." Falkenberg swept his hand across the map. "It's pretty easy to live there, too. Not much native land-life, so the Package worked quite well. All too well, perhaps." The Standard Terraforming Package included everything from soil-bacteria and grass seeds to rabbits and foxes; where the native ecology was suitable it could colonize whole continents in a generation. "There's even a fairly substantial trade in hides and tallow from feral cattle and such. Scattered ranches, small mines—plentiful minerals, but no large concentrations—poor communications, not enough money for good satellite surveillance, even."

Owensford nodded. "About like the Old West, sans Indians," he said. "You think some of the bandit activity is political?"

"Of course it's political. By definition, any large coordinated action is political. But if you mean connected with off-planet forces, possibly not. Fleet intelligence says no, anyway. Of course Sparta is a long way away." The Legion had strong, if clandestine, links to Sergei Lermontov, Grand Admiral of the CoDominium Fleet.

"Mostly it's insurrection, which can't be too big a surprise. The involuntary colonists and convicts Sparta gets are a cut above the usual scrapings. They'll be unhappy about being sent to Sparta. Ripe for political organization, and when there's an opportunity, a politician will find it."

BuReloc had been shipping the worst troublemakers off Earth for two generations now . . . *except for the Grand Senators*, Owensford thought mordantly. Earth could not afford more trouble. The CoDominium had kept the peace since before his grandfather's birth, the

United States and Soviet Union acting in concert to police a restive planet. The cost had been heavy; an end to technological progress, as the CoDo Intelligence services suppressed research with military implications . . . which turned out to be all research.

For the United States the price of empire had proved to be internal decay; the dwindling core of Taxpayers grimly entrenched against the swelling misery of the Citizens in their Welfare Islands, kept pacified by arbitrary police action and subsidized drugs. Convergence with the Soviets even as nationalist hatred between the two ruling states paralyzed the CoDominium.

By the time they destroy each other, there won't be any real difference at all.

They. Them. The thought startled him; he had been born American and graduated from West Point. *Legio Patria Nostra,* he quoted to himself. *The Legion is our Fatherland.*

"Yes, I expect most of the deportees who make it to Sparta bribed the assignment officers," Owensford said. Which indicated better than average resources, of money or determination or intelligence. There were planets like Thurstone or Frystaat or Tanith where incoming deportees ended up in debt-peonage that was virtual slavery. A few like Dalarna where the Welfare provisions were as generous as on Earth, though God alone knew how long *that* would last. On Sparta able-bodied newcomers had the same civil rights as the old voluntary settlers, and the same options of working or starving.

"So," Falkenberg said, "I don't have anything specific, but something doesn't feel right. And Sparta is just too damned important to Lermontov's plan."

"Our plan," Owensford said carefully.

Falkenberg shrugged. "If you like."

"I thought you were an enthusiast—the Regimental Council approved it, mostly on your insistence."

"Correct. Don't misunderstand," Falkenberg said. "Lermontov is our patron. Whatever the problems with this scheme, we don't have anything better—so we act as if it's going to work and do what we have to do for it."

"But you're not happy even so."

Falkenberg shrugged. "We don't control Sparta, and it isn't our home. I'd be happier with a base we do control—but we don't have one. So we go on putting out fires for the Grand Admiral."

Owensford made a noncommittal sound; Grand Admiral Lermontov's private policy-making was a dangerous game. Essential when the Russki-American clashes paralyzed the Grand Senate, but dangerous nonetheless. Falkenberg's Legion had defended Lermontov's interests for decades, and that too was dangerous.

"Unfortunately, putting out fires isn't enough anymore," Falkenberg said. "The CoDominium is dying. When it dies, Earth will die with it; but I like to think we've bought enough time for civilization to live outside the Solar System. The Fleet can't protect civilization and order without a base."

"And Sparta looks to be it."

"It's the best we have," Falkenberg said. He shrugged. "Who knows, we may find a home on Sparta. People don't usually have much use for the mercenaries they hire, but the Spartans may be different. Given time, who knows? Lermontov doesn't expect things to come apart for ten years, twenty if we're lucky. When the crash comes it's important to have Sparta in good shape."

He paused, finished his drink and frowned at the rapidly melting ice cubes in the bottom of the glass. "I suspect it will take luck to keep things going ten more years."

Peter nodded slowly. "Whitlock's report. You put a lot of confidence in him—"

"It's been justified so far. Peter, what's important is

that Sparta stays committed to the Plan, that they see us—the Regiment, and the Fleet, and the rest of us—as part of their solution and not more problems. Otherwise we'd end up with another insular regional power like Frystaat or Dayan or Xanadu, not a seed-crystal of . . . call it Empire for lack of anything better."

Owensford chuckled. "Colonel, are you saying the future of civilization is in my hands?"

Falkenberg grinned slightly, but he didn't answer.

"All right, why me?"

"An honest question," Falkenberg said. "Because you'll get the job done. You won't be ashamed to take advice. Just remember, you won't be alone in this."

"I hope not—John Christian. Who else is in on this conspiracy?"

"Not so much a conspiracy as people who think alike. An alliance. Incidentally, including some people from our side. I've just got word, Colonel Slater will reach Sparta about the same time you do. You'll remember him."

"Yes, sir."

Falkenberg smiled thinly. "Don't worry, he's not there to outrank you. Hal's mission is to set up the Spartan War College."

"He's recovered, then?" Lt. Col. Hal Slater had been shot up badly enough that he'd been forced to retire from the Legion and go back to Earth for therapy.

"Well, maybe not completely," Falkenberg said. "But enough that he can command a war academy. Hal even managed to get himself a Ph.D. in military history from Johns Hopkins while the medicos were putting him back together."

"He was with you a long time—"

Falkenberg nodded. "Since Arrarat. Before I was posted to the Forty-second. I have a request."

"Request, sir?"

"I'd like to swap you a company commander.

George Slater for Brainerd. Only you'll have to ask, I wouldn't want it thought I'd set this up myself."

"No problem. I'd rather have Hal Slater's son than Henry in a training command anyway."

"Right. Thank you."

Owensford looked away in embarrassment. Falkenberg didn't often ask for favors. *Hal Slater must be his oldest friend, now that I think of it.*

"As to the conspiracy," Falkenberg said, "there aren't any secret passwords, nothing like that. Just people who think alike. Lermontov and his immediate staff. Most of the Grant family. The Blaines, although they hope the CoDominium will survive the collapse, and they work in that direction. The Leontins." Falkenberg took a message cube out of a drawer. "The file name is BIGPLAN. The password is 'carnelian.' Don't forget that the file erases itself if you try to access it with the wrong password. Study it on your way. Then erase it."

"Yes, sir. Carnelian."

"The most important allies from your point of view are Prince Lysander and his father. His Majesty Alexander Collins First was one of Admiral Lermontov's first partners."

Owensford nodded. Sparta had a dual monarchy like the ancient Greek state. There were two royal families, the Collinses and the Freedmans; three generations away from being ordinary families of American college professors, but any royal line had to start somewhere. It was a change from the usual lucky soldier as a founder, anyway.

"But the Freedmans are inclined to isolationism. So you see it's not *just* a training command I'm giving you."

"Well," Owensford said, finishing his drink and picking up his swagger stick. "At least we won't have the Bronsons to worry about."

*   *   *

EARTH:

". . . and we both know you're a pompous, spoiled, inbred, insufferable *fool*," Grand Senator Adrian Bronson concluded. He was a tall man, still erect in his eighty-fifth year; the blue eyes were very cold on his grandnephew. "Did you have to make it known to the entire *universe*?"

A hint of Midwestern rasp roughened the normally smooth generic-North-American accent. The Grand Senator represented a district that included Michigan and several other states in the CoDominium Senate, and led a faction whose votes were the subject of frantic bidding in that perpetually deadlocked body. That was power, even more power than the Bronson family's wealth could buy. The quarter-million acres centered around this Wisconsin estate were more symbol of that authority than its source, but on this land Adrian Bronson governed more absolutely than any feudal lord. A man who angered him sufficiently here could disappear and never be heard of again.

The Honorable Geoffrey Niles swallowed and unconsciously braced to attention, a legacy of Sandhurst. He was sixty years younger than the man on the other side of the table, blondly handsome and muscular, but there was no doubt about who was dominant here.

"Really, Great-Uncle—"

"*Don't remind me!*" Bronson shouted, slamming a fist down on the polished teak of the table. The crystal and silver of the decanter set jumped and jingled. "Don't remind me that my little sister's daughter managed to produce *you*! *I* won't die of the grief, but by *God* you may!"

He turned to the other men present; there were three, one in the plain blue overall of a starship captain, the other in a trim brown uniform with a pistol at his belt, a third elaborately inconspicuous.

"Captain Nakata," he said. "Report in this matter."

The spacer was Nipponese, from Meiji; Bronson

had hired him away from that newly independent planet's expanding space navy. His loyalty was expensively bought and paid for, but would be absolute for the duration of his contract.

"Sir," he said, bowing. "While in orbit about Tanith, waiting to receive the shipment of borloi"—the perfect euphoric drug, and vastly profitable—"Lieutenant Commander Niles, on his own authority, contacted the authorities in Lederle for, ah, a hunting permit."

"A hunting permit." Bronson waited a moment, meeting his grandnephew's eyes. They were steady. *No coward, at least,* he thought grudgingly.

"Mr. Wichasta," Bronson continued. Chandos Wichasta coughed discreetly into a hand; he was a small brown man, a confidential agent for many years.

"Senator, until this communication—apparently a bureaucrat flagged it as a routine measure and grew curious—until this communication, our agents in Governor Blaine's office had kept the Governor and Colonel Falkenberg in complete ignorance of *Norton Star*'s presence. Apparently, the request began a chain of discoveries which led to Governor Blaine and Falkenberg's mercenaries discovering that Rochemont plantation was the headquarters of the rebel planters and *their* mercenaries. And that we were in contact with the rebels and planning to lift the borloi they had denied the official Lederle monopoly. The timing was very close; if your grandnephew had not made that call, we would in all probability have been able to secure the drugs, and we certainly could have destroyed them."

"Captain Hertzimer," Bronson said. The man in the brown uniform saluted smartly. Officially he was an employee of Middleford Security Services; in fact, he was an officer of Bronson's household troops.

Household troops, Bronson thought sourly. *Recruited from my estates. God, how did America come to this?* The tenants here knew they owed their farms to him; if the

Bronson family had not been prepared to keep them on the land, this area would be corporate latifundia like the rest of the Midwest. No independent farmer had the resources or the political clout to survive on good land, these days; without the Bronsons, the farmers would have been lucky to get enough to emigrate off-planet. Quite likely to have ended up on a Welfare Island.

"Sir," Hertzimer said. "On Lieutenant Commander Niles's instructions, I loaded the security platoon and the Suslov class armored vehicle on the shuttle that was to fetch the borloi. When we arrived unexpectedly, there was nearly fighting with the plantation troops and mercenaries."

"Barton's Bulldogs," Wichasta said.

"When the shuttle was hijacked by Falkenberg's infiltrators, Mr. Niles ordered the tank to open fire on it. Unfortunately—"

"He *missed*, to top it all off." Bronson sighed, and poured himself a small brandy. "You're all dismissed. Not you, Geoffrey."

The big room grew quiet as the three employees took their leave; snow beat with feather paws at the windows behind the curtains, and the fire crackled as it cast its light over the pictures and the spines of the books. Pictures by Thomas Hart Benton and Norman Rockwell and Maxfield Parrish, visions of a people and a way of life vanished almost as thoroughly as Rome. And the books, his oldest friends: *The Federalist Papers*, Sandburg's monumental *Lincoln*, Twain's *Life on the Mississippi*.

The brandy bit his tongue gently, aromatic and comforting. *My world is dying*, Bronson thought, looking at the younger man. *Nothing left but a few remnants*. He had known all his life that the Earth was turning to slime beneath his feet; once he had wanted to do something about it, to halt the process, reverse it. When had he realized that no man could? But the death of a world is a gradual process, longer than the lifetime of a man. . . . *And perhaps something can be saved. The Bronsons, at least.*

"Geoffrey, what am I to do with you? Unless you'd rather go back to England and take a post in Amalgamated Foundries with Hugo. Wait a minute." He raised a hand at the younger man's frown and thinned lips. "Your father does good work there, important work. You'd have a decent place. I know you see yourself as a second Lawrence of Arabia and another Selous rolled into one, with a dash of Richard Burton and some Orde Wingate on the side, but this isn't the 19th century . . . or even the 20th."

"No, sir," Geoffrey Niles said. A hesitation: "Does this mean you're . . . going to give me a second chance, Great-Uncle? I say, that *is* decent of you."

Bronson smiled coldly. "No it isn't, Jeff. You see, I *know* there's the making of a man somewhere inside you, under that dilettante surface. They tell me you were steady enough under fire. You didn't miss that landing craft, did you?"

"No, sir. I hulled the ship, but Barton's people hit us before I could get off another round."

"Were you hit?"

"Yes, sir."

"I'm pleased to see you're no braggart." Bronson took papers out of a drawer. "I have the medical reports. Apparently you were three weeks in the regeneration stimulators. And you still want another try?"

"Yes, sir."

"All right. But no more command positions for a while, Jeff. No more relative-of-the-boss. If you want to play with the big boys, you'll have to earn it."

He picked up a pipe from the table and began the comforting ritual of loading it.

"You see," he continued softly, "your little fiasco on Tanith did more than cost me several hundred million CD credits. It gave me a public black eye—oh, not to the chuckleheads who watch the media, but to the people who really know things." His hand closed tightly on the bowl of the corncob.

"That damnable hired gun Falkenberg!" Bronson's eyes went to a picture framed in black: Harold Kewney. Barely twenty, in the uniform of a CoDominium Space Navy midshipman. His daughter's son, the chosen heir . . . dead thirty years ago, holding a rearguard while then-Lieutenant John Christian Falkenberg escaped. Escaped, and then—

"And the Blaines and the Grants behind *him*, and that Russki bastard Lermontov, God *curse* the day I went along with making him Grand Admiral of the Fleet. They've all of them cost me time and grief before, the hypocrites. . . . Do they think I'm a *fool*, not to know that Tanith drug money's underwriting the Fleet? We all know the CoDominium won't outlast even my lifetime"—he ignored Niles's look of shock—"and I know *their* cure: a coup by the Fleet, with Lermontov calling the shots and the Grants and Blaines providing a civilian cover. And from what happened on Tanith, the Spartans are in it up to their 'idealistic' eyeballs. That so-called Prince Lysander of theirs was the one who hijacked the shuttle from under your nose."

He pressed a control, sourly watching the mixture of hatred and envy flicker across the young Englishman's face. The hijacking had been exactly the sort of exploit Geoffrey Niles dreamed about. *And perhaps could accomplish, if he learned some self-discipline first,* the Senator thought.

The door opened silently, and a man entered. An Oriental like Nakata, but without his stiffness, and dressed in a conspicuously inconspicuous outfit of dark-blue tunic and hose. Geoffrey Niles looked at him and returned the other man's smile, feeling a coldness across his shoulders and back. A little shorter than the Englishman, which made him towering for his race, sharp-featured and broad-shouldered; the hand that held his briefly was like something carved from wood. No more than thirty.

"This is Kenjiro Murasaki," Bronson said. "Owner and manager of Special Tasks, Inc., of New Osaka." The capital city of the planet Meiji.

"Mr. Murasaki has agreed to . . . take care of the Spartan problem for me. New Washington is outside my sphere of operations, but Falkenberg's Legion is *not* going to establish a base on Sparta if I can help it. I've had tentative contacts with the underground opposition on Sparta for some time; now things get serious. And the Spartans, and Grant and Blaine and Lermontov, are going to get an object lesson in what happens to people who try to fuck with Adrian Bronson."

Niles swallowed in shock. It was the first time he had ever heard the Grand Senator use an obscenity, and it was as out-of-place as a knife-fight at a garden party.

"You can join the expedition. I'll let you keep your nominal rank of Lieutenant Commander, but you'll be an aide, subordinate to Mr. Murasaki and under the same discipline as other members of his organization. Or you can return to London tomorrow and never leave Earth again except as a tourist. Take your pick."

There was a long moment of silence. Niles nodded jerkily. "If that's acceptable to you, Mr. Murasaki," he said, with a precisely calculated bow. The Meijian returned it, bowing fractionally less.

"Indeed, Mr. Niles," he said, with the social smile Nipponese used in such situations. "If one thing is understood at the outset. We will be in a situation of conflict with two organizations, the Royal government of Sparta, and Falkenberg's Legion. Capable organizations, which operate according to certain rules, the Spartan Constitution, the Laws of War. We too will operate according to rules. The Hama rules."

Geoffrey Niles frowned. "I'm . . . Please excuse my ignorance of Japanese history," he said, racking his memory.

The smile grew broader. "Not Japanese, Mr. Niles. Hama was a city in . . . the Republic of Syria, then; Northern Israel, since 2009. In the later 20th century, it rebelled against the Syrian government." Geoffrey let one brow rise slightly. "The government made no effort to pacify the city. Instead it was surrounded by armor and artillery and leveled in a week's bombardment. The survivors died by bayonet, or fire when flamethrowers were turned on cellars. Man, woman and child."

Black eyes held blue. "Hama rules. First: *There are no rules*. Second: *Rule or die*. Understood?"

*   *   *

Bronson drew on the pipe. "Something can be made of that young man," he said, glancing at the door Niles had closed behind him.

"Perhaps, excellency. Yet the best steel comes from the hottest fire," Murasaki said politely.

"If you mean, do I want him kept out of harm's way, the answer's no," Bronson said brutally. "I expect that rebellion to do a lot of damage before it's crushed, and that means fighting. It's time to see what young Niles is made of, one way or the other. This isn't a time for the stupid or the weak, and I don't want them in my bloodline. Test him; I'd be delighted if he passes, but if it kills him, so be it."

*   *   *

SPARTA:

Skida Thibodeau blinked as the light-intensifiers in her faceplate cycled down; it was fairly bright in the yard behind the ranch house, with the burning hovertruck not ten meters away.

"Smith!" she shouted. "Get that doused, do you want the RSMP down on us?"

Most of the fifty-odd ranch hands and laborers were gathered in an apprehensive clump, beneath the weapons of the guerrillas. Some wore the rough coveralls of working dress, others no more than a snatched-up blanket; they were a tough-looking lot, the sort you could hire cheap for a place a *long* way from the pleasures of town. Almost all men; there was a severe imbalance between the genders among deportees who made it to Sparta, and most women could find work closer to Sparta City than this. Some glowered at the attackers, others cringed, but none seemed ready to defy the raiders whose nightsight goggles and bandannas made them doubly terrible, anonymous in their outbacker leathers.

Others of the guerrillas were leading spare horses and mules out of the stables, fitting packsaddles and loading them with bundles of loot, everything from weapons to trail-rations and medicine. She was glad to see nobody was trying to hide anything massive anymore, or steal liquor for themselves, but . . .

The tall woman took three quick steps to where the ranch-family stood in a huddle of personal servants and the retainers who had been fighting by their sides. One of the guards had his hand under the skirt of a housemaid, ignoring the girl's squirming and whimpers. The man was one of her old hidehunters; they were nearly as much trouble as that clutch of Liberation Party deportees from Earth Croser had sent along two months back.

No point in wasting words, she thought, and whipped the butt of her rifle around to crack against his elbow. The man gave a wordless snarl of pain and crouched for a moment, before looking aside.

"Ay, Skilly, you said—"

"Keep you hands to youself," she hissed. "That for later. Be *political,* you silly mon. Now bring the haciendado and his woman out. You, Diego, take their children over to the shed and lock them in. Take the nursemaid too. And Diego, Skilly would be *angry* if anything happened to them."

The crowd grew quieter still as the couple who owned this land were prodded out into the trampled earth of the yard. *Velysen*, Skida remembered from the intelligence report. *Harold and Suzanne Velysen, Spartan-born, Citizens.* They were unremarkable. A man in his midthirties, dark and wiry; the woman a little younger, blond and as plump as you got on this heavy-gravity world. Another woman who looked to be the wife's younger sister. Harold Velysen had managed to don pants and boots, but his wife was still in torn silk pajamas that showed a bruise on her right shoulder where a rifle-butt would rest. Skida pitched her voice to carry, standing with legs straddled and thumbs in her belt:

"Now, listen. The Helots has no quarrel with you workers. The Non-Citizens' Liberation Front fights for you aboveboard and legal; we Helots does it with guns. Nobody's been hurt except the ranchero and his gunmen, hey? Not even his children. The Helots fights civ-il-ized."

She turned and extended a finger toward the group of household staff. "Any of you houseboys Citizens. Any of you want to stand over there with the bossman?" A few of the field-workers stirred before they remembered this was Sparta, where Citizen meant member of the ruling class rather than a Welfare Island scut.

Four of the house-workers moved over to stand beside the rancher; an older man and his wife, two of the surviving guards. A boy of about fourteen tried to follow them and was pushed back by the guerrillas, not unkindly. The little band had their hands roughly bound behind their backs.

"These good *Citizens* wouldn't listen when the Helots came calling," Skida continued. "No, they wouldn't listen to such rabble as us. Wouldn't listen to the workers' friends about the low pay and the bad conditions. Wouldn't pay their taxes for the people's cause." She shook her head, making *tsk, tsk,* sounds. "Thought the kings off in Sparta City would help them against such riffraff as us. Thought the Really Shitty Mounted Pimps would protect them."

The guerrillas laughed at the nickname of the Royal Spartan Mounted Police; a few of the farmhands joined in ingratiatingly.

"But then, why should they lift a finger for you?" Skida continued. She freed one hand to wave backward at the house. "Why should the *haciendado* listen to the friends of the poor? Isn't it always the way? They get the big houses and the fancy cars. They ride by and watch while you sweat in the fields? And if you object, if you stand up for your rights—"

She grinned, a glint of white teeth against the matt brown of her skin "—why, they call in the RSMP to beat you down. You aren't *Citizens,* you haven't *earned* the vote." A scornful laugh. "Learn how to pass their exams and tests—" There was a stir; most Welfare Island dwellers were not only illiterate but had what amounted to a cultural taboo against everything about the written word. "—while you're working for a living and they're living off you! Your kids can spend their lives shoveling shit, while the children of the noble *Brotherhoods* get their special schools and fancy—"

"You lying bitch!" It was the older man who had volunteered to stand with the rancher. "Mr. Velysen built this place up from nothing, and anyone can—"

Thunk. The carbon-fiber stock of Two-knife's machine gun caught him at the base of the skull. *Silly mon,* she thought as he sank to his knees and shook his head dazedly. *Skilly is giving a speech, not arguing.*

"—fancy tutors. But tonight, everyone's equal! Tonight, you see how the rich live."

A working party had been setting out tables. Now they stepped back, showing trestle tables covered with bottles and casks and heaped plates; whatever had been available in the wine cellar and the kitchens. The farm-workers moved hesitantly forward, but most of them snatched at the liquor eagerly enough. Doubly eager from fear, but they would have drunk anyway; Skida watched with carefully hidden contempt. You did not get out of the gutters on booze-dreams, or on cocaine or smack or borloi; those were for fools, like God or the lotteries or the Tri-V with its lying dreams.

Skida waited until the liquor had a little time to work, then rapped on the table with her rifle butt.

"You see who your real friends are," she said, as the guerrillas went up and down the table; they distributed handfuls of cash and jewelry. Most of the workers snatched greedily at the plunder. A few had the sense to think ahead, but nobody wanted to be a holdout.

"The Helots is your friend. The kings and the RSMP couldn't protect their friends, but the Helots can protect and punish. The Helots have its eyes and ears everywhere; here and in Sparta City, in the government, in the police, we know everything. The government is blind, it strikes at the air but it can't catch us; we cut it and turn away, cut it and turn away, and soon it will bleed to death and we be the government. Look around you! We didn't harm a hair on your heads. We didn't touch the tools or workstock or barns . . . because all this will belong to *you* when the people rules."

She smiled broadly. *And if you gallows bait believe all that, Skilly has this card game she could teach you.* "And look what else the Helots gives you!" she said, signaling. Guerrillas pushed the rancher's wife forward, and the two other women who had come to stand with her. The rancher began to shout and struggle as they were stripped and thrown down on the rough planks of the trestles.

Skida signaled to Two-knife as the screaming began, from the women and the men. "The other women, house servants and the workers, give them a shotgun and put them in a room with a lock," she said. "It is *muy importante*, understand. Just before we leave, we lock the other workers back in their barracks."

Two-knife blinked at her. "*Sí*, Skilly, if you say so. The gringo Croser, he say that?"

Skida sighed. "No, my loyal fool, he has taught Skilly much of the way of fighting the guerrillero, the little war, but Skilly put the books to work. See, if we let these animals loose they will rape all the women, burn down the ranch and then start killing each other. That makes them just criminals who the RSMP will hang. This must be a political thing, not a bandit raid."

The Mayan frowned and pushed back his broad-brimmed leather hat to scratch his bald scalp. "But the RSMP will hang them anyway," he said reasonably.

"If all share the crime, then none will talk for a while at least," she said patiently. "They will themselves kill any who would. They will say that we did it, that they were helpless before our guns, but among themselves they will know. They will feel they must support us, because they are as guilty as we, and they fear our spies among them."

She made a throwing gesture. "Many will run before the police come. Some the RSMP will catch and hang; these will be martyrs for our cause. Others will scatter to rancheros who ask no questions of a man willing to work. They will talk in secret in the bunkhouses, and all those who hate their masters will dream of doing as was done here—perhaps some will. The haciendados will hear as well, by rumor; they will fear their workers, and be twice as hard on them, which will turn more to us. You see?"

The man stood, frowning in concentration. He was far from stupid, simply not very used to abstract thought. She slapped him on the shoulder as he nodded agreement. The screams had died to a broken sobbing. Skida cast a critical eye at the tables. Unlikely that the haciendado's women would survive; best to have the rancher and all of his supporters shot just as the guerrillas left, though.

"Two-knife, you will take the first Group and any recruits we get from here back to Base One," she said. "All the Group leaders are to make for their drop camps and lie low until I return. Work the new ones hard, but do not kill more than is necessary. McMillan may begin their instruction."

Two-knife snorted; Skida nodded agreement; the Liberation Party theorist was something of a bore, but necessary. She found his cranky neo-Marxism even more ridiculous than the religion the nuns had taught her, but it was a lie with power.

"You would do well to learn his words also," she said. "I must attend a conference of regional leaders. The kings are bringing in help from off-planet. Mercenaries." *And we will have help as well, but that is a secret even from you for a while,* she thought.

Skida frowned thoughtfully down the rutted dirt road that lead away from the ranch house; it joined a gravel track down toward the Eurotas. Her mind threw a map over the night; the Torrey estate was there, older and larger than this and too formidable to attack as yet. Then came the switchback down into the valley of the upper Eurotas. The guerrillas had a Group there, about the size of a platoon, to serve as a blocking force, and then as her cover for the trip to town.

"And I might as well leave now," she added. "Adios. Meet me in the usual place in three weeks."

CHAPTER TWO

Crofton's Encyclopedia of Contemporary History and Social Issues (1st Edition):

The CoDominium emerged almost by accident as Earth's first world government; many of the consequences were unplanned and unanticipated.

One of the most notable was the emergence of a far less competitive world society. The founding powers of the CoDominium had an effective monopoly on military power, and an absolute monopoly on space-based weapons. After a series of crises convinced the United States and the Soviet Union to work together, smaller states could no longer play the Great Powers off against each other. Maintaining that power monopoly became a goal in itself.

An early result was CoDominium Intelligence suppression of research; first military and then all technology began to stagnate. Likewise, private corporations could no longer escape the power of one state by moving; instead, the worldwide regulations imposed by the Alliance, later the Grand Senate, came more and more to favor established economic interests with lobbying power. In turn, the Grand Senators and their clients accumulated increasing wealth based on patronage and politically allocated contracts. Earth of the 21st century saw unprecedented economic concentration in the hands of a dwindling number of oligarchs.

Political-social stasis also settled on the rest of the world. The CoDominium allowed no international wars after the final

Arab-Israeli conflict of 2009; hence, regimes no longer needed
to win the support of their populations against outside
enemies. Revolt against a government supported by the
CoDominium was impossible; even guerrilla war was futile
without external arms supplies and sanctuaries. At best,
developed states became junior partners. In what was once
known as the "Third World" utterly corrupt gangster regimes
became the norm (for 20th-century analogies see *Haiti*,
Liberia, *Rumania*), presiding over despair and famine. Only
the mass deportations of BuReloc, combined with the release
of viral contraceptives and the distribution of tranquilizing
agents such as borloi, maintain the present situation. . . .

*[This article was removed from the 2nd edition by order of
CoDominium Intelligence and its author was last seen in a group of
involuntary colonists embarking for Fulson's World.]*

*   *   *

TANITH:

"Soft duty, you lucky bastards."

The words had come from a unit of the First
Battalion, trudging in from night patrol past the
waiting ranks of the Fifth. It was only an hour past
dawn, and already hot enough to make the
camouflage paint run in sweat-streaks down the
soldiers' faces; the Fifth Battalion were lounging on
their personal kits, fresh from the showers and in
walking-out khakis, ready for the ground-effect trucks
to take them to the shuttle docks. The sun was a
yellow-brown glare through the ever-present haze of
Tanith's atmosphere. Some of the other remarks were
more personal and pointed.

Battalion Sergeant Sergio Guiterrez looked up from
his kit and grinned as he jerked one of the
hotter-tempered new troopers back; a local kid from a
jungle village, with a log-sized chip on his shoulder.

"Cool it, trooper, unless you want to spend the first
month on Sparta doing punishment detail," he said

genially. "And Purdy," he continued, pointing to the recruit's rifle, "if I *ever* see you let your weapon fall in the dirt like that again, you will *suffer*. *¿Comprende?*"

The recruit looked down. His New Aberdeen 7mm semi-automatic had slipped off the lumpy surface of his duffel bag and was lying on the hard-packed dirt of the parade square. Appalled, he hesitated for an instant before scooping it up.

"Sss . . . sorry, Battalion Sergeant," he began, bracing to attention. "I, ah, I was—"

"Is that an *excuse* I'm hearing, Private Purdy?"

"Oh, *no*, Battalion Sergeant."

"Good. Present arms for inspection."

Flick-click-snick. The trooper swung the rifle up, extracted the magazine and held the weapon extended across his palms with the bolt locked open.

The noncom ran a finger over the surface of the bolt head. "See this?" he said, rubbing forefinger and thumb together. "Gun oil picks up dust, and that erodes the working parts. Clean it."

Good kid, he thought, watching the earnest black face. *Plenty of brains, and Mother of God, but he can move through bush.* Purdy was one of several brothers and cousins from a jungle settlement here on Tanith, born to time-expired convicts who'd moved out into the bush to start on their own. They'd all been posted to the Scouts, and would be useful on Sparta.

"Battalion Sergeant?"

Guiterrez turned and saluted. "Ma'am?" he said.

It *did* feel odd to be saluting a redheaded chit only just turned eighteen, but he did it willingly enough. Cornet Ursula Gordon might not have saved the Legion's ass, exactly, but the story was that she *had* furnished the information that let them fulfill their contract with the Governor. What was for certain was that the Legion had bought her contract of indenture from the Hilton Hotel. *Entertainer.* Guiterrez snorted. It had been pretty clear what kind of entertainment she'd provided. Not that she'd had any choice in the matter. They might call it indentured service to repay the Hilton's costs for her education, but it was slavery right enough.

Damned if I know why she wants to go for a soldier, Guiterrez thought. The word was that Governor Blaine had offered her a good job in administration here on Tanith. *Maybe she wants to make a fresh start.* He could understand that; Sergio Guiterrez had started out running with a gang in San Diego, and had been lucky enough to catch the attention of a CD Marine recruiter looking over the newcomers to a relocation center. It was the Marines or a one-way trip to Tanith. *Got me here anyway. But not as a slave.* Smart girl, and a looker too, with that heart-shaped face and enormous green eyes; a little more athletic than he liked, but on a heavy-gravity world like this you got a workout just walking down to the corner.

"Well, it's confirmed I'll be coming to Sparta with the Fifth," she continued, returning his salute. It was a little awkward, like the way she wore the blue and gold of the Legion, but she was trying. "Captain Alana wants me to arrange a cross-training schedule on the Armor Company simulators while we're on shipboard."

"Yes, Ma'am. I'll take care of it. Welcome to the Fifth," Guiterrez said. He liked the smile he got back. *Maybe she'll do.*

*　　*　　*

Did the Governor have *to hold the going-away party in the Hilton?* Ursula Gordon thought.

She surreptitiously wiped her palms on her pocket handkerchief and smoothed down her dress-white jacket. The Tanith upper-classes never wore white, because white jackets were the uniform of convict trustee laborers; but Falkenberg's Legion wasn't about to change its customs. No one was going to mistake one of Falkenberg's officers for a convict. Not more than once, anyway.

It was only mildly hot in the screened and sunroofed porch of the Lederle Hilton, with the overhead fans whirring and cool water trickling down the vine-grown screens of Gray Howlite stone spaced about. *My palms would be sweaty if it was air-conditioned.* This building had been her home since the Hilton company bought her contract at the age of four; children of convicts had been automatically indentured then, back before the current Governor's reforms. Her place of work from the day she turned fifteen and became a fixture of the luxury suites, until Prince Lysander checked in. Three short months ago, and now she was seeing it for the last time. As a guest.

She sipped at her iced soda water and watched her fellow officers mingle with Governor Blaine's bureaucrats and planters; the planters included some former rebels, here to show their humble gratitude for the amnesty. *Sweating to please,* she thought coldly. *Learn how it feels, you slave-driving bastards.*

Blaine himself was being determinedly friendly to all. . . . It was his main weakness, a desire to be liked. Fortunately, he knew how to control it. He broke free of the circle of former enemies and came over to her. "Good-bye." He gripped both her hands with his.

I think he really will miss me.

Blaine was a tall man, over 190 centimeters, and thin enough to look almost skeletal to someone Tanith-born; his sandy brown hair was thinning on top and tousled as always, and he wore the inevitable blue guayabera shirt with the CoDominium seal on the left pocket.

"I still wish you'd taken my offer," he said. Second Administrative Assistant in the Department of Labor; a glorified executive secretary, but it was in the line of promotion, a good position for someone as young as she was. "I hate to see Tanith lose anyone with your abilities; we need all the smart, tough people we can get. Perhaps something else? Name it." Blaine was eccentric that way; he had *requested* posting to Tanith, when every previous governor had taken it as a punishment post. For that matter most planters and company executives dreamed of making a killing and moving somewhere else.

"No, thank you, sir," she said. Then she smiled; it made her look younger than her eighteen Earth years. "That's the second serious proposition I've declined in the last week; it's refreshing."

"Proposition?" he said, looking protective.

"Well, the other one was of marriage," she said. "Captain . . . ah, an officer of the Legion."

Blaine nodded, looking away slightly.

What romantics men are, she thought. It made them easy to manipulate, if you knew. Women had to; some men learned. Colonel John Christian Falkenberg III was as expert as she; military romanticism was as powerful a way to lead men by the nose as the sexual variety.

"Spare the pity, please, Governor," she said a little sharply. "It wasn't all bad here, and I'm not scarred for life, I assure you." Though there were some memories that still woke her shivering in the night; that couple from California . . . She pushed the memory aside.

"Actually, the worst thing about being a . . . " She considered; prostitute was not exactly accurate. For one thing, *she* had never seen any of the money, except for tips and gifts. For another, she had been carefully trained to offer a number of services besides the sexual. ". . . a geisha was that you had to be so damned *agreeable* and *nice* all the time. In the Legion, nobody gives a tinker's curse if I have the personality of a Weems Beast, as long as I get my job done and stand by my comrades."

"Well—"

"Look, sir, I appreciate your concern—and the

gentleman who asked me to marry him—but *I don't need any more rescuing*. Right now, I'm getting a fresh start away from Tanith. I know you'll make Tanith a better place to live, but not for *me*. And I've got a movable home and family going with me, the Legion. It's a tough place, but you *earn* what you get, you don't *wheedle* somebody to *give* it to you." She shrugged. "And if I get a husband someday, it won't be someone who wants to protect me because I'm young and pretty and look vulnerable. Hell, maybe *I'll* rescue *him*."

Blaine laughed. "I understand," he said. "I hope you like Sparta, too. Bit drier and cooler than you're used to, I hear."

Ursula laughed back at him, still feeling a slight stab of satisfaction that she could laugh because she *wanted* to. "I'm looking forward to it, to getting out of this sauna."

*   *   *

Major Peter Owensford sipped at his drink; it was the perpetual gin-and-bitters of Tanith. There was the rum-based liqueur made with Tanith Passion Fruit, but that was too sweet for lunchtime, and anyway it was rumored to be a mild aphrodisiac. *That's the* last *thing I need right now,* he thought dismally, looking over at Ursula where she stood talking and laughing with Blaine . . . *Cornet Gordon,* he reminded himself. Who had politely but firmly put him in his place; a favored uncle's place . . . *God damn it all.*

"Feeling sorry for yourself?" Ace Barton said.

"Not really, Anselm." *Captain* Anselm Barton, he reminded himself. It was going to be difficult, with Ace along. He had been senior too long; with the Legion, and then an independent merc commander for nearly a decade. *And my commanding officer on Thurstone, a lifetime ago.*

"Now I *know* you're pissed, you never call me that unless something's got your goat."

Owensford relaxed. "Oh, all right, Ace; yes."

"Smart and gorgeous, but too young for you. The problem is," he went on, resting a hand on the younger man's shoulder, "you're getting those settling-down feelings. Endemic, once you turn thirty."

"You don't have them?" Owensford replied.

"Oh, yes, but I lie down until they go away." A wink. "Works fine, provided you lie down with the right woman."

Owensford snorted laughter. "Frankly, Ace, I'm nervous about this command as well. The rest of the Legion's going to be a *long* way away." Then he winced inwardly; he had never had a detached command before, and the older man *had*.

Barton shrugged. "What's to worry about? We go set up schools. Which works fine, because we've got the older troopers. Maybe they can't march fifty klicks and fight when they get there, but they can sure train others to do it."

Besides the raw Tanith recruits, Falkenberg had taken the opportunity to move a lot of men near retirement into the Fifth. Tanith was a good place to recruit, you had to be tough to survive here, and there were plenty of broken and desperate men. The Legion as a whole was over-strength, particularly the rifle companies. His unit would include the standard six hundred or so, but twice or three times the proportion of men over thirty-five. Many of them monitors or sergeants or centurions nearing retirement, rock-steady men but tired. There would be near a thousand women and children and pensioners as well.

"Fine for training," Owensford agreed. "On that score, just got the word. Hal Slater's going to Sparta. To set up their staff college. Which means we'll be taking George as well as Iona."

Barton raised an eyebrow but didn't say anything.

"OK, so we got the old ones," Peter said.

"The old, the halt, and the lame," Barton agreed.

"But not the stupid. Given my druthers I'll take what we got. Hell, Pete, it's just a training war anyway."

"Training war?" Lysander Collins said from behind them.

They turned to greet the heir to the Collins throne of Sparta. Prince Lysander was a tall young man, 180 centimeters in his sandals; about twenty, a broad-shouldered youth with cropped brown hair and hazel eyes that looked somehow firmer than they had when he came to Tanith a few months ago.

"We were just discussing the sort of recruits we'll be getting on Sparta, for your new army. We're not used to Taxpayer enlisted men. Sorry," Owensford corrected himself. "Recruits from the Citizen class, I meant." He would have to remember that: on Earth, Citizen meant a member of the underclass, the welfare-dependent or casual-laboring lumpen-proletariat. Better than half the population of the U.S., and more elsewhere. On Sparta a Citizen was a voter, a member of the political ruling class. Not necessarily socially upper-class, but solidly respectable at least.

"Well, not all the recruits will be Citizens or from Citizen families," Prince Lysander said. "It's a big planet and not many people and there's a lot to do, if you've got some sort of education. A lot of the deportees BuReloc sends us are illiterate and have never held a job; there's plenty of unskilled laboring positions open, but I think some of them will join up for the Field Force as well."

He frowned slightly; a serious young man for the most part, thoughtful. "I'd have thought our Citizens would be easier to train," he added. "The schools on Sparta are pretty good, and there's a lot of paramilitary training through the Brotherhoods' youth-wings."

"True enough," Owensford said. "The Legion's training schedule is pretty much the same as the CoDo Marines, though. With the sort of street-toughs and

gang warriors we get, you break the recruit to build
the soldier; everything they've learned all their lives is
wrong, except for pack loyalty and aggressiveness."

Which was why nine-tenths of Marine recruits had
records; the sort who just sat in front of the Tri-V
screens and stirred only to get more booze and borloi
were little use.

"The new recruit is silly,
'e thinks o' suicide
'e's lost 'is gutter-devil
'e hasn't got 'is pride—"

Lysander quoted softly. "It makes better sense, now.
He knew his stuff, didn't he?"

"Certainly did," Owensford replied. He had
discovered Kipling on his own. The man had long
since been purged from what passed for an
educational system in North America, but Lysander
had mentioned he was by way of a national poet.
Sparta promised to be full of surprises like that.

They all lifted their glasses for a moment to Kipling's
memory.

"We'll manage," Ace Barton said. "Soldiers do."

"Not only soldiers," the Prince said quietly; his eyes
flicked toward Ursula Gordon and then away.

Owensford felt a brief stab of irritation mixed with
pity. Sparta seemed to be a pretty straight-laced sort of
place, at least at the upper levels, and Ursula had hit
the young man like a ton of cement. First love and first
adventure, that daredevil stunt with the Bronson's
shuttle and a beautiful damsel in genuine distress,
heady stuff. Doubly bitter when he realized that he
could have neither; back to the strait confines of duty,
and a marriage arranged by his elders.

At least she would have said yes *to you,* Owensford
thought ironically.

"You'll probably see more soldiering," he said kindly
to the young man. "Don't mean to sound
cold-blooded, but this little guerrilla-bandit problem

will be perfect for providing on-the-job training for your new Field Force, and it's an old tradition for crown princes to hold commissions."

"Yep." Ace finished his drink; there were times when Arizona sounded clearly in his voice, under the accentless polish an officer acquired in the CoDominium service. "Nothin' like hearing a bullet and realizing there's someone out there trying to *kill* you to put the polish on a soldier."

Lysander grimaced; his own baptism of fire had been quite recent, and his Phraetrie-brother Harv had been badly wounded, nearly killed.

"I could do without it," he said.

"That's exactly the point, Prince. Exactly the point."

*   *   *

SPARTA:

"Hey, Skilly, what-a you got for us? Where's Two-knife?"

"Gots good stuff this time, Marco," Skida said genially, walking down the landing ramp with her knapsack, taking a deep lungful of air that held slight traces of smoke and massed humanity, if you concentrated. She had been born a city girl and grown up on streets, however squalid. After a while in the outback the silence and clear air got to you. "Two-knife coming downriver with the bulk product."

The stamped steel treads rang under her boots, and the blimp creaked at its mooring tower above her. The landing field was down by the water, in the East Haven side of Sparta City, along with the fishing fleet and the river barges from up the Eurotas and coastal shipping; the shuttle landing docks and the deep-sea berths were on the other side of the finger of hilly built-up land. The pale sun was high, and crowds of seagulls swarmed noisily over the maze of concrete docks, nets, masts, warehouses and cranes along the waterfront. A good dozen airships were in, long cigar-shapes of inflated synthetic fabric with aluminum gondolas and diesel engine-pods; the one behind her had *Clemens Airways* painted on the envelope. Two more were leaving, turning south and east for the Delta with leisurely grace; out on the water a three-masted schooner was running on auxiliaries. Then the sails went up, lovely clean shapes of white canvas; the ship heeled, and her prow bit the water in a sunlit burst of spray.

"What exactly?" Marco said, as she stepped to the cracked, stained concrete. Five of her hidehunters followed, big shaggy men in sheepskin jackets, open now in the mild heat of the seafront city, their rifles slanted over their backs.

"Got twenty-five tons good clear tallow," she began, as they walked toward the street entrance.

Marco followed beside her, making unconscious hand-washing gestures; he was a stumpy little man, bald but with blue jowls. A fashion designer from Milan in his youth, swept up after the riots against the Sicilian-dominated government and handed over to BuReloc.

"One fifty tons first-grade spicebush-smoked beef jerky," she continued. "One-twenty venison. Twenty-two hundred raw cowhides, two-thousand-fifty horsehides, horns and hooves appropriate, 'bout the same deerhides, some elk. Five hundred twenty good buffalo hides, do for robes. Beaver and capybara, five hundred and seven hundred. One twenty red fox, seventy wolfhides, twenty cougar. One hundred-twenty-two saddle-broken mustangs from the Illyrian Dales, *really* saddle-broke and to pack saddles as well. Holding the horses in Olynthos, but Skilly can get them downriver if you know a better market."

They pushed through the exit gate of the landing field, and into the crowded streets of dockside; it was convenient, how Sparta had no internal checks, no waiting to have your papers cleared every time you got on or off something. There was a row of electric runabouts, little fuel-cell-powered things that ran on alcohol and air; she waved dismissal at the hidehunters and handed the attendant a gold coin. He knew her well, and there was no nonsense with bank machines that recorded where you were and what you did. Another convenient thing about Sparta.

Skida noted these matters; they were all things that would have to change, when *she* was in charge. She paid the hidehunters off in Consolidated Hume Financial Bank script; Thibodeau Animal Products Inc. used them as their bank of deposit. They also handled her modest but growing investment portfolio; under other names, they administered some of the accounts she had on Dayan and Xanadu, as well. *Skilly's just-in-case money*, she thought, dumping her knapsack beside the bundles the hunters had left in the backseat and ushering Marco to the passenger side.

"See you at the Dead Cow in three days," she said to the men. They nodded silently; she had picked them well. "Any of you gets into trouble before then, Skilly bails him out of jail then cuts off his balls, *¿comprende?*"

"Sure, Skilly," the oldest of them said. "I'll watch them."

"I can get you two-fifty crowns for the beef," Marco said, as the car pulled silently out onto the street. He was always a little nervous while the hidehunters were around. She headed uphill, to the Sacred Way, which ran down the ridge-spine of the city from the CoDo enclave to Government House Square. The road went up in switchbacks, through a neighborhood of stucco family homes over embankments planted in rhododendrons. "Standard rate for the tallow, but the hides are up two-tenths. And I can get you six crowns apiece for the horses here in town."

She raised her brows. Those were excellent prices; agricultural produce was usually a glut, and only the low costs of harvesting feral stock made the hidehunting business profitable at all.

"The Crown, he's-a buying," Marco explained, then blanched slightly as she cut blindside around a horse-drawn dray loaded with melons, in a curve that lifted two wheels off the pavement. "These soldiers they bring in, and the new army, you hear?"

"Skilly knows," she said. "OK, sounds good, regular commission." She grinned broadly; there was a certain irony to it, after all. Like charging someone for the ammunition you shot them with; the Belizian government had done that when she was a youngster.

The commission would be fair, five percent. Marco was broker for half a dozen hidehunter outfits, although Thibodeau Inc. was his biggest customer. They had had no problems, after the first time she caught him shorting her; obviously he had not expected a deportee to know accounting systems. Unfortunately for him, Skida Thibodeau had been in jail for most of her first eighteen months on Sparta—a little matter of someone hurt in a game of chance she was running for start-up capital—and she had divided her time inside between working out to get used to the heavy gravity and taking correspondence courses from the University. A simple fracture of the forearm had reformed the broker's morals, that and the cheerful warning that next time she would send Two-knife around to start with his kneecaps and work upward.

"What's this good stuff you got for me?" the Italian continued.

Skida pulled the car to the curb on the Sacred Way; Sparta City had plenty of parking, cars still being a rare luxury. This was the medium-rent district, not too close to Government House Square. A few four-story apartment houses, with restaurants and shops on the ground level; there were showrooms, headquarters of shipping or fishing firms, doctors' and lawyers' offices.

The broad sidewalk next to their parking spot was set with tables, shaded by the big jacarandas and oaks that fringed the main street: the Blue Mountain Café. Run by a family of Jamaican deportees, and set up with a loan Skilly had guaranteed. It was useful, and she had wanted at least one place in town where you could get a decently spiced meat patty. There were all types on Sparta, but the basic mix was Anglo-Hispanic-Oriental, like the United States.

"Here," she said, pulling a fur from one of the bundles in the rear seat and tossing it across his lap.

"Oh, holy Jesus!" he blurted. It was a meter long and a double handspan broad, a shining lustrous white color, supple and beautiful. The ex-fashion designer ran his hand over it reverently. "What *is* this?"

"Some of Skilly's people were working the country northeast of Lake Ochrid, you know, the Hyborian Tundra?" Remote and desolate, almost never visited. "Turns out those ermine the CoDo turned loose to eat the rabbits been getting *big,* mon."

Marco made a soundless happy whistle. There were excellent markets for furs, even Earth now that the Greens had less influence . . . especially Earth; after they had lost their commercial value nobody had bothered to preserve many of the fur species.

"Seventy-five, maybe eighty each," he said, his voice soft with the pleasure of handling the pelt.

"And this," she continued. What she dumped in his lap next was a kilo-weight silver ingot, stamped with the mark of the Stora Kopparberg mine.

"*Shit!*" he said, in a falsetto shriek. The metal disappeared under the seat. "Oh, no, not again!"

Skida grinned with ruthless amusement. So few people seemed to realize that once you made a single illegal deal you were in for good. Especially a family man like Marco, so concerned for the three children he hoped to see make Citizen someday. Every parent on Sparta got educational vouchers, but there was no law saying a prestige school had to accept the children of non-Citizens. With enough money, everything was possible, of course.

"Yes. But doan worry, this de last time."

"Oh, Mother of God, you mean that? They hang us all, they hang us all!"

"Not unless they catch us, mon," Skilly soothed. "Of course I mean it. All legitimate from now on." Skida Thibodeau believed firmly in never welshing on a business deal; it was too much like peeing in the bathwater. Besides, they were moving into big-time money now, and the fencing would have to be handled through the political side. "Coming downriver nice and safe in the tallow; besides, they never know what happen to that blimp from the mine. Bad weather, maybe."

A stowaway named Skida Thibodeau with a small leather sack full of lead shot had happened to it, but there was no point in burdening Marco with unnecessary information. Much of the vessel had been useful to the Helots—high-speed diesels were not easy to come by—and the rest had joined the crew in a very deep sinkhole.

"OK," Marco said, wiping his brow with a handkerchief. "You want me to fix you up a place at-a my house?" he said, with insincere hospitality. Skilly had more than enough to rent or buy a place in town for her visits, but that would have offended her sense of thrift. As often as not she dossed down on a cot in Thibodeau Inc.'s single-room office.

"No, Skilly going to catch a curry patty and a beer here and then meet her boyfriend," she said. Take another car out to his place, rather, but there was a mild pleasure in teasing the factor.

Marco shuddered again. "Skilly, he's a Citizen and First Families, and he's in politics and the government don't like him," he said half-pleadingly. "Why?"

"Love be blind, my mon," Skilly said. One reason she avoided it, but an affair was surprisingly good cover.

The founders of Sparta had had a privacy fetish that they built into the local culture. She reached over and pinched the Italian's cheek. "You leave a message for Skilly as soon as you find a way to wash the silver money, hey?"

CHAPTER THREE

Crofton's Encyclopedia of Contemporary History and Social Issues (2nd Edition):

THE EXODUS

The great outburst of interstellar colonization in the early 21st century paradoxically led to the reappearance of economic and social problems which Earth had thought vanished. Fusion-powered spaceships, mass-driver launchers and the virtually energy-free Alderson drive brought transport costs between systems down to levels comparable to those of 20th-century air freight, but they were still not cheap. New colonies were chronically short of the hard currency they so desperately needed to pay for imports of capital equipment. Human labor was plentiful—the Bureau of Relocation would furnish it whether the recipient wanted it or not—but everything else, from transport to machine tools, was chronically scarce.

Earth's markets were jealously guarded by the cartels which dominated the planetary economy; and there was a well-founded suspicion that those cartels and the shipping lines they controlled conspired to maintain the colony worlds as dependent markets. Some metals and drugs could bear the costs of interstellar transport, along with extrasolar rarities and luxury goods, but bulk agricultural produce was shipped only to mining systems without habitable planets.

The stable elite of colony worlds—Dayan, Xanadu, Meiji, Friedland, Churchill—were those where wealthy parent governments or corporations provided cash and credit enough to finance self-sustaining industrialization. With plentiful resources and fewer social problems, by the late 21st century these planetary states had populations in the 10-50 million range, higher per capita incomes than most Earthly nations and, were taking advantage of the CoDominium's retreat to establish sub-imperialisms and trade spheres of their own. Some planets (see *Haven*) remained mere dumping grounds, sustained by Colonial Bureau largess; *Hadley* was an interesting example of such a world escaping mass die-off after CoDominium withdrawal.

Many of the less well-financed colonies, launched by "Third World" nations or private organizations—some religious, some secular—with only enough funds to pay for transport, lapsed into a virtually pre-industrial existence of peasant farming and handicrafts; see *Ararat, Zanj, Santiago*. A common pattern on intermediate planets was the emergence of a severely hierarchical society, with a dominant elite using access to interstellar technology to rule an impoverished mass; see *Frystaat, Thurstone, Diego, Novi Kossovo*.

Constant political and social unrest resulted from this situation. See *Sparta* for an interesting case-study of an attempt to deal with these problems through careful planning; while partially successful, it . . .

*   *   *

SPARTA:

Major Peter Owensford looked up from his laptop computer to the viewport of the shuttle. It was a Royal Spartan Airways custom craft, on continuous orbit-to-ground runs; rather different from the assault boats he was accustomed to, which had to be small enough to be carried within a starship's hull. Certainly more comfortable, with the seats in facing pairs and lavishly padded. The orbiter was low enough to switch to turbojet mode, a difference in the subliminal hum that came through the hull. Below, the surface of the Inland Sea was bright-blue, speckled with islands;

even from fifteen thousand meters it looked clear and inviting. A welcome change from the livid yellow and green of Tanith's seas, always warm as blood and full of life-forms more active and vicious than anything Earth had bred. You could swim in Sparta's seas.

Both planets had high gravity, twenty percent greater than Earth. Otherwise very little on Sparta was like Tanith. Sparta had little land, but what it had was rugged, with high peaks and active volcanoes. There was hardly a mountain on Tanith.

The hook-shaped peninsula that held Sparta City on its tip came into view; off to the east across Constitution Bay was the vast marshland of the Eurotas Delta, squares of reclaimed cropland visible along its edges. The shuttle made banking turns to shed energy and descend. Most of the city was on a thumb-shaped piece of land that jutted out into the water. Owensford could make out docks at either side of the thumb's base, the characteristic low squares and domes of a fusion plant in the gigawatt range, factory districts more extensive than on most planets. Lots of green, tree-lined streets and gardens, parks, villas and estates along the shores south of the city proper. Very few tall buildings, which was typical even of capital cities off-Earth; an entire planet with barely three million people was rarely crowded. Ships at the docks, everything from schooners and trawlers to surprisingly modern-looking steel-hulled diesels.

And a big section on the western side reserved for shuttles, buoys on the water marking out their landing paths. There were two more at the docks; a big walled compound topped a hill nearby, with the CoDominium flag at the guardhouse by the entrance. That would be the involuntary-colonist holding barracks. The major road ran south from that, to a cluster of parks and public buildings around a large square.

Owensford looked up at the man opposite him and smiled at his attempt to hide the obvious emotion he felt.

"I envy you, Prince Lysander," he said. "Having a home to return to."

"Yours as well, now," Lysander said. His Phraetrie-brother Harv was beside him, staring out the viewport with open longing on his face.

"I hope so, Prince; I sincerely hope so," Owensford said. *Phraetries*, he thought. *Brotherhoods*. It was another thing he'd have to get used to; Spartan Citizens were all members of one; being accepted was a condition of Citizenship. A Phraetrie was everything from a social club and mutual-benefit association to a military unit, and the Spartan militia was organized around them.

"Reminds me of California," Ace Barton said beside him, as the shuttle's wings extended fully and it touched down in twin plumes of spray.

There was a faint rocking sensation, then a *chung* as the tug linked and began towing them toward the docks. Owensford nodded; the houses on the low hills above the quaysides were mostly white stucco over stone or brick or concrete, with red tile roofs. None of them was very large, apart from the old cluster around the CoDominium center; even the colonnaded neoclassic public buildings were only a few stories high.

The style was appropriate enough; the local climate around the Aegean Sea had the same rhythm of warm dry summers and cool moist winters as the Mediterranean basin. And a fair proportion of the original settlers had been from the North American west coast as well.

"Before they mucked it up, Ace, like California before they mucked it up."

"May I ask an awkward question?" Lysander asked.

"Considering that you're paying our bills, you can ask just about anything you like," Owensford said.

"Well—I've never been a mercenary. Maybe this happens a lot, but not long ago Captain

Barton—Major Barton then—was the enemy. And outranked you. Now he's your subordinate. Isn't this a little strange?"

Ace Barton shrugged. "Maybe not so unusual as all that. And it's OK by me."

"Ace and I go back a long way," Peter Owensford said. "I guess I told you the story one night."

"I remember some of it, but that had been a long night," Lysander said.

"I remember," Peter said. "Anyway, rank isn't a big deal in Falkenberg's Legion. Hell, nearly everyone is a captain. The chain of command depends on what post you have."

"First names in the mess," Barton said. "Sort of a brotherhood. Like yours, Prince Lysander."

"Ah. Thank you," Lysander said.

Peter nodded thoughtfully. This command would have its problems, but Ace Barton wouldn't be one of them. Ace had recruited Peter Owensford into the Legion. Peter flinched at the memory. It had been after a fiasco in the Santiago civil war on Thurstone, when he had ended up on the losing side. The memory was mildly embarrassing; you expected young men to be stupid, but that had been nearly terminal. Opting for the CoDominium service at West Point, when anyone who read the papers knew the Fleet Marines were disbanding regiments and had forty-year-old lieutenants in some outfits. No chance of a U.S. Army commission when he'd shown he was a commie-coddling CD-lover, either. Then letting the Liberation Party's people recruit him for that blindsided slaughterhouse. . . .

Ace Barton had been in it for his own reasons, and a damned good thing. Without him Owensford would have been shot half a dozen times by the Republican Commissars. Or by the Dons when the Republic went down in defeat; Barton had passed the defeated volunteers off as mercenaries entitled to protection under the Code, and then gotten Christian Johnny to take them on spec. Ace went on to ten successful years skippering his own mercenary outfit before getting smashed by the Legion on Tanith. "So," Peter said. "Another beginning."

"My grandfather said Sparta was a second chance in more ways than one," Lysander said.

Owensford smiled thinly as he stood and adjusted his kepi; the troops back in the belly of the shuttle were in dress blue and gold, and so were the officers. Noncombatants and most of the baggage would be coming later, but it was important to make a good showing for the reception committee. Important for the men as well as impressing the locals . . . and after all, it was not that often that *two* kings came to greet a unit of Falkenberg's Legion when it staged down from orbit. Even on those occasions when they didn't come down in assault boats to a high-firepower reception.

"Odd that you should say that, your Highness," Owensford said. "I was just thinking that a fresh start is the commonest dream of men past their first youth, and the hardest of things to find. We carry too much baggage with us."

Lysander looked past the older man, not quite letting his eyes settle on Cornet Ursula Gordon as she stuffed the printouts and textbooks she had been studying into her carryall. Peter Owensford suspected that both parties would have been much happier if Cornet Gordon had shipped out to New Washington. An untrained and exceedingly junior female staff officer—not much more than an officer candidate, really—did not serve the needs of the Legion on that war-torn planet, and so there was another case of convenience yielding to necessity.

For that matter, he would have preferred to be on New Washington himself. The Legion had been hired on by the secessionist rebels who wanted to free their planet from its neighbor Franklin. A desperate struggle against long odds to begin with, and Franklin had hired mercenaries of their own to boot. Covenant Highlanders and Friedland armor, at that; Christian Johnny's plan would get into the textbooks with a vengeance, if it worked. While Major Peter Owensford built a base camp, trained yokels and chased a few bandits through the hills.

No, there are no clean endings, Owensford thought. *Or fresh beginnings. But we do our jobs.*

*   *   *

Dion Croser leaned back in the armchair and stared into the embers of the coal fire, holding the brandy snifter in one hand, his pipe in the other. Cool air drifted in through the French windows to his left, the ones that opened out on the gardens, smelling of eucalyptus and clipped grass. The study was a big room, paneled with slabs of dark native stone; there had been little wood available when Croser's father built the ranch house, in the early days of settlement on Sparta. A coal fire burned in the big hearth, casting flickering red shadows that caught at the crystal decanters on the sideboard, the holos and pictures amid the bookcases on the walls. One big oil portrait, of Elliot Croser as a young man on Earth, standing before the library of the University in Berkeley. Back when Sparta was a plan, something talked about in student cafés and in the living rooms of the faculty.

He raised his glass, meeting the eyes of the painted figure. *They twisted your dream, father*, he thought. Twisted it, denied him the place he'd earned as one of the founders of Sparta. Drove him into exile on this estate, into drink-sodden futility. *I'm going to set it straight.* The face in the painting might have been his, perhaps not so high in the cheekbones, and without the slanted eyes that were a legacy from Dion's Hawaiian-Japanese mother. Without the weathered

look and rangy muscle that forty years spent outside
and largely in the saddle brought, either.

A discreet cough brought his attention to the door.

"Miss Thibodeau," the butler said, disapproval plain
beneath the smooth politeness of his tone. Chung had
worked for his father back on Earth, and his
grandfather before that, and Skida Thibodeau was *not*
the sort of person a Taxpayer in California would
receive.

"Ah, you re*mem*ber Skilly," she said ironically to the
servant, handing him her bulky sheepskin jacket and
gunbelt, before pushing through into the study and
walking over to pour herself a glass of wine.

Dion rose courteously for a moment and nodded to
her, feeling his breath catch slightly; they had been
political associates for ten years, lovers for five, and it
was still pure pleasure to watch her move. Nearly two
meters tall—and the tight leather pants and cotton
shirt showed every centimeter to advantage, moving
the way he imagined a jaguar might in the jungles of
her homeland. With a sigh she threw herself into the
seat across from him, hooking a leg over one arm; that
pushed the high breasts against the thin fabric of her
shirt. He swallowed and looked up, to the
chocolate-brown face framed in loose-curled hair that
glinted blue-black. High cheekbones and full lips, nose
slightly curved, eyes tilted and colored hazel, glinting
green flecks. Her mother had been Mennonite-
German, he remembered, a farmer's daughter from
the colonies in northern Belize kidnaped into
prostitution during a visit to Belize City. Father a
pimp; and both had died young.

"Dion my mon," she said, raising her glass.

"Skida," he replied, not using the nickname.

"Skilly hears Van Horn met with the accident she
recommended," she said. "Bobber in line for his
job?"

Croser winced slightly; setting up an assassination

squad reporting directly to himself had been her idea. Skilly had been eclectically well read even before she arrived on Sparta, but sometimes he regretted introducing her to the classic works on guerrilla warfare and factional politics. Van Horn had been necessary, of course, once he had brought his toughs into the Movement. Head of the Werewolves, the only real street gang in Minetown—gangs were difficult on Sparta, where you went to school or worked as a teenager—but not loyal. Still . . . she saw the expression and smiled indulgently.

"Mon, in this business, you doan fire people," she pointed out. "Retire feet first is the only way."

He nodded; even with the cell-structure, Van Horn could have done the Front too much damage if he had gone to the RSMP; not least because he was one of the links between the NCLF's above-ground organization and the Helots. Discipline had to be enforced, especially now that direct-action work was increasing. Far too many of the recruits were Welfare Island street-gangers, the leaders had to set an example.

"You think Bobber may resent what happened?" he said. "She and Van Horn were . . . close."

Skida laughed. "Bobber de one tell me Van Horn dipping the till excessive," she said. "Bobber and I came in on the same CoDo ship; she a cool one. Van Horn a stepping stone for her, and beside, Bobber likes girls better. Good hater, she a real believer in the Movement." She shrugged indifferently. "And she from Chicago; that useful now we getting so many *gringo* gangers off the transports."

He sipped at the brandy and took another pull at the pipe, the comforting mellow bite at his tongue.

"Congratulations on the Velysen raid," he said. "Ah . . . Skida . . . what happened to his wife and sister-in-law is creating a lot of indignation."

"Just what Skilly wanted; Dion, you know we not getting these ranchers to *like* us, whatever. And just killing them, it make them mad only and want to fight us." She extended a hand palm up, then curled the fingers. "Threaten they families, and we have them by the *balls*, mon."

He sighed again; the basic strategy was his, in any event. "I know; and they'll push for harsher measures on the non-Citizens, which drives them into our camp."

"*The worse, the better*, that what that Russki mon Lenin say, no? Very nice statement you make to the *Herald*, denouncing violent splinter faction and then blaming oppression for driving us to it." She took another slow sip of her wine; he had taught her that, to appreciate a good vintage. "How things going at the University?"

"Slowly, but we've got a structure there now. Particularly in the Sociology and Humanities divisions; there're a lot of scions there who're worried about making their Citizenship tests. Plus the usual hangers-on."

"Many ready to go Helot?" she asked. It was a bother, keeping the other recruits from eating the student types alive, but the survivors were valuable when they'd toughened up. Too many of the rank-and-file NCLF fighters broke into a sweat if they had to think more than a week ahead.

Dion's face creased in a bleak grin. "There will be, after we provoke the next riot. Sore heads and sore tempers, and once they're committed . . . " They toasted each other. "I've gotten another half-dozen CoDo Marine deserters for you, too, and another officer."

Skilly thumped the arm of the chair in delight. "Good mon!" she said. Trained cadre willing to work for the Helots had always been a problem; there were plenty of CoDo officers up on the beach, but most of them were picky. *Too squeamish to be useful*, she thought. The ones who weren't tended to have other problems that restricted their usefulness.

"Roughly, what else are we going to need in the next year or so?"

She frowned. "Dion, we got as far as we getting without serious outside help, like we discussed. Plenty recruits and enough arms"—Sparta exported the simpler infantry weapons and equipment, and the Movement had been diverting a percentage of that for years—"money coming in steady, but raids and holding up trucks not enough; we need electronics, commo gear, heavy weapons, this precision-guided stuff. Better network in Sparta City and the Valley towns, too. And techs, and a secure conduit off-planet. Not just to those Liberation Party *grisgris*, either. Even *with* help, going to be long time before we can slug it out with the Brotherhoods."

He set down glass and pipe and tapped his fingers together beneath his chin. "We've got it."

Skida raised an eyebrow. "Money?"

"Money, yes."

"Enough to pay your debts? Who we owe for this?"

Croser ignored the first question. Neither he nor his father had been very good at financial management. The Revolution would take care of the situation, but that wasn't any of Skida's business. "A lot more than money. From the Senator." A snort. "It was the Royal government hiring Falkenberg's people that decided him to do more for us than the trickle we've gotten so far. Weapons, shipping out for what the NCLF takes in, loans—*big* loans—technical personnel. . . . A group from Meiji is arriving next week." This time his grin was a wolf's. "Full conference of the clandestine branch section heads as soon as the Meijians have been briefed."

Skida's teeth showed dazzling white against her skin. "That my mon! " She raised her wine. "To the Revolution!"

He leaned over to clink his snifter against her glass. "To the Democratic Republic of Sparta!"

"To the first *President* of the Republic, Dion Croser!"

"To the first Minister of Defense"—the Royal government had a Ministry of War—"Skida Thibodeau!" he said.

They emptied their glasses and she uncoiled to her feet, walked over, braced her hands against the armrests of his chair and leaned forward until their faces were almost touching. Lips met; her mouth tasted of wine and mint. The man's nostrils flared, taking in the strong mixed scents from her clothes and skin, woodsmoke and sweat and leather and horse. Dion reached for her.

"No, not yet," Skida said huskily; her eyes glittered in the firelight. "Skilly wants a shower first. And then we lock the door for a day. Skilly has been in the outback too long. Skilly is so horny goats and girls and even my hidehunters were starting to look good."

She drew back with taunting slowness, and looked over her shoulder. "Scrub de back, mon?"

CHAPTER FOUR

Crofton's Essays and Lectures in Military History (2nd Edition)

Professor John Christian Falkenberg II:
Delivered at the CoDominium University, Rome, 2080

"The principal military states 'own' perhaps ninety-five percent of all military expertise, if that can be measured by the number of publications on the subject. They have even managed to turn that expertise into a minor export commodity in its own right. Officers belonging to countries which are not great military powers are regularly sent to attend staff and war colleges in Washington, Moscow, London, and Paris . . . the principal powers themselves have sent thousands upon thousands of military 'experts' to dozens of third-world countries all over Latin America, Africa, and Asia.

"The above notwithstanding, serious doubt exists concerning the ability of developed states—both such as are currently 'liberating' themselves from communist domination and such as are already 'free'—to use armed force as an instrument for attaining meaningful political ends. This situation is not entirely new. In numerous incidents during the last two decades, the inability of developed countries to protect their interests and even their citizens' lives in the face of low-level threats has been demonstrated time and time again. As a result, politicians as well as academics were caught bandying about such phrases as 'the decline of power,' 'the decreasing utility of war,' and—in the case of the United States—'the straw giant.'

"So long as it was only Western society that was becoming 'debellicized' the phenomenon was greeted with anxiety. The Soviet failure in Afghanistan has turned the scales, however, and now the USSR too is a club member in good standing. In view of these facts, there has been speculation that war itself may not have a future and is about to be replaced by economic competition among the great 'trading blocs' now forming in Europe, North America, and the Far East. This volume will argue that such a view of war is not correct. Large-scale, conventional war—war as understood by today's principal military powers—may indeed be at its last gasp; however, war itself, war as such, is alive and kicking and about to enter a new epoch. . . . "

—*The Transformation of War*: Free Press, 1991

The above was written by Martin van Creveld and published shortly before the United States began the largest conventional military action of the second half of the 20th century. We are now to consider where Creveld, one of the best military historians of the last or indeed any century, was correct—and where he went wrong.

* * *

"That was an impressive show, Major," Alexander I said as the last of Fifth Battalion clambered aboard the trucks in the square below.

They were locally made, diesel-powered flatbeds with wheels that were balls of spun chrome-steel alloy thread. Primitive compared to ground-effect machines, but better than the horse-drawn wagons found on many worlds. There were plenty of draft animals on the streets of Sparta City, but there were electric runabouts and diesel-engined vans as well, and even a few Earth-made hovercars.

Here in Government House Square where the mercenaries had paraded for their employer's inspection the town looked much like a Californian university campus of the older type, complete with tiled walks, gardens, and neospanish architecture. The Hall of

State could have done for a convocation, with its green copper dome and pillars; the Palace was a rambling affair that might have been the Dean's residence.

"I hope you don't mind our detaining you and your officers," Alexander said. He was a tall spare man in his fifties; much like an older Prince Lysander, except that his gray-shot hair was blond and worn ear-length in a cut fashionable on Earth two generations before. And for the infinite weariness around his eyes; Owensford knew it for the look of tension borne too long.

"By no means, sir," Peter said. He bowed slightly, reflecting that the Spartan monarchy was an informal affair, at least so far.

David I, the Freedman king, was already seated at the briefing table. Crown Prince David, actually, but his father Jason was quasi-retired, victim of a debilitating disease, and David was Freedman king for all practical purposes. David was a stocky man, dressed like his colleague in brown tunic and knee-breeches of extremely conservative cut; one of the more elderly bureaucrats near him wore a suit and tie, old-fashioned enough to be bizarre. Another man had a shaven-bald head, monocle, quasi-military tunic and riding crop; that would be *Freiherr* Bernard von Alderheim. His father had been from what was once Königsberg, East Prussia, then Kaliningrad, and now Königsberg again; his daughter was Prince Lysander's fiancée, and he was the most prominent industrialist on the planet. He was also titular head of one of the largest and most important Phraetries.

Considered eccentric, Owensford remembered from the briefing. *All in all, you can certainly tell we're seven months' transit from Earth.* He took his seat among the Legion officers.

Uniforms on one side of the square, civilians on the other, except for the man in the dull-scarlet tunic and blue breeches of the Royal Spartan Mounted Police.

From the look of his boots, the "mounted" meant exactly that.

"The junior officers and NCOs can handle encampment easily enough," Owensford said. "You will understand, we're anxious to get the basic facilities in place before our noncombatants and families arrive." Some next week, and the rest over the following months. "The Legion's accustomed to being fairly self-contained, and billeting might create problems."

Alexander cleared his throat. "I don't anticipate any trouble with that," he said. "We've got the first five hundred recruits for the Field Force standing by, and there's earth-moving equipment we can make available."

"And anything else you need, I can find for you," Baron von Alderheim said. "Will you also need workmen?"

"Thank you, no, Baron," Peter said. "Learning camp construction is as good an introduction to military discipline as any."

Ace Barton nodded agreement.

"Very good," von Alderheim said. "Castramentation. The first lessons for a Roman soldier."

Peter smiled slightly, unsure of what to say. "Sire, shall I introduce my officers now?"

"Please do," Alexander said.

"My chief of staff, Captain Anselm Barton. Captain Andrew Lahr, Battalion Adjutant. Captain Jameson Mace, Scouts commander. Captains Jesus and Catherine Alana, Intelligence and Planning and Intelligence and Logistics, respectively. George Slater, our senior company commander."

Alexander I raised an eyebrow. "Slater?"

George Slater grinned. "Yes, Sire. My father will be your War College Director when he gets here."

"Ah. Thank you. Mr. Plummer—"

"Yes, Sire." The speaker was a small man, elderly, conservatively dressed but with a splash of color in his scarf. "I'm Horace Plummer, secretary to the cabinet. This is the Honorable Roland Dawson, Principal Secretary of State. Mr. Eric Respari, Treasury and Finance. Sir Alfred Nathanson, Minister of War. Madame Elayne Rusher, Attorney General. Lord Henry Yamaga, Interior and Development. General Lawrence Desjardins, Commandant of the Royal Spartan Mounted Police."

The gendarmerie chief was a blocky man with a thin mustache, with the heavy-gravity musculature most Spartans shared and a dark tan that must have taken work under a sun this pale; not a desk man by preference, Peter estimated.

"This is the War Council," Plummer said. "In formal meetings the Speaker of the Senate would be present, and others can be invited to attend if their expertise is required, but these are Their Majesties' key advisors. Your military orders will come directly from Their Majesties. For administrative purposes you will report to Sir Alfred. Their Majesties ask that you make your initial presentation now."

"Thank you." Peter stood and went to the display board. "I gather from the reports Mr. Plummer has been sending us ever since we entered the Sparta system that things are not quite what we expected here," he said. "Some of this may need adjustment, but I think it important that we all agree on just what the Legion's mission is."

"Yes, of course," Plummer said.

"With your permission, I'm going to lecture a bit," Peter said. "Sparta has always had an enviable militia system based on the Brotherhoods, but until recently the Kingdom hasn't had any need of a standing army or expeditionary forces. That's changing due to the unstable political situation, and you've thought it wise to acquire both."

"To be blunt," King David Freedman said, "we can only afford the one if we have the other. We'll need to rent out expeditionary troops which we hope we can count on at need, because we certainly can't afford to keep a big standing army."

"Just so," Peter said. "Now, the original plan was to bring the entire legion in, let it clone itself, and hire out the clone. That would take care of an expeditionary force. Meanwhile, we would build the infrastructure for doing that trick several times over. By hiring out some units, and bringing selected experienced units home, Sparta would bootstrap up to having the equivalent of a regiment factory. With any luck they'd hire out for enough to support themselves while remaining loyal to Sparta."

"Put that way, it doesn't sound like a very good deal for the soldiers," Roland Dawson said.

"Actually, it could be," Peter said. "Depending on how it was done. Majesties, my lords, my lady—"

"With Madame Elayne's permission, 'gentlemen' will suffice as a collective," Alexander said.

Peter grinned. "Thank you, Sire. To continue. Sparta has considerable experience with militia, but not so much with long service professionals. The professional soldier, for the early part of his career, is quite different from the citizen soldier. Later, though, the differences tend to vanish. There are exceptions, but for the most part the troops may join for glamour, and fight for their comrades, but their real goal is acceptance and respect from someone they respect. A chance at honor, perhaps a second career, and a decent retirement. Sparta can provide all that."

"Pensions," David I said. "They can be expensive."

"Yes, Sire, they can be, but if you want troops loyal to Sparta, as opposed to freebooters, that's ultimately what you have to offer. I do point out that you have a growing economy, so that by the time the pensions are due you should have more than enough to pay them with. Also, you have land, and community resources. I think you may find that retired long service troopers make a net contribution to your economy even with pension costs."

"Yes, yes, of course—"

"So," Peter continued. "If it is still the goal to build long service expeditionary quality units, there will be a number of intermediate objectives, all interrelated. Take weapons systems as an example. They must be designed to take advantage of Sparta's production facilities, but also the troop capabilities—education, schools, quality of the officer corps. What weapons are available will influence how the men are trained. Naturally all this has to fit into your industrial policy.

"Staff officers. I'm sure you know there's a lot of difference between troop leaders and military managers."

"I'd always thought so until I worked with Falkenberg," Prince Lysander said.

Owensford nodded agreement. "The Legion is a bit special, Highness. Even so, you mostly worked with Colonel Falkenberg's staff, who alternate between planning and troop leadership. We also have officers who never leave their units—don't want to. Some of the best leaders you'll ever find. Soldiers should be ambitious, but not so much so that the troops wonder why they they should fight for a man anxious to leave them.

"Also, what you saw was the Legion on campaign, which, I grant you, we seem to be most of the time. What you didn't see was in the background. Schools, technical training, social activities, weapons procurement, financial investments, mostly done by non-combatants. And for all that we're a self-contained force, we're only a regimental combat team. What Sparta needs to build will be considerably larger, and thus more complex."

Peter shrugged. "A lot of that will be in Colonel Slater's department, of course, but I do want you to be aware of it."

"Yes, I see," Alexander said. "It's a bit daunting put

all at once, but we knew we were in for a major effort. I think we're still agreed?" He looked around the table and collected nods of assent.

"Yes," David said simply. "Only things are not quite what they were. Perhaps we should let General Desjardins talk about the security situation. General—"

"You knew we had a security problem," the constabulary commander said, touching the controls of a keypad. Everyone shifted in their seats as a three-meter square screen on the wall opposite the windows came to life. "It's gotten considerably worse since the last packet of information we sent your Colonel Falkenberg."

A map of the main inhabited portions of Sparta sprang out; the city, and the valley of the Eurotas and its tributaries, snaking north and west from the delta. A scattering along the shores of the Aegean and Oinos seas, and on islands. Dots showed towns; Melos at the junction of the Eurotas and the Alcimion, Clemens about a third of the way up, Dodona in the Middle Valley and Olynthos at the falls where it left Lake Alexander. That was a *big* river, half again as long as the Amazon. Another river and delta on the west coast opposite the Bay of Islands, with the town of Rhodes at the mouth; that one was about comparable to the Mississippi.

Red spots leapt out across the map; there was a concentration on the upper Eurotas and in the foothill zones flanking it on either side. A lighter speckle stretched west into the plains and mountains of the interior of the Serpentine continent, among the isolated grazing stations and mines and hunters' shacks. There was a clear zone in the lower Eurotas, but a dense scattering in Sparta City itself.

"We've always had some banditry in the outback," Desjardins continued. "Worse lately, and you can imagine why."

"Scattered population," Ace Barton said. "Vulnerable communications."

"In spades," the policeman said grimly. "There's still plenty of good land near the capital—even here on the peninsula—but it takes money to develop it, which we don't have. Agricultural prices so low that there's no profit if you need much capital investment. And a lot's locked up in big grants from the early settlement."

David I stirred. "The government has always had more land than money," he said, in a slightly defensive tone.

"Sir," the police chief said, nodding acknowledgment. "So people swarmed up the Eurotas, and into the side hills. Miners too: there are pockets of good ore, silver and gold, copper, thorium, whatever, over most of the continent. None very big except for up near Olynthos, but enough . . . Everyone in the outback has a horse and a gun, and if you know what you're doing you can live off the land pretty easy. Lot of tempting targets. The RSMP has been able to keep a lid on things, mostly; the Brotherhoods help. Until recently. This is the latest: the Velysen ranch."

A picture sprang out, an overhead shot taken from an aircraft, of the smoldering ruins of a big two-story house amid undamaged outbuildings. The screen blinked down to a ground level receptor with the slight jiggle of a helmet-mounted camera, and men in khaki battledress and nemourlon body-armor moved against the same background. A row of blanket-shrouded shapes lay beside trestle tables. Hands reached into the line of sight and lifted one covering. The corpse was that of a woman, and it was obvious how she had died. The soldiers leaned forward with a rustle of coiled tension, and one of the civilians retched.

"That's Eleanor Velysen," the policeman continued, in a voice taut with suppressed anger. "The other woman's her sister." He paused. "None of the remaining women on the ranch were molested; Arthur Velysen was shot, and his foreman and two other Citizens, and the place was pretty effectively stripped. Not much vandalism, and the Velysen children weren't harmed." The camera panned again, to a wall where **HELOTS RULE OK** had been spray-painted in letters three meters high.

"Terrorism," Owensford said softly. "Not bandits, terrorists. Helots?"

"What the terrorists call themselves these days. The same graffiti has gone up here in the city. They're *effective* terrorists, though," Desjardins said with a grim nod. "Over the past year, more than two dozen attacks fitting this pattern. Sixteen in the last two months alone, from south of Clemens to north of Olynthos, and as far west as the upper Meneander. Plus dozens of reports of intimidation, demands for protection money, pamphlets . . . and some of the ranchers and mine owners *are* paying these Helots off, I swear it."

One of the bureaucrats stirred. "If the RSMP were more active—"

Desjardins's fist hit the table. "Madam Minister—with respect—I've got three thousand police, that's *counting* the clerks and forensics people and the ones who maintain the navigation buoys and the technicians and the training cadre. I've got a grand total of *ten* tiltrotors, and *thirty* helicopters, so when we get to road's end everyone walks or rides or takes a steamboat or blimp. If I split the five hundred or so Mobile Force personnel up, the Helots will eat them alive! This gang that attacked the Velysens's place, there were sixty of them—they blew the satellite dish and cut the landlink to the Torrey estate and had an ambush force emplaced to block the road in."

"Classic," Ace Barton said.

"Seems so," Owensford said.

"You've faced this kind of thing?" General Desjardins asked.

"Oh, yes," Peter said. He nodded to Barton.

"So far it's late Phase One guerrilla ops," Barton said. "To stop it, you can't sit and wait for guerrillas to come to you. They'll destroy you in detail. You have to be *more* mobile, and let militia do the positional defense."

Desjardins laughed without humor. "That's what the Velysens thought," he said. "They had a dozen armed guards and electrified wire. My forensics people are pretty sure the six guards who died were killed by their buddies, and the sabotage was an inside job too."

Owensford and Barton exchanged a glance and a thought: *so much for a peaceful training command.*

Alexander spoke. "So you see, gentlemen, we need the Legion more than ever, which is one reason we kept the rest of it on retainer. Unfortunately, we're less able to *pay* for it than ever, as well."

Catherine Alana looked up from her notes. "Your Majesty—sir—surely this hasn't reduced your revenue *that* much?"

"Not yet," his co-monarch answered; the Freedmans had been economists, holders of the professorships at Columbia and the CoDominium University in Rome. "But Captain, the economic justification behind the Field Force—yes, I know the strategic arguments, Alexander, but we have to cut our coat to fit the cloth—the economic rationale is that it will *help* our foreign currency situation."

Peter nodded agreement. Many of the newly independent planets defrayed the costs of their national armies by hiring them out, with a little low-budget imperialism on the side. For some like Covenant and Friedland, it was their major industry. Sparta had planned to get into the game. Foreign exchange aside, it was necessary in order to develop and maintain the kind of military force that would make it *obvious* to the likes of Friedland that here was no easy prey.

David sighed. "Ideologically, we're free traders here, Major Owensford; bureaucracy and regulation were what our parents came here to *avoid*, after all. But—'Needs must when the devil drives.' All foreign currency is allocated through the Ministry of Trade, and luxury imports—anything but capital equipment—are highly taxed. It's one of the slogans the NCLF use to whip up the non-Citizens, they say they want imported luxuries and more welfare."

Captain Jesus Alana smiled thinly; he was a dark man, a few inches shorter than his red-haired wife, with a trimmed black mustache. "There was much the same on Hadley. Your opposition will be the . . . Non-Citizens' Liberation Front?" he said. "Mr. Dion Croser?"

"*Citizen* Dion Croser, and that's half the problem," Desjardins said. "And a son of one of the Founders, which is even worse. Sir, I'm morally certain he's in this up to his well-bred neck. Just let me pull him in, and—"

Alexander made a sharp gesture. "No. Not without evidence linking him to these Helots. Which I don't believe; Dion Croser's misguided, but he *is* Anthony's son, after all. 'Liberty under Law,' General Desjardins." He turned to the soldiers. "Croser's got some following here in Sparta City, mostly among the recent immigrants and unskilled workers; and a few at the University." A wry smile. "Our founders were political scientists and sociologists, but they underestimated the effect of an underemployed intelligentsia when they founded our higher educational system."

"Layabouts," David snorted. "Hanging around the campus and complaining they aren't allowed to mind other people's business in the civil service. Major, our government has only a few thousand employees and contracts most of its limited functions out—" He stopped his impulse to lecture with a visible effort.

"The fact remains, that to fully equip the Field Force regiments we must expend hard currency, and that's hard to come by. We need more export earnings. If we have soldiers employed off-world and we collect their pay in Dayan shekels or Friedlander marks, that is one thing. If they have to stay *here* and fight . . . " He shrugged.

" 'Opulence must take second place to defense,' " Owensford recited; the Freedman king looked mildly surprised to hear a mercenary quoting Adam Smith. *You'd be surprised what Christian Johnny gets us to do*, Owensford thought. *His father was a history professor, after all.* "You have indigenous munitions manufacturing."

"Small arms and mortars, nemourlon under license from DuPont; weapons are one of our main processed exports, along with intermediate-technology equipment for planets even less industrialized than we are. We can make armored cars and tanks, but there won't be a lot of output. No electronics to speak of; we've been negotiating with Xanadu and Meiji for chip fabricators, but . . . " He shrugged again; everyone knew the prices were kept artificially high. "We have the people and the knowledge, energy and resources and opportunity, all the classic requirements, but we're at the tools-to-make-the-tools-to-make-the-machines stage.

"We need *time*."

"Which is one commodity we can buy you," Owensford said. "Soldiers do a lot of that. Well, the bright side is that if you don't have much in the way of electronics, neither will the enemy. Jesus, I'd be grateful if you'd see to increased security on all the Regiment's equipment. Some of our advanced gear will be very much on the rebel want list."

"Yes, sir." Alana scrawled a note on his pocket computer.

"We are going to need air transport," Peter said.

"You can't send aviation into a battle area, but it's very often the key to making battles happen where you want them, rather than where the enemy wants them. I'll ask you to do what you can to ramp up production of helicopters. They needn't be fancy."

"Ja," Baron von Alderheim said.

"And not just in the one firm," Peter said. "Aviation is too important to be a point failure source—uh, for there to be only one supplier."

"I see," von Alderheim said. "You wish me to help my competition?"

"I'm afraid that's exactly what I wish," Peter said. "Understand, we don't need to make everything ourselves, but it sure helps if we're self-sufficient in big ticket items."

"That makes a great deal of sense," the Minister of War said. "If Baron von Alderheim will agree—"

"Oh, I agree," von Alderheim said. "Civic duty and all that. Besides, if Major Owensford is successful, there will be plenty of orders for military equipment, and hard currency as well."

"That is certainly the goal," David I said.

"A goal the enemy may have made easier," Peter said.

"Ah?" Sir Alfred looked puzzled.

"One difficulty in expanding a military force is leadership," Peter said. "Many of our first wave of recruits will have to rather quickly become noncoms and junior officers for the second group. Combat experience, even in a low-intensity war like this, will help a lot."

"I doubt Eleanor Velysen thought it was low intensity," Roland Dawson said.

"No sir, of course not," Peter said. "I don't mean to be flippant." He shrugged. "But that's still what we have here. A training war."

"So far," Desjardins said. "But it has been escalating."

Peter nodded. "Right, but we'll soon be set to deal with that, I think. Now, we're all right on technology. It's not as if we had to worry about off-planet forces with high-tech gear. Eventually we'll want troops capable of taking on a Line Marine regiment, but fortunately we don't have to ask that of them just yet." He looked at the map display. "Lot of water here. I presume we can shut down rebel water traffic."

"Lots of boats out there," Desjardins said. "Fishing, cargo hauling, even some yachts."

"They aren't likely to be smugglers. Nothing worth smuggling, is there? So surely all boat owners are loyalists."

"Or say they are," Desjardins muttered.

"You have reason for suspicion?" Barton asked.

"Fear, sir," Desjardins said. "Terrorism can be an effective recruiting device. Especially when all you're asked to do is look the other way."

"That much we can handle. We won't be recruiting any traitors. Security is Captain Catherine Alana's department and she's good at it."

Catherine smiled acknowledgment of the compliment and said, "General Desjardins, I strongly suggest an armed Coast Guard Auxiliary, river and sea. Give it responsibility for seeing that water traffic is ours or neutral."

"It might work," Desjardins said.

"Have them do random sweeps in strength," Ace Barton commented. "And be sure they have good communications, both with the RSMP and the Fifth." He grinned mirthlessly. "It's not likely, but the rebels may be stupid enough to concentrate their forces."

"Precisely," Peter Owensford said. "I doubt General Desjardins is worried about defeating the rebels in battle—"

"Well, there are a fair number of them," Desjardins said. "And the RSMP isn't trained for set piece battles. But no, we're not worried, especially now that you lot are here. It's finding them that's the real problem. Captain Alana, I'll be very happy to work with you in setting up the Coast Guard."

"And I," Baron von Alderheim said. "The fishing village on my estate can furnish the nucleus. They are all armed, they will only need instructions."

"Close off water transport and we'll have a good part of the problem licked," Owensford said. He turned to King Alexander. "Sir, you do understand, we will need some kind of registration system. A way to identify legitimate boats—"

"We have that now," Prince David said. "We believe in freedom, Major, but with freedom come responsibilities." He shook his head. "I presume you want authority for your Coast Guard to intercept vessels and search them at random."

"Yes, sir."

"That won't be popular," David said. "But I believe we can get the Council and Senate to agree. As a temporary measure, of course. I suggest one year, with full debate required before renewal of the law. Alexander?"

"I'll agree to that."

"Thank you. I'll have it drafted," David said. "Major, you said you could assure the loyalty of the Coast Guard Auxiliary. I'd like to know how."

"Ah—we have equipment—"

"Lie detectors?" Alexander asked. There was an edge to his voice.

"Something like that, sir," Prince Lysander said. "They're—" He looked to Peter Owensford. "Perhaps I'd better not say? It's non-intrusive. Nothing anyone can object to."

"Hah." Baron von Alderheim looked thoughtful.

"Sir," Peter said. "I presume everyone here has taken some kind of oath of office? With criminal penalties?"

"Yes, yes, of course, everyone here is sworn to the Privy Council," David said.

"Fine," Peter said. "Then we can begin here. And we may as well start now."

"Start what?" Elayne Rusher asked.

She was a woman of indeterminate age. Peter guessed fifty, but he would have believed anything between forty and sixty. She was attractive but not especially pretty, and gave Peter a feeling of confidence. *Like having a competent big sister.* "Loyalty testing, Madame Attorney General."

She frowned. "How do you propose to do that?"

Peter shrugged. "It's simple enough. What part of Sparta do you come from, madam?"

"I have always lived in the City," Rusher said. "And how will knowing that help?"

"You'd be surprised at what helps, madam," Peter said. "Do you know any rebels?"

"Dion."

"Of course, and his supporters. Who else?"

"No one else—"

Peter looked to Captain Alana. "Catherine?"

Captain Alana had been staring at her oversized wristwatch. "Loyal, but defending someone. She suspects someone. I'd guess a close relative, but perhaps a friend of a relative."

"Why—What in the world makes you think that?"

Catherine smiled. "A good guess, but it's true, isn't it?"

Rusher sighed. "Close enough. My daughter Jennifer is seeing a young man from the University. There's something about him—but it's nothing I could justify investigating. How have you found out all this? You've hardly had time—"

"You just told them," General Desjardins said. "Voice stress analyzers. I've heard about them, but I didn't think anyone but CoDominium Intelligence had them."

"That's what everyone thinks," Peter said. "And we want them to go on thinking it. Mr. Plummer, do you know any rebels?"

"Of course not. Other than Citizen Croser." He smiled thinly. "I take it I'm being tested now? Should I be concerned?"

"Just relax, sir," Catherine said. "Would you mind telling me your mother's maiden name?"

"All clear," Catherine Alana said. "See, that wasn't so bad."

"I can't say I like the implications," Henry Yamaga said. "As if you suspect us—"

"Sir," Peter began.

"Let me, sir," Ace Barton said. "With all due respect, my lords and ladies, this is a war of information. Determining who is and is not trustworthy is most of the battle. If your rancher—"

"Velysen," Desjardins said.

"If Mr. Velysen had known who among his guards were traitors, he'd be alive, and so would his women. Frankly, I'd think speaking a few sentences into a computer would be a small price to pay for peace of mind. While we're at it—Madame Rusher, I'm sure we'll all feel much better if Catherine were invited to dinner the next time your daughter brings her odd friend home."

"It's a bit distasteful," Rusher said. She paused a moment. "But yes, thank you. Captain, could you and your husband join us for dinner the day after tomorrow?"

"I'd be delighted," Catherine said.

"So. One less thing to worry about," Peter said. "Now, I presume that you were planning on recruiting mostly transportees for the Field Force?"

The civilians looked at each other, embarrassed; it was a little like what BuReloc did to troublemakers on Earth, with the added refinement that Sparta intended to use them as cannon fodder and make a profit on them to boot.

Alexander sighed. "Our Citizens are mostly native-born now, family people, and we have an open land frontier for restless youngsters. The people BuReloc dumps on us are mostly single adults, six-tenths men," he said.

"And many of them come from four, five, six generations who haven't worked, haven't got the *concept* of work anywhere in their mental universe. We tell them to work or starve, and it *takes* starvation to make them work—or military discipline, we presume. Some younger Citizens will be volunteering as well; we'll pass the word through the Brotherhoods, and Prince Lysander's exploits on Tanith have made the Legion pretty glamorous on the video." He looked with fond pride at his son; Lysander had been brooding at the gruesome pictures from the Velysen ranch, but he blushed slightly at his father's words.

Owensford nodded. "It's infiltrators *I'm* worried about," he said frankly, glancing over at the Alanas. They nodded. "One thing has to be understood," Owensford said. "A legionnaire has no *civil* rights."

Freedman raised an eyebrow. "And what does that mean, Major?"

"Literally what I said, Sire. Your Citizens, your non-citizens, your civilians have various civil rights which we'll do what we can to get our troops to respect; but once they've signed up as soldiers, we expect their loyalty, and that loyalty includes cooperating with our investigators to determine that they *are* loyal."

"Yes, of course. And I suppose that includes the RSMP. It doesn't appear that General Desjardins has any objections."

"On the contrary, Majesty," Desjardins said. "I'm quite confident of the loyalty of my men, but it can't hurt for everyone to be certain."

A clock chimed in the background. "Other duties," Alexander said. "We'll continue this tomorrow, but I take it we are all agreed that the primary mission of the Legion has not changed? Thank you. David?" The two kings rose, and the others in the room followed. "Until this evening, Colonel," Alexander said. "We've laid on a welcoming banquet at the Spartosky, that's our local social center." He spread his hands. "Political, I'm afraid, but necessary. The food's decent, at any rate."

*   *   *

Geoffrey Niles leaned back against the rear of the booth and took another sip of his drink, coughing slightly at the taste of the raw cane spirit. The Dead Cow was hopping tonight; it was autumn, after all, and the outbacker hunters were mostly in town with their summer haul of tallow and skins. Money to pay off some of their debts to the banks and the backer-merchants, money to burn in a debauch they could remember when they were freezing and sweating in some forsaken gully in the outback. There was a live band snarling out music, and a few tired-looking women in G-strings bumping and grinding in front of them; more were working the tables. A solid wall of noise made most conversation impossible, although not innumerable card and dice games. The fog of tobacco, hash, and borloi smoke, plus the strong smells of leather and unwashed flesh, went a fair distance toward making breathing impossible, too.

"Interesting, sir, eh, what?" Niles said to the man beside him. Kenjiro Murasaki smiled thinly and kept his eyes on the crowded chaos of the room.

Damned wet blanket, Niles thought.

You couldn't find a place like this on Earth anymore. Oh, there were dives enough if you had a taste for slumming, but an Earthside slum was a dumping-ground for the useless, the refuse of automation and the gray stagnation of a planet locked in political and economic stasis by its ruling oligarchies. There was a raw energy here, the sort he imagined might have been found on America's western frontier or the outposts of the Raj two centuries ago. These were not idlers, they were hard men who went out and wrested a living from a wilderness still imperfectly adapted to Terran life. He looked at the stuffed longhorn steer on the wall behind the long bar, lying toes-up and flanked by wolf heads, legacy of some demented Green back in the early days.

To adventure, he thought with a tingle of excitement, lifting his glass. Murasaki made a noncommittal noise; he was taciturn at the best of times, and the implants which altered the shape of his face were still a little tender.

A group had walked in, past the bouncers in their military-style nemourlon armor and helmets. *That's them*, he thought. Only one he recognized from the briefing, the tall black woman in scuffed leathers. *Stunner*, he thought admiringly. A big bald Indian-looking man with twin machetes over his back and a bowie down one boot-top, similarly dressed. Several others in the black leather jackets, red tights and metal-studded boots of the Werewolves, the gang whose turf included the Minetown section of Sparta City. Heads turned in their direction, then away; this was not the sort of place an uptown civilian could go safely, but the habitués mostly had a well-developed sense of personal survival.

Not all of them. One raised his head out of a puddle of spilled rum, stared blearily and made a grab for the black woman's crotch. She pivoted on one heel, her hands slapping down; the whinnying scream the hidehunter made was audible even over the background roar of the bar, and that dropped away to relative silence as others noted the byplay.

"Ugly, *ugly* mon," she said; her fingers held his hand in a come-along hold Niles recognized, the wrist twisted to lock the joint and a thumb planted on a nerve-cluster. "Say sorry to Skilly, ugly mon."

The bearded face blinked and twisted up, half in pain and half in astonishment. "Oh, Jesus, Skilly, sure I'm sorry, didn't fuckin' *recognize* you, honest!" He relaxed slightly as she smiled whitely.

"Not sorry enough," she said, grabbing his thumb with her free hand and jerking sharply backward.

His eyes bulged, and his free hand scrabbled for the automatic at his waist. Skilly released his hand, and her elbow moved in a short chopping arc that ended on his temple; there was a *thock*, and another as he collapsed back into the chair and his head dropped limply to the table. There were nervous grins from the other cardplayers, hoots and guffaws from all around; the woman moved through the throng slapping palms and backs, calling greetings and declining offers of drinks as she led the others to the door at the back of the room.

Niles swallowed. "Well, I'm certainly not going to press uninvited attentions on *that* lady," he said, fiddling slightly with the catch of his Jujitsu laptop. It would be ten minutes before they could join the others.

Murasaki looked up from doing calculations on his wristcomp; this time his smile showed real amusement. "Let us hope, Niles-san, that *she* does not choose to press her attentions on *you*."

Niles took a swallow of his drink. Grand-Uncle had promised him an experience that would show what he was made of. So far, it was living up to the advance billing. Collecting himself, he glanced at the ceiling. Time for the conspirators to meet and plan; he smoothed back his fluffy blond mustache with a finger and practiced his grin.

Adventure, complete with exotic dusky maiden, he thought. *I'll just remember not to offer her a thumb.*

*   *   *

"Excellent," Kenjiro Murasaki said. "As a beginning."

It was a small meeting: Croser and Skida on the one side, the Meijian and his equally stone-faced aide on the other. The small upper room smelled of wine and spilled beer and sweat; there were stains on the blankets that covered the cot in the corner, and a scribble of names knife-carved in the broad pine planks. There were no papers on the table. A first-rate memory was a condition of leadership in work like this.

The Meijian continued. "I am particularly pleased with the slow, careful preparation for overt action, the building of funds and organization."

"Protracted struggle," Croser said. He did not like the Meijian; the man was a mercenary, someone who made war for money, not principle. But there was no doubt of his competence; Grand Senator Bronson—*Earth Prime, remember that*—did not spend good money on incompetents.

"Exactly," Murasaki nodded. "Now, Capital Prime, with the assets I have brought, we may proceed much more rapidly from the phase of organization and low-intensity guerrilla struggle to that of large-scale destabilization. Indeed, I believe we must work quickly. The reports of the War Cabinet meeting today indicate that Major Owensford has already begun mobilization."

"You can overhear War Cabinet meetings?" Croser asked.

Murasaki bowed slightly. "Let us say they are not as secure as they believe. You will understand, Capital Prime, my men are specialists and technicians, not soldiers in the strict sense of the term. What we can do is give you secure communications, subvert the enemy's communications and computer networks, and provide a small but crucial increment of highly advanced weapons to offset those employed by the Spartan government. Occasional direct action of a limited nature."

"That's the *Royal* government," Croser corrected. "The Movement is the legitimate government of Sparta."

"As you say. Now, despite this, the enemy will maintain superior conventional military power almost to the end. As your own plan outlines, we must keep the struggle on a political level as far as possible." He smiled, an expression that went no further than his lips. "In this we are aided by the nature of reality, and the arrow of entropy. It is always easier to tear down than to build, to make chaos rather than order, to render a society ungovernable rather than to govern effectively.

"So. First, we must weaken and immobilize the governing class, the Citizens. Split them along every possible fault line. Next, we must detach as many of the non-Citizens who are loyal to the regime as possible, by driving the *Royal* government into a policy of *ineffective* repression. This will not be difficult; to create an atmosphere of fear through terrorism, we need only a small organization and limited support. The countermeasures, if clumsy or made to appear so, will furnish us with our mass base.

"In conjunction with this, we strike both covertly and overtly at the economy; for example, this planet is desperately short of capital, so capital assets must be destroyed, particularly those which generate foreign exchange. Earth Prime will be assisting, of course, with financial manipulations which the enemy has no effective means of countering. Once the economy is locked in a downward spiral, the NCLF and its Movement will become the only factor to *benefit* from chaos and decay. The Royal government's own diversion of resources to the police and military will work in our favor. In this stage, the NCLF can establish its own shadow regime, its no-go areas, and eat the Royal administration up from below. By then we will have built a guerrilla army capable of denying territory to the Royal forces, which we will infiltrate and subvert as well. Then, victory, and you may proceed to establish your own regime of peace and enlightenment."

The last was delivered deadpan, but Croser stifled a

glare. *Easy for you to be sarcastic,* he thought. *Meiji's a rich planet. You can't make an omelet without breaking eggs!* He had to admit there was a certain grisly fascination in hearing his own thoughts mapped out so bluntly.

"Best I keep the above-ground NCLF in operation as long as possible," he said. "In fact, I think I may be representing it in the Senate quite soon. Technically as the delegate of the Dockworkers' Union." Which would give him a position of considerable legal immunity. "We don't have much support there, but there's enough to create considerable deadlock, with a little skillful horsetrading."

"Yes," the Meijian said, warming to his topic; there was almost a tinge of enthusiasm in his voice. "Also for your al-ready-skillful disinformation campaign. If enough plausible lies circulate, truth becomes lost and all men begin to fear and doubt. The easiest environment for conspiracy is one where conspiracies are suspected everywhere. May I suggest that part of the funds I brought with me be used to make additional purchases of media and transport companies?"

Croser nodded. "We'll have to be careful," he said. "The Finance Ministry is already checking my books."

Skida sipped at her fruit-juice; the others were drinking wine, and she had always found it advisable to have her head straighter than the company.

"Skilly likes all this if it works," she said. "But the outback operation is as big as it can get without doing some serious fighting, especially now that the enemy bringing in mercs. Skilly needs to get out from under their spy-eyes, faster communication, and something to counter their aircraft."

"My technoninjas can provide all that," Murasaki said. "Of the two hundred who accompanied me—" many on the BuReloc transports that landed every month "—approximately half will return with you to the outback, Field Prime. From now on, your situation will be very different. For example, on Meiji we have developed a method of long-distance tightbeam communication, bouncing the message off the ionization tracks of meteors."

Of which Sparta had more than its fair share; the hundred-kilometer circle of Constitution Bay was the legacy of one such, millennia ago.

"Soon also, we will be reading the enemy's transmissions as soon as they do. You will have abundant computer power to coordinate your logistics, and we will be able to manipulate the enemy's accounting programs to conceal our own shipments. Also, we can degrade performance of automatic systems, the surveillance satellites the Royal government has put up, similar measures elsewhere."

"Skilly likes, but when we start popping, they going to know we getting stuff from off-planet," she said. "Then they start looking physical."

"Olympian Lines uses the Spartan system for transit to Byer's Star," Murasaki said enigmatically.

The outermost colonized system, reachable only by a complex series of Alderson Point jumps from Sparta and a full year's journey from Earth. It had a quasi-inhabitable planet; Haven, the second moon of a superjovian gas giant, a unique case. Croser remembered reading of it, and nodded to Skida. There was a CoDo relocation colony there, and some minerals.

"Earth Prime controls the Olympian Lines and has interests in the shimmerstone trade with Haven. While transiting this system, parcels can be released on ballistic trajectories. Given stealthing, and some minimal interference with the local surveillance computers, they will appear to be normal meteorites."

Croser clapped his hands together. "Won't *that* be a lovely surprise for Falkenberg's killers," he said. "Speaking of which, how's he doing?" Grand Senator Bronson had excellent intelligence, from his own resources and his leads into the Fleet.

"They are expected to land on New Washington

shortly," Murasaki said. "With luck, while we destroy the Fifth Battalion here, the Friedlanders and Covenanters will do the same for the rest there."

Croser grunted skeptically. Falkenberg's Legion were some of the best light infantry in known space. Scum soldiers, but well trained, well equipped and well lead; and Falkenberg had a reputation. Men like that made their own luck. *Men like me*, he thought. Still, New Washington was five months' transit from Sparta; they ought to have ample warning of any move.

"We'll see," he said. "Now, the other half of your people will be integrated into my clandestine operation in the towns?"

"Yes; the companies our sponsors own will provide excellent cover. I myself and my closest aides, with your permission, will form the cadre for the extension of your *Spartacus* organization." The inner-circle hit squads. "We can begin operations against enemy targets almost immediately."

"A little early for that, surely?" Croser said.

"I think you are underestimating the element of *ju*," Murasaki said.

Croser blinked for a second. *Ah, "go-with,"* he thought. The Meijian was fond of using martial-arts metaphors for political struggle; only to be expected, of course. The man was a mercenary, with a professional's emotional detachment. *All to the good. You need a cold head.* Anger was like compassion; for afterwards, when the struggle was over and it was time for the softer virtues of peace. You made the decision, you *had* to make the decision, from your heart. Grief at what his father's dream had become; rage at the smug fools who ignored him when he warned, when he pleaded, when he *showed* them and they wouldn't believe. After that everything had to come from the head; anything else was a betrayal of the Cause.

"Granted that it is too early and our network in the towns too incomplete for a comprehensive campaign of terrorism—"

People's justice, damn you, Croser thought, with a well-concealed wince. There was such a thing as taking detachment too far.

"—selective action against the proper figures is possible at once. Indeed, Capital Prime, it will be valuable training for your death-squads and their integration with my specialists."

"Who did you have in mind?" Croser asked, intrigued despite himself.

The books all said the most efficient strategy was to go for the cadres of the government: village mayors, local policemen, sanitation officers. To demonstrate the government's impotence, to blind its eyes among the populace, and to leave a vacuum the insurgents' political apparatus could fill.

"Certain of the Pragmatist leaders."

"Hmmm." Croser frowned. "Won't that just provoke . . . ah, I see."

"Yes. Either they will force through ill-conceived repressive measures, increasing our support, or they will become locked in political conflict with the Loyalist faction. In either case, we benefit."

"I'd better accelerate work on the front organizations, in case the whole NCLF has to go underground," Croser said meditatively. That would not be for a while, but when the Crown proscribed it . . . nothing like being declared an outlaw to force people to *commit* themselves.

"I authorize your suggestion," Croser said. Murasaki bowed. *And it takes care of certain other problems,* the Spartan thought. A guardian corps within the Movement was all well and good, but who would guard the guardians? These mercenaries had no local roots, and no possibility of taking over the structure he had built. With them in charge of his enforcers, his back would be safe. "Now, about the computers."

"Croser-san," Murasaki said. "Penetration of the local net has proved surprisingly easy. You will understand, we cannot *use* the data gathered too often, or the enemy will suspect and begin countermeasures. The University has a surprisingly strong software engineering section."

Croser nodded. "Policy," he said. "They wanted to begin basic research in the sciences, but that means counter-sabotage work."

CoDominium Intelligence was tasked with suppressing scientific research; their most effective method had been a generations-long effort to corrupt every data base and research program on Earth. Few of the colony worlds had the time or resources needed to undo the damage. Besides, there were few trained scientists left anywhere after four generations. Nobody wanted to live under the lidless eye of BuInt all their lives, with involuntary transportation to someplace like Fulson's World as the punishment for stepping over the line. Mostly what were left were technicians, cookbook engineers who might make a minor change in a recipe if they were very daring.

"Yes. Similar effort on Meiji is underway."

Croser held up a hand. "We can also use the information to sow suspicion—make them think we have more agents in place than we do." Murasaki smiled, a rare gesture of approval, and rose for a second to make a short bow. "My thoughts exactly, Mr. Croser. We will identify their best operatives, and then . . . for example, incorrectly hidden bank accounts with suspicious funds. Then we reveal by action we know data that this agent has access to. Synergy."

The discussion moved on to technicalities: peoples, places, times. At the last, Skida spoke.

"The Englishman. Skilly wants him."

The men both looked at her. "He a trained officer, isn't he? Skilly is going to need a good staff, and that the hardest type of talent for us to find; Skilly read the books, but got no hands-on training except learn by doing."

Murasaki nodded slowly. "He does have the training," he said slowly. "Sandhurst, and some naval experience as well. Also, he is intelligent if extremely naive. Not suitable for urban operations, I think. Too squeamish. But in the field, yes."

Croser looked at the woman narrowly; she met his gaze with an utterly guileless smile. *And he's nearer your age, and remarkably handsome*, he thought. Then: *No, Skida never does things on impulse.* As passionate as you could want . . . but underneath it the coldest pragmatist he had ever known; literally unthinkable for her to act without considering the long-term interests involved.

"I authorize it," he said. There was no time wasted on amenities, not among them; they walked through into the adjoining room, where their aides and staff sat in disciplined silence.

"Hope you like riding, English-*mon*," Skilly tossed over her shoulder, as she and Croser paused at the head of the stairs, arms about each other's waists.

Niles was blinking in bewilderment at Murasaki as Skilly's clear laugh drifted back up the stairs.

"Did you not speak of your admiration for the great English explorers and adventurers?" the Meijian asked. Niles nodded. "Consider yourself in my debt, Niles-san. I have found you as close an analog as exists in the universe."

There was something extremely disquieting in the technoninja's grin.

CHAPTER FIVE

Crofton's Essays and Lectures in Military History (2nd Edition)

Professor John Christian Falkenberg II:
Delivered at Sandhurst, August 22nd, 2087

The main constraint on the size of states is speed of communication. The Empire of Rome rarely stretched more than two weeks' march from the sea or a navigable river, simply because water was the fastest way to ship troops and messengers—force and information, the basic constituents of state power. The Mongol realm established by Genghis Khan and his descendants was a tour de force, a unified state stretching from Poland to Burma; it fell apart in less than two generations, from sheer clumsiness. Where a message might take six months and an army a year to travel from one end of the empire to another, it was simply too difficult to enforce the Khan's will in the border provinces—too difficult for the Khan's officials to collect the data they needed to make effective decisions. With mechanical transport and electronic communications, these constraints were removed; the series of wars and great-power rivalries which racked Earth from the early 20th century on were a recognition of this fact. A planetwide, later solar-system-wide, state had become possible. With the CoDominium we acquired one, in a stumbling and half-blind fashion.

The Alderson Drive gave us access to the stars at superluminal speeds—but not instantaneous transportation. In addition, there is no faster-than-light equivalent of radio;

messages carried by starship are the fastest means of interstellar communication. With the farthest colonies up to a year's travel time from Earth, the CoDominium faces many of the problems encountered by the maritime empires of Western Europe during the era of the sailing ship. Once more, distance and scale limit the effectiveness of the superstate, diffusing its strength. Smaller but more tightly organized and quick-reacting local organizations can bring more power to bear in their own neighborhoods. As long as the CoDominium remained strong and its Fleet held a monopoly of significant space warships, this mattered little.

Now that the Grand Senate is effectively paralyzed and regional powers such as Meiji and Friedland have navies of their own, the CoDominium is faced with insoluble problems. Despite the cutbacks, the Fleet is still stronger than any of its rivals—but it must scatter its strength, while the outplanet navies can concentrate. As always when an empire dies, an era of chaos intervenes until a new equilibrium of forces is born.

Similar effects may be seen on individual planets, as the unity and concentration imposed by initial settlement and CoDominium power are removed. . . .

*   *   *

"Well, *this* looks familiar enough," Peter Owensford said dryly, as they emerged from the front door of the Spartosky Ole. Sparta's twenty-hour cycle had moved far into night while the official banquet continued, and the narrow canyon of street was dimly lit by the fiber-optic marquee of the Spartosky and the glowstrips five stories up on the surrounding buildings. The red and gold light from the signs scattered over the faces of the densely packed demonstrators and mingled with the flamelight of the torches some bore along with their banners.

"*Freedom! Freedom!*" the crowd chanted; the surf-roar of their noise bounced back from the concrete walls. There were several thousand of them, filling the narrow street outside the line of cars and the cordon of

Milice, police reservists from the Brotherhoods called up to keep order. Banners and placards waved over the mob, ranging from a misspelled **FUCK THE CITYZENS** through **DOCKWORKERS' UNION FOR REFORM** to a cluster of professional-looking variations on **NCLF DEMANDS UNIVERSAL SUFFRAGE NOW.** Almost all of them had versions of the NCLF banner, a red = sign in the middle of a black dot against a red background.

Ace Barton chuckled. "I particularly like those two," he said, pointing. One read **PRODUCTION FOR THE PEOPLE**, while its neighbor proclaimed **ECOLOGY YES INDUSTRY NO.**

Peter nodded absently as he studied the crowd. The ones with the printed signs seemed to be the heart of the demonstration; they had a quasi-uniform of crash helmets and gloves, and the staves carrying their signs were good solid hardwood. The mob was growing by accretion, like a crystal in a saturated solution; many of the people on the fringes wore what looked like gang colors, or the sort of clothes you saw in an American Welfare Island. A cold knot clenched below his breastbone, and he felt a familiar papery dryness in his mouth. *This isn't a demonstration*, he thought. *It's a riot waiting to happen.*

"Nice to be loved," Owensford added dryly. Some of the signs read **MERCENARY KILLER SCUM GO HOME** and **MONEY FOR THE PEOPLE NOT WAR WHORES.** "As you say, Ace, positively homelike."

"It isn't familiar to me," Lysander said grimly. "I've never seen anything like *this* on Sparta before. Melissa, stay back." He was angry; his Phraetrie-brother Harv Middleton had naked fury on his face.

The girl at Lysander's elbow pushed forward to stand by him, studying the crowd.

"I realize you're a hero now, but try to contain it, Lysander," she said. Melissa von Alderheim was a determined-looking person, not pretty but good-looking in a fresh-faced way that suggested horses and tennis; she took after her mother's side of the family, who had been from Oxford. Even in an evening gown, with her seal-brown hair piled under a tiara, there was a suggestion of tweeds and sensible shoes about her. She and the Prince had been seated with the mercenaries and the two kings during the formal dinner and the speeches that followed; she had been coolly polite to all the officers, but teeth had shone a little every time her glance met Ursula Gordon's.

Owensford looked around. The Spartosky Ole was one of a set of fifteen-story fibrocrete buildings not far from the CoDominium compound, part of the oldest section of Sparta City and bordering on the Minetown slums. The others were plain slick-gray, but the Spartosky had a portico of twisted pillars and a marquee of glittering multicolored fiber-optic display panels.

"Who built this neighborhood, anyway?" he said, as a car pushed slowly through the crowd and the police lines. It was a simple local job converted for police use with a hatch on the roof and armor panels. It rocked and lurched as the protesters thundered their signs on the roof or grabbed for the fenders and tried to rock it off its wheels.

The two kings and their party came up beside the mercenaries. "GLC Construction and Development Company," David I said. "Why?"

"I recognize the style," Owensford said. His eyes were on the rooftops. *I'd have cover teams there if this were my operation*, he thought. "Grand Senator Bronson owns it. They never alter the plans; the Colonial Bureau built them on thirty or forty planets." Nothing but a pair of news cameras on the roofs, avid ghoul-vulture eyes drawn to trouble.

A new chant had started, among the helmeted demonstrators. "*Dion the Leader! Down with the Kings! Up the Republic! Dion to Power! Dion to Power!*" Jeers and catcalls rang as the demonstrators saw the royal party; the cleared pavement was growing crowded as more of the guests left the Spartosky.

A Milice officer pushed up out of the roof-hatch of the police car; he was wearing full battle armor, and landed heavily as he slid to the pavement and trotted over to the kings.

"Your Majesties," he said. "Sorry about this, but it . . . they had a permit, we thought it would be just the usual couple of dozen University idiots, and it just *grew*. Sirs, if you'll come this way, we've secured the rear entrance."

"No," Alexander said sharply. "I'm not in the habit of running away from my people, and I don't intend to start now."

"Your people?" a man said, with contempt in his voice. Owensford noted him without turning; Steven Armstrong, leader of the Pragmatist party, the faction in the Legislative Assembly who wanted more restrictions on the convicts and deportees. A bull-necked man, heavily muscled even by Spartan standards, owner of a small fishing fleet he had built up from nothing. The Pragmatists were the loyal opposition, more or less; the kings both backed the Foundation Loyalists. "Your Majesty had better take care your *people* don't assassinate you, since they're allowed to pick up weapons the minute they leave the CoDo prison."

Alexander acknowledged him with a curt nod, then turned back to the police officer. "Saunders, what's your estimate of the crowd?"

"Sir—" the man looked acutely unhappy. "They're pushing, but no more than the usual arms."

The Legion officers had gathered in a loose clump around their commander and the Spartan monarchs; some of them had unobtrusively buckled back the covers of their sidearms. Those were light machine-pistols, Dayan-made Microuzis. Owensford found himself estimating relative firepower; the Milice were in riot gear, truncheons and shields, but they had auto shotguns or rifles over their backs. Most of the guests had pistols of some sort—it was a Citizen tradition here—and few of the mob seemed to be carrying firearms. That meant little, though. They could be concealed.

"Sir," he said. "I'd advise you to take this officer's advice. Quickly."

Alexander Collins's mouth clenched. "Not quite yet, Major Owensford," he said.

Peter turned and caught Jesus Alana's eye. He jerked his head toward the rear door. Alana nodded and left the group.

Collins turned to the militia officer. "Saunders, this is in violation of the permit, isn't it?"

"Yes, sir," the policeman said. "Excessive numbers, obstructing traffic, half a dozen counts."

"Hand me your 'caster," the king said.

The policeman pulled a hand-unit from his belt; Alexander took it, keying it to the loudspeakers in the police car and stepping up on the base of one of the Spartosky's columns to make himself visible to the crowd.

"Get the crowd-control car ready," he said to the policeman. Then he drew breath to speak to the crowd.

*   *   *

"Two-knife," Skida said. She was lying on her back below the window, studying the crowd through a thin fiber-optics periscope. "Bobber. Now. And Bobber, Skilly would be very happy if you keep the Werewolves from getting too antsy. Important the *cam*eras get good shots of nasty policemons whipping on heads before it starts. We provoke them to provoke us, understand? On the word."

Niles looked over at Bobber. This suite was supposed

to be the offices of Universal Exports, and the female gang leader looked wildly out of place in it with her red tights and silver-studded knee boots. The chain-decked black leather jacket was unfastened to her waist, half-baring breasts far too rounded to be natural. Both bore a one-word tattoo: SWEET on the left, SOUR on the right. She stood, the tall fore-and-aft crest of hair on her shaven head nodding with the motion that had given her her street name; the rocket launcher was cradled protectively in her arms.

"Yo, Skilly," she said, wrapping it in cloth and trotting out the door. The squad of feral-eyed youths in Werewolf colors followed at her heels, and then the huge Mayan.

A snarl came from below, and Niles felt the small hairs on his spine try to rise; instinct deeper than thought told him that the pack was on his heels. He grinned past the fear, vision gone ice-clear with the wash of adrenaline, and Skida smiled back at him. Her eyes took him in again, with flattering attentiveness.

"You expect the police to attack the crowd?" he said quietly. They were alone in the room except for one of Murasaki's men, who might have been a statue as he sat at the tiny console of his portable com unit. The Englishman shifted his grip on the silenced scope-sighted carbine. "Rather brutal bunch, eh?"

"Skilly expects the police to be good and frightened, Jeffi," she replied. "They only shopkeepers and clerks, mon. Respectable people, not used to this. Frightened peoples act stupid. We take it from there." A chuckle. "Then the RSMP come kills *us*, if your Nippo friend's toys doan work."

"MY PEOPLE," a voice called from the street below, amplified echoes bouncing off the buildings. "WE ARE ALWAYS READY TO HEAR YOUR PETITIONS. REMEMBER THAT LIBERTY CAN COME ONLY TO THOSE READY TO BEAR ITS BURDENS—"

* * *

The crowd howled when it saw Alexander; and again, when he began to speak. The sound was huge, almost enough to override the amplifiers. Then another megaphone spoke, from among the demonstrators.

"FUCK THE KINGS! FUCK THE KINGS!"

Owensford was close enough to see Alexander flush, and then his lips move in a prayer or curse as the mob took it up. He was also close enough to see the anger on the faces of the Milice. They began to surge forward, pushing with batons held level, until their officers called them back; hauled them back physically, in some cases.

The twist in his stomach grew; there was more here than met the eye. Peter Owensford had been a soldier for all his adult life, very little of it behind a desk, and he knew the scent of trouble. Events were moving to a plan, a plan laid by somebody who meant no good.

"Saunders," the king said. "Read them the Act and clear the street. Minimal force, but don't endanger lives hesitating."

"*Sir!*" the policeman said with enthusiasm. He took the handunit and began—

"CLEAR THE STREET AND DISPERSE! YOU ARE IN VIOLATION OF THE PUBLIC ORDER AND ASSEMBLIES ACT AND SUBJECT TO ARREST IF YOU DO NOT DISP*SKKREEEEEEE*—"

The deafening feedback squeal continued until one of the Milice ripped the wires loose from the speaker on the car's roof. Jeering laughter rippled from the crowd among the chants, and a few bottles and rocks arched forward to bang against the shields. Owensford saw one man stagger out of the police line, hands over a smashed nose. There was a momentary gap; through it he could see two of the helmeted protesters, a man and a woman. Boy and girl rather, in their late teens. Well-dressed in a scruffy sort of way, and grinning as if this was all a game.

It is, he thought bleakly. *But not the sort you imagine.*

"Sir, the unit won't work at all, we've got no commo."

Owensford met his second-in-command's eyes; they nodded.

"Sirs," Peter said to the two kings. He had to shout. "I must insist that you return to the building, otherwise I cannot be responsible."

"The back entrance," Saunders said.

"No. Too risky, it might be covered. Captain Alana has secured the lobby. *Now*, if you please, sirs." Several of the Legion officers grouped around the kings with pistols drawn and began backing towards the entrance, carrying the protesting monarchs along willy-nilly.

"Clear the street," Saunders was screaming in the ears of his officers, who relayed it verbally to the Milice.

They raised their batons and linked shields, pushing forward. The glowstrips blinked out, and the marquee of the Spartosky, and the street was suddenly plunged into darkness. Then another light came on, a narrow-beam illuminator from the news cameras, flicking across the line of Milice and incidentally into their eyes. Owensford shaded his, and saw several of the protesters fling themselves forward on the line of clubs. He bared his teeth; they were not trying to fight, just cowering dramatically and holding up their hands as the police instinctively lashed out with their truncheons. One of the protesters turned as if staggering, and the camera light caught a mask of blood across his agonized face.

Razor cuts, Owensford knew. Flicked open to give the appearance of dramatic wounds. "Get all these people back inside," he shouted to the remaining mercenaries. The guests were milling and shouting on their own. Different from an Earthling crowd, though;

many were drawing weapons and pushing their way to the front, and there were few shrieks. A gunfight, *just* what was needed. "You, you, you, get the doors open and start pushing people into the lobby. Move!"

More bottles arched out of the crowd, some of them Molotovs trailing smoke, which burst in puddles of flame on the pavement. The police scattered away, and knots of disciplined rioters burst through, lashing out with the poles of their signs. Again they seemed more interested in being beaten than really fighting. . . .

"Jamming," Ace spoke into his ear; he had one of their own communicators in his hand, they were all carrying one in a pocket of their dress blue and golds. "I'm through to the base camp. Jesus is bringing in some MPs."

"Right. Get everything you can," Owensford said.

"Mission?"

"Cover our retreat," Peter said. "We don't understand the politics, and we sure don't have time to learn. I want everyone out of here alive and unhurt. Preferably without inflicting casualties."

"Roger," Barton said.

"The crowd-control car, thank God," Saunders muttered.

A turbine hum echoed back from the walls, and a vehicle floated into sight. It was Earth-made, a Boeing-Northrup Peacemaker: essentially an upright rectangle, supported by six powerful ducted-fan engines on either side. Nozzles protruded below the control bubble on the forward edge, and they could see the operator in the armored nacelle within. Hot exhaust air washed over them, rippling the clothes of the crowd.

"Hurry up, dammit!" Owensford barked. His men had gotten the guests moving, but it was a painfully slow process, the more when many wanted to stay right where they were.

Fresh howls rose at the sight of the riot-control

vehicle; many of the Welfare Island types would recognize it from Earth, where they were used to put down slum riots daily. Shots rang out, and bullets ricocheted from the armor panels in bursts of sparks. The Milice line was buckling, and the gang members from the outside of the crowd had waded in; Owensford saw chains and iron bars whipping through the air in deadly arcs, and then a shotgun went *thump* five times in as many seconds. The riot car turned in midair, ponderously graceful, and a nozzle swiveled. Bright yellow gas shot out, a thick jet under high pressure that bounced from the crowd and dispersed in a dense fog.

"Guiltpuke gas," Ace said. The area behind the police line was finally clearing. Owensford swiveled his head. Lysander, and what *was* his fiancée doing there; she had the back of one hand to her mouth . . . guiltpuke gas, a nausea agent with an indelible dye mixed in, so you could identify the suspects later. The sick-sweet smell of vomitus filled the air, and underlying it came a tang he recognized, the salt-iron-shit smell of violent death.

"Ace, get those troops in here NOW. I don't like this at all."

"Nor me," Barton said. "Only one problem. They've got our frequency too. With better gear than we have."

Better than we have? How? "We'd better—" he began. The world came apart in a slamming roar.

*   *   *

"Field Prime says *now,*" Two-knife said. He and Bobber were waiting perilously close, around a corner that gave on a parking lot. The gray fibrocrete wall was pockmarked, and slashed with graffiti; variations on WEREWOLVES FOREVER, mostly. And a new one: HELOTS RULE OK with the red = sign. He shrugged off the fifty-kilo load of rockets and began handing them out to the other gang-members; they seized one each and dashed or crawled off into the darkness.

"Me first," Bobber said. "Remember that, Werewolves."

Better you than me, defiling bitch, Two-knife thought, going down on one knee and drawing the pistol-shaped designator as he lowered the goggles over his eyes. They were nightsight devices and more, also showing the red line of the designator's laser, invisible to the naked eye. He held the communicator to his face and spoke, in Mayan. Not likely anyone else on this world spoke it, beside him and the *señora.*

"All in readiness here," he said.

"*Go.*"

Bobber had unwrapped her launcher, a molded plastic tube with pistol grips and a scope sight; Friedlander-made, a one-shot disposable. Her smile was wide and wet as she pivoted around the corner and raised the launcher to her shoulder. Two-knife dropped flat and scuttled sideways, taking up the slack of the designator's trigger. He could see the Spartosky clearly now; a police groundcar was parked in front of it, with a man in the hatch signaling to the vehicle floating above. The red blip of the designator settled effortlessly on the control bubble: only seventy meters; he could usually put four bullets out of five in a man-sized target at that range.

The first rocket was Bobber's; it *whumped* out of the tube, propelled by a light charge and balanced by the shower of plastic confetti that blasted out of the rear. Then the sustainer motor cut in, with a scream like a retching cat.

*   *   *

"Down!" Owensford yelled. Needlessly for his own men; as he dove to the pavement he saw Cornet Gordon trip Melissa, Lysander's fiancée, and throw herself over the older girl before drawing her pistol. Lysander and Harv hit the dirt and rolled into the gutter in well-trained unison, their sidearms out and eyes searching for targets.

The mob was running now, but that was the least of their problems.

The flight path of the rocket was a bright streak across his retinas. Where it struck the Peacemaker a pancake of fire expanded as the shaped-charge warhead slammed its lance of incandescent plasma through the armor. The big vehicle lurched in the air, then forward. It caromed into the side of the building opposite the Spartosky with an impact that made the paving stones of the forecourt shudder beneath his stomach like the hide of some huge beast shuddering in its sleep. Then it pinwheeled end over end to strike the empty roadway a hundred meters farther down. Fuel tanks ruptured, spraying vaporized kerosene into the air; Owensford buried his head in his arms and held his breath. The curve of the walls protected him from the wash of flame, that and the pillars that ringed the area under the marquee and the stone lip at the end of the roadway.

Savage heat passed over him, and a soft strong *whump* of shockwave that tried to pick him up and roll him; the exposed areas of his skin were tight and painful. He raised his head as soon as it was safe, to see the police groundcar settling back on its springs; it had taken the main force of the blast. Saunders was still in the hatchway, burning and screaming and waving his arms. For a few seconds, and then two more rockets blasted into the groundcar. The top blew off in a vertical gout of fire, metal slashing into the walls and into the backs of those Milice not incapacitated by the burning fuel. Saunders was silhouetted for a moment against the fireball, until he struck the opposite building with enough force to turn his body into a lose sack of ruptured cells and bone fragments inside the armor.

Owensford turned, his vision jumping in snapshots of relevant data. Barton and most of the remaining

Legion officers were behind pillars, the stocks of the Microuzis extended as they scanned the windows opposite for movement. Gordon was just pushing Melissa back through the door of the Spartosky; a junior lieutenant was using his uniform coat to smother the flames in the hair and gown of a guest. He staggered, grunted, fell; still moving, but grasping at a bullet-wound in his thigh.

"You Milice," Owensford called. Some of them were still on their feet, and they had all abandoned the useless riot gear for the guns on their backs. "Get the wounded in here under cover. You, Sergeant, get me ten, we've got to secure the building across the way."

The police-militia noncom turned, a look of grateful relief on his face that *someone* was taking charge. His mouth opened; then he staggered, a red splotch opening on the front of his jacket, and dropped bonelessly to the ground.

"Cover, cover!" Owensford called.

"I'll clear the building," Lysander said. He dashed forward, diving and rolling as bullets chipped the pavement at his feet, Harv skipping sideways behind him and snapping off covering shots at the windows. The Milice rallied and followed, driving into the dead ground at the base of the building across the street. The prince kicked in a door and dove through, the militia of the Brotherhoods at his heels.

Ace Barton was firing controlled three-round bursts from behind a pillar. "Fifth floor, second from the right," he shouted as he ducked back behind the stone to reload. Return fire pocked the column; he dodged down and to the other side, snapping off another burst.

"Where the hell is the battalion?"

"Coming."

*   *   *

"*¡Mierda!*" Skilly said, dropping down behind the window ledge.

Light pistol-caliber bullets hammered at the stone below; she rose and squeezed off the five rounds left in the clip, *phut-phut-phut-phut-phut*.

"Somebody down there too good a shot," she said with respect, slapping another magazine into the well in the pistol-grip of the carbine and stepping back out of the line of fire. "That enough, everyone out!"

The dark-clad Meijian at the com unit snapped it closed, picked up his personal weapon and darted to the door. "Niles!"

The young Englishman squeezed off another round and turned. "*Got* one, by god!" he said.

"Good," Skilly replied impatiently. "Doan matter, we gots nice pictures, cameras knocked out just before the first rocket. Papers will tell, but people we interested in doan read, is all. Hoped we'd get the kings . . . you take rear, my mon. Go, go, *go*."

The corridor outside was cool white silence, insanely distant from the fire and blood outside. Niles crouched, his weapon covering the long hallway as the others dashed toward the staircase; the corridors were shaped like a capital "I," with elevators in the middle and stairs at either end. He skipped backward crabwise, conscious of the steadiness of his hands and the bright concentration in his mind. *Read about* this, *Grand-Uncle*, he thought. *Tell me I'm a useless playboy now, father.*

They were to the stairs; he could hear the thunder of feet on the metal slats. And the door at the other end of the corridor was opening.

"Hostiles!" Niles shouted, dropping into prone position. Elbows on the ground, and the stock smacked into his shoulder, *squeeze* off two rounds. Star-shaped holes in the frosted glass, and a scream of pain. Then the door opened again, just enough to let a muzzle through. Shots blazed, a military automatic rifle, ugly *crack* sounds above his head, hammering into the plasterwork and leaving stinging dust in the air.

"Come on, mon, we leaving," Skilly said behind him.

Niles shook his head, fired again. "Got to give them something to think about," he said. "Grenade, please?"

She handed one forward to him, a standard plastic concussion-model egg. He waited until the opposite door began to open, then pulled the tab and lobbed it with a cricketer's expert overarm snap; it bounced into the narrow gap between door and wall and exploded, tearing the door from the hinges.

"Another, fragmentation," Niles said. Skilly handed it to him as they scuttled backward into the stairwell; there was something of a surprised look on her face.

Niles let the door close, pulling a roll of electrical tape from a pocket of his new hidehunter leather costume. The door was a simple rectangle of pressed metal, with a frosted glass window and a U-shaped aluminum handle. Moving with careful speed, he taped the grenade inside the metal loop, then ran a strip of the tape from the pin to the top of the stair railing. Finally he drew his knife and used the point to straighten the split ends of the pin, where they bent back on the other side of the grenade's lever; the slightest pressure would strip it out, now.

"Hoo, Skilly *like* that," she said, with new-found respect, slapping him on the shoulder. He found himself smiling back.

A bellow from below. "Skilly! *¡Vamonos!*"

They turned, taking the stairs a dozen at a time and whooping like children.

*   *   *

"They *didn't* cut the line, sir," the Legion electronics tech said, looking up from her equipment. The glowstrips blinked back on. "Something with the central power control computer, I'd say." They had flown her in in one of the RSMP tiltrotors, along with the reaction company who were securing the area, and Fifth Battalion medics to help with the wounded.

There were enough that they still had to be triaged. Peter Owensford walked over to where someone was bandaging Prince Lysander's shoulder. *A nice romantic wound in the extremities*, he thought. A demonstrator looked up as he passed; he recognized her, the pretty girl who had been grinning when the bottle hit the policeman. She was not smiling now, as she sat with her dead companion's head in her lap, and her face was less pretty for the streaks of blood drying on it.

"Murderer!" she shrilled. "You'll pay for this, you'll *pay*—" Then she slumped, as a passing medic stopped to press a hypospray against the back of her neck.

Lysander had heard the exchange. "Somebody will pay," he promised, looking around the street. Wreckage still smoldered, and bodies were lying in neat rows under blanket covers. "Somebody definitely will."

"Bad?" Owensford said, nodding at the wound.

"Just a flesh wound," he said. "What really hurts is that I was putting a field-dressing on it when the men with me charged down that corridor. The door was booby-trapped. Five of them died, and whoever it was got away. We'll do better the next time, sir."

"*I* call *you* sir, sir," Owensford said. A squad of Legionnaires in synthileather battledress and nemourlon combat armor moved down the street.

"Major, the Field Force is going to be under your command, and right now the best service I can do Sparta is to be part of it. Sir."

"As a beginning," Owensford said. "We'll create a Prince Royal's Own, which you can command in the field long enough that the men learn to trust you. After that, it's staff schools." Peter grinned hollowly when Lysander winced. "Someone has to lead when all this is over."

* * *

"Thank you," Melissa said, across the body. "This one's dead."

"You're welcome," Ursula Gordon said, as they moved on to the next.

Pressure bandage, Melissa thought. They ripped the Milice trooper's tunic free and wadded it over the long cut in his thigh, pressing the flesh closed and binding it with twists of cloth. The Spartan found herself breathing through her nose; it was not that the smell was unfamiliar, gralloching deer was pretty much like this, it was just that when she thought of it together with *people*—

"*Out of the way, out of the way!*" the paramedics shouted.

Melissa and Ursula jumped back; the white-coated team from the latest ambulance moved in, one setting up a plasma drip and slapping an antishock hypo on the man's arm.

"I think—" Melissa started to brush a strand of hair back out of her eyes, then stopped; in the glowlight it looked as if she was wearing gloves to the elbow, of something dark and glistening. She swallowed. "I think that's the last; they can handle it now."

"Water," Ursula croaked.

There was a fountain in the center of the Spartosky's lobby. They pushed through the thinning crowd that still milled, some shocked-silent, some hysterical, some getting first aid for minor injuries while the professionals saved those on the edge of death. The kings were in one corner with a communications tech and a knot of uniforms, mercenary and RSMP, grimly busy. Water bubbled clear and cold from the fretted terracotta basin; Melissa and the woman in uniform rinsed their hands until they were clean enough to scoop up a handful. For a long minute they waited, letting stress-exhaustion slump their shoulders.

"Thank you again, for saving my life," Melissa said. She shivered slightly, remembering it again; the roar of fire, the screams, the sudden flat *crack* of bullets.

"It's my job," Ursula said. Her eyes met the other woman's; Melissa wondered how her own looked now. *Glazed, probably. Not as steady as hers.*

"I'm . . . sorry, I've been . . . impolite," she continued. Her skin flushed, embarrassment and anger at having to say what honor demanded; the feeling was welcome, pushing away the sick knot of fear and disgust in her stomach.

"Miss von Alderheim," Ursula said calmly. Her eyes moved to one side, ever so slightly. "It's perfectly understandable. Lys—The Prince—goes to Tanith, nearly gets killed, and nearly gets snatched by a designing whore. Perfectly understandable that you should be angry, especially when she shows up here to remind everyone of it."

"I never said you—"

"Well, I was. A whore, that is, if not designing. Not my career of choice, but there it is. My lady, I never had any slightest belief the Prince would stay with me. I wanted it, yes, but I never believed it. The Prince dreamed about it; he's a romantic to his bones, but he knew better too."

"But that's it, isn't it?" Melissa said with quiet bitterness. "He loves you, you love him, but he'll *marry* me, out of *duty*." Her mouth twisted in something that might have been a smile. "A designing woman and an infatuated Prince would have been much easier on my pride, I think. I may get what I want, but not the way I want it."

Unexpectedly, Ursula smiled, an almost tender expression, and reached out to touch the Spartan on the shoulder. "He will, if you let him." she said. "Love you, that is; he's that sort of man. Besides, that's not the important thing."

"Easy for you to say."

"Well no, actually, it's rather difficult. But it's true. We were in love, or thought we were, and that's about all we had in common, apart from a few books. My mother was a drug addict and a prostitute and a petty thief, until they sent her to Tanith; who my father is or was, God only knows. I grew up on a prison-planet that lives from drugs grown by slaves, and it's just the sort of place you'd expect it to be. All I was taught was enough to make me pleasant company. You grew up with him, you've got a shared *world* in common, the beliefs and the feelings and the little things like knowing the jokes and songs . . . and something important to work on together. Opposites may attract, but it's the similarities keep people together."

Melissa blinked at her and slowly sat on the coping of the fountain. "Now I really *am* sorry," she said. "I forgot how difficult it must be for you."

"I'll heal," Ursula said. "Mostly I already have. I'd have preferred to go somewhere else, but—" She touched the Legion crest on her shoulder. "There's more choices in this business than in my old trade, but not a whole lot more. The Prince will heal too, if you help him, Miss von Alderheim."

"Melissa," the other said impulsively, holding out her hand. They clasped palms, smiling tentatively. "How old *are* you, Cornet Gordon?"

"Ursula. Eighteen standard years and six months. Going on fifty."

"You certainly make me feel like a babe in the woods, Ursula!"

"Never had a chance for a childhood," Ursula said. "But look at it this way: you're still more grown-up than most men of fifty." They shared a chuckle. "Not all, of course. Colonel Falkenberg's quite adult—but then, he *is* fifty-odd."

The chuckle grew into a laugh; a quiet one, that died away as they grew conscious of a man standing near.

"Why, Lysander," Melissa said, rising and taking his unwounded arm. "Ursula and I were just talking about you."

The Spartan prince looked a little paler as they walked away; Harv followed, giving Ursula a glare as he passed.

The mercenary sighed, rising and looking down at the ruin of her dress uniform. *Amazing*, she thought, suddenly a little nauseated with herself. *Twenty-odd people just killed, and we find time for emotional fiddlefaddle. That's humanity, I guess.* There was a line of caked, crusted blood under her fingernails, where she had had to clamp hard.

"Cornet Gordon?"

A Legion trooper, face anonymous under the bulging combat helmet, body blocky and mechanical in armor and mottled synthileather. He carried a smell with him, of gun oil and metal and burnt powder, impersonal and somehow clean. "Captain Alana wants you in the manager's office, they're setting up debriefing, ma'am."

"Thank you. Carry on." Manager's office would be up the sweeping double stairs, all marble and gilt bronze. She took a deep breath and forced herself to stride briskly, but paused at the top to look back. There was a good view out the big doors; he was holding open the door of a car as Melissa climbed in.

Just like him, she thought. *Shot in the shoulder, and he holds the car door for her.*

There was something in her throat; she coughed and swallowed. *Client number 176, not counting family groups,* she told herself coldly. *After all that, a few years of celibacy and hard work are just what you need, Cornet Gordon.*

You could believe anything, if you repeated it to yourself often enough.

*   *   *

Peter Owensford shuffled the pile of paper from one side of his desk to the other. Most of it was routine, but it could be important to set up the right routines. Or avoid the wrong ones, anyway.

Personnel decisions. Munitions design. Military industrialization with extremely limited resources.

Schools for the Legion's children. Commissary, laundry, home construction, perimeter defense, training schedules. Reports for Falkenberg, who wouldn't get them for months. Use of aircraft. Communications. Medical supplies. Much of it had nothing at all to do with strategy or leadership, but it all had to be taken care of, and some of it *did* have an impact on strategic decisions. More important, though, was that strategy had to drive the details, rather than the other way around.

And just now I don't have a strategy. Just objectives.

Captain Lahr knocked at Peter's office door. "Colonel Slater's here, sir," he announced.

"Thanks, Andy. Send him in. Give me a few minutes, then we'll need to see you."

Peter stood to greet his visitor. Hal Slater walked with a cane; there was only so much that regeneration stimulators could do when the same tissues were damaged time after time. Slater's handshake was firm, and his eyes steady.

"Good to see you again, sir," Peter said. "Damned good. Glad to see you recovered so well."

"Yes. Thank you. Surprising how little all that titanium in there bothers me. Of course given my druthers I'd take a low-gravity planet—"

"Sit down, please."

"Thank you, I will."

Peter eyed Slater's conservative suit. "Still in civvies?"

"Well, I wanted to check with you," Slater said. "They say they've made me a major general, though that's more title than rank. And of course I've still got a Legion suit with oak leaves—"

"You'd be welcome here either way," Owensford said. "Of course you knew that."

"Thank you," Slater said. "I figured as much, but it never hurts to touch the bases properly. How is John Christian?"

"A little heavier, hair a little grayer, otherwise much

the same," Owensford said. "He said to give you his regards. Care for a drink?"

"Not just now, thank you," Hal said. He looked around the office.

"Pretty bare," Peter said. "But the electronics are here."

"Yes, and so is the paperwork."

"You know it."

"It looks like you've enough to do," Hal Slater said. "I know I'm up to my arse in Weems Beasts. They seem to have given you plenty to work with from what I saw on the way in."

"Quite decent," Peter said. "I think they actually like us."

"Seems that way," Slater agreed. "Certainly they gave me decent facilities, I'll say that for them. Right near the University. Good library. Fair computer, but I brought better. Anyway, we're setting up, and I'll be having some kind of opening ceremony one of these days. I'd appreciate it if you'd come help."

Peter grinned. "Sure. I'll bring Centurion Hanselman. He wears enough fruit salad to impress the yokels." Peter waved at the stack of paper on his desk. "You can't start turning out staff officers soon enough for me!"

"Well, it will still take a bit of time—"

"Yeah." Peter paused for a moment. "Did you get a chance to look over the reports on the riot?"

Dr. Slater nodded. "Yes. Very interesting."

"Interesting."

"Perhaps I should say revealing," Hal said.

"Yeah, well they showed us some unsuspected capabilities all right," Peter said.

"Perhaps a bit more than that," Hal Slater said. "They told us a bit about themselves, too. For instance, what did they expect to accomplish?"

"Eh? I'd have said they did very well," Peter said. "They showed they can disrupt a Royal gathering. Scared the militia, killed some of them. Stood up to us, and got headlines and TV pictures showing them doing it. I'd say they racked up some points."

"Yes, of course," Slater said. "But think about it. They showed us they have far more capability than we suspected. More important, they revealed they have considerable off-planet support—"

"I doubt they intended that we learn that."

"So they underestimated us," Slater said. "All the more interesting. So they gave us all that information, and to what end? They haven't harmed the Legion. They've made the kings furious, and they convinced most of the waverers in the Brotherhoods that the threat is serious. They let us know they have professional competence in crowd manipulation, and that they can assemble a larger and uglier crowd than the RSMP suspected. They told us they have fairly sophisticated military equipment and the ability to use it. And with all that capability they destroyed one crowd control car and killed no one irreplaceable."

"Hmm. I didn't think of it that way. All right, Hal, what do you make of it?"

"First, since they aren't complete fools, look for them to have a great deal more capability that they didn't show," Hal said.

"Hmm. Yeah. Right. You said they told us about themselves. What?"

"I think they're amateurs," Slater said. "Academics."

"If you'd seen that fighting retreat you wouldn't say that."

"Oh, I grant you they're competent enough," Slater said. "But even so there's a decided flavor of book learning. Peter, I think they're operating right out of the classical guerrilla war theory manuals. People's War, People's Army. Mao's Basic Tactics. Enemy advance, we retreat. Enemy halt, we harass. Enemy retire, we attack."

"All that from one riot?"

"Well, of course I'm guessing."

"Pay attention to your hunches," Falkenberg said. *Only I don't have a hunch. Hal Slater has a hunch, and Hal Slater isn't Christian Johnny.*

"Ok, I'll think about it," Owensford said. "Now, let's get Andy Lahr in here and go over just what I can do to help you get set up properly. . . . "

CHAPTER SIX

Crofton's Encyclopedia of the Inhabited Planets (2nd Edition):

Eurotas, river. [E-ur-o-tas], named for river in southern Greece, Earth. (see *names*, Mythological, Graeco-Roman)

Largest river on the planet *Sparta* [see *Sparta*];

Length (main stream): 9,600 kilometers
Drainage basin: 8,225,000 sq. kilometers
Maximum volume: 860,000,000 liters
Minimum volume: 475,000,000 liters

Description: The Eurotas is customarily divided into the Lower, Middle and Upper Valleys, respectively, and the Delta. The Delta proper flows northward into the nearly circular Constitution Bay, encompassing an area of approx. 25,000 sq. kilometers of silt and peat-soil marshes, undergoing reclamation for agriculture in some areas. The Lower Valley runs north-south between the *Lycourgos Hills* fronting on the Aegean Sea in the west, and the twin ranges of *Parnassus* and *Pindaros* on the east, separating the Eurotas from the Jefferson Ocean (q.v.). Lying between the river-ports of *Clemens* and *Olynthos* is the Middle Valley, occupying a low-lying fault zone between uplifted blocks on the north and south. To the west, the upper portion of the Middle Valley is flanked on the south and west by the *Illyrian Dales*, a region of limestone uplands, and beyond these by the *Drakon Mountains*. North of Olynthos the river descends via the *Vulcan Rapids* from *Lake Alexander*, a body of water comparable to Earth's Lake Ontario. From the

Vulcan Rapids the Upper Valley runs generally north-south to the slightly smaller *Lake Ochrid*, the formal source of the Eurotas.

The Middle and Lower Valleys are essentially silt-filled rift depressions, whose drainage link is geologically recent. Gradients are therefore small, and vessels drawing up to 3 meters may navigate the Eurotas as far inland as Olynthos, 6,400 kilometers from the mouth of the river. Flooding, siltation, breaks in the natural levees, marshes and ox-bow lakes are common. The Upper Valley is an area of rejuvenated drainage and exposed basic rock, with frequent steep falls.

Climate and Hydrology: The Delta has a humid-Mediterranean regime, with mild rainy winters, warm dry summers and a nearly year-round growing season. The Lower Valley is similar but slightly more continental with increasing distance from the sea; the Middle Valley is comparable, on a larger scale, to the Po basin of Italy, Earth, with cold damp winters with some snow, and warm summers with occasional convection thunderstorms. Winter cold increases westward and northward, until the Upper Valley ranges from cool-temperate semiarid to subarctic north of Lake Ochrid. Lakes Ochrid and Alexander are both frozen for several months of the year, as is the Upper Valley as a whole. The Eurotas reaches maximum flow in the late winter or early spring; summer flow is largely sustained by snowmelt from flanking mountain ranges. More than half the dry-season flow is derived from the snowmelt of the Drakon Range, and most of this flows underground through the 1,000,000 sq. kilometer area of the Illyrian Dales, with their extensive near-horizontal limestone formations.

*   *   *

"*Hunf!*" Geoffrey Niles grunted, beginning to regret accepting Skida's offer to spar. His forearms slapped down on the boot just before it hit his midriff, and his hands twisted to lock on the foot. Skilly spun around the axis of the trapped foot, tearing it out of his hands before the grip could solidify and then rolled backward off her shoulder, out of his reach and flicking up, then boring back in. The circle of hidehunter faces around the campfire watched with mild interest, jaws moving stolidly as they scooped up stew.

It's going to be difficult to win this without thumping her, he thought; he had not expected that. The Belizean was a big woman, very strong for her weight, but he had fifteen kilos on her and none of it was fat. *She must have had some training.* There would be bruises on his upper arm, where she had broken a clamp-hold by stabbing at the nerve cluster. . . .

Flick. Snap-kick to his left knee. He let the right relax, and gravity pushed him out of the way; then he punched his fist underarm toward her short ribs. She let the kicking foot drop down and around, spun again with a high slashing heel-blow toward his head; the punch slid off thigh muscle as hard as teak, but his other palm came up hard under her striking leg to throw her backward. *Street-warrior style, those high kicks*, he thought critically.

She went with it, backflipping off her hands and doing a scissor-roll to land upright facing him. Then she surprised him, coming up out of her crouch, shrugging with a grin and turning away toward the fire.

Thank goodness, he thought. She was so damned *fast*, sooner or later he'd have had to hurt her, and that would be unfair, undermining her in front of her people. And—

Even then he almost caught the backkick that lashed out, the long leg seeming to stretch in the dim light. But there had been no warning from her stance.

"Ufff," he croaked, folding around his paralyzed diaphragm. She caught the outstretched hand in both of hers, twisted to lock the arm. A boot-edge thumped with stunning force into his armpit, then the leg swung over to lock around his elbow, and they were both going down. The ground sprang up to meet them with unnatural heavy-world swiftness, jarring every bone from his lower spine up as she landed half across him with a scissor on his right arm.

The Englishman writhed, turning on his left and reaching behind; there were three ways to break that hold, or with strength alone. . . . He froze as a hard thumbnail poked into the corner of one eye.

"Lie still," the liquid voice said from behind his ear; he could smell the sweat that ran down her face, and the mint she chewed. "This heavy planet, a real gentlemon always let de lady get on top."

"Your point!" he said hastily. He had been around the Upper Valley hidehunters long enough now to know why so many were one-eyed.

"Sure, just a friendly match," Skilly said. She rolled off him and erect, offering a hand and pulling him up after her. They dusted themselves off; the campside was a sandy dried riverbed, with little vegetation. "You not bad, Jeff-my-mon, just . . . Skilly hasn't fallen for *that* trick since she was ten. You fight too much like a *rabiblanco*, you know?"

They walked over toward the fire; the fuel was some native plant like a dense orange bamboo, which burned low and hot and gave off a smell of cinnamon. The camp was simple, a ring of saddles and buffalo-hide bedrolls around the hearth. Horses stamped and nickered occasionally where they were tethered a few meters away, and in the distance something howled long and mournfully. Cythera was full, nearly half again as large as Luna, silver-bright against a sky filled with stars in constellations subtly different from Earth's. Meteors streaked across it every few minutes, multicolored fire.

"Rabiblanco?" he said. No Spanish that he recognized.

"Oh, nice clean gym, nice flat mats, pretty little white suits and colored belts, hey?"

Too academic, he translated mentally. *Well, she has a point*. The shoulder felt stiff, and he rotated it gingerly.

"Yes, but what does it *mean*?" he asked. They leaned back against their saddles, nearly side by side, and one of the others handed them plates of stew and metal cups of strong black coffee from the pot resting on the edge of the fire.

"Rabiblanco?" she said. Her teeth showed in a friendly grin. "White-ass."

"You're quiet today, Skilly," Niles said.

"Skilly is thinking," she said. "We nearly there."

That was a bit of a relief. Not that she chattered; it had been more like a continuous interrogation nearly every day, starting two hours after breakfast, once she learned of his background at Sandhurst. A grab bag of everything he had sat through in those interminable lectures: leadership, communications, how to parade a regiment, logistics, laser range-finding systems, how to hand-compute firing patterns for mortars, how to maintain recoilless rifles, tactical use of seeker missiles . . . She had taken notes, too. Afternoons and they were back in the saddle and she was grilling him on how to *use* it, comparing it with things she had heard from others or read in an astonishing number of books, making up hypotheticals and hashing out alternative solutions. Evenings around the fire it had been about *him*. His relations, who knew who, how were you presented at court, what were the rules about giving parties, schools, table manners. . . .

It had been two weeks since they left the Upper Valley plains and rode into the hill country called the Illyrian Dales, and he was feeling pumped dry. It was like being picked over by a mental crow, all the bright shiny things plucked out and sorted into neat heaps and tirelessly fitted together again. He had mentioned the thought to her, and she had given that delightful laugh and said: *Bird that know the ground doan get into stewpot*, and begun again.

What a woman, he thought contentedly. Not exactly what you'd bring home to mother—he blanched inwardly at the thought—but absolutely riffing for this caper. From hints and glances, even more delightful when they had some privacy. *Burton and Selous should have had it so good*, he thought. Although Burton would probably have made more of his chances; the man *had* translated the Kama Sutra, after all.

"Jeffi, you smiling like the jaguar that got the farmer's pig," Skida said, coming out of her brown study.

"Beautiful country," he said contentedly, waving his free arm around.

That was true enough. The Illyrian Dales were limestone hills, big but gently sloped, endlessly varied. Most of the ridgetops were open, in bright swales of tall grass gold-green with the first frosts. The spiderweb of valleys between was deeper-soiled and held denser growth. Sometimes thickets of wild rose or native semibamboo so dense they had to dismount and cut a path with machetes, more often something like the big maples that arched over their heads here.

Those were turning with the frosts too, to fire-gold and scarlet, and there was a rustling bed of leaves that muffled the beat of hooves from the horses and pack-mules. Afternoon light stabbed down in stray flickers into the gloom below, turning the ground into a flaming carpet of embers for brief seconds. Sometimes there would be a hollow sound under the iron-shod feet of the animals, or they would have to detour around sinkholes; the others had told him of giant caves, networks that ran for scores of kilometers underground. Few rivers, but many springs and pools. West and south on the horizon gleamed the peaks of the Drakon Range, higher than the Himalayas and three times as long. The air was mildly chill and intensely clean, smelling of green and rock.

Best game country I've ever seen, too, he thought happily. Whoever was sent on ahead to make camp could count on finding supper in half an hour; there were usually a couple of fat pheasant or duck or rabbit waiting to be grilled, and the hidehunters had grumbled at having to eat venison four days in a row when one of them snapshot a yearling buck from the saddle.

"Thinking like a *rabiblanco* again," Skilly said, gently teasing. "Outback is bugs and boring, *solamente*, you know? Skilly is here because of her job, then it's city life for her."

"Incorrigible white-ass, that's me," Geoffrey laughed.

Ahead and to their right he could see a herd of bison on a rise in the middle distance, about a kilometer away. A few of the bulls raised their heads at the sound of hooves, and the clump of big shaggy animals began a slow steady movement away, flowing like a carpet over the irregular ground.

"I'm surprised there's so many big grazers after only, what, eighty years?"

"CoDo," Skilly shrugged. "They seeded the plants, did the gene-thing with some of them to grow faster, you know? Then the animals, sent all females and all pregnant, and screwed around with their genes too, so they have only one bull to ten cowbeasts for a while. No diseases and plenty room, grow by ge-o-metric progressive. Only last couple of years the meateaters start to catch up." Those had come from zoos, mostly; the Greens had had a lot of influence back in the 2030s, enough to override local protests and have bears, wolves, dholes, leopards and tigers and whatnot dropped into remote areas. No point in trying that on Earth, the former ranges were jammed with starving people who would gladly beat a lion to death with rocks for the meat on its bones.

"Quiet now."

The valley opened up slightly, glances of blue noon sky and Sparta's pale-yellow sun through the canopy above. Skida halted her mount with a shift of balance, touching its neck with the rein to turn it three-quarters on.

"Skilly sees you," she said in a bored tone of voice.

Niles blinked, as two figures rose from the hillside. Both had been invisible a few minutes earlier; they were covered from head to foot by loose-woven twine cloaks stuck with twigs and leaves, and the scope-sighted rifles cradled in their arms were swaddled in mottled rags. Farther up the hill the ground moved aside under the roots of a pine, and a man vaulted out and skidded down the slope to the mounted party. This one wore leather breeches and boots, a camouflage jacket over that, and webbing gear. A machine-pistol was slung across his chest and there were corporal's stripes on his sleeve; the military effect was a little offset by the black pigtail, bandanna and brass hoop-earring.

"Corporal Hermanez," Skilly said, returning his casual salute.

"Field Prime," he said, obviously pleased that she had remembered his name. "How did you spot my scouts?"

"Leaf piles doan scratch their arse." The guerrilla noncom turned to glare briefly at one of the men, who stiffened. "Two-knife?"

"Off popping the virgins, Field Prime—another fifty recruits in yesterday."

"Carry on."

The valley narrowed again. Alerted, Niles thought he saw movement now and then, once something that *might* be a sonic sensor input mike. The skin on the back of his neck crawled slightly. Then the thickly grown rock flared back on either side of them, into a hummocky clearing of gravel and rock and thin grass several hectares in extent, scattered with medium-sized oaks and big eucalyptus trees with peeling bark. Camouflage nets were rigged between the trees at a little over head-height, mimicking the ground. Across the way was a taller hill where the shell of limestone rock had collapsed inward. Water fell over the lip to a pool at the base, and he could see several dark spaces in the light-colored rock that reached back out of sight.

"Home," Skilly said. "Base One."

Men in the same uniform came and led the horses away at a trot. Niles followed Skida as she ducked under one of the tarpaulins and walked toward the falls, trying not to be too obvious as he looked around. *Not my idea of a rebel encampment*, he thought. There were dug-in air defense missiles, light Skyhawks and frame-mounted Talons; CoDo issue, or copies. Plenty of people moving around; not a spit-and-polish outfit, but they all seemed fairly clean and to know where they were going. Crates and boxes were stacked in neat heaps, and there were half a dozen circles around blackboards or pieces of equipment, familiarization-lectures. A pile of meter-diameter cylinders lay on a timber frame. He stared at them in puzzlement and then recognized a Skysweeper, a simple solid-fuel rocket that could loft a hundred-kilo load of ball bearings into the orbital path of a spy satellite.

His lips shaped a soundless whistle. *Not too shabby*, he thought. A squad jogged by, rifles at port; Skilly returned their leader's salute, the same half-casual wave, and then slapped palms with a figure he recognized: the big Indian he had met briefly in Sparta City, with his twin machetes over his back. Here he also carried a light machine gun, dangling from one hand as if it were no more than a rifle.

"Yo, Two-knife. How it go?"

"Yo, Skilly. Not bad. Your little yellow men got here with their toys, setting up now." He jerked a thumb at the caves.

"Toys may save our asses, Two-knife. Any trouble?"

"Discipline parade for offenders, and taking in the

fresh meat. Got them kit, ran them up and down hills all yesterday, usual thing like you say." The blank black eyes turned on Niles, and the Indian said something in a choppy-sounding language, not Spanish.

"He's a trained officer, not just a pretty face," Skilly replied; Niles felt oddly flattered, and returned the bigger man's gaze coolly. She slung her rifle. "Let's go. Niles should see our discipline."

*   *   *

The stench almost made Niles gag as they walked past the row of a half a dozen pits. Each was just wide enough to hold a man and deep enough that only the faces showed; none of them looked up.

"We got this from the CoDo Marines," Skilly said, watching him out of the corner of her eye. "Make them dig a hole and then live in it for a week. Next step up from punishment drill. Lot of our original trainers were ex-Marines"—*mostly gone now*, she thought but did not say—"and we had a bunch of our Movement people do hitches with the CD and some of the other armies."

"Second offense, not cleaning rifle," Two-knife said, kicking dirt in the direction of the first pit and walking on to each in turn. "Stealing. Second offense, refusing to wash. This one didn't want to learn to read. Backtalking his squad leader. Smoking borloi. Lighting fire in the open."

Beyond the row of pits were two upright X-frames made of saplings, with men lashed to them spreadeagled. Odd-looking bruises and dried crusted scabs covered their naked bodies.

"Gauntlet," Skilly explained. Niles kept his face carefully blank; that meant running between lines of your comrades while they flogged you with their belts. You could not have an army without discipline, and a guerrilla army like this had no system of laws and courts to fall back on. Not to mention the type of recruits they would have to depend on, men on the bad side of the law to begin with.

"Asleep on watch," Two-knife said of the first man. "Striking an officer," of the second. "Got an offender among the virgins, too," he went on.

They were near the C-shaped bowl that fronted the clearing; the waterfall was a hundred meters away, at the center of the curve, and its sound was a burr of white noise in the background. Here the ground ran down to the base of the cliff in a natural amphitheater. Fifty or so men and a few women were squatting on the rocky ground, in uniform but looking awkward in it, and groggy with exhaustion where they were not tense with fear. Very out of place, as well; you could tell these were men who had spent their lives in cities, and on their streets. A few armed troops stood by, not quite guarding the recruits; two more flanked a bound prisoner at the base of the slope, very definitely guarding *him*. A short woman stood nearby, glaring at the one under guard.

"The virgin's name is Carter," Two-knife continued. "The other one is Werewolf. He caught Williams in the third back warehouse cave, tried to hump her. She caught him a couple and he whipped on her *muy mal*, then ran when the patrol came."

"Williams . . . Citizen family, University, come in right after we blow the Peacemaker? Her squeeze killed by Milice?"

He nodded and Skilly fell silent, taking in the parties as she walked down toward them. Then she turned to face the recruits, ignoring the judicial matter for the moment.

"This," she said, indicating herself with a thumb, "is Field Prime. Field Prime commands the Spartan People's Liberation Army. We call ourselves the Helots; pretty soon you learn why. Helots are under the direction of the Movement Council and Capital Prime. Field Second," she continued, turning to Two-knife, "repeat the charge."

When he had finished, she turned to the woman. Girl, rather; about nineteen, but it was difficult to tell anything else because of massive purple-and-yellow bruises that covered her face.

"Yes."

"Louder, Helot."

"Yes! I told him to go away and he grabbed me and I kicked him and he started hitting me and—" She turned away, arms tightly crossed over her chest.

"So, Carter," Skida continued, to the prisoner. "What you say?"

"Lies," the man said. He was not much older than his victim, still in gang colors, a thin acne-scarred face and darting eyes. "Them University cunts, they'll spread for anything. Stuck-up bitch probably has the crud, anyway."

Skida looked at Two-knife, then took the girl's chin between thumb and forefinger for a moment to examine her injuries. A slight nod and the guards stepped away from Carter, who smiled and stood taller. Skida was wearing a Walther in a cross-draw holster below her left breast, with the butt turned in. Her hand did not seem to move with any particular haste, but the echoing crack of the first shot rang out before Carter's eyes had time to do more than widen. He jerked back, folding as if an invisible horse had kicked him in the gut. The flat slap of the 10mm bullet hitting the muscle of his stomach was just audible under the gunshot, and she held the second until he clapped his hands to the spreading red patch and moaned in shock. The next bullet left a black hole in the middle of his forehead and snapped him erect again for an instant while the back of his skull blew out in a shower of bone-chips and pink-gray jelly.

"Take this shit away and throw it down a hole," she said, holstering the weapon.

"First lesson!" she continued to the recruits. "Only two ways out of this army!" Skida held up a fist. One finger shot up. "One, when we marches down the Sacred Way in the victory parade." Another finger. "Two—feet first. This the Revo*lu*tion. The Revolution not a tea party; it not so kind, so gentle, so reasonable as that."

She paused to let the recruits absorb that; one was retching, and a few were looking shaky. Most of the rest sat stock-still, but the smell of their fear was rank. After a moment she tapped herself on the chest.

"Skilly—that Field Prime to you—Skilly knows you. Knows all the secret of you dirty little souls. You think you baaad, eh? Think the world give you a hard *time*, think the world *owe* you something. Now you going to go *take* it, eh?" Mutters of approval. The tall woman sneered.

"Well, Skilly tells you something; you half right. Yes, the world shit on you all your lives. The Welfare officers, the CoDo, the rich, the taxpayers back on Earth, Citizens here—all of them fuck you over from the day you born. What does that make you?"

She paused, then spoke in a tone thick with scorn. "Shit yourselves, is what." Another murmur, hostile this time and quickly dying under her glare. "Yes! You everything the bossman ever tell you you are. You *worthless*, you *useless*, no good to yourself or anybody. They *laughing* at you, mon."

"But here"—she tapped a booted toe against the rocky earth—"here, you *maybe* become something. Here you learn how to take what the world owe you." She crossed her arms. "How? Not by sitting in a bar, talking wit' you friends about how you do something *next month*, for sure. Not by rolling drunks and beating up on tourists and cutting each other. Not by pushing shit into your arm or up your nose.

"Here, you learn to *fight*. Here, you learn to be an *army*. That is *power*, mon! Who wants that? Who wants power, who wants to fuck the people that been up your ass all your life?" They cheered at that, a raw savage sound. Niles felt his stomach clench with the sudden realization that it was directed at *him* and people like him.

Alarming, he thought. And exhilarating, the same wild excitement you got on a fast powder-snow slope.

"Shut up! Shouting won't get it for you; lying under a tree won't, nohow. *Work* get it for you." There was dead silence now; Skida's grin was gaunt and knowing. "Yes, *compadres*, here you *work*. You work harder than field-hands cutting cane, you work until the brains run out your nose like sweat. And you *learn*." She stooped, and caught up a glob of semiliquid gray. A tuft of hair and bone was still attached to the glistening string of matter. Skida swung her arm in an arc, spattering it at the feet of the crowd, grimly amused as they shrank back.

"Look at that! Brains, and never used for anything but holding two deaf ears apart. Brains that wouldn't *learn*, wouldn't *listen*. At least now the ants eat them, get some use out of them. You want to be like that? No? So that the next thing you do here, you learn to *use* the brains. You *stupid*, now. Too stupid to *know* you stupid; now, we fix that.

"One last thing. Look at each other." She waited a moment, until their heads turned uncertainly from side to side. "These people your *compadres*. These are the peoples you live with, eat with, work with, *fight beside* from now. Field Prime isn't your mother; Field Prime doesn't care if you love each other. You can hate each other like brothers. But when we finished with you, you will be tighter than brothers—you will save your *compadre*'s ass, because you know he will save *yours*.

"And when you've done all that, *then* you'll have the power. The power of an *army*. Do you understand?"

"Answer, *Yes, Field Prime!*" Two-knife shouted; it was an astonishing sound, loud enough for a powered megaphone.

"*Yes, Field Prime!*"

"Louder, so Field Prime can hear you."

"*YES, FIELD PRIME!*"

*   *   *

"And this your place, right next to mine," Skilly said.

Niles nodded, a little dazed. The tour had been exhaustive, and combined with a running staff meeting and a series of introductions; he sensed that was a test too, of his ability to assimilate information quickly and not lose his feet. The network of caverns was enormous; on Earth it would have been a famous tourist attraction. Here it was being put to more practical use: stables, armories, kitchens, barracks, infirmary, machine-shop, a hydro-generator running on an underground stream, classrooms, even a small computer room with a commercial optical-disk system capable of holding almost unlimited data. The Meijians had been setting up shop next to that; farther back were caves stacked high with hides and tallow and jerky, part of the operation that provided cover and additional funds.

"This . . . must have taken years," he said.

"Near ten years. Skilly found it just after she got here"—over a decade—"but she was *really* running a hide-hunting business then." She waved a hand into the darkness. This stretch of corridor was lit by fluorescent tubes stapled to the rock. "Plenty more place like this in the Dales. About four hundred Helots here now, most training, and then we push them out to the other bases, keep everything dispersed. Duplicate all the *fa*cilities here, too, stuff in various place, if we ever have to move out fast. Building up the numbers now, got the frame*work* and just need the warm bodies."

"Well, ah, yes, Field Prime," he said. She was leaning against the doorway of her quarters, set into the fissured rock, smiling slightly.

"Field problem in the morning," she said, looking at the chronometer-compass on her wrist. "Oh," she added, just as she closed the door. "Connecting door from your place inside. Not locked."

*   *   *

This is ridiculous, Geoffrey Niles thought, staring at the doorknob.

His room was a simple bubble in the rock, roughly shaped with pneumatic hammers; the floor was covered with mats of woven quasibamboo, and there was simple furniture of wood and metal that looked as if it had been knocked together in one of the workshops and doubtless had been. There was a jug and bowl on the dresser and a field phone beside the bed, which was covered in furs that would have been worth a fortune on Earth and were probably what the poor used on Sparta. Someone had unpacked his gear and stowed it neatly in the dressers: there were four sets of Helot uniforms in his size with Senior Group Leader's rank-badges—about equivalent to Major—hanging from the wooden rod that served as a closet, a complete set of web gear, and boots that fitted him. No excuse to linger beyond washing up and changing his clothes.

Also a bottle of brandy and some glasses in a cupboard. For a moment he considered taking a shot . . . *Don't be ridiculous*, he told himself again. *You're twenty-four years old, not some schoolboy virgin. You've had plenty of experience with women.* His palms were sweating; he wiped them, and looked at the door again. Saw Skilly's face as she shot the man in the stomach this morning, bored disinterest. Saw it as they ran down the stairs in Sparta city, laughing as the grenade blew and shrapnel licked at their heels amid the screams and curses. He shivered slightly with a complex emotion he could not have named, and wiped the back of his hand across his mouth.

"So she's not a debutante," he muttered.

The door swung open noiselessly. There were two chambers on the other side; the first was an office, tables of neatly stacked papers, filing cabinets, a retrieval system and desk; all dim, lit only by the reflected light of a small lamp in the next. The only ornament was something that looked like an Indian figurine about six inches high, a six-armed goddess dancing.

He walked through. The bedroom was larger than his, but scarcely better furnished, except for one wall that held racked bookcases and a veedisk player. A big Japanese-looking print beside that, but he paid little attention to it. Skilly was lying reading on her bed, the blankets and ermine coverlet folded down to the foot of it. She was entirely naked, and there were two glasses of brandy waiting on the night table. "Well," she said softly, putting aside the book. Some distant part of his brain noted the title: *Seven Pillars of Wisdom*. "Skilly was beginning to think you not mon enough, Jeffi."

She slid down from the pillows and stretched; her chocolate-colored skin rippled in long smooth curves as she linked her hands behind her head. Her breasts were high and rounded, the nipples plum-dark and taut. He felt his hands open and close convulsively, and when he spoke his voice was hoarse with the pulse that hammered painfully in throat and temples and groin.

"I think you'll find me man enough and more."

She laughed, with a child's gleeful malice in the tone. "Come show Skilly, then. Show me what you made of."

*   *   *

The Englishman murmured slightly as Skida slipped out of bed; she waited for a moment until he turned over and burrowed his head into the pillow. Chuckling soundlessly, she pulled the ermine coverlet up around him before slipping into her pajamas and out the door.

This was officer country and safe, but she tucked a small automatic into the back of the trouser-band just the same; habit, and good habits kept you alive. She gave a contented yawn as she padded down to the wardroom and over to the cooler unit set against one wall, taking out a tall glass of milk and a plate of her favorite oatmeal cookies before flopping down on a couch. The wardroom's style was deliberately casual, to encourage the command cadre to develop a club spirit. Not very likely anyone would be here at this hour, though; Base One rose with the dawn, and Sparta's nights were short.

She sipped and nibbled contentedly, thinking, smiling to herself.

"Skilly looking happy," Two-knife said. "You going to drop Croser?" He knew she seldom had more than one man at a time; Skida Thibodeau hated mess and confusion and unnecessary trouble.

"Not right now, but it time to put us on a more *pro*fessional footing," she said lightly.

Two-knife walked over to the cooler and fixed himself a plate of cold chicken, popping the cap off a beer bottle with one thumb. He was wearing only cotton-duck trousers, and the faint glowlight emphasized the heavy bands of muscle over shoulders and chest and stomach; he was taller than her, but broad enough to seem squat. She smiled affectionately, remembering the time a pimp in Mayopan had decked her from behind with a crowbar during a negotiation session over territorial rights; Two-knife had grabbed him by wrist and neck and done a straight pull until the man's arm came out at the shoulder socket.

"What joke?" he said.

"Remembering old times," she said; they dropped back into a familiar mixture of Belizean English, Spanish and low-country Mayan. "Remember the time RoBo was going to shoot you?"

Two-knife laughed, a rumbling sound. "Never forget it. The look on his face when you broke his neck! Ah, those were the days, Skilly." There was a companionable silence. "How long you going to keep the Englishman?"

"Permanent, Skilly thinks," she said. At his look of surprise: "Well, Croser not the one I want for keeps. Hard man, him, maybe too much to handle up close. Besides, Skilly don't like cutting throats in the family, and if . . . " She made a gesture, and he nodded: it had long been obvious there would be an endgame after the Revolution, if they won.

"Jeffi perfect; got the right connections, smart enough, make good babies"—she had had several hundred ova frozen a couple of years ago—"just what Skilly need to put on the polish when she move up in the world. Anyway, going to be busy for a while."

Two-knife grunted. "Yes. There's going to be a lot of dead white-asses soon."

"Hey," she said playfully, "no race prejudice in the Helots—that a gauntlet offense!" They both laughed. Of course, there *was* a regulation to that effect; there had to be, given the polyglot nature of the force. Two-knife made a show of despising everyone but Mayans from his home district, anyway, and for that matter, the term meant "naive fool" as much as anything specifically ethnic.

"Besides, Skilly's momma was a white-ass."

"I, Two-knife, will forgive you for that. Even forgive you that your father was a damned Black Carib pimp."

She finished her milk and licked her lips. "Hey, Two-knife, serious, mon; remember after we win, we gots to put this place back together and *run* it." She looked at him from under her eyelids. "Ah! Skilly will find you a nice widow—widows be plentiful then—with yellow hair and big tits and good hips and a big hacienda, she teach you how to take off your boots in bed and eat with a fork, so Skilly won't have to hide you in the closet at the fancy parties."

"You want to *kill* me, woman?" he asked, shaking with laughter again; then his face fell, as he realized she was half-serious. And when Skilly made a plan . . . "You told the Englishman he's getting married?" he said.

"No," she said, dusting her hands as she finished the last cookie. "Skilly will train him up to it gradual."

CHAPTER SEVEN

Crofton's Encyclopedia of the Inhabited Planets (2nd Edition):

Sparta: Sparta (originally Botany Bay) was discovered by Captain Mark Brodin of the CoDominium Exploration Service ship *Lewis and Clark* during the Grand Survey of 2010. Alderson point connections to the Sol system are via Tanith, Markham, Xanadu, GSX-1773, and GSX-2897. Further connections exist to Frystaat, Dayan and Haven. Initial survey indicated a very favorable native ecology but no exceptional mineral or other resources. A Standard Terraforming Package was seeded in 2011, and the Category VI Higher Mammal Package followed in 2022.

Circumference: 13,600 kilometers
Diameter: 13,900 kilometers
Gravity: 1.22 standard
Diurnal cycle: 20 hours
Year: 1.6 standard
Composition: Nickel-iron, silicates
Satellites: Cythera, mass 1.7 Luna

Atmosphere is basically terrestrial, but with 1.17 standard sea-level pressure. Total land area is approximately half that of Earth, with extensive oceans; much of the land, c. 28,800,000 sq. kilometers (18,000,000 sq. miles), is concentrated in the Serpentine Continent, an equatorial landmass deeply penetrated by inland seas . . . Native life is mainly marine; the high concentration of dissolved oxygen in the oceanic waters, and the extensive shallow seas, permit a very active oceanic ecosystem with many large piscoid species. Land-based forms are limited to primitive vegetation and analogs of simple insects; terrestrial species have largely replaced the native on the Serpentine continent and adjacent islands. Total illumination is 92% of standard, resulting in a warm-temperate to subtropical climate in the equatorial Serpentine continent, shading to cold-temperate and subarctic conditions on the northern shores.

Initial settlement: A CoDominium research station was established in 2024, and shipment of involuntary transportees began in 2032. In 2036 settlement rights were transferred to the Constitutionalist Society (conditional upon continued receipt of involuntary colonists), a political group centered in the United States, and settlement began in 2038. Internal self-government was granted in 2040, and the Dual Kingdom of Sparta was recognized as a sovereign state by the Grand Senate in 2062; the CoDominium retained an enclave in Sparta City, and involuntary colonization continued as per the Treaty of Independence.

*   *   *

"Well, I'm glad we won't be doing a full review just yet, sir." Battalion Sergeant Sergio Guiterrez said. There was heartfelt relief in his tone.

"His Majesty Alexander isn't coming; General Alexander Collins will be here instead, Top," Peter Owensford said. "A useful fiction; Prince Lysander came up with it, some historical thing from Britain." Their vehicle was waiting at the steps of the General Headquarters building, but Owensford stopped for a moment to look at the camp.

The Fifth Battalion's camp was a hundred kilometers south of Sparta City, at the base of the peninsula that held the capital and on the western fringe of the Eurotas delta. The main road from the city ran by along the sea, but that was merely a two-lane gravel strip; most traffic was by barge or river-steamer. Marsh and sandy beach and rocky headlands fronted the water, with a screen of small islands on the horizon. Inland were the Theramenes Hills that ran north to the outskirts, not really mountains but tumbled and rough enough to suit; between hills and sea was a narrow strip of plain. Eight weeks of Sparta's short days ago it had been bare save for a thin covering of grass, a useless stretch of heavy adobe clay.

Now it was the base camp of the Fifth Battalion, Falkenberg's Mercenary Legion—and the newly formed First Royal Spartan Infantry, King Alexander's Own Regiment: Fort Plataia. Men and machines had thrown up a five-meter earth berm around an area a kilometer square; radar towers showed at the corners. The capacitance wire and bunkers and minefields outside did not, but they were there and ready, and beyond them signs warned intruders that the camp was protected by deadly force.

Within was still an orderly chaos. The essential buildings had gone in first: revetments for air defense, bunkers, shelters. Dug-in armories, the generators, stores, roofed with steel beams and sandbags. This HQ building, Officers' and NCOs' mess, kitchens, all of the same adobe bricks and rammed earth stabilized with plastic and roofed with utilitarian asbestos cement. Married quarters were just going up in a separate section in the southeast corner, and there were peg-and-string outlines for barracks.

Many dependents, most of the troopers, and all the continuous inflow of recruits were still in tents. They had *made* the tents, under the direction of the veterans of the Fifth, each maniple of five issued canvas and rope; learning to cook and clean for themselves, to work as a unit. Not that they spent much time in the tents; the recruits lived in their leather and cotton-drill uniforms, out in the field in all weathers with nothing but their greatcloaks for protection. Two weeks of conditioning and close order drill and basic military courtesy, then they learned to make their battle-armor of nemourlon and live in *that*, night and day. Small arms training, maintenance work, unarmed combat; field problems, live fire exercises. The recruit formations shrank under the brutally demanding training, but more flowed in. Street toughs just off the CoDo shuttles, fresh-faced Citizen farmboys from the Valley. . . .

All done quickly, and done well. Peter nodded in satisfaction. Then he caught the Sergeant Major's faint grin. Owensford swung into the jeep. "Let's go," he said.

*   *   *

"Again, I'm rather impressed," King Alexander said, returning Peter Owensford's salute and nodding toward the bustle about them.

He had come by helicopter, and was dressed in the uniform of a General in the Royal Spartan Army, which meant minimal ceremony. It was a new uniform, since Sparta had nothing but the Brotherhood militias and a company-sized Royal Guard until the Legion landed. Melissa had designed it; there was a high-collared tunic and trousers of a dark sand-gray, pipped along the seams in silver, with Sam Browne belt and boots, and a peaked cap. Owensford rather liked it; less showy than the Legion's blue and gold, but sharp, and men needed to feel like soldiers in garrison situations where battledress and weapons were ridiculous.

"Thank you, sir. We've been turning adversity to advantage. I'll fill you in at the briefing. If you'll come this way?" The Spartan monarch was looking older, and much more tired; his skin seemed to have coarsened in the weeks since he had greeted the Legion.

General Desjardins of the RSMP was with him, and some of his officers; a few civilians, including Melissa von Alderheim. *I suppose she thinks Lysander could get back to the city more often,* Owensford thought, a little wistfully. In his thirty-sixth year he was growing more than a little envious of his married comrades. . . . *Although I suppose any marriage a prince makes will be more a matter of duty. At least there aren't any more stories about the Prince and Cornet Gordon.*

The main landing field was outside the kilometer-square perimeter of the base, but not outside its circle of activity. A company-sized group of young men in uniform trousers and T-shirts jogged by down a newly made dirt track behind a standard-bearer with a pennant, their booted feet striking the gravel in crunching unison. Their heads were cropped close, and sweat ran down their faces, made the cotton singlets cling to their muscled chests despite the cool wind from the water. The man with the pennant was at least forty, or possibly half again that with regeneration treatment, but he showed no strain at keeping up with youngsters raised in this gravity.

"Heaow, *sound off!*" he barked.

A hundred strong young voices broke into a song that was half-chant:

"Kiss me good night, Sergeant Major,
Tuck me in my little feather-bed,
Kiss me good night, Sergeant Major—
Sergeant Major, be a mother, to meeee!"

The king smiled. There was a good deal else going on. A regular *crack . . . crack . . .* came from a firing range further inland. In the middle distance mortar teams were drilling, *schoomp* as the rounds left the barrels, *pumpf* as they burst several thousand meters to the west. Officers and noncoms in Legion uniforms stood nearby to supervise mortar crews. Fatigue parties in gray overalls were at work, digging or repairing heavy equipment. A column of armored vehicles was leaguered in a square to one side of the roadway. There were six-wheeled battle cars, with turrets mounting a 15mm gatling machine gun, or a single-barreled model and a grenade launcher or mortar. Turretless versions were parked within the leaguer; hatches and rear ramps showed they were intended as personnel carriers.

"From the von Alderheim works?" Alexander said, as he climbed into Owensford's jeep. It was a safe bet; the AFVs had locally made spun-alloy wheels, and the armor was welded steel rather than composites. "Quick work."

"Yes, sir," Owensford said. "Miss von Alderheim has been most helpful."

Melissa blushed as the two men turned to look at her. "Well, it's the all-terrain truck chassis and engine," she said. "You know, Uncle Alexander, I trained on the CAD-CAM computer Father brought in for the University?" Not really needed, when most of what Sparta's major vehicle company turned out was standard models built to obsolete designs. And there was a waiting list for *them*. "I just . . . ran up something. The machine does most of it, really."

"Which reminds me," Peter said. "Until we get the aircraft construction going, I'll need another way to loft Thoth missiles. Dumb solid rockets should do. Not quite in the von Alderheim line, but shouldn't be too difficult."

"Thoth missiles?"

"Well, that's the code word. Small smart missiles. Usually rolled out of a cargo aircraft just over the horizon from the target, but that's a bit hard to do here without airplanes. A rocket booster system would be trickier, but the Alanas think they can do it."

"I'll get someone on that," Melissa said.

"No point in spreading this around," Peter said. "Who knows, we might surprise someone."

The jeep swept past the gate, as guards in the blue and gold of the Legion and the gray of Sparta brought their rifles to salute. *I'm a damned tour guide*, Owensford thought, as he pointed out the important features. Here too there were endless groups of marching men, most in mottled camouflage fatigues and bulky nemourlon armor. One group of such were double-timing with their rifles over their heads; lead weights were fastened all over their battle harness.

"Punishment detail," Owensford explained. "When you're working men as hard as we are, you have to come up with something a little more severe to act as a deterrent."

* * *

The rest of the command group were waiting at the Headquarters building. There was a flurry of salutes and handshakes before they moved into the staff conference room.

Peter Owensford felt an almost eerie sense of *déjà vu* as he took his seat at the head of the table. The room was a long rectangle, one wall dominated by maps, the other by a computer display screen; the officers were in the standard places for a staff meeting. Enlisted stewards brought coffee, then retired behind the guarded door. A Royal Army corporal-stenographer sat in one corner, her hands poised over the keyboard.

"Ten' '*hut*!" Battalion Sergeant Guiterrez said.

"At ease, gentlemen, ladies," Owensford said. *Odd. How often have I seen Christian Johnny do this?* "General Collins is here as a participant observer." Hence not in the chain of command, and seated to his right. "We'll begin with the readiness report. If you please, Captain Barton?"

"Sir." He nodded to the "general." "The Fifth and its noncombatants are now fully settled. Expansion and training is proceeding as follows."

He touched the controls and an organizational chart sprang out on the computer display screen to the left of the table.

"We've received approximately thirty-seven

hundred recruits, of which four hundred and eight have proven unsuitable. An unusually low ratio, considering that we're training the cadre for larger units.

"We've shifted the least physically fit members of the Fifth into four training companies, configured as cadre units to handle basic training, and a technician's course largely manned by pensioners and noncombatants. That hasn't presented a major difficulty in unit continuity, because they wouldn't be in combat units to begin with. Four additional rifle and one heavy-weapons company have been formed, using many of our remaining enlisted cadre and local recruits; we've concentrated the, ah, less socially desirable individuals into the new Legion formations."

"Your appraisal?"

"The five new companies are now combat-ready. There's not as much unit cohesion as we'd like, but they'll shake down. The new personnel have received the full basic training except for space assault and non-terrestrial environment practice. We've got the nucleus of a good combat force here."

"So you've cloned your battalion," Alexander said.

"Well, the new units haven't the experience, of course," Owensford said. "Normal Legion procedure is to organize with no more than one recruit in each maniple. In the present situation we may have as many as three, and some of those have monitors who aren't long past being a PFC." He shrugged. "We make do with what we have, but frankly, I'm not so sorry that the rebels have been active lately. Combat's just what we need to make regulars out of these units."

"Ah. And what of our Royal Spartan forces?" Alexander asked. There was eagerness in his voice.

"Approximately five hundred recruits are still in the basic training pipeline," Barton said. "Two thousand three hundred have completed basic and in some cases advanced training, and have been formed into three infantry, one mechanized and one support battalion, plus headquarters units and armored-cavalry squadrons. One of the infantry battalions is the Prince Royal's Own, and we've tried to post some of the best troops into that. When we get more aviation assets we'll turn it into an air assault unit."

Another chart took form. The table of organization was based on the Legion's, essentially similar to a CoDominium Marine regimental combat team: Headquarters company; Scouts; signals platoon; combat engineering platoon; two heavy-weapons companies with mortars and recoilless rifles; transport company—mules, in this case, with some unarmored versions of the von Alderheim 6x6; aviation company, and medical section.

"There are conspicuous gaps, of course," Barton concluded. "No aircraft, so aviation company is only a shell. Light on artillery. Communications aren't what we'd like them to be. However, I can say that the first Field Force regiment of the Royal Spartan Army now exists, and we can add combat battalions as we get them. As you can see"—arrows sprang out, linking the Spartan regiment with the structure of the Fifth—"our primary limiting factor is leaders, both officers and NCOs. Of the two, the shortage of experienced NCOs is more difficult. Junior officers are in sufficient supply; a number of officers from the Brotherhood militia units have enlisted, and more than forty former Line Marine personnel resident on Sparta have offered their services to date."

Sparta was a popular retirement spot for CoDo officers; many of them on early retirement, with the cutbacks. The social atmosphere appealed to them, you could get quite a reasonable estate for very low prices, and even a meager pension in CoDominium credits went a long way here. Much further than on Churchill or Friedland, even, if you were prepared to live without the high-tech gadgetry.

"For the rest, we have filled the senior NCO slots and

most of the company, battalion and HQ positions by lateral transfer from the Legion, usually involving brevet promotions. Wearing two hats, as it were."

A temporary promotion, to allow the mercenaries to command their theoretical equals in the larger Royal Army formation.

"If I may, Major?" General Collins's voice. Owensford nodded.

"Of course, sir."

"My—that is, the two kings have been informed of the matter of brevet promotions. We have decided that for the duration of the Legion's stay such personnel will be carried on the Royal Army rolls and receive the pay and other privileges attendant on their rank. Which of course will become permanent if any choose to remain with the Royal forces when at liberty to do so."

"Thank you, sir, on behalf of my men," Owensford said. "They'll very much appreciate it." Many of the Legionnaires were nearing the end of their terms of enlistment, retirement age, or both. *And if the plan works out, the Legion or part of it may well be based on Sparta.*

Alexander Collins smiled. "Including Captain Barton and yourself, of course," he said, holding up a hand. His aide placed two small wooden boxes in his hands. "Your other hats, gentlemen." A colonel's eagles for him, and a lieutenant-colonel's oak leaves for Ace.

"Again, thank you, sir." *And now is not the time to lecture about rank and brotherhood and ambition. . . .*

"Furthermore, an Order in King and Council has been made that a full five-year term of service in the Royal army will constitute fulfillment of the public-service portion of the Citizenship examinations. Three terms of service with honorable discharge, or award of the *coronea aurea* award for valor during service, or promotion to commissioned rank, upon honorable discharge will constitute full qualification for Citizenship."

"We are in your debt." There were murmurs from the other mercenary officers; not many host-worlds were that hospitable. Many regarded hired soldiers as in much the same category as whores: paid professionals filling a necessary but unmentionable service. Offer of citizenship and a home was more important than rank inflation, and by a lot. *They clearly took us seriously when we talked about loyalties and incentives. The Colonel's going to be pleased. I wonder how much of this is Lysander's doing? Probably a lot.*

"The nominal commander of the First Royal Infantry is, of course, His Majesty Alexander First," Ace Barton said. "The professional commander for the moment is Major—Colonel Owensford, with Lieutenant Colonel Arnold Kistiakowski as deputy."

Kistiakowski, a militia officer, had been an accountant in civil life, but did seem to have a flair for military command. He was also the son of one of the First Families, and an elected Senator. He nodded acknowledgment.

"Captain—Major Barton," Owensford said, "is chief of staff to the First Royal as well as to me as nominal chief of staff to the Minister of War." The Spartan chain of command sounded more complex than it was. Peter could hardly blame the Spartans for wanting to retain control over the military machine they were constructing.

"Major, are the First Royals ready for combat?"

"Low-intensity combat only, sir. The First is lacking in battle computers, secure communications gear, nightfighting equipment, range finders, modern artillery—the artillery battalion is using locally made one-twenty-five- and one-sixty-mm mortars—antiaircraft and antitank capacity. It also has no organic air transport, and the combat engineers are underequipped. None of that is fatal, but you wouldn't want to throw them up against experienced troops with full equipment."

"General comments?"

"Sir . . . as recruits, the recruits are of excellent

quality; the standard of literacy and general mechanical aptitude was particularly notable. About half the men are of Citizen background and half not." As opposed to seventy-thirty in the general population, and about eighty-twenty in the relevant age groups.

He smiled: "There was some friction at first; they thought of each other as hick sissies and gutter thugs respectively. Going through basic has cured a good deal of that."

At least while they were in ranks. There was a more basic culture clash; the Citizens seemed to be very like what the old middle class of America had been, before it fissured into Taxpayer and Welfare Island Citizen. Respectable people, stable personalities from stable families. While the transportees came from a brutally chaotic background of illiteracy, illegitimacy and instant gratification.

"What they need most now is some experience to convince them that they're really soldiers; that would shake them down, solidify unit esprit, and help us identify potential leaders, which is our main restraint on further expansion at the moment."

"Thank you," Peter said. "Next item, logistics and technical support. Captain Alana?"

Catherine Alana touched her own keyboard, and a series of boxed equipment mixes appeared on the computer screen.

"As Captain Barton reported, the main shortage is in high-tech equipment. Local industry makes high-quality gear, but the variety is restricted. We're working with designers to overcome that. Basic equipment is excellent, as are ammunition supplies. We get smart weapons in sufficient quantity for training, and we're building a stockpile, but there are never enough."

"And won't be," Alexander said. "Until we begin earning hard currency. Which will expend those munitions—"

"Yes, sir, bootstrap operations tend to be slow," Catherine agreed. She shrugged. "So we do the best we can. As presently equipped, the First would already be suitable for employment in some off-planet situations. New Washington, for example, if Colonel Falkenberg needs more troops. Particularly as light infantry in unroaded situations, they could already command better contract terms than most Earth-based outfits."

There were a few snorts; nobody thought much of Earthling mercenaries these days. The best recruits were going to the growing national armies, as the CoDominium grip weakened.

"I've shown here four alternate add-on weapons and equipment kits, with their probable price ranges, and the degree to which they'd enhance effectiveness. It's my estimation that with certified combat experience, the First—excuse me, the Royal Army, I'm not used to thinking in these terms—the First could secure an equipment loan from Dayan or Xanadu against a lien on their first few contracts." Those powers offered specialist mercenary units of their own, but also acted as escrow agents and financed turnkey operations. "We've got plenty of technical personnel here, and I've assigned each of them two Royal Army understudies. By the time the equipment comes in, the people to operate it will be there too."

Owensford nodded. "Well done." He meant that. Building a regimental-sized fighting force in such a short time was a considerable accomplishment. "Fortunately, we don't have to provide all the managerial and staff service training. General Slater's War College is doing an excellent job of that.

"What we here must do is develop combat capability. That's more than simply honing individual skills. It's a matter of working with what we have, to blend weapons and skills and capabilities into fighting units. Captain Jesus Alana will elaborate."

"If I may lecture for a moment," Jesus Alana said. "The available weapons, Sparta's industries, and financial limitations all dictate that whatever we eventually add to the mix, Sparta will for some time to come specialize in infantry. This is not necessarily a disadvantage. Infantry has dominated war in many eras, and can be decisive today.

"Since we have little choice but to develop infantry teams, we need to understand what infantry does. There are two major objectives to infantry action. One is to take ground and hold it. The other is to kill or disable the enemy.

"These are generally achieved in quite different ways. The best way to take ground is to move in when it's not occupied, and get there with enough force that no one wants to dispute it.

"The best way to kill enemy troops is to make him break his teeth assaulting prepared positions. Of course, it doesn't take too bright a commander to know frontal assaults against strong positions aren't a good idea, so it follows that the best tactic is to make him think there aren't many of you out there. No big target for him to shoot at. Then hit him with real firepower he didn't expect. The United States developed that into a fine art in Vietnam just before the politicos closed them down: small patrols able to spot for long-range artillery and missiles. The enemy couldn't fight back because he couldn't get at the artillery and missile bases, and the patrols weren't a very good target because they were small enough to stay dug in. They were also well armed and trained for close combat."

"Doesn't that take high technology we don't have?" Alexander asked.

"Not so high as all that, sir," Catherine Alana said. "And again we make do with what we have. Jesus and I have worked out something. Should be quite a surprise to the enemy."

"That would be a pleasant change," Alexander said. The frowns on the faces of the king and General Desjardins brought Owensford back from the pure professional satisfaction of doing a difficult job, reminding him of exactly why it had been so necessary to hurry.

"So," Jesus continued. "Our goal, then, is to develop light and agile forces accustomed to digging in and defending themselves against close in enemies, while bringing in fire support to deal with everything else. We then tailor our training to that end—and of course that decision affects our weapons procurements, which impact industrial decisions.

"As to the technological skills, first we teach them to be military officers, leaders, then we send them to General Slater's War College, or the University. Or both. In this way we bootstrap up to larger units." Jesus shrugged. "Unit cohesion suffers, of course, but we can stabilize assignments to troop units once we have developed all the skills required. After that it's a matter of sane replacement policies."

"If we live that long," Desjardins said.

Peter Owensford nodded. "I'm coming to that. Captain Alana, please give us a strategic appreciation. Begin with the political background, if you please."

"Sir. First, the good news," Jesus Alana said. "The Foundation Loyalist and Pragmatist factions—not really parties yet—have agreed on the tax increases necessary for the security program." The Spartan constitution included discretionary funds always at the disposal of the Crown, but new taxes required Council and Senate approval. "As long as they pull together, the situation is serious but not desperate."

"The bad news," he went on, "is that the NCLF is making political hay with the massacre at the Spartosky. They brought criminal charges against the Milice, the kings, the Legion individually and collectively, even Miss von Alderheim here."

Somebody laughed down the table; Owensford sent a quelling glance.

General Desjardins snorted. "After twenty police were killed! Cases thrown out of court." Spartan law was quite unequivocal on the subject of deadly self-defense. Grudgingly, he added: "Some of the crowd *were* shot in the back as they ran. The Milice had never been under fire before, and they panicked."

Jesus Alana smiled. "Ah, but General Desjardins, the news cameras were disabled before the rocket attack. To the NCLF's target audience, pictures are truth and written words automatically lies. Street demonstrations have become a daily occurrence. The Dockworkers' Union has staged several sympathy strikes, and there has been loss of produce on the docks to spoilage. And Mr. Dion Croser—let me rephrase that—*Senator* Dion Croser is now their representative in the legislature."

Alexander sighed. "I wouldn't have thought the Citizens in the union would tolerate it," he said.

"They know they're outnumbered, and they know Croser's goons know where their families live," Desjardins said bluntly. "You will not let us use those measures against him, but he is free to use them himself. The end result is, he's now got a perfect platform and Legislative immunity from libel laws. He's spent the last two months up and down the Valley, organizing in the riverport towns. The bastard can make a speech, I'll grant him that. Even got some farm-workers signed up, won't *that* be lovely when he takes them out on strike in the middle of harvest in the sugar country, say."

Jesus Alana coughed. "Yes. Unfortunately, we also have nothing we could take to court to connect the NCLF with serious illegal activity. Of which there has been a steady increase." He touched the controls, calling up a map of the Eurotas Valley, a shape like a horizontal S running four thousand kilometers from northwest to southeast as the crow flew. Much more in terms of river frontage, of course. For most of its length it was an alluvial trough, flanked by hills and mountain ranges; those culminated in the Himalayan-sized Drakon Range in the west.

"More Helot attacks on isolated ranches. Also trucks, transport, economic targets—weirs, power stations—and most recently, a small RSMP post here in the Middle Valley. Most of the troopers were out on patrol, but four were killed and considerable weapons and equipment seized. So far, retaliatory action has not been . . . very effective."

Desjardins stirred. "My men are doing their best, but they're impossibly overstretched," he said. "Just the Valley is over two million square miles! By the time they've gotten to the site of one incident, the trail is cold and there's another alarm somewhere else. What prisoners we've taken are useless, and deny any knowledge of a connection between the Helots and the NCLF."

"Yet it seems conclusive," Owensford said. All eyes turned to him; it was a lonely feeling. "This is not bandit trouble. This is the beginning of a classic two-level guerrilla war, of a pattern quite common on Earth during the Cold War period, before the CoDominium. Quite classic, almost as if it were taken from a book. The directors of this war—it can only be called that—know what they're about. We are facing an able, determined and ruthless enemy."

"One singularly well equipped," Catherine Alana said. "We've been analyzing the jamming signals used during the riot. Highly sophisticated. Definitely off-planet equipment, and probably personnel."

The Spartans looked up quickly. "Who?" Alexander asked.

"Nothing definitive," Catherine said. "But if I had to say for the record, I'd guess one of the Meiji technoninja outfits."

"But you're not sure?" Desjardins said.

"They're blooming expensive," Jesus Alana said. "We can't think who hates Sparta enough to pay that price. This planet doesn't have that sort of enemy."

"Croser does," Alexander said. "So long as his creditors don't call in his debts and ruin him."

"Which perhaps we should arrange," Catherine Alana said quietly.

Jesus grinned. "Then there is another matter."

"Yes?" Desjardins prompted.

"The atrocities," Catherine Alana said. "If the rebels do have off-planet help, it is from an organization that does not recognize the Laws of War. A lot of the Meijian outfits don't, but they're mostly espionage and clandestine-operations oriented. Outside the mercenary structure entirely."

Jesus Alana shrugged. "So. We have guesses as to who, but there is no uncertainty about what: the enemy has high-tech off-planet support. That being true, they probably have other capabilities we have not seen."

"A timely warning," Alexander said.

"Indeed," Jesus Alana agreed. "More timely, I think, than the enemy suspected. Moreover, General Slater has the opinion that these people have been closely studying the classic works on guerrilla warfare. I am inclined to agree. And while the classic patterns are classic because they have been effective, they do have the disadvantage of being well known. From here on, we should have clues as to what the enemy will do next."

"Precisely," Peter Owensford said. "Now. Here's the situation as I see it."

He touched the keys to call up checklists and organization patterns. "The first principle is that political action is as crucial as the strictly military. That is as true for us as for the enemy. Therefore, we will begin counterespionage operations in coordination with the RSMP and General Slater's schools. A first priority will be to prove the links between the NCLF and the Helots. Second, we must learn the means by which they obtain. And tighten customs inspections, of course."

Everyone nodded; the weapons captured after the Spartosky affair were mostly of Friedlander and Xanadu manufacture but that meant little, since both those powers had a cash-and-carry policy and did not require end-user certificates.

"Now, in strictly military terms, the essentials of counterguerrilla warfare are intelligence, mobility and interdiction. The closest possible coordination of police, militia and military activities in each area is essential. With the Royal government's permission"—a nod from Alexander—"I am appointing Captain Barton as liaison officer and Inspector-General of Militia. Captain Barton, you will see to the organization of a three-tier system in each canton of the affected areas; police, home guard and local reaction forces."

Ace nodded; there was a faraway look in his eyes, the expression of a man marshaling himself for a difficult job.

"This will provide patrols, point-security and raw intelligence data. We will also use this structure to cut off the guerrillas as far as possible from contact with the civilian population, and from their sources of supply."

"The First RS Infantry, and the four available companies of Legion troops, will be the active military element in our strategy. Using active patrolling, SAS teams"—Special Air Services, the traditional term for deep-intrusion scout forces behind enemy lines; they were a specialty of the Legion—"and the intelligence data funneled through Captain Alana's office, we will find, fix and destroy the guerrilla bands operating in the Middle and Upper Valley districts. Once we have significant aviation assets we can be even more aggressive, but there is no reason why we can't start some operations now." Peter grinned. "If you have one problem, you have a problem. If you have several, they can sometimes be made to solve each other. In our case we need to give combat experience to our troops, and simultaneously we have an enemy trying to initiate classic guerrilla operations against us. Questions, gentlemen?"

There were; mostly technical, directed at the staff. He leaned back in his chair. *No reason it shouldn't work, in theory,* he thought. Falkenberg had required them to study enough examples, from the brilliant successes like Sir Gerald Templar's in Malaysia in the 1950s, through military victories and political defeats like that of the French in Algeria and the Americans in Vietnam, to outright disasters like the First Indochina War. Plenty of rebellions out among the colony worlds as well.

Interesting factors here, he thought: *unique, like every war.* The land-population ratio was higher than any comparable situation he could think of, for example. Nor could he think of another case where the population was mostly rural but of urban origins. Very little in the way of aviation assets, as yet, but what he did have was probably reasonably safe from sophisticated antiaircraft weapons. Very little in the way of mechanical transport at all; mounted infantry would probably be valuable. The enemy would certainly be using them. A cavalry guerrilla. *Interesting.* There were recent precedents; and further back. . . . *The Boer War, of course. And Southern Africa about a century ago, or a little more.*

"I think that's all, then," he said at last, and turned to Alexander Collins. "Comments, sir?"

"Yes, Major." The older man leaned his hands on the tabletop; there was a slight tremor in the left. "Two things. First, I have received notification from the CoDominium Bureau of Relocation, through the commandant of the local CD enclave . . . Sparta's quota of involuntary convicts is to be doubled over the coming fiscal year."

That brought everyone bolt upright. "Sir," Jesus Alana said. "We were expecting it to be *reduced*."

The king nodded. There was a slight sheen of sweat on his brow, although the room was cool. "Yes. Of the planets receiving deportees, only Haven is farther from Earth. BuReloc has been steadily shifting to the closer worlds to cut expenses." Since it was being systematically starved of funds by the deadlocked Grand Senate, outright sale of involuntary convicts on worlds where that was legal had become an important source of BuReloc's budget. "There has been a reversal of policy."

"The fix is in," Jesus Alana said flatly. "The NCLF bought a Grand Senator."

"Or already had one," Catherine added thoughtfully.

"I do not think so," the king said, rubbing a hand across his brow. "I always felt that Earth would not allow the Spartan experiment to succeed, to expose its ancient corruptions, that there were forces moving secretly . . . " He stopped with an effort, then shrugged: "You see, though, what sixty thousand new untrained, unskilled, possibly unemployable refugees carefully trained to hate all authority dropped into Sparta City will do. Especially with the new taxes restricting employment."

There was silence for a moment. Everyone *did* see; it was a cruelly well-aimed blow. *The CoDominium kept Earth from suicide,* Owensford thought, *but the price is damned high.* Sparta could not refuse, of course. The action was technically within the provisions of the Treaty of Independence, and Sparta had no navy and little in the way of planetary defenses. A single Fleet destroyer would compel obedience, and even Sergei Lermontov could not fudge a direct order from the Grand Senate.

The king collected himself, relaxing slightly. "This . . . emergency has come up so quickly that a few of us are inclined to panic. To see conspirators and traitors under every bed."

A wry smile. "I find myself doing so, in the small hours of the night. Nevertheless, we must remember that the vast bulk of the population—including the non-Citizen population—are *not* conspirators, are *not* traitors. Our enemy—the true enemy, the few malignant minds behind this unspeakable thing—will attempt to divide us. Citizen against non-Citizen, employer against employee, outback against city, old settler from new immigrant. Our enemy wants us to hate, to fear, and to lash out blindly. *We must not do so.* Because if we do, we will *create* the divisions the enemy falsely claims exist; we will drive whole segments of our people into the enemy's camp."

"True enough," Owensford said. "The people are on our side, something we have to remember. Guerrilla operations are painful, but they can't win against determination. Even the importation of barbarian elements from Earth can't defeat a strong civilization. Sparta has overwhelming strength in the Citizen militia. It's our job to do as much of the fighting as we can so the nation doesn't have to. We'll do that job."

*   *   *

"*Gracias,*" Jesus Alana said, as Ursula handed him a cup of coffee.

They all had one in front of them, along with their readout screens and notes. *Husband, wife and protégée,* Ursula thought ironically. *And probably the future teacher for Michael and Maryanne Alana when they're older. . . . However they've managed it, what these two have together is worth learning about . . .*

The Legion was pretty much of a family business, at that. One window in the thick adobe wall was open, and they could hear faint construction sounds and the *heep, heep* sound of someone counting cadence. Intelligence Central was a big office, more than enough for their three desks and filing equipment, with maps and charts pinned to the whitewashed walls.

"Now, let us implement some of the fine theories we talked about to the kings this morning," Jesus Alana said. He called up a map of the western portion of the Middle Valley district, and his finger tapped the Illyrian Dales. "Notice the relative concentration of guerrilla attacks on the south side of the Eurotas, and between the area just above Clemens and around Olynthos. All within striking distance of the Dales, which are themselves little-known and without permanent habitation. And are also larger than all the Spains. Cornet Gordon, what other relevant information do we have about the Dales?"

He only calls me that when he's putting me on the spot, she thought. Then—

"Limestone, sir."

"Limestone. Precisely. Why?"

"Limestone is water-soluble, which means caves, and with the amount of outflow coming down from the Drakons and reaching the Eurotas, there must be a *lot* of caves. Underground river-systems, in fact. Excellent concealment from satellite surveillance."

"And from everything else," Catherine said.

"So that is point one," Jesus said. "Then you let the computers chew on the statistical data, and you get—what?"

Ursula nodded enthusiasm. "Direct correlations between guerrilla activity, length of settlement, percentage of Spartan-born and Citizen population, average size of rural holding and land values."

"Excellent," he said dryly. "In other words, in the Lower Valley there is little guerrilla activity, many Citizens, relatively smaller ranches and farms. In the Middle and Upper Valleys, newer and larger ranches, more non-Citizens, more recent immigrants, and more guerrilla incidents. What exceptions are there to this?"

"Ahh . . . the area of the Upper Valley, between Olynthos and the Cupros Mountains. There've been mining and support settlements around there since the early days, but there's a good deal of guerrilla activity reported there as well."

Jesus Alana relaxed. "Inquisition ended. You should have looked more carefully at the data about the Upper Valley; first, the mines employ many unskilled laborers. Second, there is a new fringe of settlement in adjacent areas, to supply the growing industrial population. *And* it is very close to the Dales, again. Remember, patterns of *detail*.

"Cathy, what does PhotoRecon say about the spysat of the Dales area?"

"Not much, Jesus, but Lieutenant Swenson doesn't think much of the hardware they've got. She says it's basically weather and geosurvey oriented, and badly out of date at that; not very maneuverable, and there are only two eyes. If you know their orbital ephemeris, and you've got good satellite observation security, you could fox them. Mostly what it shows is wildlife, the odd forest or grass fire, and occasional hunting camps. What *should* be hunting camps."

"We should recommend low-level aerial survey," Jesus said. "But with care. Have Swenson set up a team of technicians, and we will borrow some of the RSMP tiltrotors—blimps if we must—and do some intensive sidescan and IR work. Land parties and do seismic mapping at intervals as well."

"I'll coordinate with Major Barton," Catherine said.

"And Captain Mace. His scouts may be glad of the opportunity."

"Right. Anything else?"

"Yes." He touched his controls, and the area around Olynthos sprang out; it was a city of about forty thousand, just below the exit from Lake Alexander. Smelters originally, more recently general industry, and many of the outbacker hunters operated out of there. "The Scout Company of the Prince Royal's Battalion is going to base out of here when they move out. Have Sweeny run some of them through on her depth-sounding equipment, and then issue it to them when they begin practicing their SAS games up in the Dales. If you can pry the stuff loose."

They both smiled; Senior Lieutenant Leigh Swenson guarded her remote reconnaissance equipment with the brooding intensity of a hen with one chick.

"That should turn up some interesting data," he said meditatively, finishing his coffee. "Which leaves the question of the NCLF and Sparta City. On the one hand, that's more the Milice and RSMP's territory. On the other, I agree with Desjardins: the NCLF as a whole may not be with the Helots, but their leadership *is*. Pity this is a constitutionalist planet."

On most worlds—on anywhere directly ruled by the CoDominium Colonial Bureau, or for that matter in the United States—they would simply disappear Mr. Dion Croser and sweat the facts out of him.

"No it isn't, or had you forgotten we were supposed to be based here permanently?" Catherine Alana said. "I wouldn't want our children to grow up on that sort of world, Jesus."

"But if they don't get moving, this may *become* that sort of world," he replied. "Personally, I don't find the NCLF's political program very reassuring."

Ursula cleared her throat: " *'If you fight dragons long enough, you become a dragon: if you stare into the Abyss, the Abyss will stare back into* you.' " Nietzsche, and on her required reading list. Along with all the rest of the canon, in case she was bored in her munificent four hours of free time daily.

"The fact remains, the Milice and the RSMP have no

political intelligence to speak of," Jesus continued sourly. "They are trying to remedy that lack, but you know the problems."

"Philby," Ursula said. "But isn't your lie detector gear—"

"It's good but not that good," Catherine said. "What we can detect is stress. If we're lucky, and especially when we surprise people, we can get differential stress —stress indications where there shouldn't be so much, that sort of thing. Casual use against well-prepared subjects, that's another matter."

"So we may have infiltrators," Ursula said. She had been doing a good deal of reading in the classical espionage cases. How the West German counter-intelligence chief in the 1980s had been a Sovworld plant, and one reason the Israelis had overrun the Levant so quickly in 2009 was a deep-sleeper who was head of Military Intelligence Evaluation for the Greater Syrian Republic.

"Well, not in the Legion itself. Certainly not among the officers. What I would like is a source of information of our own." He called up a map of Sparta city, clicking in on the lower southwestern corner. The spacious grounds of the Royal University of Sparta filled the screen. "We know that the NCLF has an active student chapter. The usual thing: boredom and guilt and excuses for failure among the spoiled children of success. Not as much here as most places—this is a frontier planet—but enough." A grim smile. "Odd, how guilt is inversely proportional to real culpability. On Santiago"—his home, one of the three nations of Thurstone—"where there is real slavery, most university students are fanatic Carlist reactionaries."

"The ones here probably don't feel really afraid," Ursula said clinically. There had been clients like that, back on Tanith in the Lederle Hilton, who had been sorry for her. They usually expected something extra for it, too.

"Yes. And we also know that there have been disappearances among members of the student chapter of the NCLF. Half a dozen immediately after the Spartosky incident, for example. Educated people would be one of the chokepoints for a guerrilla force recruited mainly from transportees. They will need junior officers."

"Well, then we should obviously try infiltrating through there," Ursula said. "Who did you have in mind—oh."

Catherine Alana reached over and patted her hand. "You *do* need some more formal schooling, dear," she said.

"Oh." She looked down at her hands, with a sinking feeling. The structured, ordered life of the Legion was a little confining sometimes, but wonderfully secure. "Well, I do have acting training," she said dryly. "But Mata Hari I am not, with respect, sir, ma'am."

"Mata Hari we don't want," Catherine said. "You'll be a student on detached duty taking courses in cartography and statistics, both of which are quite relevant to your career. Who you date is your business, not ours. Except that if you meet any of the militants there's no point in being rude to them."

"Oh. But—"

Jesus shook his head. "I am not sure this is a good idea," he said.

"I'll be fine," Ursula insisted.

"Perhaps. But we have no wish to cause you embarrassment. You need not reveal anything at all about your previous experience. Merely tell them that you were recruited on Tanith, and you have been sent to the University for formal training. Then be careful, because you will almost certainly be approached by the enemy in the hopes that you will let slip something of value."

"Only I don't know anything—"

"That is not strictly true," Jesus said. "In any event, I think I can guarantee that at least one of those who pays attention to you will have ulterior reasons. What you do about that is your business, but be certain, we are not asking you to play Mata Hari."

"Would it help if I tried?" Ursula asked.

"My dear," Catherine said, "I should think you know the answer to that. The Legion needs nice, healthy young officers, not psychological wrecks. Learn and observe, that's all. We're soldiers, not spies."

CHAPTER EIGHT

Crofton's Encyclopedia of the Inhabited Planets (2nd Edition):

Aegean, sea. [Ae-ge-an], named for enclosed portion of eastern Mediterranean, Earth. (see *names*, Mythological, Graeco-Roman)

One of two linked inland seas on the planet *Sparta* [see *Sparta*];

The Aegean, with the larger *Oinos sea* (q.v.) to the south, forms the great inland embayment which separates the northern and southern lobes of the *Serpentine Continent*, Sparta's principal landmass. Roughly rectangular in shape, the Aegean covers approximately 510,000 sq. kilometers; geological investigation shows that it was formed by a complex process of subsidence, attendant on the crustal plate movements which accompanied the raising of the *Drakon Mountains* (q.v.) In general terms, the Aegean is therefore relatively warm, shallow (few areas over 500 meters depth) and characterized by a rough balance between sediment deposition and subsidence of the sea floor. Characteristic terrain on all sides of the Aegean consists of coastal plains of varying width, backed by hills or mountains; the northeastern corner offers a lowland corridor to the valley of the *Middle Eurotas* (q.v.) The main river draining into the Aegean is the Eurotas, which reverses its lower course and drains northward through its delta into *Constitution Bay* (q.v.), a nearly circular impact crater associated with an asteroid collision of circa 50,000 BCE. The large volcanic islands of *Zakynthos* (q.v.), *Leros* (q.v.), *Keos*, (q.v.) *New Crete* (q.v.) and

Mytilene (q.v.) are products of the same astrophysical event.

Marine life is abundant, and is based on native equivalents of plankton. Common species include the *grunter*, notable for its great numbers and resemblance to the terrestrial cod, the multiclawed *rockcrawler*, much in demand as a delicacy offworld, and the *torpedofish*, a predatory species up to 10 meters in length, which attacks its prey by ramming with its bone-armored nose. All vertebrate piscoids are gill-breathers but have pseudomammalian features such as four-chambered hearts, and are viviparous. The *tangler kelp* is the sole source of Ez-e-Mind™, Lederle AG's vastly profitable "morning after" contraceptive. Introduced terrestrial species include the common dolphin and the orca (killer whale), both wild and domesticated.

*   *   *

We have fed our sea for a thousand years
  And she calls us, still unfed,
Though there's never a wave of all her waves
  But marks our English dead:
We have strawed our best to the weed's unrest,
  To the shark and the sheering gull.
If blood be the price of admiralty,
  Lord God, we ha' paid in full!
                    —Rudyard Kipling

*   *   *

Steven Armstrong pushed his chair back from the table and loosened his belt. *Been doing that a lot lately*, he thought. Growing a bit of a pot, to offset the massive shoulders and bull neck and the barrel chest that bulged out his roll-necked sweater. . . . He grinned and tossed back thick rough-cut hair the color of butter, only lightly streaked with gray. Once he took the *Alicia* out of harbor and north to the Thule Sea, he'd work that off soon enough, no matter how good Cookie's hash was. The air was full of the odors of good solid cooking, with an overtone of pipe tobacco and damp cool air from Constitution Bay below; they were close enough to the docks to hear the gulls, and the clacking sound of the cranes.

"Ladies and gentlemen!" he said, standing and raising his stein. "I give you—the Alicias, both of 'em! The ship, and the lady who made her possible!"

There was a cheer from all the tables he had rented in the Neptune; hearty cheers, though nobody had been drinking more than enough to put a little edge on. Most of them would be sailing with him in an hour or so, after all. All eyes had turned to his wife at the other end of the table. Alicia Armstrong was smiling and wiping at her eyes at the same time, as the guests began to applaud her. She was a round-faced woman with a close-cropped head of tightly curled hair, and eggplant-black skin that set off her gold seashell earrings. Three children from four to ten were seated next to her; they leaped up and began clapping too, with high-pitched shouts of *"Mommy! Mommy!"*

"I—" she began, as cries of "speech, speech" rang through the taproom. Then: "Oh, let Steven make the speech—he *likes* doing it."

More laughter; Steven Armstrong had been Senator-legate of the Maritime Products Trade Association for a year now, and was famous for a rhetorical style that included thumping lecterns hard enough to break the wood at Pragmatist rallies.

"OK, I promise not to damage Mrs. Kekkonen's tables, at least," he began, looking around until he caught the proprietor's eye and winked. She winked back; the Armstrongs and the Neptune Inn went back a long way. It was the sort of place he enjoyed; not fancy, just a taproom and kitchen with an outdoor terrace for summer and some rooms above. A workingman's place, where you could get a good solid mess of grunter fillet and yam or a twenty-ounce steak and potatoes and pie for an honest tenth-crown; the sort of place you could bring your family, too. "Actually, I hate giving speeches."

"Then you must love to suffer, bucko!"

"Shut up, Sven. Where was I . . . Armstrong & Armstrong's come a long way," he said. "When Alicia and I got married, we honeymooned here at the Neptune because we couldn't afford anything else—"

"Well!" the widow Kekkonen said, mock-indignant.

"—and all we had was these hands"—he held them up; massive and reddened, scarred and callused with hooks and nets and lines—"Alicia's brains and one rickety overgrown dory with an engine that worked, sometimes. I busted my butt, and Alicia kept books better than the computer we couldn't afford—found out that the Meijians would pay through their noses for rockcrawler claws—and we saved every penny. Now we've got four trawlers and damned good ones, and best of all—the *Alicia*. You all know what it'll mean, being able to tap the Thule Sea shoals; off-planet exchange, for one thing. No reason to let the Newfies get it all."

Cheers and jeers; nobody much liked the secretive and clannish settlers of New Newfoundland, the big island in the gulf where the Oinos Sea met the outer Jefferson Ocean.

"I'd like to thank everyone who helped make it possible," he went on. "Even Consolidated Hume Financial." More laughter, sheepishly joined in by the representative of the bank in his conservative brown tunic and sash and knee-breeches. *Well, nobody loves a banker*, Armstrong thought. Especially not on a planet starved for capital and with a strict hard-money policy. "And the great people from Huang, Lee and Parkinson." The shipbuilders; his sincerity came through. "My friends from the Association, who paid as the only way to shut me up and get me out of Sparta City"—cries of protest and a few half-eaten rolls flew past his ears, with the odd "damn straight"—"and most of all, my wife. My only regret is she isn't coming with us—but she's got the best excuse I can think of."

Six months of pregnancy, now showing considerably. She put her hand on her stomach and met his eyes.

"Yeah, Armstrong, but when's *yours* due?" Sven Nyqvist said, poking a stubby finger into his captain's midriff. Steven Armstrong's booming voice led the laughter.

"Thank Christ *that's* over," he muttered, standing beside the wheel of the *Alicia*. Dockside was a kilometer to the west now, Sparta City a sprawl of white and pastel and greenery across its hills. And the dockside crowds, and the reporters.

The *Capital Herald*'s little newsblimp was still overhead, with the irritating buzz of its twin engines; he was strongly tempted to give it the finger. *No.* The cameras could count the hairs in your nose from 800 meters. *Too many watching*, he thought. *Ignore them.*

As he'd ignored the reporters with their asinine questions. *"Why do you want to enslave the transportees, Senator Armstrong?"*

"Assholes."

"Sir?" from the helmsman.

"Steady as she goes. Just glad to get out of town. If I never see another equals sign, it'll be too soon."

"Amen," said the helmsman.

Enslave the transportees, Armstrong thought disgustedly. *Sweet Christ, I* married *a transportee, didn't I?* Many of his best workers were transportees, and he had sponsored a half-dozen into the Brotherhood of Poseidon after helping them make Citizen. Even the common ruck of them weren't too bad, once they learned they couldn't sit in the gutter and live on handouts here. He snorted again; anyone who starved on Sparta deserved it; you could eat for a week on two day's wages for casual labor. *Hell, you can walk out of town and throw rocks at the rabbits.* He'd done that himself as a boy, when times were *really* hard.

No, it was the real scum that needed attention. Not those scooped up by BuReloc for being in the wrong place at the wrong time, like Alicia's parents; the real criminals, the pimps and street-gangers and whores. Bad enough they cut each other up down in Minetown, dropped their bastards in the gutters without even caring enough to take them to the nuns. Now they were swarming into that son-of-a-bitch Croser's NCLF, outnumbering the real workingmen in the Dockworkers' and half a dozen other unions. Strikes—only last month he'd lost fifteen tons of rockcrawler while they struck the packing-plant over some idiot political thing. Killings, like that mess at the Spartosky. Thank *God* Alicia hadn't been there.

"Aaah, enough politics," he muttered.

He pushed the captain's cap back on his head and worked the cigar to the corner of his mouth. One of cookie's stewards brought him a cup of coffee the way he liked it, black and sweet, and he cupped his hands around the thick white china. The *Alicia* was making good speed, seven knots; not wise to go much faster; Constitution Bay had enough sandbars and shallow water to give a strong man the willies. She would do better out in the open ocean, though. He looked around with pride: fifteen hundred tons, good von Alderheim steel for the hull, decking and upperworks of redwood. Two thousand-horsepower diesels with electric transmission, burbling their song of power through his feet. Deck-winches, nets, processing-holds and bunkrooms, all the best that Sparta City could make, and that was damned good. Even off-planet electronics, echo-sounder and radar.

The horseshoe bridge with its consoles and dials smelled of paint and seasoned wood and very slightly of the vegetable-oil fuel burned by the engines; he liked it, would like it even better when she'd been battered a little by the ocean swells, and smelled of salt and piscoid. The shallow Aegean and Oinos swarmed with good eating-fish, far more than Sparta's limited population could use. The *Alicia* was bound for bigger game: the huge piscoids of the cold and dangerous Thule Sea; that was what the rocket-harpoon launcher was for. Lustrous metallic-scaled hide, mouth-ivory more beautiful than the vanished elephant herds of Earth. Complex oils with a dozen uses, from perfumes to drugs.

"Sir."

He jerked out of his reverie, looked around: It was the radio watch, Maureen Terwonsky. Looking worried, which was not like her.

"It's a radiotelephone call, sir. They want to speak to you personally. They won't give a name."

He pulled the cigar out of his mouth and considered the chewed wet end. "If it's those news people again, tell them to go bugger themselves," he said. She began to speak into her equipment.

"Captain . . . Captain Armstrong, he says if you don't listen you'll regret it, and your family will too."

Something cold and limp touched his spine. He leaned forward quickly, touching the control that shut off the speaker for a moment.

"Get to the auxiliary in the radio room, *and get the Milice on the line*. Move!"

He took up the handset with a deep breath. "This is Captain Armstrong," he said; his voice was deadly flat with the effort of control. "Who is this?"

"This is the voice of the workers, *Captain* Armstrong," the voice said. "This is the voice of the ones you think are tools to be used and thrown aside, to make your riches."

This can't be serious, he thought. A crank call; the voice sounded a little nasal, probably North American. Not a slum dialect; educated, but not Spartan-born either.

"What the hell are you talking about?" he asked,

playing for time. With a little luck, the Milice would trace the call back through Broadcast Central. "You can't—"

"Oh, but we can, *Captain*. Hear the voice of the tool. We've heard your voice, making speeches. Trying to grind the common people down, make them suffer even more. Now you're going to feel our anger, now *you're* going to suffer from the just wrath of the people."

"What the fuck—" Static hiss; Terwonsky stuck her head through the hatch at the rear of the bridge.

"Milice got it, they're working on it, Cap," she said.

"Don't worry, probably just a crank—" he began.

The *Alicia* jerked and stopped dead in the water, almost as if she had hit a shoal. Echoing silence fell as the engines cut out, broken only by yells from startled crewfolk. Lights flickered, then came on more dimly as the emergency batteries cut in. Armstrong lunged across the bridge, balance telling him the ship was already down by the stern and to starboard. His hand slapped down on the communicator, and a screen lit with a view of the engine room.

Armstrong's stomach clenched, and he could feel his scrotum contract and try to draw his testicles up against his stomach. Nothing lit the engine compartment but the red emergency lights, and they shone on a scene out of hell. Water plumed in through the floor gratings, from a slashing cut that must run the full length of the compartment; no, beyond it, into the rear hold. The deck was already awash. The engineering crew were scrambling around the main hatchway in the bulkhead just below the pickup, battering and prying with crowbars and hand-tools.

"Sven!" Armstrong shouted. "What's going on?"

A desperate face turned up, blood and water running down it from sodden hair and a cut across the forehead. "Jesus, it just went like a bomb! Both the hatchways are sprung, she's flooding, we'll be under in three minutes."

"Hold on!" He slammed the all-stations button, and his amplified voice bellowed out throughout the *Alicia*.

"Now hear this! The black gang is trapped in the engine-room, and it's flooding. McLaren, whoever's near there, get the cutting lance down there now, d'you hear. Now!"

"Jesus, Steve, it's flooding faster, we can't budge this bastard." Panting, and an iron *chung* as a prybar broke under the desperate heaving of three strong men. Some of the others were shouldering in to try with their bare hands, screaming in panic.

Hurry up, hurry up, Armstrong pleaded.

"Jesus! *Jeezzzuussss—*"

"Sven's dead," Armstrong said hoarsely, throwing off the blanket somebody was trying to put around his shoulders. There were Milice cordoning off the dock; out on the waters he could see divers jumping from a hovering helicopter.

"Oh, honey, *no*," Alicia said.

"I saw it," Armstrong mumbled. Then he shook himself, stood erect. "Come on, we're getting you and the kids home and then I'm going to get some *answers*, by God."

They pushed through the awestruck crowd toward the family van: a six-wheeler they used for vacations at their cottage up in the hills. A cameraman tried to work through to them; one of the Milice tripped him, then stamped a boot through the equipment. The sight brought a tiny sliver of chill satisfaction, something to put between himself and the vision of his oldest friend floating dead before a pickup camera. . . . Soothing the children was better, forcing him out of himself.

"Honey, you sure I shouldn't stay?"

"No, not in your condition. Get them back to the house, Fred's sending some of his people over"—his brother-in-law, and a commander in the police—"and *stay* there until I call. OK, sweetheart?"

She bit her lip, nodded, kissed him and slid into the driver's seat. He waited until the big vehicle was safely out of the parking lot, before he turned and looked at the death of a lifetime's dream. *Half an hour,* he thought, dazed. *Half a flipping hour. It's impossible.*

The explosion was not quite enough to knock him down; it did send him staggering half a dozen steps forward. Even as he turned and ran, the van blossomed in a circle of fire as the ruptured fuel-tank blew. He could hear his children screaming quite clearly over the roar, as he wrenched at the burning metal.

Steven Armstrong was screaming himself as they pulled him away from the wreckage where nothing lived, although not from the pain of his charred hands or the third-degree burns across most of the front of his body. He was still screaming as the paramedics dragged him back, until they hyposprayed enough sedative into his veins to turn a bull toes-up.

*   *   *

"I am ashamed. I have failed," the Meijian said.

Murasaki nodded; they were alone in the plain white room of his lodgings, which with the equipment he had brought was as secure as any building on Sparta. The floor was covered with local bamboo matting; his futon was neatly rolled in one corner, and beyond that there was only the low table between them, an incense burner, and one spray of willow-buds in a simple jar. Sandalwood perfumed the air; a cricket chirped from its tiny cage of silver wire.

"I must expiate my shame," his follower said.

They knelt facing each other across the table, dressed in dark kimonos. The technoninja drew a knife and laid the smooth curve of it on the lacquered wood before him, then began to tie a handkerchief tightly about the base of the smallest finger of his left hand.

"Wait," Kenjiro Murasaki said. For some time they did only that, moving solely to breathe. At last:

"You are in error. You have not failed."

"*Roshi*," his follower said, bowing his head to the mats between his palms. "Yet Armstrong lives."

"Beware of the illusions of specificity. Although Armstrong lives, circumstance is such that he will serve our purposes none the less. For the Armstrong we wished to die, has died; in his place is born another.

"So."

"So."

Silence stretched.

CHAPTER NINE

Crofton's Encyclopedia of the Inhabited Planets (2nd Edition):

Sparta, Royal University of: Institution of postsecondary education, sole university of the *Dual Monarchy of Sparta* (q.v.). Founded in 2040, only a few years after the arrival of the first settlers of the *Constitutionalist Society* (q.v.), the University of Sparta embodies many interesting organizational principles and fulfills a number of functions.

The University is organized as a cooperative corporation, with the Crown, the faculty and individual professors holding shares. Some state revenues are "dedicated" to the University; other sources of income include endowments, extensive property holdings, fees, service charges for research work, and patent revenues. Individual faculty are paid a basic salary, with bonuses determined by number of students enrolled and by a complicated, results-oriented testing process. Some chairs are separately endowed, and the endowing individual or authority may nominate the holder subject to a Dean and Faculty veto.

Enrollment is by two methods; scholarship examination, and fee payment. The scholarship tests are severely selective, but confer free tuition, preference for work-study occupations, and in some cases rent-free student accommodations and a stipend. Those entering via fee payment need not take the entrance exams but may and often are disqualifed during their course of study; fees are not refunded. Additional supplements are also offered to those willing to contract for public service work (e.g., primary school teaching in remote locations) after their graduation.

All the common courses are taught, together with some unique to Sparta such as Introductory Military Science; there is no law school, as formal qualifications are unnecessary for practice on Sparta. The University is affiliated with St. Thomas Royal Hospital and the McGregor Oceanographic Institute; it cooperates closely with the research departments of many private businesses, and undertakes contract and freelance research work on an extensive basis. The University also operates an extensive correspondence degree section, and many students take the academic portions of their courses by mail or Tri-V link, coming to the campus only for laboratory work or oral examinations.

There are no sororities and fraternities, although the Candidate Sections of the *Phraetries* (q.v.) fulfill many of the same functions.

Current enrollment (2090): students, 8,000; post-graduate students and teaching assistants, 2,000; faculty, 998.

*   *   *

"God Almighty, that's gruddy," one of the students said. "Overload gruddy."

Ursula Gordon nodded as she relaxed back into the wicker chair in the student commons. The 'caster himself was obviously shaken as he showed the bodies being recovered from the burnt-out wreckage of the Armstrongs's van.

"I don't know what the planet's coming to," one of the observers said disgustedly, taking another pull at his beer.

Observe, Ursula told herself. *That's what you're here for.* That and the classes, and hers were over for the morning. They had been interesting . . . odd mixture of people, too. Mostly young, but with a solid sprinkling of older types; evidently the University ran extension-courses all over the settled portions of the planet, not difficult with satellite communications. No problems about enrolling, either; if you paid your way, you could sign up for any course that had room for you, although the fees were quite high.

There were plenty of scholarship students as well, often from poorer Citizen or even transportee families. They *did* have to pass entrance exams, stiff ones, but their tuition was free and they got first crack at the service-staff jobs that would let you live with modest comfort while you studied. It was a tempting arrangement: leave the Legion, go to the University, and eventually become a citizen of Sparta. *But there's a job to be done first.*

The viewer switched to underwater shots of divers pulling bodies from the wreck of the *Alicia*, with voice-over commentary on the long slash that peeled open her hull for half its length. Ursula looked aside, out the arched windows. You could tell what the priorities of the Spartan Founders had been; the University had been started almost as soon as the prefab shelters went up. It occupied an inordinate stretch of high-value land, too, down on the southwestern shoreline of the city. Georgian-brick dormitories and white neoclassical lecture halls, flagstoned paths and gardens that were quietly spectacular, without the harsh flamboyance she had been accustomed to on Tanith. From here you could see students strolling along the pathways, sitting on stone benches under trees, eating or flirting, people-watching themselves or indulging in the perennial undergraduate arguments about the Nature of Things.

A sailboat was skipped across Sparta Sound, its sails gaily blue and yellow against the forest green of the offshore islands. The air of the winter afternoon was chilly enough to make the walking-out khakis and wooly-pully sweater comfortable; shirtsleeve weather to the others on the verandah.

"Yeah, it's tragic, but . . . " someone was saying. He had a button on his tunic, black with a crimson rim and a red = sign. Then his voice went higher: "Hey, Senator Croser's on!"

The lean Eurasian face filled the screen; that was set into the wall to imitate a crystal display unit, but it was actually a locally made cathode ray set-up with no Tri-V capacity at all.

"Quiet everybody! Listen!" That from Mary Williams, an intense girl who'd taken little part in the earlier discussions.

". . . NCLF and I, personally, denounce this abhorrent crime, and demand that the Royal administration bring the perpetrators to justice," he was saying.

Sincere looking, Ursula thought judiciously. Being interviewed in his study, from the bookcases and shabby-elegant furniture. Looking very professorial in a dark-blue tunic with leather elbow-patches, knee-breeches, and matching sash. *No. A little too hard-faced*, she decided. An outdoorsman's look, body fit even by Spartan standards; and yes, that was a snow-leopard head on the wall behind him. Beaky Anglo face with slightly tilted blue eyes, gray-streaked black hair.

"At the same time, and without condoning such atrocities or the sick minds that conceive them, this senseless violence is exactly what the Non-Citizens' Liberation Front is doing its best to stop—and which the so-called Pragmatists are fanning. Extremism breeds extremism. A new deal for our oppressed classes is the only way to restore true peace and social harmony to Sparta."

"Are you saying that Senator Armstrong provoked this attack?" the interviewer asked sharply.

Croser shook his head. "Please, I *insist* that you not read words into my mouth." He leaned forward, making a clean, spare gesture with one hand; his voice was deep and sincere, the eyes level and intense.

"I am simply saying that the Pragmatist proposals—to forcibly indenture convicts for the length of the sentence the CoDominium imposes, or involuntary transportees who don't immediately become 'self-sufficient'—this is not only wrong, stupid, a step on the road to slavery—it's a source of the very violence the Pragmatists complain of." His voice grew passionate for a moment: "Our parents and grandparents didn't come here to live in an armed camp, or for cheap labor; they came for *freedom*. We didn't come to be the CoDominium's partners in oppression. We've lost sight of that, and we're paying the price."

"By 'we,' do you mean the Pragmatists, or the Citizen body as a whole?" the interviewer continued.

"Pragmatists and Foundation Loyalists both; the ugly and benign faces of repression. Oh, I grant the good intentions of the most of the Loyalist leadership, even of some Pragmatists, poor Senator Armstrong among them. But look how the Crown and its Senate and Council hangers-on is reacting to the current crisis! Hiring off-planet paid killers and raising armies, when the same funds devoted to the welfare of the less fortunate would buy us *real* peace."

He smiled sadly. "There's a very old joke from Earth. A Minister of State goes to his king and says: 'Sire, in your new budget I notice you spend *billions* for weapons and not one *penny* for the poor.' The king replies: 'Yes, when the revolution comes, I'll be *ready*.' "

There was a chuckle through the common room; even the interviewer's voice seemed more friendly when he continued:

"You don't advocate revolution, then, Senator Croser? Some of your followers seem more radical."

Croser chuckled. *"There go my people; I must hurry to get ahead of them, for I am their leader,"* he quoted. "Mahatma Gandhi. The moderate leadership of the NCLF—of which I am only one—are Sparta's best guarantee *against* revolution. It's the Citizens who obstinately cling to outworn aristocratic privilege, who prate about self-serving and exploded slogans such as the separation of state and economy, who are risking everything. The true radicals look on the NCLF as the greatest obstacle to a bloody revolution, and driving the NCLF underground would be the best gift the Crown could give to the real rebels—to the extent that there are any."

"You don't agree there's a real security threat?"

"Yes! Of course there's a threat: and it is the inequitable distribution of power and wealth on Sparta, not a few extremists in the hills, or the type of fanatic who perpetrated this action today. We won't discuss the ludicrous tales of massive conspiracies the Government is putting about to justify its preparations for war on the people."

"Senator, some have pointed out that you, yourself are a wealthy man with extensive landholdings and mineral interests. . . ."

Croser nodded and began loading a pipe. "Quite true. And if I gave it all away, the process of economic concentration would continue; we're breeding an oligarchy here, based on nothing better than the luck of being born into an old-settler family. If you look at the record, you'll find almost all my income goes into the NCLF, free of charge. And"—he waggled the pipestem admonishingly—"the NCLF stands four-square for private property; we just want more people to have the privilege! John Stuart Mill himself said that excessive concentration of wealth is a provocation to leveling legislation."

"Thank you, Senator. This is Jerric van Damm of the Spartan Herald Service, interviewing Senator Dion Croser, legate of the Dockworkers' Union on today's terrorist attack which resulted in the death of Mrs. Alicia Armstrong and her three children, and the severe injury of her husband, Senator Steven Armstrong. Senator Croser, any closing remarks?"

"Thank you, Citizen van Damm. Just this." The camera panned in, until the blue eyes filled the screen. "I appeal to *you*, my fellow citizens of Sparta, to wake up and realize injustice can never rest secure. In your hands lies the power to avert tragedy—and the price is reform. Act now!"

"Now, *there's* someone who knows what's going on!" one of the students said, pushing his glasses back with his thumb.

"Horseshit," another said. She was sitting with a young man, and they were both in the gray sweatsuit outfits of Brotherhood militia training. "You boil that little speech down, and what it amounts to is that somehow we're all guilty because a bunch of scum-suckers burned a pregnant woman and three children to death; not to mention the sailors on that boat. C'mon, Ahmed, we'll be late for drill."

"Brainless jocks," the student with the glasses muttered; not, Ursula noticed, until they were gone. "That's the only type the Brotherhoods are letting in these days; I thought Sparta was founded by people like *us*." Glasses was in sociology.

"Ahmed's folks were transportees," someone said.

"Ass-kisser," Glasses sneered. More politely: "What did *you* think of the Leader's speech, Ursula?"

"Well, I'm certainly against slavery," she said sincerely. Many of the others looked embarassed, especially Glasses—*McAlastair*, she thought—who had tried to kiss her in the stairwell at the faculty-student mixer last week. His wrist had healed nicely. *Tanith certainly has a reputation here,* she thought. If possible, worse than the actuality. Interesting that somehow everyone seemed to know all about what she did on Tanith.

"Then why are you in that Legion?" Mary Williams said sharply.

"Because I owe them for rescuing me from slavery."

"I heard the mercenaries owe you," the Williams girl said. This one was altogether more serious than the rest of the crowd of parlor pinks and NCLF-groupies she'd fallen in with. "For helping put down slave revolts on Tanith."

"There weren't any slave revolts on Tanith, just

outlaws who robbed and killed convicts because it was easier than attacking the planters. Catching and hanging them did everyone a favor."

McAllistair frowned and made to speak, but Williams laughed and laid a hand across his mouth.

"At least you're honest," she said. "I like that. And not so squeamish as the rest of these crybabies."

"I am *not* squeamish!" McAllistair said. "Look, Croser himself—"

"Croser's heart is in the right place, but he's blind to some things too—that massacre at the Spartosky, people shot down in the streets!" *Ah, yes, she was there with the demonstrators,* Ursula thought. *Dropped out of sight for a while, pretty broken up, her boyfriend was killed.*

Williams was continuing passionately: "Can't you see that the time Croser's warning about, when refusal to reform brings on revolution is . . . oh, forget it, Andy. Anyway, Ursula, we're going down to Ptomaine Heaven to grab some grunter sticks and fries. Want to join us?"

"Love to," Ursula said. *And keep talking, the meter is running.*

*   *   *

Horace Plummer, Secretary to the Council, struck a pose. "His Majesty Jason the First, being unable to attend and having need of the assistance of Prince David, has designated King Alexander the First as his representative at this meeting, which is therefore an official meeting of the Council empowered to approve all measures. All rise."

King Alexander came into the Council chamber and took his seat at the head of the big table. He nodded to the Council and the military staff. "Thank you. You may begin."

Lysander stared at his father as they all took their seats. What he saw was shocking. He had been in the field with his battalion so that this was the first time he had seen the King in a month. *I knew he was working too hard, but this—!* Alexander Collins looked to have aged a decade in the last few months; the lines in his boney face were graven deeper, and there was a disturbing nervous glint in his eyes, a hint of desperation as he looked around the War Council. The meeting was in the Government House chamber where they had held the first briefing by the mercenaries three months ago. Today the chill seemed deeper than the mild seacoast winter beyond the windows could account for. Rain fell steadily from a soft gray sky.

"I gather you've got something for us?" The king was speaking more slowly than usually, as if he were fighting a speech impediment, but there was an edge of impatience in his voice.

"Colonel Owensford, please begin your presentation," Plummer said.

"Your Majesty." Peter stood. "We have a great deal to cover today. First, a summary: The First Royal Infantry is fully qualified to take the field, and I shall shortly recommend that we do so."

"That sounds encouraging," Alexander said.

"Yes, Sire," Peter said. "Captain Alana, please give your report."

Jesus Alana had been trying to hide a frown while looking at King Alexander. Now he stood and took his place at the display screen.

"We have found the satellite systems oddly ineffective," Jesus said. "But yesterday we finally found something worthwhile." Images formed on the screen. "The location is the Rhyndakos river, about twenty kilometers upstream from Dodona." The screen briefly flashed a map, locating the area as a south-bank tributary of the Eurotas, in the western part of the Middle Valley; Dodona was a small town at its juncture with the main stream. "Lieutenant Swenson will explain."

"Sir. Your majesty, we wouldn't have gotten anything

if the leaves weren't off the trees, and there isn't much even so, but look here."

The screen changed. The image outlined in black was something that could be barely made out as the lines of a small river-steamer's hull, a flat wooden rectangle with a rear-mounted paddle wheel. A little out of date now that diesels were becoming more common, but they were cheap and simple to make, able to put in anywhere and hundreds of identical models plied the Eurotas from the Delta to Olynthos.

"Here's the computer enhancement."

The image was still coarse and grainy; even the Legion's computers could do only so much with the data input offerred. What did show was glimpses of men in bulky clothing unloading coffin-sized boxes and carrying them down the bow-ramp to waiting animals, pack-horses or mules, where others lifted them on to the carrying saddles.

"Next sequence is interesting," Swenson said; her voice had a technician's satisfaction in getting better performance than could be reasonably expected from second-rate equipment.

This time it was a smaller, square box, and it had broken when it fell. The contents had spilled free, some of them out of the cylindrical wicker containers. Dull-gray metal cylinders about the length of a man's arm, with conical tops and a rod coming out the bottom.

"Mortar bombs," she said, with a prim smile. "Specifically, for your Rojor 125mm rifled medium mortar. There is," she added pedantically, "no stencilling on the crates, but there isn't much doubt where they came from, either."

"Olynthos or Sparta City," Owensford said. Those were the only two places on the planet with forging and machining shops capable of doing the work. "Probably Olynthos, given the location."

Alexander's voice was thin with fury as he rose and

turned to General Desjardins. "*What is your explanation for this?*"

The constabulary chief stuttered, paling. "Your Majesty, I, ah—"

"And how long has this been going on?" The king's voice rose to a shriek: "*Who is the traitor?*"

"Your Majesty," Owensford said. Then more sharply: "*Your Majesty!*"

Alexander Collins caught himself and wiped a handkerchief over his mouth. "Colonel," he said, sitting again.

"Your Majesty, until quite recently Sparta had only the most cursory controls on weapons movement," Owensford said. His face was blankly expressionless; Lysander had been with him long enough to know what *that* meant. "This could have been going on for quite some time, I'm afraid. With enough money, it wouldn't have been hard to organize."

"Export shipments," Jesus Alana said. "Thurstone has been buying from here for half a decade now." The five-sided civil war there had been going on for twice that length of time. "Mother of God, even the CoDominium Marines on Haven use Spartan-made light arms. Just shaving a few percentage points off each would get you a respectable amount, provided you weren't expending them. You'd have to fiddle the weight allotments, but it could be done if no one was looking hard. Just for an example, you could overweight something else going up with the same load, and it'd look fine."

"Yes, yes," the king said. "What do you propose to do, Colonel Owensford?"

"Treat this as an opportunity, Your Majesty." He called up a map. "We now have two battalions of the Legion. The Fifth is eager for duty, and has already been send upriver. The First Royal is also on route to the Mandalay–Olynthos area. The seismic-testing teams have begun operations, and scouts can be sent into those hills immediately.

"I propose that we take to the field in full force. Three battalion-sized columns, with Brotherhood first-line milita in support, will move into the Dales on converging vectors."

Worms of colored light writhed into the hills from the Valley.

"This will be a reconnaissance in force. That's often a polite way to say 'we have no objective,' or in this instance 'training war,' but in fact we do have an objective. The enemy has probably been accumulating heavy equipment for years. We also know that they recently acquired off-planet support, which very likely includes computers, radars, possibly considerably more. All that requires a base. I propose to find that base and destroy it."

"Bravo," Alexander said.

"So in this case we really do have a reconnaissance in force," Peter said. "Strong enough to fight anything they can put against us, and mobile enough to cover a lot of ground. We go in searching. Depending on the information we gain, we'll modify the directions of attack, attempting to corral and destroy any Helot forces we contact."

"Do you think you can destroy the . . . " the king was reluctant to use the enemy's own designation, "the guerilla forces?"

"That depends on how mobile and well-organized they are, and their leadership," Owensford said. "Also how many, and how good their reconnaissance and intelligence is. They don't know what we're up to yet, but when we begin to move they'll see us coming." He pursed his lips. "The truth is, I don't know what we will accomplish. At the least we should be able to make them abandon a good part of their heavy equipment, and we will kill some of their cadre. That, I think, is the worst case. General Slater will discuss what else we might accomplish."

Hal Slater stood with some difficulty. Everyone had

tried to get him to remain seated when giving his reports and lectures, but he never did. Hal limped to the briefing stand and faced the Council.

"Gentlemen. I believe we are facing amateurs. Of course that's true on the face of it—clearly they haven't brought in any large military professional units without our knowledge. I think they *have* brought in some off-planet consultants, and we're fairly certain they recruited some retired CoDominium officers as advisors, but the important point is that the Helot movement is headed by amateurs.

"Croser," Alexander said.

"Croser for one," Hal Slater said. "And some I can't identify, but I've been studying the patterns of operation, and I think I know those commanders better than they suspect I do. In particular, I am certain I know what books they have studied."

Aha! Lysander thought about the implications of that. *I wouldn't make much of it, but I can see how Slater might.*

"I will be glad to discuss this further if you like, but let me state my conclusion: I believe the Helot organization thinks itself ready to step up to the next phase in the classic guerrilla sequence. If that is so—and the pattern of their terrorist activities makes me quite sure it is—they will be extremely reluctant to abandon their heavy equipment."

"No sanctuary," Ace Barton muttered.

Hal Slater smiled thinly. "No political sanctuary, so they have attempted to build themselves a geographical sanctuary. When we violate that sanctuary, their leaders, following the classic pattern, will say to themselves that they should retreat, abandon their base—but they will not *want* to do that. Far less will their troops want to do so. Even the lowest dregs of humanity has some need for personal space and ownership. Moreover, that heavy equipment is the key to continuing on their schedule.

"Gentlemen, Madam, I believe they will fight on far

longer than they should. They will tell themselves they
are trying to give us a bloody nose, to punish us, and
they will believe that. They will tell themselves they are
going to hit us and run, and they will believe that. But
they will always be more eager to resist than to run."

"And the upshot?" Peter Owensford prompted.

"They will stand and fight long after they should
have quit. They will take more casualties than they
expected to. There's another point."

Hal Slater's lecture, or something, had had a visibly
relaxing effect on Alexander I. "Yes, General?" he
prompted.

"Amateurs make elaborate plans," Slater said. "They
concoct schemes. Often quite complex schemes. They
rely on gimmicks. Their notion of surprise is sneaking
up on someone, hitting him with an unexpected
weapon, that sort of thing. It often works—against
other amateurs."

"We wouldn't want to underestimate the enemy,"
Henry Yamaga said.

"No, my lord," Peter said. "But we don't take counsel
from our fears, either. This campaign is unlikely to be
decisive, but we should do them considerable damage.
Throw them well off balance. Pity the transport
situation will hinder us so badly, but there it is."

Most of the Middle and Lower Valleys were pretty
much a sea of glutinous mud at this time of year, apart
from the natural levees and some artificially drained
portions. The westernmost end of the Middle Valley
where the Eurotas turned northwest toward the
Vulcan Falls was just as muddy, with the addition of
occasional heavy snows that generally melted within a
week or so and added to the saturated ground. The
Illyrian Dales were a little better, since the porous
limestone was free-draining, but they were very
broken, and the rain-laiden winter winds from the east
rose and dumped blizzard after blizzard when they
met the hills and the mountains behind.

"If we had more air transport, we could drop blocking forces and round more of them up," Owensford said. "As it is, a number of them will escape. If General Slater is correct, not as many as they think, but without aviation we're much hampered." He shrugged. On most planets there would have been a scattering of private helicopters owned by the rich, at least, and available for emergency use; on Tanith, for example, most planters owned at least one. Sparta had forbidden that, with wise forethought, putting the money into importing production goods and relying on lower-tech transport. Now she was seeing the unintended consequences of her planning. The new industrial plan called for production of military helicopters, but they wouldn't have them in quantity for more than a year.

"In any event, the objective is to force them to choose between fighting and abandoning equipment which will be hard to replace now that security's been tightened; and to demonstrate that they have no sanctuary from the Royal government forces."

"Yes, by all means," Alexander said. His shoulders slumped slightly. "I almost envy you, Colonel, taking the field against an open enemy. While I sit here, fighting shadows, shadows." His eyes began flickering from side to side again. "Their spies are everywhere—if not Croser's, then that *fool* Armstrong's! Everywhere! The Royal government leaks like a sieve, trying to get anything done is a nightmare, wading through glue while they close in around me."

His voice was growing shrill again. "But I'll destroy them yet, do you hear me, *destroy* them." He panted slightly as he pushed two folders of documents across the polished black wood of the table to Owensford. "The first's the authorization to raise three more regiments, together with a notification to the Brotherhoods that we're in a state of apprehended insurrection. How soon can the Second RSI be ready?"

"With luck, ten weeks, Your Majesty." Owensford

nodded in satisfaction. The notice to the Brotherhoods meant that they were put on formal notice to meet their Obligations to the Crown. Spartan Citizens took that very seriously indeed; he could expect a new flood of recruits, and more importantly men who had military experience or who had been through the excellent Spartan ROC, Reserve Officer Course.

"And here's a Royal Rescript—I had the devil of a time getting David's assent, is he *blind*—anyway, this is a Rescript declaring a State of Emergency in the Province of Olynthos." Owensford nodded again, more grimly. Virtual martial law. "Now get out there and *kill* them, Colonel."

"Yes, Your Majesty. Up to now these Helots have had it their way. They are very experienced in terrorism. We will now show them something they don't know about. We will show them war."

The King stood and waved dismissal. The officers rose and left, leaving the monarch staring moodily at the wall map. Royal Army sentries in the hall outside snapped to salute, and Owensford returned it absently as he pulled on his gloves. When he spoke to the Prince it was in a low murmur.

"My Lord Prince, has your father been seeing a physician?" he said.

"I don't know, sir. I'll certainly look into it."

"Do so, Lynn. Do so." He looked at his chronometer. "Landing ground at 0600, Captain Prince."

*　　*　　*

"Good *God*, Melissa, what's *happened* to him?" Lysander asked, in a furious whisper.

Melissa von Alderheim looked overworked herself; and she had flung herself into his arms with an enthusiasm that startled him. Especially since the nook they were in was not strictly private. Her father, *Freiherr* Bernard von Alderheim, was notoriously strict.

She snuggled closer within the circle of his arms. "It's

the strain," she said. Her voice tickled the underside of his jaw. "Oh, Lynn, I've missed you so!"

A breathless moment later: "Isn't he seeing a doctor?"

"We've had a specialist in, but he couldn't find anything organic wrong."

"It's not like Father," Lysander said stubbornly. "I've never seen him—he isn't the type to crack under pressure."

"There's never been pressure like this before," she said.

"Keep an eye on him, will you? Try to get him to rest more." A thought. "What was that he said about *Armstrong's* spies?"

"You didn't hear? Steven Armstrong got out of regenn two weeks ago—earlier than he should have, the doctors say—and vanished. Until yesterday, of course."

"Darling," he said. "I've haven't slept in twenty hours, we've been planning—what *did* happen yesterday?

"The NCLF offices on North Sacred Way were bombed. Two people were killed, and someone phoned in to the police. They said the Secret Citizen's Army was responsible, that the Secret Army would do what the Royal Army couldn't. The Milice . . . the Milice think Armstrong's behind the Secret Army, Lynn."

Lysander closed his eyes. *Every time I think things are getting better, they get* worse *instead,* he thought. *Is this planet under a curse?* It was enough to make *him* start believing in conspiracies.

"Just what we need," he said wearily. Then he smiled down into her face. "Funny, we haven't had much time together, and yet . . . well, we feel a lot closer."

"We've been working together for the same thing, Lynn," she said.

True. Melissa was more than the heir to the von

Alderheim works, and future Queen; she was a very talented hand at the computerized design machines. The best they had, and needed more than ever with the sudden demand for new military products.

"Don't work yourself to death over at the War College," he said gently, taking her head between his hands. "And there's only a few hours before we move out. I don't want to spend them talking about the war"—*how naturally we start to use the word*—"or, or anybody else."

"I know," she said. "That's why I had dinner for us sent up to my rooms."

"What will your father say?"

"I don't really care." She took his hands between hers and kissed the palms. "I just . . . want to make sure you have a good solid memory to remind you of your reason for staying alive."

And something to remember you by if you don't come back, went unspoken between them, as they walked toward the stairs hand-in-hand.

CHAPTER TEN

Crofton's Encyclopedia of the Inhabited Planets (2nd Edition):

Illyrian Dales, The: area of hilly terrain, named for areas of the Balkan peninsula now part of Serbia, Croatia and Albania. (see *names*, Mythological, Graeco-Roman) Notable feature of the planet *Sparta* [see *Sparta*];

The Illyrian Dales cover an area of approximately 1,400,000 sq. kilometers (875,000 sq. miles) between the western extremity of the Middle Valley of the *Eurotas* river (q.v.) and the *Drakon Mountains* (q.v.). The Dales take the shape of a blunt pyramid, with its base pointing northward and its apex lying along the course of the *Rhyndakos* river (q.v.), a south-bank tributary of the Eurotas.

The Dales are geologically recent, composed of sedimentary marine limestones deposited while the present Middle Valley was a shallow inland sea, prior to the collision of crustal plates which produced the Drakon Range. Buckling and rapid water-erosion has produced a landscape of low hills and gentle ridges, occasionally punctuated by intrusions of harder metamorphic or volcanic rock, which form "plugs" remaining above the peneplain-like surface surrounding them; limited areas of steeper slope have developed semi-karstic formations. The Dales' limestones consist essentially of calcium carbonate, with high concentrations of potassium, phosphorus and other trace elements. Similar formations on Earth include the Nashville basin of Tennessee, and the central ("Bluegrass") basin of Kentucky. No formation of this size would be possible on Earth, but the greater liquidity of the Spartan magma and higher internal heat from gravitational contraction and the decay of radioactives produces more rapid and uniform patterns of deposition and uplift. (Thus accounting for the prevalence of high mountains on a planet with such active erosive forces). Altitude ranges from 300 (in the southeast) to 1,200 meters above sea level in the northwest. After allowing for the 18-month Spartan year, the climate is comparable to the mid-latitude temperate zone of Earth's northern hemisphere, having warm to hot summers and cold winters with (depending on area) three to six months of continuous snow cover. There is little surface drainage, but artesian springs and underground water are common, as are sinkholes and caves.

Description: As with much of Sparta, the native vegetation has been largely replaced by introduced Terran varieties. Initially covered with tall-grass prairies (largely greater bluestem, panicum and canegrass) it has increasingly been colonized by broad-leafed trees ranging from tulip poplar and magnolia in the south to rock maple and birch on the northern fringe; forest cover is more plentiful to the south. Rainfall increases from north to south and from east to west, reaching a climax on the lower slopes of the Drakon range; the southernmost areas receive 180 centimeters per annum, dropping to 80 centimeters per annum on the northern fringe where the Dales give way to the level formations of the *Hylas Steppe* (q.v.). Animal life is almost exclusively Terran, and includes feral cattle, sheep, horse and beefalo, wild swine, various deer species, elk, wapiti, European and North American bison, and brown and black bear. Carnivores were a somewhat later introduction and include wolves (Siberian timber wolf varieties), bobcat, wild cat, lynx, leopard, ounce (snow leopard) and Siberian tiger. Ecological conditions are chaotic, as the introduced species eliminate the less-evolved natives and seek a new equilibrium. (see *Planetary Ecology*, *Terraforming*.) To date, there is no resident human population due to transportation difficulties and superior opportunities elsewhere, and exploitation is limited to harvesting of wildlife, with limited timbering and quarrying on the eastern border.

*   *   *

When first under fire an' you're wishful to duck
Don't look nor take 'eed at the man that is struck.
Be thankful you're livin', and trust to your luck
And march to your front like a soldier.

* * *

"Hey, Top."

Sergio Guiterrez lowered the field glasses; there wasn't anything to see, anyway.

"Yeah, Purdy?"

He'd known it was one of the Legionnaires; the Spartans in the First RSI were calling him Sergeant Major, which was his brevet-transfer rank. To a member of Falkenberg's Mercenary Legion, there was exactly one RSM among Legionnaires; and that was Regimental Sergeant Major Calvin, just as Falkenberg was the only colonel.

"This river ever end?"

"They say so, Purdy; supposed to be today. I can't see much sign of it."

Not *much* of anything to see all the weeks upriver, just the Eurotas getting smaller in stages so tiny you couldn't notice them. Riverbanks with trees, riverbanks *without* trees, views of farm fields, views of grassy prairie and swamp and bare mud and tangled forest. Animals and birds, of course, like something out of the zoo or an old flat Tri-V documentary. Damned few people even the first few days out of Sparta City, so the wildlife was something welcome, something to look at. That and the other troops on the big flat barge, and every now and then some little town where they stopped to take on fuel or run the troops around to keep them from losing their edge. Wet and cool down on the Lower Valley, wetter and colder as they went west along the Middle, which was the same as the Lower except there were fewer people. Wettest and coldest since they'd turned southwest up this tributary, the Rhyndakos.

"Top?"

"Yeah?"

"Something I can't figure," the Tanith-born Legionnaire said.

"Ask away, kid," Guiterrez said. Purdy liked to figure things out, which was one reason he'd made monitor so quick, that and being able to read and having a way with machinery.

"What I can't figure, is why does anyone on this planet want to rebel? It doesn't figure, you know?"

The noncom pushed himself into a sitting position against the pile of supplies and looked around. The barge was a wooden box ten meters by twenty, one of a string pulled along by a puffing little stern-wheeler boat. A dozen more boats and barge-strings further back, where the Brotherhood militia battalions they'd picked up in Dodona were following. About half of this one was taken up by supplies, mostly a battery of heavy 160mm mortars, three-meter tubes on wheeled carriages, and boxed Legion electronics, counterbattery radars and suchlike. The rest was filled with a company or so of the First RSI; they'd rigged up tarps over the hold of the barge, so everyone was pretty dry, and lit low-coal fires in steel drums, so you could get warm. Some of them were cooking things, fish they'd caught or chickens from the last stop, or brewing coffee, and the quality of the wine ration was better than he'd had anywhere else.

He grinned. They had kept the troops busy as possible, classes and even small-arms practice at things passing by, but it was still soft duty. A few of the Spartans had had the gall to complain about conditions, until they saw the Legion veterans laughing at them.

Wait until they're up to their balls in mud and eating monkey, he thought. "You can get rebellions in most places," he said. "They don't like the people running the place, I guess. Your folks moved off into the jungle back on Tanith to get away from the planters and the government, didn't they?"

"Yeah, but Top, they'd have given their right foot to have a place like this. Except it's so cold. No jungle, no Purple Rot, no Weems Beasts or Nessies, lots of good eats, you can pick who you want to work for without slaving your sentence term on some plantation, or hell, just get away from the river a ways and start farming."

Guiterrez laughed softly; there was no sting in it, but Purdy looked slightly abashed.

"It's alright, Purdy, keep thinking that hard and someday you'll be giving *me* orders. See, kid, you're thinking like Tanith. Somebody straight from a Welfare Island on Earth—like I was—it's not so hot. Sure, you don't have to eat protocarb glop, but they *like* glop. Taxpayers eat meat, and they're not taxpayers. There's no Tri-V here, and no Welfare either—no borloi, come to that, or free government booze. Say you're a street-gang warrior like I was, you don't get far here either, the people are all ironed and it's mostly a losing proposition to run in a gang. So it's work for a living or starve, and sure, *you're* used to that—your folks raised you that way, and they learned the hard way—but the convicts aren't. Aren't used to country living, either. Make's 'em feel hard done-by."

One of the First RSI troopers looked up from loading a magazine. "Nah," he said. "It's the girls."

"Girls?" Purdy said, half-turning.

"Sure. Like, I'm a transportee, right? So there's, say, seven pricks to three gashes on those CoDo transports landing here. Studs lined up waiting for them, the transportee gash gets snapped up damn fast, you bet. And you can't get alongside much Citizen cunt even in Sparta City, and if you're outback in a bunkhouse, nothin'. So unless you like men, you might as well get yourself killed 'cause life ain't worth living, right?"

Purdy looked around. The banks of the Rhyndakos were low and swampy for the most part, covered in dead brown reeds; beyond them were thickets of oak and beech, bare and gray-brown as well; to the south and west, very distant, they could see the white glaciers of the Drakon range catch the afternoon light. A hawk hovered overhead, and apart from the chuffing of the tugboats' engines the only sound was wind in the branches. Thick flakes of damp snow were falling from a sky mostly clouds, melting almost at once when they touched the barge. On the shore above the reeds it lay half a meter deep, and the hills to the north were domes of white. The last farmhouse had been yesterday.

"There sure aren't any girls out here," he said.

"Nah, but you can kill somebody and take out your mad, see?" The soldier grinned, showing yellowed teeth. "Me, I figure on being a hero when I get back, get some fine patriotic Citizen to give it to me, see?"

Another trooper laughed. "You wish, Michaels. Maybe some woman *dies*, leaves it to you in her *will*, that's the only way *you* ever going to see any isn't bought and paid for."

The steamboat rounded a corner, and sounded three sharp hoots on its whistle. Guiterrez pushed himself erect; his battle armor was feeling a little tight around the gut, but a couple of days humping the boonies ought to cure that. "Fall in, get ready to disembark! And Purdy," he said.

"Yes, Top?"

"You're lucky. In the Legion, you don't have to know *who* the enemy are, or *why* they're there. All you have to know is how to get them in your sights."

The steamboat let go the towing hitch and turned, the reversed paddlewheel churning the surface of the Rhyndakos into white foam. On shore, the advance party fired a light mortar with a special attachment to carry a line; it trailed coiling through the air and landed across the bows with a wet *thwack*, scattering troopers.

"Dog that line to the brackets," Guiterrez said.

A dozen hands rove it through metal eyelets along the notional bow of the barge, and on shore a working party ran the other end through a block and tackle braced to a tree and heaved in unison. The lead barge in the chain grounded on the soft silt with a shuddering crunch, and the others closed up as the troops on board hauled in the connecting cables.

"Form up!" Guiterrez said, and the company NCOs echoed it. A plank landing ramp splashed over the side. Then there was a whining screech from the shore, as the First's pipe-band prepared to play its soldiers ashore and into the bridgehead.

Operation Scrub Brush was under way.

*   *   *

Geoffrey Niles blew gratefully on the surface of the coffee cup and took a sip. The Command Group post-exercise criticism session had broken up, and he was *still* chilled from the last two days of winter maneuvers. Sighing, he sank back in the chair and looked around the cave, inhaling the scents of wet wool and limestone and coffee.

It's not the cold out there, it's the bloody damp, he thought. Thick snow, and more coming when you least expected it. All made harder by the draining pull of heavy gravity.

The inside of the base was all well back from the entrances, which meant it was not much more dank and chill than it had been in summer. Dimly lit by a few glowtubes stapled to the rock, and if you wanted to get warm you went to your room and moved the heater in under the blankets with you. There were heat sensors all over, and thermal camouflage discipline was enforced with a ferocious disregard for the privileges of rank. The officers were all bundled to the ears . . . *Not a bad lot,* he thought. Friendly enough now that he had proven himself able to keep up and not one to presume on a consort's influence. *Hard men, though,* he decided, studying their faces. *Dangerous men.* Which was all right with The Honorable Geoffrey Niles, since he had always aspired to being a hard and dangerous man himself.

Not exactly top-hole, though, these johnnies. Not gentlemen at all. Except for a couple of the ex-CD types like von Reuther, and he suspected they had been broken out of the service. It was the first time he had ever associated with members of the lower classes so intimately, except with servants. Strange, in some ways; rather like being in the monkey-house at the zoo. They were intelligent enough, a few of them even well-read, but they simply had very little in common, from backgrounds so alien.

Still, I feel good, he decided. The past month and a half had been the hardest work he had ever done, physically and mentally. He felt hard and fit from the relentless drill; balanced and confident inside. *For once nobody gives a damn who my pater or Great-Uncle is,* he thought. *They don't even know.* Whatever respect he had won here was his and his alone.

Not to mention, he mused happily, looking over at Skilly. She was talking to von Reuther, the artillery specialist, probably about the latest shipment from offworld and the wonderful surprises it had brought. She felt his gaze and flashed him a smile; he returned it and raised his cup.

"Field Prime," the orderly said. Skilly raised a hand to stay von Reuther. "The consultant"—*mercenary* was not a word the Spartan People's Liberation Army used for its off-planet helpers—"says there's a priority message for you, ma'am."

Skida's stance did not change, but Niles knew her well enough now to see the sudden tension in her leopard gracefulness. Conversation died as she stalked out of the cave and into the next chamber. A thick waiting descended, until a scream rang out.

Niles blinked. He knew that exultant catamount

screech very well, and the usual cause for it, but somehow he doubted Skilly was having an orgasm in the radio shack. The others exchanged glances, grins; Two-knife turned and slammed the heel of one palm into the rock, manic exuberance from him. When the guerrilla commander stalked back into the room it fairly crackled from her. "The mountain has moved! *They took the bait!*" She shoved one fist into the air. "Long live the Revolution!"

Niles felt his skin tighten; it was an eerie sensation, as if he was trying to bristle like a mastiff that had caught the scent. Words ran through his mind, ancient words—

> But word is gane to the land sergeant,
> In Askerton where that he lay—
> "The deer that ye hae coursed sae lang
> Is seen into the Waste this day."

And perhaps it was wrong to think so of hunting men, but at this moment there was no place in the human universe he would rather be.

The officers stood and cried her hail; out of conviction, or for sheer relief that the waiting was ended. When she spoke again it was with crisp decision.

"General alert. Group Leaders, concentration points as per plan Triphammer. Takadi"—directed at the Meijian liaison and technical expert—"get your surprises ready. Two-knife, we start reeling in their little picnic parties as soon as we sure they not modifying their plan. After that, first thing Skilly wants is to hurry them up a little and put them off-balance. Senior Group Leader Niles, you take—"

* * *

The militia battalion commanders of Operation Scrub Brush, Task Force Erwin, were gathered around the command caravan with their staffs and the RSI officers; Owensford was using its internal map-projector on the dropped rear ramp of the converted APC.

"And you'll need observation posts here, here and here," he said to Morrentes, the major in charge of the stayback force at the bridgehead, pointing to positions on the map in a semicircle about the landing stage. High ground for calling in fire.

It was nightfall on the Rhyndakos, but there were arc-lights playing on the improvised landing stage, as men surged off the barges and manhandled equipment through roots and mud and onto firm ground; mules were being lead down ramps, and their mournful braying echoed along the silent banks of the river. Empty barges were lashed together into makeshift docks covered with planking brought along for the purpose, and in the middle of the hundred-meter width of the river steamboats were maneuvering to bring their strings to the outermost links. Wheels and hooves trundled thunder-hollow as the Brotherhood Citizen-soldiers poured onto the banks. There was an occasional sharp *crack* as someone felled a tree with a string of detcord around the base, and the snarl of chainsaws. Two militia infantry battalions were digging in around the bridgehead; cleared fire zones, trenches, log-and-dirt bunkers, machine gun nests and revetments for their mortars, minefields and wire. A corduroy road had been laid down from the bluff to the water's edge, and the last of the marching column's equipment was being trundled up and loaded onto the waiting mules.

"I'll run a practice-fire program," the Brotherhood officer said thoughtfully. "We'll do some selective felling and booby-trapping out a klick or so from our perimeter."

Behind him a Legion technician squeezed a small plastic bulb. It inflated into a neutral-colored sphere the size of two beachballs; he slung a piece of plastic machinery beneath it, fastened it to a spool of wire the size of thread and let it unreel as the balloon rose.

"That'll give you real-time overhead surveillance," Owensford continued. A small camera-pickup, with the optical processor relatively safe down at the bottom; hence the balloon units were so cheap you could use them prodigally. "Lace the woods around here with communications thread and cameras, it'll make your perimeter security more redundant. We're going to spike camouflaged laser-relays to the trees, so we'll have a way of talking to you without breaking radio silence. This base is absolutely crucial. Keep the drones ready, but don't use them unless you have to."

Major Morrentes was a rancher, a man of medium height with a weathered tan and the bouncy rounded muscularity that second-and third-generation Spartans seemed to have.

"Still wish I was going with you, Colonel," he said ruefully. His lips lost what appeared to be a habitual smile. "My spread's just down from Dodona; they killed two of my vaqueros, good men and Phraetrie brothers, last spring. Not to mention the stock run off and stolen or equipment destroyed, and the convicts who took my boat and came here, I think."

"You may see some action, Major," Owensford said. It was a little disturbing, the sullen anger the Brotherhood soldiers felt toward their opponents. *You've been a mercenary too long*, he thought. *Remember what a grudge-fight is like*. "Just don't forget that your primary tasking here is to keep the river open behind us."

"Sir."

"Now, the rest of us are advancing by battalion columns."

The lead element would be a battalion of the First RSI, heavily reinforced. Twelve of the von Alderheim armored cars, and two dozen of the APCs. Not

carrying infantry, but towing heavy mortars, fuel,
counterbattery radar and communications gear from
the Legion stocks. A command car on the same model,
with his staff and gear. Then the rest of the First
Battalion, First RSI; eight hundred men, more or less,
with their supplies on pack-mules. Six more battalions
of first-line militia, seven to nine hundred men each.
Enough distance between to give each other room and
cover a reasonable amount of space, close enough for
immediate mutual support if—when—they ran into
something.

"Every half-day's march"—fifteen kilometers, more
or less—"we'll drop off one company and two mortar
batteries on these locations." Hilltops with good fields
of fire, available water, and favorable placing to act as
patrol bases. "With rocket-assist, the heavy mortars
will give overlapping fields of fire all along the route.
As reinforcements come in upriver, we feed them up
the line and relieve the dropoff units to rejoin their
battalions. Task Forces Wingate and *Till Eulengenspiegel* will be doing likewise."

"By the time we reach here"—he placed a spot of
light about three hundred and twenty kilometers
north—"the enemy'll have to either fight or run; in
either case, our satellite observation will spot them as
soon as they're forced to move substantial units and we
can reconcentrate and either destroy them or chase
them west into the Drakon Range foothills. They've
evidently got excellent overhead surveillance security,
but the fact they haven't been spotted much puts an
upper limit on possible numbers."

Unlikely that the Royalist force would be able to
catch the guerrillas, if the insurgents abandoned their
heavy equipment, although he had brought enough
horses to equip a substantial force of mounted infantry
in that event. But of course if they captured or
destroyed the enemy equipment, the exercise would
be a success no matter what else was accomplished.

"That done, we can convert some of our firebases into permanent patrol outposts, rotate the militia garrisons as needed, and move the First and the other Field Force regiments in to clean more territory." Guerrillas would still be able to infiltrate, but it would be infinitely more difficult and dangerous once they had to start from bases further away from the Eurotas. "Any questions?"

"Sir." Captain Prince Lysander, code name Kicker Six, who would be leading the scout element. "It's unlikely we have tactical or strategic surprise." Impossible, with troops steaming up the river from Sparta City and militia being mobilized all through this part of the Middle Valley. "Why haven't the rebels done anything yet?"

"I don't know, Captain. I expect we will find out presently."

*   *   *

"We are facing a three-pronged attack," von Reuter said, in accented Anglic with the slightly pedantic twist of a CD veteran. "North, center and south, as vas indicated by our preliminary intelligence. Probably due to our disinformation, the main *schwerepunkt* is in the south, with the northerly force acting as a mobile anvil and the central pozzibly as a strike reserve."

His pointer moved from opposite Olynthos in the north to the middle Rhyndakos in the south, stopping on the way to tap at the box-figures representing the Royalist forces' central landing on the right bank of the Eurotas. "Mobilized militia units are standing by on t'Eurotas to act as blocking forces and general reserve, with mobile mechanized reserves in Olynthos and Dodona."

"Zis attack vill take the form of a closing concentric ring, attempting to constrict our movements. The elements are widely spaced—distances of several hundred kilometers—and t' enemy is relying on superior communications and reconnaissance to immobilize us and prevent our timely concentration against any of his columns, and superior artillery and command and control to overpower zose units of our forces he does encounter. Current intelligence indicates the spearheads of each enemy column are composed of troops of Falkenberg's Legion and the First RSI, wit' substantial numbers of Brotherhood militia in support. Total enemy attack forces are in the range of fourteen to seventeen battalions."

He clicked heels and handed the pointer to Skilly. Niles felt a tightly controlled excitement as she leaned forward into the light that shone over the map table; beyond her the caves of Base One were a kicked anthill of activity, as the Helots prepared to go to war.

"Thank you, Senior Group Leader," she said seriously. "OK. We know more than the Royalists think we know; they haven't changed their battle plan much and we going implement the first contingency for Triphammer."

The pointer skipped south. "This column under Owensford is most important one. They coming through pretty thick country, not too many ways they can go. Group Leader Niles, you take the fast reaction force and stop their lead elements here." She stabbed the pointer into a spot about five days march from the Rhyndakos. "Day before that, they have to commit to one of three alternative pathways, you got twenty hours or so to get ready. That get them good and far from base; when they hot and bothered dealing with you, Skilly will swing in with the forces from the bases along the route, the Base One elements, and the prepositioned equipment.

"Von Reuter, you has the northern wing. They got more mechanized stuff there and the ground more open, but looks like heavy weather. We wants them in good and deep so we can delay them once the southern column is disposed with. You—"

The briefing continued, the officers mostly silent, scribbling an occasional note on their pads; there was a brief question-and-answer session period.

"So," Skida said at last. "Now, you, Tenjiro." The Meijian mercenary bowed slightly. "When we come in contact, they going know we fudging the recon satellite data if they got reports from their troops and the pictures doan show. You gets the Skysweepers ready. Niles," she continued, "Tenjiro's people feeding you the locations of the Royalist SAS teams as they reports. Niles, everyone, Skilly really upset if those teams make any contacts. Be ready to take them out just before we is engaged. Be sure to send enough stuff to do it right."

"Do it right," Niles said. "I can tell you those people are good." They had driven Barton to distraction on Tanith. "We're not going to take them out with any small units."

"So send big ones. Skilly think they like those people, gonna hurt them when they die."

Niles nodded assent.

"Field Prime," one of the other officers said. "They're going to know we're in their communications link when we silence the SAS people. And once the satellites are down, we're as blind as they are to further movement."

"Balance of advantage to us," Skilly said. She bent the pointer between strong brown fingers, looking down at the map with a hungry expression. "We gots their basic positions, and our fixed sensors. They going to be off-balance and hitting air." She raised her head, met their eyes; Niles felt a slight shiver at the feline intensity of it.

"One last thing Skilly want clear: we not fighting for territory, that *their* game. This going to be a long war; unfair one, too. So long as we doan lose, we win; so long as they doan win, they lose. Hit them hard, hurt them—the Brotherhoods particular—but preserving your force is maximum priority." A deep breath. "Let's do it. Let's *go*."

                    *   *   *

"Ready to move out, sir," Lysander said.

"All right, Prince Captain," Owensford said, nodding. "Find them, laddie. We'll be right behind if you run into trouble. Good hunting."

Lysander saluted and turned. The men of his company rose to their feet silently, weapons cradled across their chests. One hundred and twenty, a fifth of them seconded Legionnaires, because this was point duty and crucial. Bulky and anonymous, the gray of their fleece-lined parkas and trousers and body-armor hidden by the mottled-white winter camouflage coveralls. Bulbous helmets framed their faces; the mercenaries and officers were wearing Legion gear, with its complex mapping and communications capacity, the sound and light amplifiers; the ordinary First RSI troopers made do with a built-in radio and nightsight goggles. Everyone had heavy packs, half their own mass or more, because no mules were coming with *them*.

Marius's mules, he thought. *That's what Roman soldiers called themselves.* After Gaius Marius reformed the Republic's army around 100 BC, abolishing the cumbersome baggage trains and giving every legionnaire a bone-crushing load. *Some things in war never change.*

The dying didn't change either.

You'll be in tight-beam communication via the aircraft, and you can't get lost, Lysander told himself. With aviation assets so sparse the seismic-mapping units were doing double and triple duty, reconnaissance and forward-supply as well. Still, they had satellite communications and navigation, and good photomaps.

I wonder how Falkenberg felt the first time he led troops out.

Was he scared? Interesting. It's worse this time than back on Tanith. On Tanith it was just me and Harv I'd kill if I mucked it up.

"Move it out," he called; the platoon commanders and NCOs echoed him. The first platoon filed into the waiting woods, and in less than a minute were totally invisible. "Follow me. With our shields or on them, brothers." *Nothing ahead of us but the SAS teams,* he thought; it was a lonely feeling, almost as lonely as the weight of command on painfully inexperienced shoulders. *If there was anything big, the satellite's IR scanners or the SAS would have caught it. And you've got a whole battalion of the Regiment behind you.*

Harv closed up beside him, moving easily under the burden of pack and communications gear. He pulled the screen down before his face and keyed it to light-enhancement; they moved off into the deeper darkness under the trees, white shadows against the night.

*   *   *

Sergeant Taras Hamilton Miscowsky handed out the packets of pemmican, and the other members of his SAS squad huddled together in the lee of the fallen oak; his tarp had been rigged over the roots to cover the hollow made where the big tree had toppled. Doctrine said it was possible to light a well-shielded mini-stove buried in the earth, and God knew some coffee or tea would be welcome with the wet cold, but he was taking no chances right now.

He looked out into the night-black woods. *Dark as a tax-farmer's soul,* he thought.

The forest around him would have looked half-familiar and oddly strange to someone used to the temperate zone of Earth; the trees were of too uniform an age, none more than seventy or eighty years. Too thickly grown with an undergrowth that included everything from briars to feral rosebushes, and an occasional patch of native pseudomoss with an olive-gray tint fighting its loosing battle against the invading grass. Many of the trees had fallen, grown too high and spindly to bear a gravity a fifth again as high as that for which their genes prepared them. *Chaotic ecology*, was what the briefing veedisks had said.

None of it bothered Sergeant Miscowsky; he had been born on Haven, where it was always cold and almost always very dry and all forests were equally alien to him, problems to be learned and solved.

What *was* bothering him was the fact that he had discovered nothing in a week's scouting. Nothing, zip, nada, zilch. He looked at his wrist. 0130 hours, coming up on time to report.

"Andy, rig the tightbeam," he said.

Andy Owassee was a Legion veteran, who'd made the SAS just before they left Tanith. The other two were locals. Good men, outbackers who'd done a lot of hunting, but he wished he had more veterans with him, the men who'd gone with the bulk of the Legion to New Washington.

"Isn't that a risk?" one of the RSI newlies asked; in a whisper, mouth pointed down.

"Not much," Miscowsky said. "Line of sight from the blimp." There were several patrolling along the Eurotas northeast of here. "Nothin' sent back or forth except clicks, until they lock in—feedback loop. And it's all coded anyway." Tightbeam to the blimp, blimp to satellite, then satellite to whoever needed to hear it.

Out in the dark something yowled. *Something big and hungry*, Miscowsky thought. At that, at least the local predators didn't hide in mudholes to sink their fangs in your ass as you stepped over like the ones on Tanith. Earth stock anyway, and Earth carnivores were all descended from a million years of ancestors with the sense to avoid humans.

"Got it, Sarge," Owassee said, handing the noncom a thread-thin optical fiber link; he plugged it into a socket on the inside rim of his helmet, and then ducked back outside to the watch position.

"Close the tarp," Miscowsky ordered. They made sure it was light-tight, and then the sergeant touched the side of his helmet. It projected a low-light map of the terrain on the poncho folded over the uneven dirt floor of the hollow.

"Cap'n Mace? Mic-four-niner, location"—he touched the map his helmet was projecting, automatically sending the coordinates—"over."

"Reading you, Mic-four-niner. Signs of life?"

"Nothin', sir, and I'm stone worried. Plenty of animals"—they had blundered almost into a deeryard with a hundred or so whitetails—"and sign, shod hooves and old fires, might be hunters or if it's enemy then they police up real careful." They had found a body at the bottom of a sinkhole, about a year dead and looking as if nothing had gotten to it but the ants; the leg bones were broken in four places, and there were a few empty cans around it.

"This place is like a Swiss cheese for caves and holes, sir," Miscowsky went on. He paused. "Yes, sir, I know it's a big search zone but it's as if we're moving in an empty bubble. I think it's a dance, Skipper. They're playing with us."

"What's your situation?"

"Camped high. Dug in. Perimeter gear out. I been running scared all week, and—"

"*Sarge. Sound.*"

All three men froze, only Miscowsky's hand going to the tarp. He touched his helmet to cycle the audio pickups to maximum gain and background filter; the officer at the other end had caught the alarm and waited, silent on the circuit. The noncom closed his eyes to focus his senses.

Creaking, wind, somewhere far off the thud of animal hooves. Then a crackle . . . *might be a branch breaking in the wind*. Rubbing sounds, and a tear of cloth. A muffled metallic click; some dickhead waiting until too late to take off the safety. "Got something on pickup. Three hundred forty meters bearing two-nine-five. There's another. Four hundred forty-five bearing one-seven-five."

"They all around you?"

"May be."

"Stand by one."

"Hartley here," a voice said. "You're sure?"

"Sure enough."

"Call it off."

"Fire mission. Offset three hundred forty, bearing two-niner-five, moving. Offset four hundred forty-five, bearing one-seven-five, stationary. More to come."

"On the way."

A long pause, then a flare of light somewhere off toward battalion. A big rocket flashed high, arced toward them.

"Comin' in, peg 'em."

Miscowsky scanned the area below him. "Goddam," he muttered. There were fifty men closing in. "It's a bloody damned race," he said.

"Think they got us located?" Owassee asked.

"Maybe not." Miscowsky began setting in ranges and offset bearings on his sleeve console. "Gonna be close—ah." A timer glowed softly on his sleeve. Fifty-five seconds. Fifty-four. "Impact in fifty seconds. Estimate where they'll be when the balloon goes up." He grinned wolfishly.

*   *   *

"Kicker Six," the voice said softly in Lysander's ear. "Third Platoon here. We found a mine."

"Halt," Lysander said, on the unit push. "Perimeter, defensive." The first thing but foot and hoofprints they had found in three days' march.

Ahead of him and to either side, men stopped and melted into invisibility. Behind fallen logs, in the shadow of bushes, simply sinking into snow until only their eyes and the white-painted muzzles of their weapons showed. There was very little noise; the odd crunching sound, a few clicks as the team-served weapons set up. He and Harv went to one knee, waiting until the guide from Third Platoon came. The trooper gave a hand-signal from twenty meters; they followed him in silence, from cover to cover. The last three hundred meters they did on their bellies.

"Sir," the junior lieutenant breathed as they crawled into the lee of a big beech; the snow was thin here, high on the other side of the tree where the prevailing east wind piled it. Ice hung from the thick branches in stalactites, legacy of what had probably been the last thaw of the year, up here in the hills.

"Monitor Adriotti spotted it."

Andriotti was a Legionnaire, a man with a dark face and scars that ran down it into the neckline of his parka. Forty years old, perhaps fifty. Alert, but with a phlegmatic resignation that went deeper than words could reach.

"Zur," he said; there was a thick accent to his words, but it was of no particular place. The accent of a man who has spent his adult life speaking Anglic as a *lingua franca* with others also not born to it. "Tere. Snow is just off the tripwire between t'ose trees."

Lysander cycled his faceplate to IR; nothing, the booby trap was at ambient, which meant it had been here for a while. He risked a brief burst of ultrasound, then froze the image. A curved plate resting on a low tripod in a clump of leafless thorny bush, impossible to spot with the naked eye. The wire ran at ankle-height, in a triangle secured at the corners to two trees five meters apart by plastic eyebolts screwed into the bark. The gap was the obvious route for anyone who didn't want to crash through brush, and anyone who had would have been shredded by thousands of fléchettes.

"All units," he said. "Remain in place and look for

mines. I don't have to tell you to be careful. Dig in. Full perimeter defence." Never a mistake to dig, if you had to stop. The books said minefields and other obstacles were primarily useful to pin a force so that it could be attacked.

"Com, patch me through to Command."

*   *   *

"*How* many?" Peter Owensford asked as Mace finished. *Contact. This is it.*

"Sir, Miscowsky and his team are under attack by at least a company. Team Z-2 doesn't report. A-1 and A-2 report all nominal. Something coming in—Deighton's under attack. And Laramie."

"Deighton, Laramie and Miscowsky. And Katz doesn't report. Bingo," Owensford said. "Well, we sent them out to find something."

Find it and kill it. Each of the SAS teams carried directional beaming equipment that could feed the team's coordinates, plus an offset, to incoming Thoth missiles. Thoth was normally launched by aircraft kept just at the team's horizon, but in this case there weren't any airplanes for that, so the birds were lofted by solid rockets. That could be expensive if the birds went out and there were no targets, but Peter didn't think that would be the problem here.

"Jamming. We're getting jammed," Mace said.

"Jamming," Owensford acknowledged. "Well, we expected it after the Spartosky. Loft the anti-radiation missiles. And keep lofting Thoth support." Thoth missiles depended on a direct line of sight communication, and employed an autocorrelation system that was nearly impossible to jam, even with brute force.

"Aye aye."

Owensford studied the map. Miscowsky was Z-1, ranging in ahead of the column of Royal troops heading north from the Rhyndakos, Katz with Z-2 likewise. T-1 and T-2 were with the central column, punching in directly west from a convenient bend in the Eurotas. A-1 and A-2 with the northern force, pressing southeast from Olynthos.

"They knew where to look," Peter said aloud. He thought about the implications of that. There was only one way they could have known that well. He turned to his adjutant, Andy Lahr. "Andy, they knew where to look. You agree?"

"Yes, sir."

"Jericho. Get the word out, all units, Jericho."

"Roger."

Peter picked up the microphone. "Mace, broadcast to all of your units. Code Jericho. Repeat, Code Jericho. Got that?"

"Roger. Code Jericho."

*   *   *

"Message, Captain." Communications Sergeant Masterson spoke urgently.

Lysander frowned. "I need to talk to headquarters—"

"They're broadcasting, sir. Jericho. Code Jericho."

"Jericho."

"Yes, sir. I got special orders on that one—"

"I know," Lysander said. "All right. Acknowledge."

"Acknowledge Jericho," the comm sergeant said. "I say again, we acknowledge Jericho. All units Task Force Candle Four, command override, your word is Jericho, Code Jericho. I say again, Code Jericho."

Jericho, Lysander thought. Assume that all transmissions are monitored by enemy. Assume that all ciphers and encryptions are compromised. All communication in future to be by code book, or in clear with enemy presumed listening.

"We're getting another," Masterson said. "This one's just for us. Kicker Six, Code Dove Hill. Code Dove Hill."

"Right. Thank you." Lysander touched his sleeve console and typed rapidly. "DOVE HILL."

"ASSUME ENEMY IN GREATER STRENGTH THAN ANTICIPATED." "Bennington," Masterson said. "Wait a second, that's not for us. Here's ours. Saratoga. Tiger. I say again, saratoga, tiger."

"SARATOGA," Lysander typed.

"DIG IN AND PUNISH THE ENEMY. UNLIMITED FIRE SUPPORT AUTHORIZED."

"TIGER," he typed.

"GOD BLESS US, THERE'S NONE LIKE US."

*   *   *

"All right," Owensford said. "Code books from here on." And thank God for a suspicious mind. Codes were not convenient. You couldn't say anything you hadn't thought of in advance and put in the code book—or personal data base, as the case might be—but they did have the advantage of being unbreakable. You'd have to capture a pocket computer intact, and even that wouldn't help for long, since the code word meanings changed from day to day and unit to unit.

"Code this," Owensford told Andy Lahr. "Teams A-1 and A-2 are to shift position and maintain radio silence unless attacked. Their primary mission is to get home alive. Relay message to Task Force *Till Eulengenspiegel*—" the central column "—entrench in place, stand by to call in Thoth, and hurt the enemy."

That wouldn't take long, since the central column was a feint, a company-strength unit making enough radio noise for a battalion. Of course a feint backed by enough callable firepower was more trap than feint . . .

"Task Force Wingate is to shift to fallback communications and maintain nominal transmission. Maximum alert; reduce movement, prepare for meeting engagement."

"Righto."

The interlock chimed, and the com technicial looked up from his board at the rear of the command-car's hull.

"Sir, priority report from Captain Collins."

"Put him through. Kicker Six, you understand Jericho?"

"Roger Jericho, sir. Sir, I've got multiple detection sensor and tripwire-detonated mine sightings all along my line of advance here."

"Merry times." Owensford looked down at his map; wheeled vehicles could advance through this section of the southern Dales, only about four-tenths of the ground was under forest, but if you counted that and very broken terrain it channeled an attack quite nicely. Channeled it down to about four alternative angles of approach within the fifty klicks on either side of the arms sighting that had started this whole affair.

"Check for command-detonated devices within your perimeter, Lynn," he said.

"Shit, I never thought—sorry."

"Quite all right," Owensford said with a bleak smile. "We're only four klicks south. You have your orders, Kicker Six. Stand by one." He turned. "Andy, how do I say 'Use explosives to clear mines. Conserve troops.' ?"

"GLOSSARY. HILDEBRAND."

"Got it. Captain, your codes are Glossary, I say again Glossary. Hildebrand. I say again Hildebrand.

"Roger. Glossary, Hildebrand. And TIGER to you, too. Out."

"Andy, check confirmation all units acknowledge condition Jericho," Peter said. "Then get me Task Force Atlas, Lieutenant-Colonel Barton." They were all wearing their Royal Army hats tonight; that was the central reserve, in Dodona. The line there at least was secure.

A wait of a few minutes. "Barton here. Ready to scramble."

"Ready. Scramble." There was a tell-tale sing-song background in his earpiece. "Scrambled."

"Scrambled," Barton confirmed. "OK. I've been following it."

"You get the same feeling I do, Ace?"

"That joyful, tingling sense of anticipation that comes just before you jam your dick into the garbage grinder? Yeah."

"How do you figure it?"

"Could be either an agent in place, a pirate tap in the satellite, or both. They know more than we thought, and they've got more force than we expected."

There was no visual link, but it took no imagination for Peter to see Barton's face, cynical grin, toothpick moving rapidly from one side of his mouth to the other. "Status of the reserves, Ace?"

"Nominal. Of course we're using up Thoth at a fearful rate, ditto ARM."

"Any effect?"

"Sure. Their jamming's just about stopped, and Miscowsky and Katz are having a field day. Between them, they've taken out the equivalent of a battalion."

"Think we got all their antennas?"

"Hell, no."

"Yeah, I agree," Peter said.

Owensford looked at the map again. Four Brotherhood battalions with his Task Force Erwin column in the south, and the reinforced battalion of the First RSI. The same with Task Force Wingate in the north. One company with the feint. The mechanized battalion of the First outside Olynthos with two squadrons of armored cars, ready to back up Wingate. Four companies of Legion troops in Dodona, with all the ground-effect transport that the Middle Valley could provide, fast enough to reinforce *either* Wingate *or* Erwin. On the map the advancing columns looked like the jaws of a beast, closing around the south-central Dales. On the ground it was fewer than ten thousand men moving through an area of rough terrain larger than many countries back on Earth.

Plenty of troops in reserve, if you counted the militia, Ace had been working miracles with them. Another full brigade of first-line mobilized Brotherhood fighters along the river ready to intervene if it must, and the twenty thousand or so of the second-line were standing to arms on the defensive, giving him a secure base. Five times that number of third-line, women and older men, not field units but ready to fight and doing noncombatant work. None of them very mobile, unfortunately. Sparta's blessing and curse, the Eurotas; it made bulk transport in the settled regions so easy that there was an overwhelming temptation to put off developing a ground-transport infrastructure.

Should I have taken more of the militia in with me? he thought. Then: *no, the reasons are still valid.* Risky enough to have them standing by as emergency reserves.

Good militia were still part-time troops, unpracticed in large-unit maneuvers. The Brotherhood fighters were first-rate in their own neighborhoods. That was one reason nobody had ever taken a serious crack at Sparta, the Brotherhoods could field better than a third of a million at a pinch. The problem with that Swiss Militia system was that if you called everyone to arms, there was no one left to do the work; and Sparta's economy was in bad enough shape as it was.

Losing too many of them could be absolutely fatal; at a pinch, Sparta could stand heavy casualties to its offensive force, but the Brotherhoods were the iron frame that kept this section of the Valley under government control.

"All right, we probe, but *carefully,*" he said at last. "This operation is primarily a reconnaissance in force, anyway." The best way to learn about an opponent was to fight him. "It all depends on what they've got and how good it is. We've already learned something about that."

"Yeah; they're pretty good, and they've got a secure communications system in there. Which is more than we do." Owensford nodded thoughtfully; it looked unpleasantly like the enemy had been preparing this for years. The whole of the Dales could be linked together with optical thread-cable and permanent line-of-sight stuff.

"The main thing is not to get hurt," Peter said. "Get that out to all units. If the other guys want to play, dig in and pound them. They're better than we thought they were, but they're still just light infantry.

"Meanwhile, let the SAS teams come home, but keep sending them fire support as long as they can spot targets. After all, it's what they're out there for."

"I ain't worried about them," Barton said. "But there's something sour about this whole operation."

"I got that feeling too."

"And we're blind. Pete, I suggest we wait for new satellite pix before we commit."

"Trust them?" Owensford asked innocently.

"Oh. Now that you mention it, no. Guess I don't."

"So we have to try something else. Bring up the birds; one with me, one with Task Force Wingate. Keep them well back." Tiltrotor VTOL aircraft, commandeered from the RSMP for the seismic-mapping project. They could transport a complete platoon of infantry; right now they were crammed with other stuff. It would not do to put them in harm's way, of course. Aircraft over a battlefield had been an impossibility since good light seeker rockets became common. The enemy certainly had those.

"You're the boss," Barton said.

"Bring up, code—" He did a quick search on his data base. "The code is Babylon."

"Babylon." A pause. "Babylon it is. Anything else?"

"That's it."

"Task Force Atlas, out."

"Out," Peter said.

Next. "Andy, let Heavy Weapons company dig in and prepare to fire support missions. Have Scout company pull all forward units inside artillery support range."

Not many proper guns, most of it was big mortars, but still enough range once the scouts drew in.

"Roger. SAS teams report enemy activity slacking off."

Peter glanced at the munitions expenditure readouts. "I should bloody hope so. Haven't you got a better report than that?"

"Miscowsky reports 'DYANAMO.' That translates as 'heavily engaged.' "

"Other teams?"

"Much the same. Heard from Katz finally. His report prior to acknowledging Jericho was 'JESUS CHRIST!' Now reports, 'Heavily engaged, am hurting enemy.' "

"Good." *The SAS teams are doing their job, but I don't like this. Ace doesn't either.* "Bring them home. Send out escort patrols to assist."

"Suggestion," Captain Lahr said.

"Spill it."

"This is all by the book," Lahr said. "They'll set up ambushes for the escorts, sure as hell."

"Gotcha. Yeah, send an SAS Thoth controller along with each escort team. With luck they'll find some targets going in while the teams kick ass coming out."

"Roger that."

"Now get me Collins again."

"Can't guarantee security."

"Understood."

"Coming up," Andy Lahr said.

There was a pause. "Kicker Six here."

"Jericho."

"Understood."

"Captain, I need an estimate of how far that mine obstacle stretches. . . . "

"About five hundred meters to my left, sir; three hundred to the right, and it's anchored in a ravine. About fifty to a hundred meters thick. We estimate a minimum of three hours to clear a path suitable for vehicles."

"Stand by one." Owensford studied the map. The western end of the minefield ran down toward a valley; there was a lip to that hill, a traversable slope beyond the mines, and then broken wooded ground down to the low point.

What was it Ace said about garbage grinders? That gap might as well have a sign on it, "Please insert male generative organ here." *Well, a trap you know is a trap is no trap.*

"Stand by for orders," Peter said.

No point in having Collins waste troops on mines. Use fuel-aid to blast hell out of the area and be done with it. The main thing was to stay out of trouble. Owensford typed orders.

"DIG IN. STAY DUG IN UNTIL MINEFIELDS CLEARED. USE ARTILLERY AND HE TO CLEAR MINE AREA. DON'T RISK TROOPS ON MINES. PREPARE TO PUNISH ENEMY ATTACKERS."

"Andy, put this through the data base and give me the codes. Thanks."

"OK. Attention to orders. Code DECEMBER. Repeat December. Code TRILOGY. Repeat Trilogy. Code ELK HILL. Repeat Elk Hill."

"DECEMBER, TRILOGY, ELK HILL. Roger."

"Code TIGER."

"Tiger it is."

"Okey Doke. Out." Peter Owensford reached up and undogged the hatch, climbing up to stand with head and shoulders in the chill air. Cythera was up, shedding patchy moonlight through scudding clouds. He cycled the facemask until the scene had a depthless brightness. The main body of Task Force Erwin was moving at the equivalent of a quick walk, no more. A dozen armored cars were leapfrogging forward, moving in spurts and then waiting in hull-down positions while the flanking infantry companies swept through the wooded areas to either side in skirmish line; behind both the bulk of the expeditionary force marched in company columns, enclosing their mule-born supply trains.

That changed even as he watched. The APCs halted

and spilled their eight-man crews to begin setting up the heavy weapons. Shovels and the 'dozer blade of the engineering vehicle began preparing firing positions for the mortars, well spaced out and downslope from the crest. Still further down, the Headquarters troops were digging in as well, spider-holes and pits for their heavy machine guns and perimeter gatlings.

"Sir, Senior Lieutenant Fissop." The commander of the HQ company. "He requests permission to blow standing timber for entrenchment purposes."

"By all means," Owensford said, studying his map again.

Assume there's a blocking force near that minefield, he thought. *Can't be too large. Now, what avenues of attack are there . . . ahh.*

"Message to Third Brotherhood. Close up to two klicks west of us and advance using this ridge"—his light-pencil traced it—"having his mortars ready for support"—mule-born 125mms—"and begin a probe here." That ought to put them right behind whoever was waiting for him to swing around the mines.

"Twenty-Second is to maintain distance on the Third's left, ready to move in support. Eighteenth is to close up to within five klicks to our rear, and Fifty-first to deploy in place for the moment on the right." A good well-rounded position, ready to attack, retreat or switch front at need, and capable of interdicting the low covered ground on all sides.

"Sir, CO Task Force Wingate."

"Patch."

"Slater here," a familiar voice said.

"Copy, George," Owensford said.

"I've run into a spot of trouble."

"Details?"

"Mines, snipers and teams of rocket launchers infiltrating between my columns. Lost two armored cars and about fifteen casualties; we've counted about five times that in enemy dead. They're willing to take casualties to hurt us."

"Interesting."

"Isn't it? Also, two of my forward support bases along the route back report harassing fire from mortars. One twenty-five millimeter stuff, shoot-and-scoot, they're working counterbombardment."

With locally made counterbattery radars; Owensford had no special confidence in them. Single-frequency, and the innards were positively neolithic, hand-assembled transistors and chipboards salvaged from imported consumer electronics.

"Stand by for orders." He looked up "Conserve Ammunition" and "Fire if target under observation and located." "Code HAWKWOOD. Repeat Hawkwood. Code ARAGON. Repeat Aragon."

"HAWKWOOD. ARAGON. Roger."

"Stand by one."

"Roger."

"Intelligence. What's on Elint?" Electronic traffic interception.

"Nothing, sir."

There were ways to handle movement without any radio traffic at all, but not many. One way was to move everything according to a prearranged plan. Like terrorists. That would be interesting. He switched back to the commander of the northern column.

"We'll know more in a bit. Hop to it."

"Roger. Wingate, out."

"Come on, birdie," Owensford murmured to himself. "Because here I sit, bloody blind."

*　　*　　*

"Senior Group Leader," the communications tech said, "Base One reports there was a three-minute lapse in enemy satellite-link commo immediately after the SAS teams were attacked. They are now using alternates, and code book."

"Thank you," Geoffrey Niles said. "Results?"

"Heavy casualties, sir. The SAS teams are calling down some sort of smart weapon bombardment, and they're all well dug-in. They've shredded our people, some have already cut and run." He touched the earphone of his headset. "The consultants say the weapons are being lofted by short-range rockets from the main enemy columns. Antiradiation missiles are giving our jamming serious problems."

"Damn." He frowned; overrunning the SAS teams would have been a significant blow to the enemy's capacities. Skilly's orders had been quite specific, though. "Break off the attacks. They'll probably try to send someone to pull the scouts out. Have the attack teams set ambushes on the likely approach paths. Otherwise, stay out of visual observation range and harass with mortar fire."

"Counterbattery hits our mortar people every time they fire."

"Poor babies." Niles looked at his chronometer; 0200. "Time to surveillance satellite overpass?"

"One hour twenty-seven minutes, sir." A pause. "Sir, Base One reports two enemy aircraft are lifting off-schedule from Olynthos and Dodona." They had agents in place in both towns. All you needed was someone with binoculars, and a zeroed-in laser transponder aimed at a spot in the hills to the west and south. A negligible chance of someone having detection gear in the path of a tight beam during the few seconds it was in use.

"Tiltrotors. Looks like they're heading for the rear zones to do Elint and remote-sensor interpretation." The pickups would be forward. "ETA forty minutes."

"Very good," he said with a fierce grin, looking back at the map. The enemy were quick on the uptake, but there were still things they didn't know. "I'm moving forward to take personal command of the blocking force. Sutchukil," he continued to his adjutant, "keep me notified of the status of the aircraft."

"Sir," the Thai transportee said; he was a short stocky man with a grin that never reached his eyes, an aristocrat and would-be artist shopped to BuReloc in some local power struggle.

Outside the tarp shelter it was growing rapidly colder in the gully under the light of the sinking moon; Niles stopped for a second to pull on his thin insulated gloves and fasten the top of his parka. Breath puffed white as the headquarters section fell in around him; there was little other movement in the rocky draw where they had left the vehicles. Those were simple frameworks of wood on skis, holding little but a light airship engine with rear-mounted propeller and a fuel tank. The troops' skis and the sleds that carried heavy equipment were stacked nearby, several layers thick against the rough limestone of the cliff wall.

"*La joue commence*," he murmured to himself.

CHAPTER ELEVEN

Crofton's Essays and Lectures in Military History (2nd Edition)

Professor John Christian Falkenberg II:
Delivered at Sandhurst, August 22nd, 2087

The nature of the societies which raise armies, the economic resources available to the state, and the nature and aims of the wars which the state wishes to, or fears it must, wage, are all mutually dependent.

Thus for the last two centuries of its existance, the Roman Republic kept an average of ten percent of its total free citizen population under arms, or half or more its adult males. This was an unprecedented accomplishment, made possible in a preindustrial world only by mass plunder of the whole Mediterranean world—directly, by tribute, and through the importation of slave forced labor—and a very high degree of social cohesion. When Hannibal was at the gates of Rome and fifty thousand of Italy's soldiers lay dead on the field of Cannae, the Republic never even thought of yielding. New armies sprang up as if from the very earth, fueled by the bottomless well of patriotic citizen-yeomen. By contrast, under the Empire a mere three hundred thousand long-service professionals served to guard the frontiers of a defensive-minded state. No longer could the provinces be plundered to support a total-mobilization war effort, and it was precisely the aim of the Principate to depoliticize—and hence demilitarize—the citizenry. By the fifth century, relatively tiny barbarian armies of a few score thousands were wandering at will through the Imperial heartlands.

Eighteenth-century Europe saw another turn of the cycle. The "absolute" monarchies of the period fought limited wars, with limited means for limited aims. They had neither the power nor the wish to tax heavily or conscript; their armies were recruited from the economically marginal—aristocrats and gutter dregs—and waged war in a formalized, ritual minuet. A few years later the French Republic proclaimed the levee en masse, and the largest battle of the Napoleonic Wars involved nearly a million men. The cycle repeated itself with a vengence in the next century; in 1840 the combined armies of Hamburg, Bremen, Lubeck and the Grand Duchy of Oldenburg numbered some three thousand men. In 1914, those same territories contributed in excess of thirty thousand men to the forces of Imperial Germany, and replaced them several times over in the holocaust that followed.

Yet the wheel of history continues to turn. The CoDominium, ruling all Earth and at one time or another over one hundred colonized planets, never had more than five hundred thousand men under arms; during its rule, most national armies on Earth declined to the status of ceremonial guards or glorified riot police. Once more, stagnant oligarchies have nothing to gain by arming the masses; small, professional armies operating according to the Laws of War conduct limited conflicts to maintain a delicate sociopolitical balance. In the colonies and ex-colonies, important campaigns are decided by tiny forces of well-trained mercenaries or professional soldiers; a regiment here, a brigade there.

And now another turn of the wheel seems to be beginning.

*   *   *

If your officer's dead and the sergeants look white,
Remember it's ruin to run from a fight;
So take open order, lie down, and sit tight,
And wait for supports like a soldier.

*   *   *

"Task Force Wingate. Slater here." A buzzing in the

background; scrambling, and Ace's people had rerouted the link though a newly laid cable up the riverbed to Olynthos. Everything through Legion equipment.

"Owensford here. What's the story, George?"

"A bit of a dog's breakfast, I'm afraid," the commander of the northern column said; Peter Owensford could hear a dull *crump . . . crump* in the background, and small-arms fire.

Dog's breakfast, he thought. One of Major Jeremy Savage's expressions. *And I wish he and Christian Johnny were in charge here instead of twenty light years away.*

"My central element ran into an infantry screen," Slater said. "Well placed; we had to deploy and put in a full attack, couldn't just brush them aside. Gave us a stiff fight and then moved back sharpish. We cut them up nicely, but then I went forward to try and keep them from breaking contact and we got caught by a mortar and bombardment rocket attack."

"Rockets?"

"One-twenty-seven mm's, the same type the Royals use." A six-tube launcher, in batteries of three. "Four batteries, widely spaced. Proximity fused, time-on-target with the mortars, and cursed well placed. Then the ones we'd been chasing came back at us, right on the heels of it, grenade and bayonet work for a while."

Owensford winced; that was a bad sign, that the enemy had troops willing to take casualties from their own artillery to push in an assault while the fire kept the defenders' heads down.

"Pretty much the same thing happened to the Forty-First Brotherhood." The militia unit on the far left flank of Task Force Wingate.

"They pursued until they were out of reach of the battalion on their right, with more enthusiasm than sense"—Owensford nodded; you wanted aggression, but only experience could temper it with caution—

"and now they're leaguered and under attack from all sides. The enemy is trying to infiltrate squad-sized units and recoilless teams down the wooded vales between my units, and it's sopping up my riflemen to stop them, turning into a bloody dog-fight down there. Plus constant harassing fire from eighty-two mm's"—platoon level mortars—"and snipers behind every bush. I'm moving the Seventeenth Brotherhood up from reserve to help pull the Forty-first out of its hole and back to the main body, and putting the Tenth"—the unit on his immediate right—"into the low ground to work their way around the flank of the people ahead of me, while the Seventh drops back and covers us both on the right."

"Appraisal of the enemy?"

"Too damned good for comfort; not up to Legion standards, but good. Their equipment's about the same as the Royals, except their radar and radar countermeasures, which are better, probably as good as ours. Off-planet stuff. Chaff and jamming, so I'm returning the favor; they've got more visual observation right now, I'm working on it."

A gatling six-barrel went off somewhere near to the mike, a savage *brrrrrrrt-brrrrrrt* sound, a hail of bullets that would saw through trees.

"They know how to use their weapons, they've got discipline and good small-unit tactics," Slater continued. A wounded man screamed, a high endless sound suddenly cut off as if with a knife. "Not bothered by armor, either; they've got plenty of light recoilless stuff and unguided antitank rockets, and they're not afraid to get in close and try to use it. I've taken damned few unwounded prisoners."

A pause. "The Brotherhood people don't seem to have taken any prisoners at all, by the way."

Damn, damn, don't they understand it'll make the enemy fight harder? Owensford thought. He would have to do something about that.

"And whoever's in charge knows his hand from a

hacksaw too. I'd swear there's a CoDominium Academy mind behind that fire mission."

"How many of them?"

"Difficult to say; they keep shooting down my spyeye balloons as fast as I put them up. At least a thousand, no more than two." Task Force Wingate would outnumber them by at least fifteen hundred men, possibly by twice that.

"I could fight through what's facing me," Slater continued, echoing Owensford's thoughts. "Why don't I think this is a good idea?"

"It's what they want you to do, of course. Bugger that. We're better set for a battle of attrition than they are. The one thing I haven't noticed in all this is logistics troops. They may be able to make infantrymen out of those street gangs, but they seem to be a bit short on supply clerks.

"Consolidate as soon as you've pulled the Forty-first out of its hole, and dig in. The mission's changed, George. To hell with moving across ground. The objective is to kill their cadres. Troops as good as those can't be all that plentiful, not to terrorists, so dig in and break their teeth. Before we're finished they'll have their battalion commanders out fighting like riflemen. And make them use up their munitions. This has just become a logistics war."

"Suppose they won't come at us?"

"They will. 'Enemy advance, we retreat. Enemy halt, we harass.' They'll think you're slowing down because you're beaten just like the Brotherhood troops," Peter said. "Let's encourage that thought. They've got some kind of complicated battle plan, and just for the moment I'd as soon they thought it was working. I particularly don't want them to think that either you or the Brotherhoods can mount an attack. And they'll think they have to attack before they run out of supplies. Or just to get ours."

"Gotcha."

"You're an anvil. Be a good one. When I've got recon

I'll put some mobility back in this battle. For now they expect you to advance, so digging in will be a surprise. But be ready to advance again when I need you."

"Understood."

"Godspeed. Out."

*   *   *

"There, Senior Group Leader," the platoon leader of the guerilla advance element said, making a tiny hand motion through the improvised blind of thorny brush. "The rest of them are a thousand meters back, digging in."

Niles slipped up his nightsight goggles and used the glasses instead, switched to x10 magnification and light-enhancement. The hundred-meter gap between the minefield and the steeper slope down to the valley was an expanse of snow stippled with the dry yellow stalks of summer's grass. A few small trees were scattered across it, and the odd bush. Nothing moved but the wind, scudding a thin mist of ice crystals along the surface of the ground. Then a man rose to one knee, motionless with a white-painted rifle across his chest. A full minute's silence, then he made a hand signal; half a dozen others rose out of concealment and moved forward twenty paces, sank to the earth again. Another six rose from behind the lead element's position and passed through, went to ground ten or twenty meters in advance.

Good fieldcraft, Niles thought. Aloud: "Open fire!"

Muzzle-flashes lit the night, twinkling like malignant orange fireflies. Men flopped, screamed, were still; a stitch of tracers curved out toward the Helot positions, and the Royalist riflemen opened return fire as well. Bullets went by over Niles's head with an ugly flat *whack* sound, and bark fell on his helmet and the backs of his gloves. He raised his own rifle and settled the translucent pointer of the optical sight on a suspicious gray rock that jutted up out of the snow.

A head and arms snaked around it, a long finned oval on the muzzle of the weapon they carried; rifle grenade. Niles stroked the trigger gently. *Crack*. The recoil was a surprise, sign of a good shot. The head dropped back and the rifle slipped back into view and landed in the snow.

God, Niles thought as a surge of excitement flowed from throat to gut. He touched the side of his helmet.

"Status of element Icepick."

"Moving out," his adjutant said.

"Execute fire mission Alpha," Niles ordered. "I'll join Icepick with the Headquarters squad. Switch to local band relay." They were moving now. Communications weren't so good. *So what? No commanding from the rear! Get out where the troops could know you weren't afraid.*

"On your own, platoon leader," Niles continued, beginning to worm his way backward. Then the sky overhead glared a violet almost as bright as day.

* * *

"*Incoming. Able Company position.*" Owensford watched the battle screen change again.

"Lysander's scouts," Captain Lahr said.

In the background Captain Sastri, the artillery chief, spoke in a monotone. "Multiple incoming. Tracking." Light flickered across the northern horizon. "Computing positions. Preparing for counterbattery shoot . . . countermeasures. Chaff and broad-frequency jamming, decoys."

Peter nodded in satisfaction. "Andy, be sure we record all this for analysis."

"Roger," the adjutant said. "The bad guys are expending a hell of a lot of ordnance, Colonel."

"Yeah. Sort of makes you wonder who paid for it all. Andy, what do you make of this?"

"Well, they had a hell of a lot more gear than we expected. It hasn't been used all that effectively."

"Not too surprising. Most of their training had to be map exercises. Dry fire."

"Yes, sir. Just as well."

"They jumped the gun, too," Peter mused. "They should have waited until we got in deeper."

"Probably scared we'd find their base."

"Could be. I still think there's some kind of plan at work here. Something complicated. Main thing is, keep them using up their heavy stuff until they notice they're running short."

Behind him the 160mm mortars flashed as Sastri sent in anti-radar and counterbattery fire. *Crump. Crump. Crump.* Twelve times repeated, and then the brief winking of rocket-assist at the high points of the shell's trajectories, thousands of meters overhead. The muzzles disappeared behind their raw-earth revetments, as the hydraulics in the recoil-system automatically lowered them to loading position; the bitter smell of burnt propellant settled across the hilltop. Inside the gunpits the two loaders would be dropping the forty-kilo bombs down the barrels . . . the tubes showed again, ten seconds to load and alter the aiming point both. *Crump. Crump. Crump.*

A rumble throught the ground, and an edge of satisfaction in Sastri's voice:

"Secondary explosions. Scratch one rocket battery."

Rockets hissed skyward, arcing northward.

"Jamming antennae down. One. Two . . . Active jamming off. Chaff continuing."

*　　　*　　　*

"Sir, Second Platoon, we're under fire." A bit superfluous, Lysander thought, since they could all hear the crackling two thousand meters to their left.

"Where's Lieutenant Doorn, sergeant?"

"Dead, sir. Three dead, five wounded. Heavy automatic-weapons fire. Maybe a whole company come after us, we'd have been dead if we hadn't dug in."

Lysander could hear the relief, and more, in the sergeant's voice.

"*Incoming!*"

Lysander ducked lower into the hole. *At least everyone is dug in.* Explosions all along the line, but a lot fell into the minefield, setting off more mines. *They thought we'd be in there. . . .*

"Alexi's hit, medic, medic!" somebody shouted.

Then the sky screamed, globes of violet light raking through the cloud towards them. The Collins prince dropped to the bottom of his spider pit and tucked his limbs in, standard drill to let the thicker torso armor protect you. A flicker of silence, and then the world came apart in a surf-roar of white noise. The rocket warheads burst apart thirty meters up, showering their rain of hundreds of grenade-sized bomblets to bounce and explode and fill the air with a rain of notched steel wire. The sound was distant as the helmet clamped down on audio input that would have damaged his ears, like a movie on Tri-V in another room of the house, and it seemed to go on forever. Something struck him below the right shoulderblade with sledgehammer force, driving a grunt out between clenched teeth.

Fragment, but the armor had stopped it. If a bomblet fell into the hole with him, well, Sparta would just need another heir to the Collins throne. He felt sick, a little lightheaded; part of him not believing this was real, a deeper part knowing it was and wanting to run away. Had it been this bad, swimming underwater to hijack the shuttle on Tanith? *No*, he decided. Then he had had one definite task to do, and Falkenberg waiting, and that had been very comforting. *Peter's a good man,* he told himself. *Good soldier. And now there are people looking for* you *to be their rock.*

A lot of the incoming barrage had fallen into the minefield. The enemy had expected to catch troops out in the open, not down in holes.

The rocket fire lifted, to be replaced almost instantly

by the whistle of mortar shells; continuous bombardments were luxuries for rich worlds with abundant mechanical transport. Lysander raised his head, automatically sorting through the messages passing through the audio circuits of his helmet. Casualties, more than he liked, but nothing like what there could have been if they'd been out there in the open.

"Shift the wounded to perimeter defense," he said on the company push. *Schoop.* A mortar firing, it might be up to a klick away. *Whunk.* A fountain of snow and vegetation and wet old earth bloomed ahead of him, in among the minefield. *Well, that's one way to clear a field. Let the enemy pound it. Bloody good thing we stopped the advance.*

Schoop. Schoop. Whunk. Whunk. The three eighty-two mm's of his own weapons platoon were back in action, firing to the direction of the Second's observers over to the left.

"Fire central," he said, switching to the interunit frequency. "I'm taking medium mortar fire. Counterfire needed."

Far above, points of light winked briefly; heavy mortar shells getting an extra kick at the top arch of their trajectory. Seconds later a heavy *crump . . . crump* echoed from the hills, mingling with the noise of explosions eight or ten thousand meters to the north, wherever the computers thought the rockets had come from.

"Sastri here." The battalion heavy-weapons company CO. "Can you observe the fall of shot?"

"That's negative, Fire Central."

"Not much point, then," the artillery officer said. "With passive sensors, there just isn't enough backtrack on mediums. If you can get drones over the target, let me know." A hint of impatience; the battalion heavy weapons were working hard to supress the enemy's area-bombardment weapons.

Schoop. Schoop. Schoop.

Lysander looked again to his left. "Patch to Colonel Owensford."

"Owensford here."

"Sir. Code JOSHUA, repeat Joshua." Owensford did not have to look up the meaning: "Permission to continue attack."

"Negative. DOVE HILL continues."

"Then give me some fire support! Some of those Thoth missiles—"

"Who's asking?"

"Kicker Six, sir, this is—"

"So long as it's not the Prince Royal, shut up and soldier. We'll know more in a few minutes."

"Aye aye, sir. Out."

Dig in. Dig in and wait, while they drop stuff on our heads. They're out there, Lysander thought. They're out there, those terrorist bastards, they're out there killing my brothers, and we could go kill them. Let me go get them, dammit. *Next time, by God, you just might be talking to the Prince Royal. . . .*

*   *   *

Lieutenant Deborah Lefkowitz frowned at the satellite photo as the engines of the tiltrotor transport built to their humming whirr. There was plenty of room inside, even with the sidescan radar and IR sensors and analysis computers the Legion had installed; this class of craft was originally designed as troop-transports for the CoDominium Marines, capable of carrying a full platoon a thousand kilometers in two hours. Room enough for the six equipment operators and her, and even a cot and coffee machine so that they could take turns on a long trip. The smell of burnt kerosene from the ceramic turbines gave an underlying tang to the warm ozone-tinted air.

That is an odd *snow formation*, she thought, calling up

a close-range 3-D screen of the picture. Down a ridgeline bare of trees, through a shallow valley where it vanished under forest cover, then starting up again three hundred meters south. Multiple sharp depressions the width of a man's hand and many meters long, running in pairs. It could be a trick of lighting, shadow played odd games when you were taking optical data through an atmosphere under high magnification. . . . She began to play with gain, then froze the image and rotated it.

Her round heavy-featured face frowned in puzzlement. *Mark it and send it back to the interpreters. But—*

Deborah Lefkowitz had been born on Dayan, a gentle world of many islands in warm seas. She had trained in photointerpretation as part of her National Service, and followed her husband into the Legion when he grew bored with peacetime soldiering on a planet too shrewd and too feared to have many enemies; he was on New Washington now, commanding an infantry company. Massaging computers was a good second-income job for her, perfectly compatible with looking after two young children. But these odd shapes in the snow tugged at some childhood memory. . . .

The aircraft was rolling forward, no reason for a fuel-expensive vertical lift here. As the wheels left the ground, Lefkowitz touched the communicator. There was a slight pause as the seeker locked on to the relay station in Dodona, and then the status light turned green.

"Commander Task Force Erwin, please."

"Owensford here."

"Major, I will be on target in thirty minutes. In the meantime, I have an anomaly in the last series of satellite photos. What look like . . . well, like ski tracks, sir."

"Ski tracks?"

"Cross-country skis." *That* had been the memory.

Jerry and she had spent their honeymoon at Dayan's only winter resort, on one of the subpolar islands. "Moving—" she paused to reference. "From a position three-fifty kilometers north northwest of your present location almost like an arrow towards you, stretching for ten kilometers or so, then vanishing."

Silence for a long moment. "How many? And how long ago?"

"Impossible to say how many, sir. Could be anything from one hundred up, or more if some sort of vehicle on ski-shaped runners was used. How long depends on snow conditions, wet snow freezing and then being covered by fresh falls . . . that could mean anytime since the first firm snowfall."

Her fingers danced over the console. "Say any time in the last three weeks. But, sir, even if they all went to ground every time the satellite came over the horizon . . . very difficult to conceal, sir. The IR scanners and the imaging radar are much less affected by vegetation, and anyway, the leaves are off the trees."

"If the satellites are giving us the real data, Lieutenant." Owensford's voice was harsh, and she felt a similar roughness in her own. On Tanith the Legion had fought rebel planters supported by the Bronson interests, and Bronson had suborned personnel in the governor's office, filtering the satellite data.

"But sir, we've had our own people in there from the day we landed! Senior Lieutenant Swenson went over it all with a fine-toothed comb; nobody's been allowed past those computers and we take the datadump right into our own equipment."

"Still, it's interesting, isn't it, Lieutenant? And those computers aren't ROM-programmed like ours. It'll be even more interesting when you get some direct confirmation. Meanwhile, I'm not real confident about those satellite pictures. Owensford out."

Lefkowitz looked up. The other's faces were bent over their equipment, underlit by the soft blue light of the display screens, but she could see the sheen of sweat on one face, the lips of another moving in prayer. They had been nibbling at the outskirts of the Dales for a month, even landing and planting sensors; so far, not a hint of enemy activity. Suddenly that seemed a good deal less comforting.

"Relay link," she said.

"Green," the radio technician replied; the tiltrotors had a feedback-aimed link with a blimp circling at five thousand meters over Dodona, ample to keep them in line of sight even when doing nape-of-the-earth flying.

"Set for continuous download, all scanners." Everything the instruments took in would be blipped back to headquarters in Dodona in real time. "Pilot," she said, "I really think we should stay low, perhaps?" Even though they were staying well short of the action, south below the horizon from Task Force Wingate, along the path it had marched.

"Ma'am," the flyer said. "Everyone strap in."

There was a flurry of activity as the technicians secured themselves and anything loose. Silence for long minutes; Lefkowitz caught herself stealing glances out the nearest port. Moonlight traced lighter streaks across dark ploughland and pasture, where the long windbreaks of cypress and eucalyptus caught and shaded snow. The last lights of the widely scattered farmhouses dropped away as they left the settled lands around the confluence of the Eurotas and Rhyndakos. The pilot brought the plane lower still, until the tallest trees blurred by underneath so closely that they would have hit the undercarriage if it had not been retracted. There were trees in plenty, then open grassland where sleeping beasts—she thought they were cattle but could not be sure—fled in bawling panic as the dark quiet shape flashed by. Swamp, where puddles of water cast wind-riffled reflections from stars and moon.

"Relay from Major Owensford. Column's under attack, rocket and mortar fire."

Then they were over hills, the ground rising steadily. More snow appeared, first in patches and then as continuous cover; the reflected light made the night seem brighter. Forest showed black against the open ground, as if the hills were lumpy white pillows rising out of dark water. The lights of the base on the Rhyndakos showed; the tiltrotor circled, then swung north toward the chain of firebases.

"Passive sensors only," Lefkowitz said. "Warm up the IR scanner." A bit of a misnomer, since it was a liquid-nitrogen cooled superconductor in large part. "Prepare for pop-up manouver. Location, pilot."

"Coming up parallel with Task Force Erwin's column of march, one-ten klicks south."

"Major Owensford, I'm making my first run. Stand by."

"Standing by, Lieutenant," the cool voice replied.

"Pilot, now."

Debbie Lefkowitz keyed her own screen into the IR sensor. It had fairly sophisticated electronics, enough to throw a realistic 3-D map and pre-separate anything not the natural temperature of rock or vegetation. Data was pouring into the craft from the sensors with the column and in the firebases along the route, free of the suspect satellite link that lay between the Dales and the Legion's analysis computers back in Fort Plataia.

"Major, you've got about . . . two thousand hostiles in your immediate vicinity," she said, as the machines correlated the fragmentary input. "Grid references follow." And relay this back to Swenson, now!

A machine beeped at her. She looked at it and her stomach clenched.

"Major, I've got multiple readings *south* of your position. South of *my* position. Readings all around," she said. *Calm,* she told herself sternly. This was certainly more hands-on than headquarters duty, but needs must. If the Royalist line of march was a bent I, the troops—they must be troops—were two parallel lines flanking it on either side, with another bar in the north closing the C. *This safe rear zone just became bandit country.* The enemy below *might* not have stinger missiles and detection gear, but they probably did. "Permission to conduct direct scan."

"South—" Owensford began, then snapped: "Denied. Get low and get *out* of there, and do it *now*."

"Sir." Gravity sagged her into the seat as the pilot turned for home and rammed the throttles to full.

"We're getting out of here soonest," she said on the cockpit link. "Might as well take a look while we're leaving. Prepare for pop-up. Stand by for sidescan."

The rotors screamed as the engine-pods at the ends of the wings tilted, changing the propellors' angle of attack. The aircraft jerked upward as if pulled by a rubber band stretching down from orbit.

"Scanning . . . down!"

Another freight-elevator drop. "Major, troops, at least two thousand down here heavy weapons probable category follows—"

Alarms squealed. "Detection, detection, multiples, frequency-hoppers—"

"*Jesus Christ missile signatures multiple launch—*"

The pilot's voice overrode it, shouting to his copilot: "Flares and chaff, flares and chaff! Those are Skyhawks!"

The *putputput* of the decoys coughing out of the slots was lost in the scream of the airframe as the pilot looped, twisted and dove almost in the same instant. The cabin whirled around her. For a moment they were upside down and flying in the opposite direction to their course two seconds ealier, and she could see two livid streaks of fire pass through the space she had been occupying. One struck trees and exploded in a globe of magenta fire as they began to turn, but the other did not. "Shit, shit, shit, *shit*," the pilot cursed.

The Lord our God, the Lord is One— Lefkowitz found herself praying, for the first time since girlhood. *Get the data stream out. Send everything we know. Nobody dies for nothing. Let them know what we saw.* Lights flashed as the computers dumped their data.

The tiltrotor was *below* the nape of the earth now, threading its way through narrow passages between trees and rocks, flipping from one wingtip to the other with insane daring as the pilot stretched the machine to its limits. Inspired flying, and very nearly enough; the missile was barely within effective radius when the idiot-savant brain that guided it sensed its fuel was nearly exhaused and detonated.

"Portside engine out, cutting fuel." The copilot's voice, metronome-steady. The aircraft lurched and turned sluggish, barely missed a hilltop.

"Starboard's losing power!" Both pilots' hands moved feverishly on the controls. "Something nicked the turbine casing, she's going to split. Shut it off, Mike, shut her *down*."

"I *can't*, we're too *low*—"

The plane surged upward, painfully, clawing for enough altitude to pick its landing-spot. The starboard engine's hum turned to a whining shriek that ended in an intolerable squeal of tortured synthetic and an explosion that sent the tiltrotor cartwheeling through the sky. Fragments of fiber-bound ceramic turbine blade sleeted through the walls of the aircraft, and lights and equipment shorted out in a flash of sparks and popping sounds and human screams, of fear or pain it was impossible to say. Lefkowitz felt something like a needle of cold fire rip down the length of one forearm.

They struck.

*   *   *

"The observation plane's down," Andy Lahr said. "Lefky bought us a lot of data. Still sending when she augured in."

"Dead?"

"Dunno. Went in from low altitude. Maybe not."

"What can we send to rescue her?" Owensford demanded.

"Not one damn thing. That area's crawling with hostiles. Which we know about only because of her, but they'll get to her long before we do."

"I see. Tell Mace. All right, let's see what she found out."

"It's a lot. One thing's certain, Major. The satellite data is thoroughly corrupted. We didn't get clue one of that force to the south, and it's far too damn big that we wouldn't have seen *something*."

"Right. Get me Jesus Alana."

"Alana here."

"Jesus, we've been snookered."

"Yes, sir, I'm following it."

"Got anything for me?"

"First cut analysis: your upper limit's blown away. The satellite hasn't been reporting properly, and we must ignore all its data. The conclusion is that we do not know what we're facing."

"How truly good," Owensford said. "What else?"

"They're trying for a giant Cannae."

"Hell, we knew that."

"Yes, sir, but they have more in place than you thought. We have been thoroughly deceived from the beginning. The satellite data were not merely incomplete, they were corrupted."

"How?"

"Someone is spending money like water," Alana said. "They have imported gear that we cannot afford, and people who can use it."

"People who didn't come off a BuReloc transport, that's for sure. OK, we have rich enemies off-planet. What do I do this morning? What's vulnerable?"

"The force to the south is not well organized," Alana said. "And they cannot be reliably in communication with their headquarters."

"Not in communication. But they're moving. So they're following a plan."

"Probably."

"OK. A giant Cannae, and they think it's working. I want to think about that. You flog hell out of the data and report when you have something. Out."

After the battle he'd have to send a report to Falkenberg. And a letter to Jerry Lefkowitz. But just now there were other things to worry about.

"Andy."

"Sir?"

"They want us to move into the jaws. We want them to think we're doing it. Have all the units out there keep up coded chatter, lots of message traffic." He typed furiously. "OPERATION RATFINK, VARIATION THREE. GET YOUR STAFF PEOPLE WORKING ON THAT."

* * *

"Senior Group Leader, we have confirmation, they're talking a lot," the headquarters comm sergeant said.

"Acknowledged." Niles grinned, and turned to the company commander. "Right on schedule. The Brotherhood troopers will be coming down there," Niles said quietly, pointing west and to his right as his left hand traced the line on the map. "Get as far upslope as you can, dig in, and hold them. You're going to be heavily outnumbered. Hold while you can, then pull out; but every minute counts."

"They'll have to come to us," the Company Leader said. "Can do, sir."

"Good man. Go to it."

That's G Company gone, the Englishman thought, as they headed into the trees.

A stiff price, but worth it. They had gambled heavily on Skilly's plan. Niles had argued that it was too complicated, and was ordered to stop being negative.

But it's working. It really is.

He had to trot to catch up with his headquarters

squad; nobody was stopping now. The three remaining companies of Icepick were moving at better than a fast walk, through the thick snow-laded brush of the swale between the two Royalist forces; you could do that, with a little advance preparation of the ground and a great deal of training. Already past the skirmish at the minefield; he could hear the crackle of small-arms fire half a kilometer away to his left.

God, I hope the rocket batteries are still up. Enough of them, at least; the Royalist counterbattery fire had been better than expected. At least they seemed to have run out of whatever they'd used to support the SAS teams, those horribly accurate rockets. . . .

Violet spheres of light floated across the sky. Six lines of three on the main First RSI position. Another six on the Brotherhood battalion to his right, that ought to give them something to think about. Six more on the unit off on the enemy's western flank. *They'll be out in the open. Should be taking heavy casualties, that will help George company.* Then the crump of mortars and the rattle of small arms; the better part of four companies of Helots putting in their attack on the flanking unit right on the heels of the bombardment. *One hour thirty minutes to the satellite*, he thought.

Group Icepick was nearly silent as it moved, only the crunch of feet through the snow and the hiss of the sleds. There were ten of those, each pulled by half a platoon, bending into their rope harnesses. The loads were covered by white sheeting that hid the lumpiness of mortars and heavy machineguns, recoilless rifles, boxes and crates. The men trotting silently through the forest undergrowth in platoon columns were heavily burdened as well, with loads of ammunition and rifle grenades, spare barrels and extra belts for the machine guns, light one-shot rockets in their fiberglass tubes, loops of det cord. They showed little strain and no confusion, only a hard intent concentration.

Well, Skilly was right, he thought; training to the point

just short of foundering them was the only way.

There was a sudden burst of small-arms fire and shouting from just ahead and to the left.

"Report!" he snapped.

"Sir, First platoon, E Company, Cit's comin' down off the ridge. 'Bout a platoon of 'em, we're engaging."

Rotten luck, he thought. Still, you couldn't expect the enemy to cooperate with the plan. *Act quickly.*

"Kolnikov," he said, keying his circuit to the E Company leader. "Detach First and Third to me, you're in charge, get Icepick where it's going and *fast*, then set up. Headquarters platoon," he continued to the men around him, "Signalers and techs, accompany Company Leader Kolnikov until I rejoin you. The rest of you, follow me. Move!"

He angled to the left and increased his pace to a pounding lope, all he could manage in this gravity with what he was carrying. The men followed, and all down the column the pace picked up as the orders were relayed. There were no cleared lanes through the brush upslope, but his men wormed through it quickly enough; visibility dropped to five meters or less, and stray rounds began clipping through the branches unpleasantly close. Grenades were going off, and he could hear the hiss of the light rockets the guerillas carried. A glance at his wrist.

0300. One hour twenty minutes.

"Sutchukil here," a voice said in his ear as he went to one knee and waved the others past him. "The enemy aircraft is down."

"Good," Niles said. Intelligence would be interested, and the "consultants" were as eager as their stoneface training allowed to get their hands on Falkenberg's electronics. A prisoner would be a bonus too, although Legion people were said to be very stubborn. *God, it's getting comfortable to think of fifteen things at once, I must be getting used to this business.* "Advise the nearest officer to send a patrol. Out."

*   *   *

"Wake her up."

A cold tingling over the surface of her skin, and Lieutenant Lefkowitz blinked her eyes open. She was lying against a packing crate, in a gully that was not quite a cave. There was a strip of faint light thirty meters up, where moonlight leaked through interlacing branches across the narrow slit in the stone, a little more from shaded blue-glow lanterns. Below the walls widened out, vanishing into darkness beyond. To her right the gully narrowed and made a dog-leg; that must be to the outside. Men were moving in and out; out with boxes and crates from the stacks along the walls—*skis and sleds, I knew it, that thing with the propellor must be a powered snowsled*—and on the other side of the cave she could see the cots and medical equipment of a forward aid-station. Nobody in it yet, the medics standing around watching or helping with the work.

The air was cold enough to make her painfully concious of the thinness of her khaki garrison uniform, and smelled of blood and medicines and gunoil and the mules stamping and snorting somewhere back in the darkness.

"She's awake." The voice was kneeling at her elbow; a woman in camouflage jacket and leather pants like all the rest she could see moving around, with corporal's stripes and a white capital M on the cuff. The shoulder flashes held nothing she recognized except a red = sign on a black circle.

"Fit to stand rigorous interrogation?" An officer, from his stance and sidearm; Asian, short and stocky-muscular. In the same uniform as the others, but without insignia, and he wore something that was either a long knife or a short sword in a curved laquered sheath at his side. She felt a slight chill as his eyes met hers. Complete disinterest, the way a tired man looked at flies.

The medic nodded. "Bruises, wrenched ankle, slight chill, no concussion," she said, as she packed her equipment and headed back to the tent with the wounded.

"Stand her up."

Hands gripped her and wrenched her to her feet; she bit the inside of her mouth to keep from crying out at the pain in her head. The enemy officer turned to a bank of communications equipment, an odd mixture of modern-looking modules and primitive locally manufactured boxes. *Very odd. None of the advanced equipment are models I could place.* Functions, yes, but not these plain black boxes without maker's marks or even the slightly bulky squared-off look of milspec. His hands skipped across a console, and a printer spat hardcopy. He held it up, looked at her, nodded and raised a microphone.

"Base One, Intelligence, Tetsuko, please."

There was a moment of silence; Debbie Lefkowitz used it to control her breathing, and the throbbing and dizziness in her head receded. Very faintly, the sound of explosions echoed in through the entrance and the opening overhead. The communicator chirped.

"Triphammer Base Beta, Yoshida here," he said. "We have a live survivor from the enemy surveillance plane; Lieutenant Deborah Lefkowitz, one of Falkenberg's people, recon interpretation specialist. Field Prime is with the advance element. Yes. Yes, sir, I'm sending all the equipment we salvaged in an hour or so with the next evacuation sled. Sir, I have no facilities or drugs for—yes, sir." The printer spat more paper with soundless speed, as the officer looked around.

"Sergeant Sikelianos," he called.

"Sir?"

"I don't have time to attend to this, and your guard

squad might as well be making themselves useful. Here's a list of information we need from this prisoner. Get it out of her, but she's got to be ready to travel in a couple of hours; Tetsuko wants to do a more thorough debriefing. See to it."

"Yes, *sir*." Sikelianos was a thickset man, you could tell that even through parka and armor, with a rifle slung muzzle-down across his back. Thick close-cropped beard and hair twisted into a braid down his neck, both blue-black. He was grinning, as well, showing white, even teeth with the slightly blueish sheen of implants.

"Remember Field Prime's Rule, Sikelianos. One chance."

"Yessir. Come on, you four."

The four soldiers—*armed men at least, if not soldiers*, she thought with contempt beneath her fear—tied her hands behind her back and hustled her into the dark area where the rock did meet overhead. Past a herd of mules within a rope corral, into echoing silence and chill; the cold was beginning to drain her resources, and she shivered slightly.

"OK, this is good enough," the guerilla noncom said. It was almost absolutely dark to her eyes; they would be using their nightsight goggles. Hands came out of nowhere and threw her back against the wall; she saw an explosion of colored lights behind closed lids. Then real light. Sikelianos had switched on a small hook-shaped flashlight dangling through a loop on his webbing belt. It underlit the men's faces, caught gleams from items of equipment slung about them.

"OK," Sikelianos said; he was smiling, and she could see him wet his lips behind the white puffing of his breath. "We got some questions for you, mercenary bitch. You going to answer?"

"Lieutenant Deborah Lefkowitz, Falkenberg's Mercenary Legion, 11A7732-ze-1 *uhhhh*." He had hit her under the breastbone, fast and very hard. She dropped to the ground, gagging and coughing as she struggled to draw air into paralyzed lungs. They waited until she was merely panting before drawing her up again.

"You going to answer the questions?" Sikelianos said, brushing his knuckles across his lips.

"Under the Mercenary Code and the Laws of War—"

This time the fist struck her almost lightly, so that she was able to keep erect by leaning against the rock. Again he waited; when she straightened up, he had drawn the knife worn hilt-down at his left shoulder. The blade was a dull black curve, but the edge caught the faint light of the shielded torch. His left hand held a pair of pliers. He laughed, putting the point of the knife under her chin; she could feel the skin part, it must be shaving-sharp. A tiny stab of pain, and the warmth of blood on her cold-roughened skin.

"You mercs and the Cits, you deserve each other." The knifepoint rose and she craned upward, head tilted back until the muscles creaked. "Now, by now even a stupid cunt like you ought to realize something. This is the Revolution, we're not playing no stinking game, and we got our *own* rules. Like, everything is either *them* or *us*, you understand? Other rules we sort of make up as we go along."

"But," he went on, "we do got a few real ironclad *laws*. Field Prime's Rule, that's one. You listening?" He leaned closer. "Outsiders get just *one chance* to cooperate. Savvy? You answer our questions, we take you back to the officer and you get a nice warm blanket and a safe trip to Base One, everything real nice, you can sit out the war in a cell. Maybe we even exchange you. You don't answer . . . well, you will. Up to you, smooth or rough."

"Lieutenant Deborah Lefkowitz, Falkenberg's Mercenary Legion, 11A7732-ze-1," she began. Then she closed her eyes and clamped her mouth tight as he gripped the collar of her jacket and slit it open down the front.

"Hey, Sarge," one of the guerillas laughed. "Goosebumps—maybe she likes it rough."

There was a shark's amusement in his voice. "I always got the pliers to fall back on."

Deborah Lefkowitz remained silent when a boot tripped her. She only began to scream when they stretched her legs wide and slashed the pants off her hips.

*   *   *

"*Goddamn it!*" Lysander swore to himself in quiet frustration, as the cry of *incoming* echoed across his position. The engineers stayed at their positions long enough to fire the breeching charges, stubby mortars that dragged lines of plastic tubing stuffed with explosives through the air across the minefield. Then they copied everyone else and dove for cover; many of them rolled under the bellies of the six armored cars that had come forward. The assault company of infantry had no such option, nor had there been time for it to dig in. They hugged the earth and prayed or cursed according to inclination; a few managed to roll into already occupied holes dug by the Scout company.

"Overshot," he murmured a moment later; there were mortar rounds falling on them, but the rockets . . . *on Peter*, he thought. *Well, he has those armored cans. . . .*

"Sir." The Legion helmet identified the speaker, Junior Lieutenant Halder, Fourth Platoon, the ones he had sent down to scout the woods. "We're engaged, ran into an enemy unit in the thick bush. They were moving south, sir, hard to tell how many, but they're loaded for bear. I'm getting heavy rifle grenade and antipersonnel rocket fire, sir."

"Calderon, switch the company mortars to support Third Command."

"Owensford here."

"Sir, Code—" he punched at the keyboard woven into his cuff. "Code ALGERNON, repeat Algernon. Code MOSEBY." Enemy forces in large but unknown strength west of my position.

"Copy. The land-line should be connected now; link to Sastri to call in fire support. Hurt them, Kicker Six, that's what you're out there for."

*   *   *

Another blast of shrapnel from the antipersonnel bomblets swept over the command caravan. *Goddamn it, I'm an infantryman, not a turtle*, Owensford thought. Although there was a certain comfort to having 20mm of hardened plate between you and unpleasantness.

Movement in the ravine. Hmmmm. Up north around Slater's column, the enemy had been using infiltration tactics down the wooded corridors. Potentially more of a problem here than there, since the proportion of forest was greater.

He looked at the map; squares were beginning to fill in for enemy units. The tiltrotor's sacrifice had been worth a lot; now they knew where to fly their drones, and they were getting more data.

So. What do we know?

The Fifty-first out on his flank had been hit hard, infantry attacks in strength right on the heels of the first bombardment; now they were gradually turning front as parties of the enemy tried to work around their rear. The Third on his left was moving east and north to cover the flank of his probe through the minefield, the Second on the far left was getting hit-and-run skirmishing and snipers and moving slowly to close up with the 3rd.

"Andy, link me up with Barton and Alana. Can we do that securely?"

"Sure can. Got a new fiber thread laid five minutes ago. Stand by one—got it."

"Ace. Jesus. Stand by to trade data sets." Peter slapped the function keys, and lights blinked. His map screens changed subtly.

"All right, Jesus," Peter said. "What are they trying to do?"

"It depends upon whether or not they are fools."

"What do you think?"

"Don't look like fools to me," Ace Barton said.

"They are not fools," Alana said. "Their plan is well executed. The problem is that they have not enough force to accomplish what clearly they believe they can do."

"Say that again."

"Colonel, they look to be trying to cut through to your base camp and destroy it. All their movements point to that. Yet they have not enough force to do it, and the result is that they expose themselves to attrition, and then to counterattack."

"First they build a pocket for you, now they stick their own dicks in the garbage grinder," Ace Barton said.

"Not fools but acting like fools."

"That's close enough," Alana said.

"Secret weapon, Jesus? Nukes?"

"It is a possible explanation."

"Damn high cost, using nukes," Peter said. "If anything would unite the CoDominium from the Grand Senate down to the NCO Clubs, that would do it. Ace, do you get the impression that things are not what they seem?"

"I sure do, Boss."

"OK," Peter said. "Here's what I'm seeing. We have three elements, two real attacks and a feint. The feint is left alone, the two real attacks are under fire within a few minutes of each other. Conclusions, Jesus?"

"Our plan, at least in outline, was known to the enemy."

"Sounds right," Barton said.

"Now they are committing major portions of their

strength in what appears to be a hopeless attack. It's not a feint, they're in too far for that already."

"Correct again," Alana said.

"All right. New mission for Task Force Wingate: fall back and regroup as mobile reserve. While they're doing that, Ace, you scramble your four companies in the hovertrucks, and get the Dodona militia moving too. I want reinforcements moving toward the Bridgehead Base *soonest*. That's where they're heading. But hang back, don't get in there and make a big target of yourselves. It's time we started playing this according to our own script."

"Aye aye. I don't like this secret weapon deal."

"Nor I. Jesus, put somebody smart to thinking about the situtation: what could they have that would justify what they're doing? Use drones as you need them. This is a priority one mission. Report as soon as you've got an idea."

"Aye, aye, sir."

"One thing," Ace Barton said. "We've learned something about the enemy commander."

"Yes?"

"Devious mind, Pete. Devious. Atlas out."

He paused for a second. *Right.* One damned thing after another, like a picador driving spikes under the hide of the bull. Nothing deadly, but designed to disorient and enrage, while the sword stayed hidden in the cloak . . . *or better still, a cat playing with a mouse.* There was an almost feline malice to the whole setup; whoever was in charge on the other side was inflicting damage for its own sake. He looked at the map again. *Particularly on the Brotherhoods.* Who were well-trained troops, but civilians-in-uniform, with families and communities that depended on them.

This is as much a terrorist operation as a battle, he thought, with a slight prickle at the back of his neck. You had to be a bit case-hardened to be a mercenary anyway, but. . . .

"Get me Morrentes." Back at the river base-camp.

"Colonel," the militia officer said. "Hear you're having problems. All quiet here, so far. No sign of the force the 'plane reported."

"Yes. I'm sending Lieutenant-Colonel Barton and the Legion companies up to join you," he said. "Possibly I'm being nervous, but I don't think so."

"I see, sir," the rancher said; his voice was slow and thoughtful.

"You're already dug in good," Owensford said. "Stay that way, but now I want you to be ready to move fast. I don't know what they have, but they're acting like it's going to turn the battle around for them. Like they can wipe you out with one blow."

"Nukes?"

"It sure looks like it, but we don't know," Peter said. "We just don't know."

CHAPTER TWELVE

Crofton's Essays and Lectures in Military History (2nd Edition)

Herr Doktor Professor Hans Dieter von und zu Holbach:
*Delivered at the Kriegsakademie, Koningsberg,
Planetary Republic of Friedland, October 2nd, 2090*

Since the development of the metallic cartridge, smokeless powder and the self-loading firearm, small-arms development has gone through a number of cycles. The original generation of magazine rifles were the result of a search for range and accuracy; they were bolt-action weapons, capable in skilled hands of accurate fire at up to several thousand meters. In the opening battles of the First War of AntiGerman Encirclement (1914–1918), the professional soldiers of the British Army delivered deadly fire at ranges well in excess of 1000 meters, at the rate of twelve aimed rounds per minute—leading the officers of the opposing Imperial German formations to suppose they were the targets of massed machine guns! By the 1930s, these bolt-action rifles were being replaced by self-loading models firing identical ammunition and of roughly comparable performance.

However, the mass slaughters and hastily trained mass conscript armies of the 20th century rendered the long-range accuracy of such weapons irrelevant. Studies indicated that virtually all infantry combat occurred at ranges of less than 800 meters, and that in any case most casualties were inflicted by crew-served weapons, particularly artillery. Accordingly, beginning with the Wehrmacht in 1942, most armies switched to small-calibre assault rifles capable of fully automatic fire but with effective ranges of as little as 500 meters; in effect, glorified machinepistols. For a few decades, it appeared that laser designators would provide an easy answer to the problem of accuracy, but as usual with technological solutions countermeasures limited their usefulness to specialist applications.

Two developments brought the return of the long-range semiautomatic infantry rifle. The first was the development of first kevlar and then the much more efficient nemourlon body-armor. Nemourlon armor of reasonable weight resists penetration by most fragments and any bullet that is not both reasonably heavy and fairly high-velocity. Since modern body-armor covers head, neck, torso and most of the limbs, experiment has proven that a cartridge of at least 7x55 mm is necessary for adequate penetration; such a round renders an infantry rifle of acceptable weight uncontrollable if used in a fully automatic mode. The second factor was the gradual decay of the mass, short-term conscript army, as small forces of highly trained professionals once more became common. Sufficient training-time for real marksmanship was available in these forces—thus increasing their advantage over less well-trained armies still more.

*   *   *

A belligerent with small regard for human life is far less sensitive to taking casualties than one accustomed to cherish life highly—-a factor that surely must enter into strategic calculations. The American practice of "body-counting" enemy casualties in the Vietnam War was mindless in innocently assuming that these deaths had a bearing on North Vietnamese capabilities and willpower.

The weight of burdens, up to some unknowable point, is relative, as anyone knows who has ever gazed at the statue in front of Boys' Town, Nebraska: One boy carrying another over the inscription "He ain't heavy, Father. He's my brother." What some consider burdens, for example digging ditches, others consider good sense and the chance to build good morale. Nor will it do to try to calculate the economic costs of each side's losses or efforts. Not only do people put different values on things, but more important, military goods are valuable not for the materials and labor that go into them, but for the strategic gains that can be got out of using them. No one in wartime has ever been struck by a piece of gross national product.

—Paul Seabury and Angelo Codevilla, *WAR: Ends and Means*

*   *   *

"Field Prime."

Skida Thibodeau woke as she usually did, reaching for the weapon resting beside her head.

"One hour, Field Prime," the orderly said, handing a cup of coffee in through the flap of her field shelter.

She took the cup and sat up, pushing aside the greatcloak and stamping her feet into her boots; all she had taken off was the footwear and the webbing gear and armor. Her eyes were sandy as she sipped. There had been a dream. . . . *Skilly was walking down a fancy marble staircase with Niles. Maybe Niles.* Whoever it was had been in a fancy uniform, and she had been wearing jewels and a sweeping gown. Trumpets blowing, and men and women in expensive clothes and uniforms bowing. The faces had been an odd mixture. The Spartan kings, and Belezian gang leaders she had known back a decade ago. The CoDo assignment clerk who had taken half her credits to get her to Sparta and tried to make her spread for him besides; the "uncle" who had raped her when she was ten. Those tourists who had made her smile for the camera before they'd give her the one-credit note. That was when she was a runner for Dimples, sixteen, no, seventeen years ago; odd she remembered it.

All the faces had been terrified; except Two-knife's and he was grinning at her in a formal suit with the machetes over his back, next to the *haciendado* woman she had promised, or threatened him with. The triumph had been sweet beyond belief. . . . Then the dream had changed, she was in an office that was somehow a bedroom and dining room too. Sitting at a table eating breakfast, with a huge pile of official-looking papers waiting beside the plate, all stamps and seals, while a nursemaid held up a baby that had her skin and hair and huge blue eyes like Niles, or her mother's.

Skilly's mind is telling her to get her ass in gear, she thought, as she buckled the webbing belt and rolled out of the shelter. *Dreams are fine for in-cen-tive.* The air was cold and full of mealy granular snow, flicking down out of a sky like wet concrete; the damp chill cut deeper than the hard cold that had settled over the northern Dales these past few weeks. Wind cuffed at her; it was still a little surprising occasionally, how much *push* the air on this planet had.

There was quiet stirring all through the spread-out guerilla camp, men rolling out of their shelter-halves—many had just lain down under them, exhausted by the trek—water cooking on buried stoves covered in improvised log blinds. Slightly risky, even in this steady light snow, but worth it for the boost; she had specified that everyone got a hot drink and something to eat before the action. High energy stuff, candy and sweets, coffee, caffeine pills for a few of the most groggy. Grins, salutes, an occasional thumbs-up greeted her.

They good bunch, she caught herself thinking, slightly startled. Then: *this isn't just like running a gang.* That was more like lion-taming, never knowing when they would turn on you. This trust stuff was infectious, like the clap. *Skilly will have to watch herself or she'll go soft.*

The command staff were waiting under a tarp stretched out from a fallen tree; these were dense woods, down at the edge of the Rhydankos floodplain, huge cottonwoods and oaks and magnolias. Skida walked toward the officers, chewing on a strip of jerky. The sort that the CoDo Marines called *monkey,* that swelled up in your mouth like rubber bands. She swallowed, followed it with a piece of hard candy, and looked at the situation map.

"Report," she said.

"We recovered a prisoner from the aircraft. She is resisting interrogation, but Yoshida reports the enemy have some warning of our location but no precise data."

"Hmm." That was an inconvenience; they would be watching, and there would be more losses from the base's tubes before they closed. Although the prisoner might be valuable later.

"Stragglers?" she continued.

"Fewer than ten percent," Sanjuki said; the Meijians were good at computerized lists. "I am surprised."

She nodded. "You doan understand how powerful a force the need to prove yourself be, mon." *Or think only Meijians can feel it.* "Can they fight?" she continued, to the unit commanders.

Nods, despite the brutal forced-march pace of the past week; they had all had a few hours rest by now, and there were the pills as a last resort. Amazing how it had not occurred to anybody that it was *easier* to move around the Dales in deep winter. Not to the Royals, although most of them came from the Valley where "winter" meant "mud." Nor to her guerillas, well, most of them were cityfolk, or from hot climates . . . she was from a tropical slum herself, but she read history. Russian history in this case: if Batu Khan could do it, why not Skida Thibodeau? Snow made it *much* easier to carry heavy equipment along, helping with the perennial dilemma of infantry; move slow and you missed the chance, move light and fast and you didn't have the stuff there when the shit came down.

She looked at the map, absorbing the latest changes. About as planned, except that the mercs seemed to have twigged faster than she hoped.

"OK," she said. "Up to now, we has been biff-baffing them—" she made a gesture, miming striking for one side of the face and then another "—because we knew exactly where they were and they couldn't find us. That about over after our next surprise. Then it just a matter of fighting, which they pretty good at when they know where to point the ends the bullets come out of. Ojinga, Raskolnikov." The two who were to attack the first firebase north, present by link rather than personally.

"Field Prime."

"You ready?"

"Green and go."

"Niles."

"Yes, Skilly?" he said, slightly breathless. She could here firing in the background.

"0400," Skida said. "Twenty minutes from . . . *mark*."

*   *   *

"Fuck, am I glad to see *you*, sir," the platoon leader said. He had a thin brown face, scarred by childhood malnutrition, desperate with worry now and bleeding from a light fragmentation wound on one cheek. There were slick-shiny scars across the nemourlon of his body armor and the battle-plastic of his helmet. "I got thirty percent casualties, more maybe, it hard to know, and these Cit cocksuckers can *fight*."

"So can we, platoon leader, so can we," Niles said. "Get your wounded out now."

A mortar shell exploded in the treetops twenty meters upslope, a bright flash through the night and *crack* and the top half of the tree toppled into the forest. They both ducked reflexively and then grinned at each other.

There was a furious close-range firefight going on in the brush just ahead and upslope, continuous automatic weapons fire, thud of grenades, the louder whut-*bang* of rifle-launched bombs, and an occasional *raaaaak*-thud of shoulder-launched rockets. Mortar shells from the Royalist forward positions were landing, beating a pathway through the forest canopy, the follow-up rounds exploding contact-fused on the floor below.

"Alexandro," he said, to one of the platoon leaders from Kolnikov's E company. "Reinforce the engaged platoon, but have your sappers start stringing improvs"—boobytraps rigged from munitions they were carrying, rockets and grenades —"right behind your line. Careful, eh? When we fall back, your people delay the pursuit while the engaged platoon passes through you and moves south. Martins," he went on to the other of Kolnikov's subordinates. "You come in on their left." From the south. "I'm going in on the other side. Hit hard, hit fast, then get the hell out when they reinforce."

He turned to the headquarters platoon around him; two dozen, spread out in small clumps. "Sergeant," he continued crisply, "deploy into skirmish line. We're going south and upslope, and be careful you don't get the end of the line visible from the top of the ridge. When I give the word, a volley of rifle grenades, then attack. Oh, and fix bayonets." A rattle as the blades went on, then another as the finned bombs were attached to the launcher clips built into the muzzles. "Follow me, *compadres!*"

                    *   *   *

"Sir, *sir!*" the desperate voice in Lysander's earphones said. He could hear the cause already, a fourfold increase in the firing to his left, down in the woods. "Sergeant Ruark here, Lieutenant Halder's dead, we lost the recoilless, they're coming in on both sides of us!"

"Steady, Brother," Lysander said, feeling an almost physical effort as he tried to pour strength down the circuit link. "Help's on the way. Call the positions. Weapons," he continued, "switch the rest of the mortars and the recoilless to support 4th. All headquarters rifle squads, prepare to move downslope. Company

Sergeant Hertzmeier, you're in charge here." He waited until the next stick of enemy mortars landed. "Let's go!"

"They told us to stay in place." Harv said.

"They told Captain Collins to stay in place," Lysander said. "Those are our Brothers down there!"

Harv grinned wolfishly. "Welcome back, Prince."

*   *   *

"Incoming!"

"For what we are about to receive, may the Lord make us truly thankful," the driver of the command caravan muttered.

What the hell *are they doing?* Peter Owensford thought, clanging the hatch shut as another volley of rockets came howling in. Only two batteries on his position now, the 160mm's had caught several, unmistakable seismic indications of secondary explosions.

"Andy, get me Jesus Alana."

"Stand by one—go."

"Jesus, what the hell are they doing?"

"I truly do not know, Colonel," Alana said. "They are sending a major force through the valley between you and the Third Brotherhood."

"Isn't that suicide?"

"It is suicide if they do not win big. Which is to say, they must expect to defeat the entire First Royal Infantry, plus the Brotherhood forces holding the river camp."

"And that's not going to happen. All right, Jesus, they think they've got something decisive. What? Nukes?"

"No, they have moved far too many troops far too close for that."

"Then what in the hell—" He was interruped by two close explosions that rattled the caravan.

"Hah."

"You have something, Jesus?"

"Yes, sir. As you ordered, I have been prodigal in

expenditures of drones. One has sent back photographs that show enemy troops, several hundred. Colonel, every one of them is carrying a gas mask. A few are wearing them."

"Gas mask. *Wearing* them?"

"Three men only. That we have seen."

"Three scared men. Gas masks. Chemical weapons. Poison gas. Is *that* what they're counting on?"

"Quien sabe? But it explains all the data we have."

"OK. Go look again while I think." An enemy willing to use poison gas. Prima facie violation of the Laws of War. You got hanged for using chemical weapons. Unless you won, of course.

The Helots expected to win. Expected to win big.

* * *

"Close in, close in, the bastid sumbitches can't mortar us if we close in!" the sergeant of Niles's headquarters squad was shouting.

Good advice, he thought sardonically, dashing forward to roll over a convenient log. Very convenient, and a Royalist machine gunner had thought so too; two of the crew sprawled around the weapon were dead or unconscious from the rifle grenade that had destroyed their position. The third was just rising; there was blood all down one leg, but his hands were steady on the machine pistol.

I'm bloody dead, Niles had time to think, before two massive impacts sledged him back sprawling against the log. Then the Royalist was twisting sideways against something that shouted and lunged behind a glint of metal. Too late, and the Helot's bayonet grated into his lower chest; nemourlon was excellent protection from fragments, moderate against blast and no good at all against cold steel. The return stroke with the rifle butt laid him out beside his comrades, and the rifle poised.

"No," Niles wheezed. "Don't kill him."

He looked around, fighting the savage pain when he

breathed, feeling at his stomach and chest. The covering of the armor was ripped, and he could feel the heat of the flattened disks of lead alloy embedded in it, digging into his skin where the tough material had dimpled inside as it came close to parting. One of his ribs might be—was—cracked, but the nemourlon had stopped both rounds. It was *supposed* to be proof against pistol-calibre, but that had been awfully close . . . *a good thing the local arms industry doesn't run to tungsten.*

"Sir, you all right?" the guerilla trooper said, flat on the ground and scanning upslope.

"Yes," Niles lied. "Here, pull the straps on my chest armor tighter. Lieutenant," he went on, touching the side of his helmet, "you have any prisoners?"

"Yeah, sir. Five anyways, all cut up pretty bad. You want I should slag 'em?"

"Negative!" Niles said sharply. *Not gentlemen at all*, he reminded himself. *But they're brave lads, and they can learn.* "I'm going to buy us a little time with them, Lieutenant. Pass the word to be ready to pull out sharpish." He looked over at the three wounded Royalists; two were still breathing. At his watch: 0410. "Man that machine gun, soldier," he said to the trooper who had saved him. It was the same type the Helots used, a Remington M-72 model 2050, and familiar enough.

"More Cits comin'!" from upslope, as the trooper wrestled the bipod-mounted weapon around.

CrashCrashCrashCrash of mortars, the soft coughing *thump* of a medium recoilless, followed by whirrrrrrr-*whomp!* as the shell landed and blasted dirt into the air uncomfortably close; a thirty-meter oak toppled back and downslope, rolling and bounding in the heavy pull of Sparta's gravity. A deep cheer, and firing. Niles touched his helmet in another combination, switching to a frequency the enemy used and broadcasting in clear.

"Royalist commander! White flag, parley!"

* * *

"Push 'em back, Brothers! Kings and Country!" Lysander shouted.

The line of RSI infantry was dodging forward; yelling like madmen and firing from the hip as they ran on the heels of their mortar fire. They were coming in on the south side of the trapped Royalist platoon, flanking the enemy flankers; well-aimed machine gun fire lashed out at the rescuers, but the forest made it impossible to keep much ground under fire. A trumpet sounded from the Royal Army line, high and sweet over the crackling of burning trees and brush.

"By squads," Lysander said. His automatic weapons were opening up, covering the short dashes of the infantrymen who then covered the forward movement of the machine gun teams. Grenades arched through the woods toward the rebels, the RSI troops taking advantage of their higher position on the hillside, white flashes that faded on nightsight goggles like blinking at the sun and then away. Suddenly it was the guerillas who were under fire from both sides.

"Royalist commander! White flag, parley!"

Lysander started violently, almost breaking stride. He went to cover with practiced skill.

"You want to surrender?" he said, switching to clear on the same band. The firefight grew in intensity as men blasted at each other from point-blank range.

"No, do you?" the voice said coolly; Lysander gritted his teeth in fury. Two of his men were dragging a third back upslope, and the wounded man's legs glistened black in the amplified light of the prince's face shield.

Recorder. Turn on the recorder, Lysander thought.

"Actually," the rebel continued—his voice was incongruously cultivated, a British accent like Melissa's grandfather—"I've got eight or ten of your men down here, badly wounded I'm afraid. Ten minutes truce to pull out our wounded, and you can have them back. This immediate area only, of course. One thousand meters radius from your position."

"Who's this?" he asked, playing out the scenarios in his mind.

"Senior Group Leader Graham, Spartan People's Liberation Army," the rebel said. "Who might you be?"

"It hardly matters." Lysander made hand signals. Continue the attack.

"It's their funeral. Your Brothers."

"No deal," Lysander said. "Harm my men and you'll hang, if you live that long." Switch to command channel. "Let's go kill that smug son of a bitch! Go, go—" He thumbed the command set again. "Get me the Colonel."

*   *   *

"All units, WIPERS, I say again, WIPERS," Owensford broadcast. "WIPERS, TRILOGY, WESTWOOD." Don protective equipment and prepare for chemical attack. All troops without protective gear withdraw from present positions. Fall back and regroup for counter attack.

"Andy, who's mobile with chemical protection?"

"Prince Royal's Own, sir."

"Where are they dug in?"

"On— They're not dug in. They're moving, in support of one of the Brotherhood units."

"Son of a bitch."

"You aren't surprised?"

"Should I be? Andy, make sure Collins acknowledges WIPERS, TRILOGY, WESTWOOD."

"Aye aye."

"Sparks, get me Morrentes."

"Morrentes." That line, at least, was secure.

"Sir."

"They're coming right at you, and it's clear they believe they'll win. We can't figure how unless they use gas, and so far as we can tell, every one of theirs has chemical protection gear."

"Holy shit, Colonel, most of my lads—"

"Right. So bug out, and now."

"Where to?"

"High ground. Group toward Barton's force. And don't get lost. We'll need you again."

"Well—Colonel are you sure about this?"

"No. If I'm wrong, I'll have let them sucker you out of a good position. That's not fatal. They may be able to raid your camp, but looting the baggage has got more than one army killed. You'll still outnumber them, and you'll be ready to counter attack. And if they are using gas, Major, if they are—"

"Yes, sir. OK, here I go."

"Barton."

"Right here, Boss."

"You been following this?"

"Better than that," Ace said. "I sent out a couple of my own drones. Jesus is right, they all got gas gear. A few have already put their masks on."

"Scared," Peter said. "Can't blame them. All right. They'll send in their gas, then what? Jump Morrentes's position, I'd guess."

"Me too. Devious mind, Colonel. Devious mind."

"It isn't going to work."

"Didn't say smart, said devious. Amateur's plan. Terrorists rehearse everything fifty times and think being prepared for friction and bad luck means you don't expect *everything* to go right. In the real world—"

"In the real world, no battle plan survives contact with the enemy," Peter said. Falkenberg's favorite military aphorism.

"Eggszactly. So I'm sending my chemical protected troops up to take good positions. When the rebels overrun Morrentes's camp, we pound hell out of them, then while they're figuring that out, we'll be in position to counterattack."

"That sounds right. I'll leave you to it, then. Hurt the bastards, Ace."

"I'll do that little thing. Out."

"Andy, get me Captain Mace."

"Mace here."

"How are your SAS units?"

"As you requested, I have four operational and standing by."

"Good. Jamey, they're about to bite off more than they can chew. When that happens they'll figure to fade off into the hills."

"Yes, sir—"

"So I want your SAS teams standing by to vector Thoth in on them when they run. Use what air transport we've got to inject those lads into good positions to cover retreat areas."

"Roger. Can do. Colonel, I have a problem. Miscowsky wants to go after Lieutenant Lefkowitz."

"Yeah, he's served with Jerry, that figures. What is that situation? Can Miscowsky's team do any good?"

"Colonel, I don't know, and that's a fact. We've got the crash site pinpointed, but there doesn't look to be anyone there. It's just damned hard to know."

"Assume she's alive. Which way will they take her if they break and run?"

"You really expect them to break, Skipper?"

"Good chance of it. They're gambling a lot on this gas attack. Or whatever they're aiming down my throat." Peter watched as his screens showed updates on the enemy positions. "And they're still at it, trying to run right down our throats like there's no tomorrow. Jamey, what the hell else could it be that would make them act like this?"

"Yeah. I expect you've hit on it. Suppose they stop and pull back now?"

"Let 'em. They've still got to run a gauntlet to get out of there. Jamey, use your own judgment on trying to rescue Lefkowitz." *Which means he'll send a team, of course.* "But have teams ready to pound on 'em when they run.

"Next. I want as many of your scouts as you can organize set up and ready to run in amongst them when they break. This battle is by God going to end with pursuit."

"Right on. I'll see what I can get ready."

"Andy, what communications are secure?"

"Everything local. If it's not on a fiber line, you'll hear the warning wail."

"Right. Thanks."

"And D Company reports contact."

Owensford nodded. That was the blocking force down in the ravine to the west, and now he would learn for sure why the enemy seemed bent on committing suicide.

"Put McLaren on." Another secure channel. The signals people all deserved medals.

"Captain McLaren here," a thickly accented voice said; from New Newfoundland, the island settlement in the Oinos Gulf. "There's a force of at least three companies comin' doon the valley at me, Colonel. They're carrying heavy weapons, but they'll nae get past if we get fire support."

"On its way, Captain," Owensford said. "Are you ready for chemical attack?"

"As ready as I'll ever be. The lads that hae the gear ha' put it oon, the rest hae moved back to hasty shelters."

"That *ought* to do it. We don't know what they have, or how much, but with luck it can't be *that much*."

"Luck goes both ways, Colonel. We're warned noo, the lads know which side of the turf goes up."

"Right. Captain, I don't mind if they get past you."

"Sir?"

"I want them to think they fought past you, but I don't want you taking casualties. When they move in, probably under cover of that gas attack, punish them as they go past, but mostly fall back on your reserves, regroup, and wait for the signal to counter attack. They're putting themselves into the bag, Captain, and I wouldn't want to stop them."

"I see. We'll be ready, then."

"Incoming," Sastri's voice said on the Heavy Weapons line. "New pattern. Incoming on *all* positions, single batteries to each of our battalions. Impact in thirty seconds."

"Looks like this is it, Captain. Godspeed."

"Sir, Morrentes calling, urgent."

"Owensford here." There was a faint but unmistakable background sound, a rising and falling wail: the line was radio line of sight, possibly secure, possibly not.

"Colonel, FAIROAK." Owensford whistled silently; *radars inoperative due to enemy antiradiation missiles*. "Ditto Firebase One, we've got movement all around. I'm lofting some of the Thoths, but there isn't enough target data to—"

"Gas!" An automatic alarm squeal, and then Sastri's voice screaming on the override push: "*GAS! ALL UNITS ARE UNDER GAS ATTACK, PROTECTIVE MEASURES IMMEDIATELY GAS GAS GAS!*"

"Morrentes here, the camp's under gas attack."

"Loft your birds high, then drop them onto your old camp, sector fiver," Owensford said. "That's where they'll be coming in."

"*GAS, GAS, GAS . . .*"

A long chilling scream from someone, that ended in retching coughs. Owensford's hands were moving in drilled reflex, as a ring of plastic popped loose around the base of his Legion-issue helmet. *Open* the armor at the neck *strip* it back *pull* the tab; a sudden hiss as the seal inflated tight to his skin and the lower rim of his faceplate. Strip the hypnospray out of its pocket in the fabric of his sleeve and press it to the neck below the seal; antidote, if it was a nerve agent.

But the Brotherhood troops and the RSI don't have Legion equipment. Except the Prince Royal's Own. And everyone has masks. It was still in the training. One reason gas wasn't used much. They have the masks, if they didn't ditch them as useless weight. Think of that as a way to weed out stupid troops. We had warning, not enough, but why am I surprised that terrorists use terror weapons? One thing for sure, they haven't any more experience with war gasses than we do.

"Command override," he said. That put him on the universal push. There was no emotion now; everything felt ice-clear. "All units, gas counter- measures." He turned to Captain Lahr. "OK, that's their big move. Stop them now, and we've won. Andy, make sure we preserve records of this. Make damned sure of that. I want evidence that will stand up in every hearing room from here to the Grand Senate."

*   *   *

"Now," Skilly said, looking at her watch. 0420. Her hand stabbed down, one finger extended.

The Meijian touched a control. The antiradiation missiles lept skyward and looped over down toward the Royalist river-base.

"Now," Skilly repeated. A second finger.

The sky lit with violet as the bombardment rockets drew their streaks across the sky. Two hundred meters above the earth they burst, and a colorless, odorless liquid volatized into gas and floated downward.

"Now." A third time. Nothing visible here, but hundreds of kilometers to the north another of Murasaki's technoninjas touched the controls before him. Two solid-fuel rockets leaped aloft and arched west as they rose; they were not capable of reaching orbital velocity, but more they had more than enough power to spew their loads of ballbearings into the path of the observation satellite. The steel would meet the orbiter at a combined velocity of better than sixteen thousand meters per second.

"Now." Fourth and last. From all around the Royalist base, men rose and rushed forward, even as the alarm klaxons wailed.

CHAPTER THIRTEEN

Crofton's Essays and Lectures in Military History (2nd Edition)

Herr Doktor Professor Hans Dieter von und zu Holbach:
*Delivered at the Kriegsakademie, Koningsberg,
Planetary Republic of Friedland, October 2nd, 2090.*

War among the interstellar colonies is a relatively new phenomenon, although civil disturbance is not. Only since the emergence of strongly independent planetary states in the 2060s has a new balance of power begun to manifest itself, with the traditional accompanying features: armaments races, offensive and defensive alliances, puppet governments and spheres of influence. This process is still incomplete, as the significant powers—Dayan, our own Friedland, Meiji, Xanadu—are still somewhat deterred by the enormous although declining and semi-paralytic power of Earth's CoDominium Fleet. Space combat remains an almost exclusively theoretical exercise. Ground warfare has been limited, with intervention in the disputes of worlds without unified planetary governments, or undergoing civil war, the characteristic form. The independent planets seek to defray the costs of raising armies and to gain combat experience by following the example of the autonomous mercenary formations and hiring out their elite troops; political influence often follows automatically, as in, for example, the close links now existing between the Republic of Friedland and the restored Carlist monarchy of Santiago on Thurstone.

As one consequence of this pattern, the significant armies

have continued to be small and usually based on voluntary recruitment, intended for deployment outside their native systems. The strong, industrialized and unified worlds have no use for mass armies, and the planets which need such have not the resources to maintain them. Thus reserves of trained manpower, and still more the organizational and social structures needed to support universal mobilization, have become virtually nonexistent. Some planets, of which Sparta is an excellent example, have attempted to raise well-trained and widely based militia systems. The primary weakness of this approach is the lack of standing forces, and hence of the infrastructure of higher command and administration; also, the lack of fighting experience, the only true method of testing the efficiency of a military system. . . .

*   *   *

We was rotten 'for we started—
  we was never disciplined;
We made it out a favor if an order was obeyed.
Yes, every little drummer 'ad 'is
  rights and wrongs to mind,
So we had to pay for teachin'—an' we paid!

There was thirty dead and wounded
  on the ground we wouldn't keep—
No, there wasn't more than twenty
  when the front began to go—
But Christ! along the line o' flight they
  cut us up like sheep,
An' that was all we gained by doin' so!

*   *   *

"Faster!" Niles hissed at the two guerillas who were supporting him on either side.

"Niles." Skilly's voice.

"Getting into position," he gasped. "Will be there."

"You'd better."

He could move, but there were limits on how fast a

man with a hairline rib fracture could run. The hypnospray was beginning to take effect, pain receding and the band around his chest loosening.

They had caught up with the bulk of the Icepick column; men were crouched next to their loads of explosive death, looking forward to the firing ahead at the enemy infantry's blocking position, or up to where the forty-kilo loads of the Royalist heavy mortars would drop on their heads from only three thousand meters away.

We're here. The cost had been high. All of his headquarters and special guards, dead or left behind to block that hard-nosed Spartan bastard who wouldn't parley. *Can't blame him, but it was worth a try.*

"Drill A, Drill A!" Niles gasped, over the command push. Maximum gain. *"DRILL A!"* His escort stopped, and he pulled open the throat of his own armor to seal the ring around his neck; the Helot senior commanders had offworld helmets with all the trimmings, for obvious reasons.

Stasis dissolved into action; nobody had explained why Drill A was practiced so often, but the movements were automatic. Helmet off. Pull the plastic bag out of its case on the belt, drag it over the head, yank the tab. Disconcerting how it plastered itself to the face and neck, but the areas that touched mouth and nose turned permeable instantly; permeable to air molecules, and nothing else. Helmet on . . . even the men probing with fire at the Royalist line ahead stopped the necessary few seconds. Or most did, from the way the sound dropped off for a few seconds, and anybody who didn't . . .

Rockets burst overhead; there were cries of alarm from the Helot columns, but no rain of bomblets followed.

. . . anybody who didn't, deserved what was about to happen to them.

"Kolnikov!" he snapped, as they came to the head of the column. "Hit them, hit them *now.*"

It was quiet ahead. All quiet. The gas must have acted more quickly than he thought. The Helots were already surging forward through the woods, their screams no less chilling for being muffled through their gas filters. Niles drove forward himself; the pain in his side was distant, he would pay for it later, no *time* to think of that. Past the enemy line, past gunners sprawled shot or bayonetted around their machine gun, helmets off and gas filters in their hands. Firing, screaming; the company behind him deploying and charging uphill, at right angles to the Royalist blockforce's position, rolling it up from the downslope flank, throwing them back toward the top of the ridge.

Grenades crumped and rifles chattered; he could see figures darting through the woods. Firing, falling; not all the enemy were down, the RSI's training was recent and the response to the gas alert quick . . . but it was enough. They were getting past the enemy. Losing troops, but they were getting past, moving faster now. . . .

"Keep moving, Kolnikov!" he said, turning from the fight and loping up to one of the sleds. The men pulling it were sprinting now, their breath harsh and rasping through the filters, faces red and contorted into gorgon-shapes. One stumbled and went down as a bullet punched into his side. His comrades ripped him free almost without breaking stride, and Niles snatched up the rope and put it over his shoulder.

"We're through, everyone move, this is *it*, *do* it, lads, go, go, *go*."

Ahead was the knoll where the weakest of the Brotherhood forces waited; the Eighteenth, the one that had been dropping off men for the firebases. Men and weapons . . .

"Go, go, go!" The sky screamed as the follow-on bombardment launched. He had lost a third of his frames to the Royalist counterbattery fire, but there were enough for these two targets.

The knoll lit with a surf-wall of flame.

* * *

"They're past us, Colonel," McLaren said. "I thank you for the warning. I've lost aye more o' my laddies than I like, but 'tis no what would hae happened if we hadna known."

"Can you see the enemy?"

"Aye, they're past and running up toward the Eighteenth's encampment."

"Excellent. Regroup and get ready to go kill them." Owensford switched channels. "Stand by to Flash Blue Peter Four," he said quietly.

"Standing by."

"Let me know when they go to ground, McLaren," Owensford said.

"Aye, that I will, Colonel. That I will, the murtherin' bastards."

"Warning."

"Go ahead, Guns."

"Colonel, incoming, our position and the Eighteenth's, *all* their batteries on those targets. Thirty seconds to impact." A second's pause. "Second launch. I should have better counterbattery after this, but we're going to be buttoned up in our holes until they run out of rockets." The mortar crews had no overhead protection, and the submunitions would slaughter them if they stood to their weapons.

"Right. Button up and stay buttoned. Andy, get me the Eighteenth."

"Eighteenth Brotherhood, Wilson."

"Wilson, they'll be battering hell out of your old position. Get down and stay down. When the bombardment's over, continue your withdrawal."

"Sir, we'd like to go after them."

"Negative. Your mission is to stay intact and stay alive. Just by existing you keep the bastards in the sack they put themselves in. They thought they'd fight through you. They don't know you're still organized and on their flank."

"Aye, aye, sir."

"Good man. Hang in there."

Whump Whump Whump Whump—the bursting charges of the rockets went on longer this time, much longer. The aching moment of comparative silence, and then the long roar of white noise. The sound of the wire shrapnel hitting the sides of the command car was like being inside a steel bucket that was being sandblasted. The seven tons of armor rocked back and forward as the bomblets cascaded off its hull.

A much louder explosion, and for a moment he thought the command van *would* turn over.

"Sastri here. We lost one of the one-sixty-mm's, something hit the ready ammunition in the pit with the tube," he said. A hint of real pain this time; like most gunners, the officer from Krishna loved his artillery pieces. "Priorities?"

"Stand by to flash the Eighteenth's former area. They'll learn in a minute that they aren't the only ones who can be clever."

"Sir, I have the Third Brotherhood on the push. Secure."

"Owensford here."

"Colonel, they—there was at least a company of them, we ran right into them while the gas attack was on, what shall I do?"

"*Stop* them," Owensford said. "You *know* where they are, you still outnumber them, just *stop* them. Don't let them through, and it won't be long. Henderson, I gather you went to their support. Report."

"Sir. Fifteen percent casualties."

"Gas situation?"

"We're all right. The Third Brotherhood took some heavy losses. Lot of them down, still alive."

"Leave 'em for the medics. If you don't hold that position, they'll all be dead anyway. Running away just gets you killed, you and everyone you left behind as well."

"Aye, aye, sir."

"Consolidate your present position, mop up those hostiles who are giving the Third trouble, then push directly south down the valley towards me, keeping the armored cars on your western flank as close to the forest as possible. Hit the force that's blocking McLaren, and roll in on the rear of the people attacking the Eighteenth Brotherhood's old encampment from the valley."

"Sir."

"Morrentes here, Colonel, the rebs are over the wire, they're over the wire, I've lost two of my observation outposts and Firebase One isn't reporting, they're using some sort of precision-guided light missile, laser or optical or something they're flying them right through the *firing slits* of our bunkers—"

"It's a damned good thing you're not in them, then. Calm down, Morrentes." Peter watched as data flowed into the map table. The scouts were doing their job, the river base was sending data. A wedge, right through the eastern perimeter of the base, driving straight for the CP and the artillery.

"You can't let them get the artillery, or we've all had it. I know we scattered your troops, now collect what you've got left and get ready to counterattack. Defend those guns. You're to hold them until Barton gets there. Less than an hour."

"Yes sir."

"Good man. Out. Ace?"

"On the river, Pete. They tried to stop us, but we had a surprise for them. ETA as per."

"Thank you."

More bomblets rattled against the command caravan. "The great thing," Peter said to no one in particular, "the great thing is not to lose your nerve."

The third wave of enemy rockets had stopped. The ridge outside was almost swept clean of snow, littered with dead men and mules—others were limping or running through the emplacement, adding their element of horror and chaos—but the flanking infantry companies were moving, deploying and heading south. There were figures moving and muzzle flashes all over the Eighteenth's former position. It was time.

*   *   *

Whunf. The 106mm recoilless gun crashed, igniting the brush behind it. The shell hammered up a gout of dirt two hundred meters ahead, and a platoon of Helot infantry threw themselves forward on the position.

"Keep moving, keep moving!" Niles said again; his throat was hoarse, but it was not safe yet to take off the gas filters; water seemed like a dream of paradise, and rancid sweat soaked his uniform inside the armor, chilling when it came into contact with the outside air.

He dashed forward himself. His troops were firing wildly, charging forward, in among the enemy bunkers—

No one was shooting back. The Royalists must have been stunned by the artillery bombardment.

"Kolnikov!"

"Platoon Leader ben Bella here, sir. Company Leader Kolnikov's dead."

Oh, sodding hell. He had been one of their CD men; only a Garrison Marine officer, but competent in a humorless Russian way.

"Are you in contact with Sickle elements?"

"Yes, sir. They're considerably disorganized, sir, the Fifty-first Brotherhood mauled them pretty bad before they withdrew."

"Well, *get* them organized, man!"

CRUMP. Shockwave, another, like hammer blows. Downslope a dozen more tall flowers of dirt with sparls of fire blossoming at their hearts. The enemy 160mm's were back in action—astonishing, with the intensity of the bombardment they'd just gone through—*and that used up the last of our rocket ammunition. Bloody hell.*

The last Helot elements burst out of the wood, a wave a hundred men strong. Niles grinned to himself; it was the right time, but also an interesting way to get men to advance—have the enemy shell them into it.

"INCOMING!"

The troops ran to the enemy bunkers.

"Fuck all, there's nobody here!"

"Empty! No bodies, nothing!"

"INCOMING!"

"Take cover!"

Niles ran toward the nearest bunker, then stopped. "Stay out of those bunkers!" he screamed. "Stay out, it's a trap, it's a trap!" Too late. His men were diving into the bunkers as the enemy artillery came in.

He dove to the ground and tried to make himself small, as bomblets and VT fell around him.

Empty bunkers. Royalist artillery registered on this position, ready to fire as soon as he got here. They'd known he was coming, and that meant that the bunkers—

A bunker ten yards to his left exploded in fire. Then another. And another.

Mines. Command detonated mines. The artillery bombardment continued, as one by one the bunkers exploded in fire and white phosphorus, and Niles's command disintegrated.

*   *   *

Skida Thibodeau dodged behind a lacework of fallen trees and turned her binoculars on the main enemy base down below at the river. Floating curves of fire reached out towards her. While Icepick fought its way through the valley, the headquarters guards units had moved parallel to them. At the last moment she came in from the North in the only helicopter available, flying low to the ground, a terrifying experience but it wasn't likely the distracted enemy would spot the machine before it dropped her off and went back to the base camp.

The Spartan river base was a semicircle backed on the river, lit like day now by burning timber, smashed wagons, the fires from the barges anchored by the shattered piers. Lights sparkled all around the perimeter of it, bulging inward here and there, bulging in furthest from the west, a wedge cut out of the half-pie. The wedge sent out licks of fire, flame-thrower fire, to the strongpoints holding out in its path. Just beyond the point of the wedge longer flashes sparked, mortars firing to support the Royalists.

Suddenly fire fell into the wedge. The men dodged into bunkers, into holes—

The bunkers began to explode one by one, killing her troops.

Kali eat they eyes, it not working, she thought disgustedly. The Helots had been relying on overrunning the base while the defenders were still reacting to the gas attack. Something had gone wrong. The Brotherhood fighters had recovered too fast and were dying too hard; the Helots did not have the weight of numbers or metal to overcome the stiffening resistance.

Or worse. *How did they know we coming? Traitors! Royals must have spies in the Helots, spies, how else could they know? It was a good plan, can't go wrong, must be spies.*

Suddenly the Royals were on the move. The big unit on the ridge above, the one that Icepick had fought past, it wasn't killed at all, and now it was coming down the hill to close the trap.

There was gunfire behind her. The Royals were moving in that way, too! *One more push.* It was a good plan, too good to give up now, just because a few things went wrong. Something always goes wrong.

She swept her binoculars around the hill. Aha! "They got observation from up there," she muttered.

It was the last of the river base's outposts, the last one holding out.

"Follow me!" she shouted. The reserve company advanced behind her. The fire from the observation base was still heavy, and she found the attack squads grouped in the last cover, huddling against the timber and rock. She rolled into the biggest hollow.

"Who's in charge here?" she said.

"F-f-field Prime!" A boy, looking pathetically young, none of the street-tough now. "I am, Field Prime, at least, Group Leader Metaxzas is dead. Platoon Leader Swaggart, ma'am."

"OK, Swaggart. Keep calm, fill me in."

Tears of frustration glistened in his eyes, but his mouth snarled. "They . . . it was so *close*, we got the gatling out with the flamethrower and started to pile in, then a mortar round hit right behind Group Leader and they came back at us, pushed us back over the wire. We tried, we really did, Field Prime."

"Skilly know, boy. Quiet." They certainly had; half the reinforced company sent to take this position looked to be out there, hanging on the wire or scattered in front of the Royalist firing positions. Strong positions, with good overhead log-and-earth cover.

She looked up the slope; the gatling was still dead, but there were functioning machine guns in the two bunkers flanking it. The covering wire had been blown with bangalore torpedoes, long tubes of explosives pushed in under it, but there might be live directional mines. *No help for it*, she said, taking a long breath. *Starting out, you knew it come to this.*

"Weapons," she said. The Meijian answered.

"Sanjuki here."

"You got those mortars silenced yet?"

As if in answer, a bright light arched through the sky from the east; it seemed to hesitate and then plunged down toward the burning chaos of the river base.

Lauched from a stubby melted-looking automatic mortar, and guided by a fiber-optic cable. There was a tiny Tri-V camera in the nose, but only fractions of a second to guide it in.

"One more down. They have excellent overhead protection, Field Prime, and only open their firing slits for a few seconds."

She gritted her teeth; Skida Thibodeau had always hated excuses. You did it, that was all.

"Field Two, how it going?"

"Hard work, Skilly." Two-knife's gravel voice. "We killing them, but the *rabiblanco's* not giving up much."

"Keep at it, I get their eyes off you." Back to the Meijian. "Fire mission, ring Base One," she said.

"Yes, Field Prime—that is very close to your position—"

"*Skilly know!* Skilly says do it, and *now!*"

"All right," she continued, switching to local push. "Skilly is here, *compadres*. What you all waiting for, the Cits to send you enough lead you can open a bullet factory? This way up!"

The rockets crashed down, and the air filled with steel. "Follow me!"

*   *   *

"Urrgk."

Private Brother Pyrrhos McKenzie spat, coughed, spat again. The fluid from his lungs seemed to be about half blood and half thick clear *something* that he didn't want to think about. Everyone else in the bunker was dead, he thought—Ken when the gas came, and Leontes with a bullet through the face in the last attack. He hung over the grips of the gatling, blood and brains from the wound and the inside of his helmet still leaking down on the metal; it sizzled, the breech-ring hot enough to fry the matter that slimed it into a hard crust.

Glad I can't smell, McKenzie thought. The radio was

squawking, but there was no time to listen to that. Breathe. Deep bubbling sounds, like air going through a coffee maker. Cough, and his mouth filled with the heavy salt warmth. Spit. A little better on the next breath. Up. Impossible to stand, haul yourself up handover . . . handoverhand. Gasping, he stumbled two steps to the firing slit and collapsed over the weapon, knocking the other militiaman's body off it.

"Sorry, Leo," he wheezed; that was a mistake, he went into another coughing fit and something in his chest felt like a hot knitting needle. *Only right.* Leo and he had been ephebes together, candidates for the Phraetrie. He was going to marry Leo's sister Antigone when they both turned twenty-three. The coughing went on a long time, but he felt a little better afterwards, though, and blinked his eyes clear while his hands fumbled at the grips of the gatling. Took up the slack on the spade grips, and the electric motor whined, spinning the barrels with blurring speed. His thumbs rested on the firing buttons on top of the grips.

God, there's a lot of them. Crawling towards him, but he was nearly level with the ground here. Lots of dead people out there, dead mules and horses, the gas had gotten them. Burning stuff, crates.

He depressed the muzzles, stroked the buttons. *Brrrrrrrt. Brrrrrrt.* The recoil surged in his arms, and he coughed again; the liquid spurted out of his mouth and hit the barrels, spraying. Rebels dropped, killed, sawn in half by the fire. The enemy scattered, rolling out of his line of fire; he walked the bursts over crates, bodies, anything that might give cover. Wood and flesh and mud exploded away from the solid streams of heavy 15mm rounds, bullets that would punch right through a mule. One hundred rounds a second, and there was a *big* bin of ammunition right there beneath the firing step.

Brrrrrt. They were shouting out there, or screaming or something. Trying to crawl closer. Closer to him and

Leo, closer to Antigone and mom. *Brrrrrrt.*

Leonidas. Megistias. Dieneces. The heroes of Thermopylae, he'd been a little bored learning that in school. *I suppose they didn't want to die either*, he thought with a sudden cold lucidity; his knees felt weaker, and the corners of his mouth were leaking. *Alpheus. Maro. Eurytus.*

Another burst. Another, swinging wide to cover the full arc of the bunker's semicircular firing slit, there ought to be a couple of automatic riflemen in support. More rebels down, others trying to crawl backward, some dragging their wounded.

Demaratus the lesser. Deonates—

*   *   *

Skida slumped to the ground, panting. The ground under her heaved slightly as the satchel charge they had thrown into the last bunker went off; flame shot out the firing slits all around.

"OK," she croaked, as much to herself as to the survivors, and used her rifle to push herself up to her knees; the wound in the leg was not too bad, just a gouge out of the muscle really. Bullets were cracking by overhead, so she crawled to the edge of the sandbags, rolled over onto the ground.

That put her next to Platoon Leader Swaggart; on an impulse she reached out to close his eyes, then surprised herself even more by bending to kiss his brow.

Shit, she thought. *Maybe Skilly should have stayed in hidehunting and hijacking.*

"Intercept one," she said, paused to swill out her mouth from her canteen. "Field Prime here. Report."

"They got past us."

"*What?*"

"They had a fucking six-tube *rocket launcher* under tarps on all the hovertruck roofs, Field Prime! As soon as we opened up they all turned and let us have it, my company is *dead* and we lost both the recoillesses! I got maybe ten effectives left."

"OK," Skida said. *Think, bitch.* She looked down at the base. "Shit again," she mumbled.

The wedge below was a sheet of fire, white phosophorus and blown bunkers. They weren't going to overrrun the Brotherhood artillery positions. Some of the other penetrations had made progress, but even as she looked tiny figures surged out of the headquarters bunkers and struck the extending flank.

Why? Traitors, it had to be. Someone back at headquarters, knowing she was coming in here, someone who wanted her dead, someone who wanted to take over the Movement, that must be it, and now the Royals were moving. *Shit, pretty soon they trap us all!* It was hard to think.

"OK, Intercept One, pull back to rendevous." At the firebase they had overrun, the first one north of here.

"Pull back with what? To what? Dis de Revo*lution*! Fuck the Revolution!"

Her phones went dead.

She changed channels. "Field Two."

"Field Two's down," a voice answered her. "Senior Group Leader Mendoza here. Orders, ma'am?" Mendoza sounded so tired he had almost stopped caring. For a moment Skida did as well.

"*He dead?*" she cried, voice almost shrill. *Two-knife?*

"No, hit pretty bad. We're carrying him." Desperation. "Orders, *please.*"

No one to talk to. Can't tell this one it's over, time to bug. Skida raised a fist and hammered it into the wound on her leg, using the savage pain to drive her mind back into action.

"Right," she said coolly. "Consolidate, throw back that counterattack. Dig in, put in supressing fire, get your wounded out. I gives fire-control over to you. Sanjuki, got that? Including you special stuff. And get those mortars hopping. All assault leaders," she continued. "Anyone about to break through?"

Silence.

"OK, Plan Beta, prepare. The relief force made it and they going be here soon." *About ten minutes. That fast thinking, those rockets. Skilly must see that officer has an accident.* "All elements on the east side of the perimeter, Field Prime authorize tactical withdrawal." Bug out. Run. Live to fight another day. "Time to talk."

She touched a preselected sequence on her helmet, one that would blurr her voice.

*   *   *

"Colonel, I have a message," Andy Lahr said. "Claims to be the Helot supreme commander."

"Hah." His command caravan was hull-down, two klicks from the former position of the Eighteenth. Forty-kilo shells from the heavy mortars were passed overhead and fell into the Helot positions. The armored cars were coming up in support.

The only thing they have left is their artillery, and they're pretty well out of rockets for that. "Where's the signal coming from?"

"Up on the ridge, where they overran the Brotherhood outpost."

"Hah. Get me Mace."

"Scouts, Captain Mace."

"Jamey, have a hard look at Ridge 503. Figure out how you'd retreat from there toward the enemy artillery base. Put one of your best SAS teams in a good position, and stand by weapons. I think they'll have targets to designate soon enough. And watch for vehicles, someone claiming to be their top leader is up there and they may send something for him."

"You got it."

"Andy, when we put the rebel commander on, I want you to listen. Patch Barton in too. Private comments to me if indicated."

"Yes, sir. Helot field commander, I have the Colonel. Go ahead."

A woman's voice answered, astonishingly enough. Blurred by an antivoiceprint device, otherwise a clear contralto with a lilting Caribbean accent.

"This Spartan Liberation Army Field Prime, proposin' a mutual withdrawal under terms, with temporary armistice," she said.

Owensford felt his lips turn in a snarl. "Interesting. What are you offering in exchange for letting you getting away?"

A laugh, cool and amused. "You can't stop us, merc. We get out of here when we want. Look, up there, we gots forces north and south of you. You attack one way, we come the other."

"I see." Peter thumbed the command set. "Get a good fix on that position, and tell Jamey to get his scouts moving."

"And you come both north and south, and we bugs out," she said reasonably. "One part of the Dales just about like another to us, mon. We got enough firepower left to keep you heads down while we be going, too. And you notice something? All your mules be dead, mon. No transport, nohows; hell, you goan have to *hunt* for the *pot*. You got visual from your river base?"

"Yes," he said, switching on a screen with an overhead view.

"Watch this. See the second mortar on the right?"

A few seconds later something like a very quick firefly darted into the spyeye's view, did a double loop and slammed neatly into the steel cover over the mortar's hatch.

"These things got a range of better than thirty klicks," the voice went on. "So you relief force not going to land here. Gots to land downstream, *fight* they way through thick woods we holding and have mined, by the time they get here we gone. You want to chase us through the woods, booby traps and ambush for a thousand klicks? All right with me, mon. No satellites for you, now, either."

"Thank you," Sastri said on the private channel. "We have located the source of that rocket. Out of our range, I fear. I will notify Captain Mace."

"Another thing," the rebel leader said. "We got, oh, two-fifty prisoners up there, another eighty-so in your Firebase One we overrun, and here at the *river*. You don't agree, we kill them all."

"Typical," Jesus Alana said. Hah, Owensford thought. Andy must have the entire staff listening to this. Good.

"Typical terrorists," Alana continued. "When things go wrong they threaten hostages."

"I will hold you personally responsible for any violation of the Laws of War," Peter Owensford said.

Laughter. "Responsible? Mon, me head in a noose already if we lose! What you do, hang me twice? This no gentlemon war, dis de Revo*lut*ion. All or nothing.

"Too, we figure you got maybe fifteen percent casualties, lots of gas-wounded what die if they doan get regenn soon. We run away, you kill a few more of us, but not much left of pretty-mon army, hey?"

"I'm listening."

"You talk sensible, we let you fly them out."

That could be crucial; the time between injury and treatment was the single most important factor in survival rates. Particularly for the ones with lungs burned by the desiccants.

"Field Prime moves a company or so out into the open, they hostages. Doan expect you to trust we. You wounded, they *me* hostages."

Owensford changed channels. "Get me Kicker Six. Fast." He switched back. "I don't have authority to make deals with you. I'll have to get a political leader."

"Mon you damn well better hurry doin' it."

"That's as may be," Owensford said. "But until I get political authorization, the answer to your request is no."

"How long it take?"

"Depends on my communications," Owensford said.

"I give you fifteen minutes. Then no deal. I call you back."

* * *

"Headquarters calling, Prince," Harv said. He held out the handset.

I don't have time, there are a million things happening all at once and I can't keep track of them— He took the instrument. "Kicker Six here."

"I need to speak to Prince Lysander."

"Sir?"

"Political decision time," Owensford said. "The enemy is offering a truce. The bait is about four hundred Brotherhood soldiers, plus letting us fly out the wounded. They'll release their hostages in exchange for a cease-fire. Otherwise they kill them."

"Will—will they do that?"

"They're terrorists. Of course they will."

"What do we lose if we take them up on it?" Lysander asked.

"Pursuit. I've got the SAS teams moving into place, and a new supply of Thoth. We have an overextended enemy, nearly exhausted, with their elite forces strung out in exposed places. They claim they can always get more troops, but that's exactly what they can't do. It takes *time* to train fanatics out of the illiterates they start with. We're the ones who can turn Citizens into soldiers in short order."

"Four hundred Brothers."

"Or Candidates. About half in half would be my guess. If they have that many. They may be lying."

"But you don't know."

"No. Our communications haven't been that good. The figure is possible." Owensford paused. "I'm more concerned about our wounded. Some were gassed.

They'll survive with prompt treatment, otherwise not."

"What would you do if they were your troops?" Lysander asked.

"I don't have to say. Every mercenary hates decisions like that. Our troops are our capital."

"What is it, Prince?" Harv demanded. "What's wrong?"

Lysander shook him off. "Colonel, you don't have to decide, but you do have to advise me. What would you do?"

"I'd win the battle. Every one of their elites we let get away is a new hero, someone to train more. But there's something else. Our troops are exhausted. I can harass the enemy as he pulls out, but what we really need is to break past their rear guards and have a real pursuit. That means more hard fighting, maybe desperate fighting. More casualties, maybe a lot more casualties, and the way the troops are placed, most of that will fall on Spartans. Not just regulars, the Brotherhood militia. I can't kid you, if we refuse the truce you'll lose men. The hostages, lots of the wounded, and more."

Lysander swallowed hard. He could hear the fighting around him. The Prince Royal's Own were still moving forward, slowed now, but still moving.

"They planned it this way," Lysander said.

"Something like that," Owensford agreed. "They had their plan, this elaborate scheme to destroy us. When that didn't work they thought to try this."

"We lose a lot if we turn them down," Lysander said. "And our men are tired too." He felt as if his head had been filled with cotton batting, then set on fire. Mostly he wanted to lie down and sleep. "Will they fight if we do? Will the Legion support us?"

"Yes."

Yes. Not maybe. No hesitation, no excuses. Yes. Lysander looked around the command post. Men dead and dying, but men doing their jobs too. And outside. Troops fought. Fought and died, but every one of them, alive or dead, was facing the enemy. He looked at Harv, who stood relaxed, but eager to move on.

Well, at least one of them will follow me. And every one of those bastards we kill now is one fewer to kill our women and children, raid our ranches— And then he knew.

"Colonel Owensford, please patch me through to the Helot commander. When I have finished speaking with him, I would be pleased if you would connect me to the command link so that I can address the troops directly."

"Aye aye. The enemy commander is a woman. May I and my staff listen in on your conversation with the Helots? We can make private comments on channel B if you like."

"Please do."

"Stand by—" There were clicks in the earphones. A voice spoke in his left ear. "This is the private channel. They won't hear anything said here." Then, "Go ahead."

"Hello. With whom am I speaking?" Lysander said.

"Dis de Helot Supreme Commander. I figure who you must be if Colonel has to ask your permission to wipe his ass."

"This is Crown Prince Lysander Collins."

"Well, smell you. Dis de Revolution. You want to join it, Baby Prince?"

"I am told you wish to negotiate."

"Truce. Evacuate wounded. Exchange prisoners."

"No."

There was a long pause, then laughter. "OK, you keep my prisoners, I give you back yours. You stay in place, I pull out of here with whoever can walk. You send medics after your wounded, take care of mine."

"I will say this once. There will be no truce. I am willing to proclaim a general amnesty, provided that all of you lay down your arms immediately and surrender. The amnesty will cover all enlisted

personnel including war crimes committed if acting
under orders. Excepted from the amnesty will be
commissioned officers accused of war crimes. They will
stand trial for those crimes. You have two minutes to
consider this offer."

*   *   *

Shit he one hard nosed bastard. Skilly looked around at the
remains of her command. Down by the river the wedge
was shrinking as she watched. Not much left there. On
the ridge opposite a whole new Royal force, one that was
supposed to have been wiped out, was forming up.

Her own forces were scattered across the Valley,
exhausted and out of communications for the most
part. There would be very little new fire support.

Not much time left. Not much time at all. She tried to
keep the mocking tone in her voice when she
answered the Prince, but deep in her throat was a
tightness. This wasn't working at all well.

*And back at the base is a traitor I have to kill, kill for me,
and Two-knife, and all these kids.* She thumbed off the
microphone. "You two, get ready to move out. We
going out of here fast and light. The rest of you, dig in,
dig in and fight. I go get more troops, I come back for
you." She cleared her throat and thumbed the
microphone on again.

*   *   *

Mocking laughter sounded in Lysander's headset.
"That no offer at all. Prince, you don' take this truce, I
cut de throats. With pictures. Lots of pretty pictures
for de TV stations, they be happy to show all your Cits
what you make happen."

"Typical," Jesus Alana said in his left ear. "Typical
terrorist. 'Look what you made me do.' Keep her
talking, Highness. They like to talk."

"If you do not accept the amnesty, then all of your
people will be dealt with as traitors," Lysander said.

"They already traitors to your government. You goin' punish them for what I do?" A chuckle. "You stallin' me. You ain't goin' to leave all these Brotherhood babies to die. Some of them coughin' their lungs up now, they going to drown in they own snot, and it's all your fault. Come on, let's stop this fight and take care of these people."

A tempting offer.

"Keep her talking," Alana repeated urgently.

"What do you want?"

"General amnesty. Forgive and forget. Peace, the war is over. We all goes home."

"So you can start killing ranchers again next week. No thank you. Lay down your arms and I will spare the lives of all your troops, and your officers."

"I notice you doan say you let ME go. Listen to this." There was a long burbling scream. "I hope you hear that all your life, that what you done to your brotherhoods."

"Make your decision. Accept amnesty or we will hunt you down and kill you."

"You done killed your people," the voice said. "And that *all* you kill." The phones went dead.

And that's that. He tried not to think about the dead and dying. *But it's cowardly not to think about them. I don't want more of this. I didn't ask to be born Prince of Sparta.*

Leonidas didn't ask to be born king, either. The Three Hundred didn't ask to go to the Hot Gates.

He thumbed the microphone button. "Give me all units.

There was a short pause. "You got it. Want me to announce you?"

"If you please."

"All units, stand by. Crown Prince Lysander Collins will speak."

"Brothers. Brothers and Legionnaires, brothers and sisters all. This is not a speech. I don't know how to make great speeches, and I'm too tired even if I did."

"I just want to say that you've won a great victory,

and I'm proud of you all, but the day isn't over. The enemy still lives. Now they want to run away, to hide in their caves so they can creep out and kill and maim and destroy. It's all they know. We see what they do and we say that's inhuman. Brothers and sisters! It is inhuman. They do inhuman acts because they are no longer humans themselves!

"For every one of them you kill today you will save the life of a Spartan, of a dozen Spartans.

"You've beaten them, thrown back the best they have, beaten them despite their poison gas and terror weapons. They are beaten as an army. We have a glorious victory—but they are not all dead. Too many live, and while they live they threaten our homes. Every one of them killed is a victory. Every one that escapes is a defeat for us.

"The way will be hard. My advisors tell me we will lose as many of our Brothers and Sisters in this pursuit as we have lost in the battle—but we will win, we can destroy them utterly.

"We have beaten them in war. Now we must hunt them down and kill them. Kill them like the wolves they are. For our homes. For our country. Kill them."

Lysander set down the microphone. There was silence for a moment, then sound, a swelling of sound, sound that drowned out the noise of battle.

From every part of the valley the troops were shouting, some in unison, most not, but across the battlefield the cries arose. "Kill them! For Kings and Country! For the Prince!"

There was a crackle in Lysander's phones, but it was hard to hear. His own headquarters troops were cheering with the rest of them. Even Harv was shouting his head off.

"Yes?" Lysander shouted into the microphone.

"This is Colonel Owensford. Awaiting orders, Prince Lysander."

CHAPTER FOURTEEN

Crofton's Encyclopedia of the Inhabited Planets (2nd Edition):

Treaty of Independence, Spartan: Agreement signed between the Grand Senate of the CoDominium and the *Dual Monarchy of Sparta* (q.v.), 2062. The Constitutionalist Society's original settlement agreement with the Colonial Bureau of the CoDominium had provided for full internal self-government, but the CoDominium retained jurisdiction over a substantial enclave in *Sparta City* (q.v.), the orbital transit station *Aegis* (q.v.), and the refueling facilities around the gas-giant planet *Zeus*. In addition, during the period of self-government a CoDominium Marine Regiment remained in garrison on Sparta and its commander also acted as Governor-General, enforcing the residual powers retained by the Colonial Bureau, mostly having to do with the regulation of involuntary colonist and convict populations.

In line with Grand Senator Fedrokov's "New Look" policy of reducing CoDominium involvement in distant systems where practicable, negotiations began with the Dual Monarchy in 2060. Under the terms of the Treaty, the Royal government became fully responsible for internal order and external defense of the Spartan system, and all restrictions on local military and police forces were removed. The transit station and Zeus-orbit refueling stations were also turned over to the Royal government. However, the treaty also stipulated that certain facilities were to be maintained, at Spartan expense, for the use of the CoDominium authorities and the Fleet; these included docking, fueling and repair functions, and orbit to surface shuttles. Also mandated was the continued receipt of involuntary colonists at a level to be set by the Bureau of Relocation, and for this purpose the CoDominium enclave in Sparta City was retained with a reduced garrison. Penalty provisions in the Treaty authorized direct intervention by the Commandant of the enclave should the Royal government fail to fulfill these obligations. . . .

*   *   *

"In the long run, luck is given only to the efficient."
—Helmuth von Moltke

*   *   *

The helicopter dipped into the valley. At its lowest point it slowed briefly, just long enough to let Sergeant Billy Washington and his four teammates tumble out to land beside the gear they'd pushed out ahead of them.

The helicopter continued on over the next ridge. Anyone tracking it from a distance would have seen it enter and leave the valley flying just above the nap of the earth, and would have no reason to suspect that it had done anything unusual while out of sight between ridges.

Sergeant Billy Washington and Monitor Rafe Skinner went up the ridge first, taking pleny of time, because they had time and it never hurt to be careful. The best surveillance they had indicated that the ridge top would be empty, but they took half an hour making sure that it was, before Skinner took up a post where he could keep watch, and Washington motioned for the others to come up.

"All clear," Washington said.

"Thank you, Sergeant Washington." Technical Sergeant Henry Natakian, like the two privates who carried the heavy gear, was Spartan, although he was a full Citizen and they were still Candidates. Because of his technical education Natakian had been posted into the communications section, Headquarters Company, of the First Royals. He'd been surprised to find himself subordinate to a Legionnaire sergeant of no particular technical education, but it hadn't taken long to learn why. Now he hoped that the black man would elect to stay with the Royals rather than return to the Legion. Billy Washington might not have all the technical skills Natakian and his Spartans did, but he understood war. Washington and Skinner had saved them from Helot traps four times in the last three days.

Washington located the precise spot he'd been given on his map. As the two privates humped the heavy gear up the ridge, Washington and Natakian set up the base tripod for their relay antenna. Ridge 602 didn't overlook the source of the Helot artillery, but it was in line of sight to a hill that did; and while it didn't have line of sight to Legion Headquarters, it could see another ridge line that did. . . .

*   *   *

The helicopter dropped Sergeant Taras Hamilton Miscowsky and his twelve-man SAS section nine kilometers from the Helot artillery base, which put him four kilometers from the hilltop that overlooked the Helot base area.

Miscowsky wasn't happy with the assignment. It wasn't that he anticipated trouble taking his objective. Miscowsky hoped there would be some of the scumbags up there on the ridge above, but it wasn't likely. The Helots couldn't guard every possible observation point, and there was nothing special about Hill 633, except that it had a line of sight to Hill 602 where Billy Washington would be setting up his relay. Another team would be moving on Hill 712, which was a more obvious place for the Legion to put an observation post. That team would probably run into trouble, but then they were expecting it.

The problem wasn't this assignment. Miscowsky

wanted to be somewhere else. He knew better, knew he was the best man for what he was doing, and that helped, but it still bothered him that he wasn't looking after his former Captain's wife. The rescue team sent to her downed airplane had found no survivors. There were four bodies, one a man with his throat cut, but none of them had been Lieutenant Deborah Lefkowitz.

Sergeant Mendota was with the rescue team. He was as good a tracker as Miscowsky. Maybe better. In this terrain, probably a lot better. If anyone could track down the slimeballs, he could. And after all, Mendota had been on Jerry Lefkowtiz's team too, but it still bothered Miscowsky that he wasn't going on that hunt.

Miscowsky didn't think they'd ever find the lieutenant alive, not unless she was here at the Helot base, and he didn't really expect that. Back at the front, the Helots were bugging out all over, abandoning their wounded and killing their prisoners, and there wasn't any reason to believe they'd taken the trouble to transport Lieutenant Deborah Lefkowitz when they left their own wounded behind. They'd probably killed her, cut her throat like her pilot and those Brotherhood prisoners one of the Scout units found. Maybe it was worse than that. Mendota's report had been sketchy, obviously left something out. They'd found something they didn't want to talk about, something having to do with the lieutenant's clothing. Miscowsky didn't want to guess what.

The blood feud tradition was strong among Taras Miscowsky's people on Haven, and he hadn't forgotten despite his Legion experiences. Hatred filled him as he sent his scouts ahead up the ridge. Cold hatred, but it didn't change his actions. The Legion's SAS people were all selected for their ability to use good judgment in high stress conditions. Hatred only fueled caution. Jerry Lefkowitz had been Miscowsky's officer when he first joined the Legion, and had

Lefkowitz not placed as much value on the lives of his men as he did on personal survival, Miscowsky would not have lived through his first battle. As it was, Taras Miscowsky expected to live long enough to settle the score for his captain. Not just those who did it. Those who ordered it. All of them.

* * *

"Observation teams in place," Captain Mace reported. "Stand by for data updates."

The displays on Peter Owensford's map table blanked out momentarily, then came up again. Many of the large blurred splotches had been replaced by smaller, more precise figures. Owensford bent over the map of the enemy headquarters area. He used a light pen to circle one section. "How reliable is this?"

"Very," Mace said. "Miscowsky has it under observation. That's real time data."

Owensford smiled thinly. "Looks like they're packing up to leave."

"Yes, sir, looks like that to me, too," Andy Lahr said. "Maybe we ought to help them—"

"No doubt." Owensford turned to Jameson Mace. "Jamey, you've got full priority on Thoth bundles one through four, secondary after that. Use 'em when your team on the spot thinks we'll get the most out of them."

"Roger," Mace said. "It's a judgment call. The longer we wait, the more chance the scouts will have of blocking their escape. On the other hand, the sooner we strike, the more we get before they bug out at all. Then there's the business of the Helot commander."

Owensford turned knobs to scroll the map to the ridge above the river camp. "Last traced to this area. I see McLaren's moving in there now. Andy, see if you can get McLaren on the line."

"Aye aye."

"McLaren here."

"Captain, what are you finding up there?"

"Dead and dying, Colonel. Little else. If they can run they've done it. And the usual. Our lads, hands tied, throats cut, or bayonetted. Or worse, I will no describe some of what we've seen. 'Tis no easy on my lads—"

"It's not supposed to be," Owensford said. "That's what the Helots are counting on. They want to turn us into beasts no better than they are. Don't let them."

"Aye."

"Easier to say than do," Andy Lahr muttered.

Owensford nodded. "Captain, any sign of the rebel commander?"

"Now, how would I know if I found such?" McLaren demanded.

"Sorry, forgot you weren't in on that conversation. The Helot commander's a woman," Owensford said. "At least the voice was contralto."

"Och. Well, there are no women up here, Colonel. No women at all, and sights here no woman should see. Except that one, and I suppose she saw it all. She's no here, Colonel."

*   *   *

Geoffrey Niles let the river carry him down past the Spartan encampments. He had lashed himself to the bleeding corpse of one of his troops. The now useless chemical protection gear kept his clothing dry. It also kept him afloat, and the current soon took him out of the combat zone.

I told them it wouldn't work, he thought. Too complex. I told them. There was no place to go. His command was destroyed. There was supposed to be an emergency rendezvous point, but he wasn't sure he wanted to go there. Would Skilly understand there was nothing he could have done? No more any of them could do? Skida Thibodeau wasn't one to take excuses for failure. *Even if the failure was hers? Because of her plan?* But she wasn't likely to admit that.

He thought of surrender, but he was afraid to do that. Gas. War gas. The books talked about hanging officers for using poison gas. *It wasn't my fault! I didn't want to do that.*

He could say they hadn't told him. It would even be true. They'd said non-lethal chemical agents in the planning sessions. Of course everyone had known better. There were no non-lethal agents effective enough for what they'd attempted. Even the war gasses, the lethal agents Murusaki used, hadn't been good enough. Nothing had been good enough.

What could we have done? They'd been good troops, all of them, they'd done all that courage could do, and it hadn't been good enough. We were so close, a little more and we'd have had his artillery, then we could have punished the Brotherhood troops, but it wasn't good enough, the plan, the gas, none of it was enough.

Should it have been good enough? It had seemed so romantic, help the poor against the Spartan aristocracy, overthrow the tyrants, but the Spartan kings weren't tyrants. Not at all. And the poor, the downtrodden—

He thought of what Skilly had ordered. Kill all the prisoners. His troops would have obeyed, but of course he hadn't transmitted that order. Some of them had done terrible things on their own, but at least they hadn't killed all those Brotherhood troops, the wounded ones they'd captured, the ones disabled by gas.

I didn't do that, anyway. But Skilly had ordered it. And worse. That female Lieutenant, the one from the airplane. Jeff hadn't been there, but he'd heard what happened.

I was on the wrong side. This isn't Lawrence of Arabia. No romance here. This isn't anything I want to be part of.

The current carried him around another bend of the river. He was far from the combat zone now. He began to shiver. The cold was seeping in despite his protective gear. It was time to get out of the water. He watched for a sandbar, some place to land.

I want to go home, he thought. But where was home?

*   *   *

"Ten' *'hut!*"

"Please," Lysander said. The command bunker was crowded, and everyone was standing to attention. Officers moved out of the way to allow Lysander and Harv to get to the big map table. When he got to the table, Lysander looked to Peter Owensford for help. "Please," he repeated.

"Carry on," Owensford said. "Welcome to the command center, Your Highness. Have you instructions?"

"Colonel, you're in command of this force—"

"Tactical command," Owensford said. "Yes, sir. Shall we review the situation for you?"

"Colonel, you're embarrassing me—"

"Prince Lysander, there's nothing to be embarrassed about," Owensford said.

"Well, I hadn't really intended to assume command—"

"You hadn't intended to, but you did, and that's all to the good," Owensford said. "Highness, unity of command is the most important principle of war. Having you as a battalion commander violated that principle. Nothing bad came of it, but something could have, and I for one am glad it's over." He shrugged. "Captain Bennington will see to the Prince Royal's Own. No one expects you to take tactical command here. I'll give the orders. You just tell me what you want accomplished."

Lysander nodded. His face was grim. "I want you to make the most of this pursuit," he said. "I've seen— I've been up on the hill where they had over a hundred Brotherhood prisoners. And in the field hospitals with the troops who were gassed." He shuddered. "The only thing worse than doing that to them would be to have done it for nothing."

"You didn't do it, Prince," Harv said quietly.

"Your Phraetrie brother is right," Owensford said. "You didn't do it. That's what these people want you to think, that it's your fault that your people were killed. It wasn't your fault. They're the ones who did this, not you."

"Yes. Thank you. All right, Colonel, what is our status?"

"Quite good, actually," Owensford said. "As is often the case, the bold course has proven to be the best. We lost a number of prisoners to terrorist crimes, but many of them would not have survived anyway. Meanwhile our assault casualties have been surprisingly light, and we have been able to inject SAS and Scout teams into positions to block enemy retreat paths. We have relay units to observers spotting in the enemy camp headquarters itself. Finally, we rescued forty-seven prisoners, all wounded, down by the river. The Helot officer there either didn't get the order to kill the prisoners, or didn't obey it."

"Who was he?"

"We don't know. He's probably dead. That unit was the spearhead of this crazy stunt, and took very heavy casualties. We're sorting through the survivors, but so far no one admits to being any kind of commander."

Lysander nodded. "Find out, please. Assuming it's possible, of course."

"Wilco," Andy Lahr said.

"Please continue," Lysander said. "Sorry to interrupt."

"Yes, sir." Owensford used his light pen to mark a region on the map table. The computer zoomed in on the area. "Their main force was here. They had been advancing prior to the failure of the gas attack. They then halted, milled around a while, and after we rejected their leader's offer of a cease-fire, dug in and resisted."

"Dug in," Lysander said. "Does that make sense? I'd have thought they would run away."

"So would we," Jesus Alana said. "My conclusion is that they were ordered to hold on to cover the escape of their leaders."

"Which worked," Owensford added. "Or something did. We haven't caught anyone higher ranking than their equivalent of a lieutenant, and both of those were wounded. But it cost them. By the time that force was ready to break and run we had not only pounded it pretty bad, but we had scout units across their line of escape. We don't think more than ten percent of their main unit got away."

"Good," Lysander said. "But those ten percent are their officers?" Owensford nodded. Lysander shook his head ruefully. "All right, what about their technical people?"

"Definitely Meiji mercenaries," Jesus Alana said. "We have found three. All dead, of course. We are hoping for more when we assault the Helot headquarters area."

"When will that be?"

"Probably not until tomorrow," Owensford said. "We've been bombarding the area, of course. We had to neutralize their artillery before we could deal with their dug-in forces. Now we're moving units into position for the actual assualt."

"Can they escape after dark?"

"Some will," Owensford said. "We've got scouts and SAS units in the area, but they'll never get all of them. That complex of caves is big."

"What about their missing leader? Will she go back there?"

Jesus Alana shrugged. "Quien sabe? But in my opinion, no. There would be no reason for her to risk her neck again. No. Highness, in my opinion she is gone. A pity, but there is nothing we can do."

"I wouldn't want her to escape."

Jesus Alana frowned slightly. "Highness, I would pray that if she escapes, as she has, she never returns. But I am afraid we have not seen the last of that one, and I do not think you will have much reason to rejoice when next we hear of her."

*   *   *

Peter Owensford laid down his pointer and looked around the Council Chamber. He had certainly had an appreciative audience as he explained the campaign to the War Council. "That concludes the briefing, Sires, gentlemen, madam," he said. "In sum: thanks to the leadership of Prince Lysander we turned a tactical win into a superb strategic victory."

"My congratulations," King Alexander said. There was a tremor in his voice. "Please, take your seat. Thank you. Colonel, alas, it was unfortunate that you were unable to find more of the technical people at the enemy headquarters."

"Agreed, Sire," Owensford said. "The materiel losses have put a heavy dent in their schedule, no doubt about that, they've been knocked back into Phase One of their plan, but it would have been a bigger blow to them if we'd captured their technocrats." Owensford shrugged. "Nothing we could do. Apparently they bugged out about the time the enemy commander did. One reason why their field troops crumpled up so easily after Prince Lysander rejected their truce offer. No tech support."

"If I may," Jesus Alana said.

"Please," Alexander prompted.

"We are wondering if this has not produced a certain tension between the Helot leaders and their Meijian employees. Each may feel betrayed by the other. Certainly there must be suspicions. Suspicions, incidentally, which we will certainly try to foster and exploit."

"Thank you," Alexander said.

"Next," Owensford said. "I expect this next item will surprise you all as much as it did me. Captain Alana."

Jesus Alana bowed slightly. He obviously was enjoying himself. "We have identified one of the Helot leaders," he said. He touched a button on his sleeve console, and a cultured British-sounding voice said, "Actually, I've got eight or ten of your men down here, badly wounded I'm afraid. Ten minutes truce—" Jesus thumbed the button and the voice cut off.

"From the events of the battle at the river camp, it was probable that this was the man who commanded the main thrust of the Helot effort. Prince Lysander"—Jesus bowed again—"instructed us to determine the identity of that commander, so we paid particular attention to the record of his attempt to negotiate a truce.

"Some of our officers believed they had heard this man before," Jesus said. "It was then simple enough to digitize his voice and set the computer searching. It found a match quickly enough." Alana touched another button, and a picture appeared on the screen: a handsome man, clean shaven except for a thin mustache. "The Honorable Geoffrey Niles," Jesus said. "Grand-nephew to Grand Senator Bronson."

"Bronson?" Henry Yamaga demanded.

"Aye, my lord," Peter Owensford said.

Someone whistled. *Freiherr* von Alderheim said, in a low voice, "Ach. Now we know who has paid for these Meiji devils to come here. But why? What interest has Bronson in Sparta?"

"I wish I knew," King Alexander said. "I very much wish that I knew."

"It makes one thing certian," Lysander said. "We aren't safe here. It isn't enough to mind our own business."

"I have always thought the CoDominium's masters

would not allow us our experiment in peace," Alexander said. "I—but there is a reason why I should not speak to this. Not at this moment. Captain Alana, Captain Catherine Alana, please make your presentation."

Catherine stood. "Yes, Sire. I will now summarize a report we already delivered to His Majesty and His Highness. The King insisted that I inform the Council."

Peter Owensford stared around the room through half-closed eyes and watched for the effects of Catherine's announcement.

"The Council will recall that His Majesty has—not been quite himself," Catherine said.

Actually, he was acting like a raving maniac there at times, Peter thought. He saw that Lysander had put his hand on his father's shoulder. The Prince's mouth was set in a grim line of determination.

"We have determined the reason for this," Catherine said. "The Palace medical supplies have been tampered with. In particular, His Majesty's normal anti-agathic shots." She waited for the buzz of alarm to die away. "Of course the physicians have been testing regularly for poisons, and examining the King after—he began to act strangely. This was something a great deal more subtle than a simple poison. A tailored virus, aimed at the endocrine glands and the hormonal behavior regulation system."

"Devils," the Minster of War hissed.

"Yes, Sir Alfred," Catherine said. "Quite a devilish trick. Meijian technology, we presume. Certainly much of the equipment Jesus found in the Helot field headquarters could only have originated on Meiji, and they are known to do a great deal of genetic engineering."

"What are the effects?" Lysander asked.

"Similar to paranoid schizophrenia."

Alexander drew in his breath sharply.

"As we told you, it is only temporary, Majesty," Catherine said.

"If I may," Alexander said. The room fell silent. "I noticed that—I was not myself, much of the time. And that I tended to improve when away from the city. But I did not suspect— My friends, I wish to apologize. I have been very cruel to many of you."

"Sire—Majesty—Father it's all right—" Everyone spoke at once.

"So," Madame Rusher said. "That's why our friend Croser has been muttering about Regency provisions."

"This is too much. Far too much," Lord Henry Yamaga said.

"Indeed," *Freiherr* von Alderheim said thoughtfully. "Perhaps this will provide the final stimulus needed in certain quarters. Croser has taken advantage of the law. He thought to make himself immune to ordinary law by taking that seat in the Senate. He forgets that there is also Law."

Alexander looked to his counselors. His eyes had a haunted expression. "My friends—My dear friends, I can't trust my own judgment. Therefore, with your permission, I appoint my son Lysander Prince Regent—"

"No, Father," Lysander said. "It's not necessary."

"I agree the formal devolution isn't necessary," Madam Elayne Rusher said. "Triggers far too many formalities in its wake. Sire, if you're concerned about your judgment, you can have the same effect by taking Prince Lysander into your confidence and having him present your will to the Council."

"Do you—do all of you agree?" Alexander asked.

There was a chorus of assent.

"David?" Alexander asked.

"I would never ask you to step aside," David Freedman said. "Welcome back, sir."

"Thank you. Then so be it. In future, Prince Lysander will, acting on my advice, speak for me to this Council, much in the same way that Prince David speaks for my colleague. In general I will also be present, but if there is a conflict between us, my son Lysander's views shall prevail, this to be so until Lysander says otherwise in a formal Council meeting at which I am not present. I wish this entered as an order in Council with the assent of my colleague. Is this agreeable to you all? David? Thank you."

CHAPTER FIFTEEN

It is not often that historians can determine the exact moment when history changes, and it would be hubris for us to assume we know precisely when the intention to attempt the transformation of Sparta from an isolated planetary state into the Spartan Hegemony first entered the thoughts of Crown Prince Lysander. Yet there are those who believe they not only know, but were present that day.

—From the Preface to *From Utopia to Imperium: A History of Sparta from Alexander I to the Accession of Lysander*, by Caldwell C. Whitlock, Ph.D. (University of Sparta Press, 2120).

* * *

The lecture theater of the Royal Spartan War College was an attractive mixture of old and new. The walls were paneled in wood or something indistinguishable from it. The seats were arrayed in rising tiers, each seat comfortable enough to avoid fatigue, yet not so well padded as to make the students sleepy. The lecture podium was behind a large computerized map table whose controls were duplicated both at the lectern and in the control booth at the top of the room. Behind the lectern were more screens, touch-sensitive so that the lecturer could draw figures that would be automatically copied for later printout. The acoustics of the room were excellent.

Cornet Alan Brady of the Second Royal Infantry came to the podium. He spoke in a clear voice, and if he was in awe of his audience his voice didn't show it.

The room was filled with officers of all ranks, from officer cadets through General Peter Owensford; and in the center of the front row sat Crown Prince Lysander Collins, wearing the uniform of a Lieutenant General of Royal Infantry. The story was that Lysander hadn't much care for the rank, but that Major Generals Owensford and Slater insisted that if the Prince wanted to appear in uniform, he had to out rank them; and they were quite prepared to resign the Royal commissions and revert to Legion rank to make their point.

Brady didn't know, and wasn't thinking much about that anyway. He was a good enough actor to play his part without nervousness, but that meant he couldn't vary much from the script.

"Highness, Lords, Ladies, and Gentlefolk, this will be the inaugural colloquium of the Royal Lectures on Strategy made possible by a grant from *Freiherr* Bernard von Alderheim under the patronage of Their Majesties. The first lecture will be presented by Major General Slater, Commandant of the Royal War College.

"General Slater."

Hal Slater limped to the podium from his place in the front row. He set down his black malacca cane with the silver double-eagle head, a present from King Alexander, and touched controls on the lectern. An outline appeared on the lectern screen. Hal didn't like to read prepared speeches, but this lecture would incorporate quoted materials, and he wanted to get those right.

He looked out at the audience. The best and brightest of the Spartan military—young officers posted to the General Staff as well as senior Legion and Royal officers. There were also half a dozen civilians, military history students at the University admitted to the lectures for their education.

Of course there's only one real target for what I'm about to say, but I need to be careful not to make it too obvious. . . .

"Highness, my Lords, Ladies, and Gentlefolk. Many

of you have recently returned from what is rapidly becoming known as the Helot War. Much of our army is still in the field.

"The campaign was a success, in that our forces destroyed much of the enemy's capabilities to wage aggressive war and harm our people. We killed or captured many of their cadre and their best troops, and we destroyed or captured a great deal of military equipment, much of it highly advanced, some advanced over anything we have.

"Unfortunately, despite this victory, the war is not over. It is quiet for the moment, but rest assured, the enemy is reorganizing. Having failed at the tactical offensive, he will assume the defensive, hide, lick his wounds, and make ready to try again.

"We may liken this battle to Thermopylae. Certainly our troops do."

There was general laughter, because, as if on cue, they could hear a section of cadets marching to class, singing, "Leonidas came marching to the Hot Gates by the sea, the Persian Shah was coming and a mighty host had he—"

"Moreover, Thermopylae as Leonidas no doubt intended, a delaying action fought to blunt the advance of the Persian army, and delay the enemy while the Athenian fleet made ready, and the rest of Greece mobilized for war. Of course it didn't work that way, and the Three Hundred went on to a glory undimmed after millennia. Yet for all the effect it will have on the future of this conflict, your battle on the Illyrian Dales might as well have ended as did Leonidas and the Three Hundred: covered with glory, but with the enemy still advancing, still able to harm our country, burn our fields, kill our women and enslave our children.

"This is the nature of this kind of war."

And that got their attention. Hal smiled thinly.

"This kind of war is called Low Intensity Conflict, or

LIC. The name is unfortunate, because it is misleading. If we are to draw the correct conclusions from our recent experience, and apply the lessons we have learned to the future, it is very important to understand the threat—and to understand that so-called Low Intensity Conflict can be and has been decisive in determining the destinies of nations.

"Low Intensity Conflicts were highly important all during the latter half of the twentieth century; so much so that one prominent military historian concluded that that kind of war was the only decisive kind of war.

"After describing conventional military forces—the sort of thing you are part of, the Legion, the Royal Infantry—after describing conventional forces and decrying their expense, Creveld said:

"'One would expect forces on which so many resources have been lavished to represent fearsome warfighting machines capable of quickly overcoming any opposition. Nothing, however, is farther from the truth. For all the countless billions that have been and are still being expended on them, the plain fact is that conventional military organizations of the principal powers are hardly even relevant to the predominant form of contemporary war [which is Low Intensity Conflict, or LIC.]

"'Perhaps the best indication of the political importance of LIC is that the results, unlike those of conventional wars, have usually been recognized by the international community. . . . Considered from this point of view—"by their fruits thou shalt know them"—the term LIC itself is grossly misconceived. The same applies to related terms such as "terrorism," "insurgency," "brushfire war," or "guerrilla war." Truth to say, what we are dealing with here is neither low-intensity nor some bastard offspring of war. Rather it is WARRE in the elemental, Hobbesian sense of the word, by far the most important form of armed conflict in our time.

" '. . . how well have the world's most important armed forces fared in this type of war? For some two decades after 1945 the principal colonial powers fought very hard to maintain the far-flung empires which they had created for themselves during the past centuries. They expended tremendous economic resources, both in absolute terms and relative to those of the insurgents who, in many cases, literally went barefoot. They employed the best available troops, from the Foreign Legion to the Special Air Service and from the Green Berets to the *Spetznatz* and the Israeli *Sayarot*. They fielded every kind of sophisticated military technology in their arsenals, nuclear weapons only excepted. They were also, to put it bluntly, utterly ruthless. Entire populations were driven from their homes, decimated, shut in concentration camps or else turned into refugees. As Ho Chi Minh foresaw when he raised the banner of revolt against France in 1945, in *every* colonial-type war ever fought the number of casualties on the side of the insurgents exceeded those of the "forces of order" by at least an order of magnitude. This is true even if civilian casualties among the colonists are included, which often is not the case.

" 'Notwithstanding this ruthlessness and these military advantages, the "counterinsurgency" forces failed in *every* case. . . .' "

"So wrote Martin van Creveld in *The Transformation of War*, published in 1990 just prior to the American adventure in the Iraqi Desert; demonstrating once again that even the most brilliant historians often draw the wrong conclusions. It is certainly the case that so-called Low Intensity Conflicts had been and could be decisive, against both the United States and the Soviet Union; but this should not have been surprising, since most of those conflicts were no more than an extension of what had been called the Cold War. If either power became involved in LIC, the other power would find compelling reasons to aid the insurgents."

Hal tilted his head down so that he could examine the room over the tops of his glasses. *Still have their attention,* he decided. He took a sip of water and continued.

"What was not noticed until the last decades of the twentieth century was that insurgency was quite often nothing of the kind, but a cover for the invasion of one nation by another, with the invading nation supported by powerful allies who enjoyed immunity from military retaliation. South Vietnam did not fall to insurgents in the jungles, but to a modern armored army employing ten thousand trucks and twenty-five hundred armored fighting vehicles; and while North Vietnam was not always a sanctuary—the 1972 offensive triggered massive bombardment of the North by the United States—China and the Soviet Union always were sanctuaries, and none of the North Vietnamese war materiel was manufactured in North Vietnam. By the same token, the weapons employed by the Afghan *mujahideen* were not made in Afghanistan, and the factories producing Stinger missiles and recoilless artillery pieces were quite safe from Soviet attack.

"Military historians like van Creveld, in considering how successful insurgency aided by one Superpower could be used against the other did not, until the end of the Cold War, consider the improbability of the success of LIC against both Superpowers acting in concert.

"Insurgency against a modern state requires powerful allies operating from sanctuary. The allies need not be of 'superpower' status; but they will require that one of the Superpowers, or both of them acting as the CoDominium, protect the sanctuary status of the supplying nation. Unfortunately, given supply of war material from a sanctuary, insurgency can be continued practically forever."

General Slater looked directly at Prince Lysander, and said, "The strategic implications should be obvious."

*   *   *

Afterwards, after sherry and coffee, after the questions and the congratulations, the audience filed out. They were all talking and joking, all but one.

Crown Prince Lysander Collins left the room alone, lost in thoughts no one wanted to interrupt.

THE END

Erma Bombeck

AT WIT'S END

Illustrated by Loretta Vollmuth

FAWCETT CREST • **NEW YORK**

AT WIT'S END

THIS BOOK CONTAINS THE COMPLETE TEXT OF THE
ORIGINAL HARDCOVER EDITION.

Published by Fawcett Crest Books, a unit of CBS Publications, the
Consumer Publishing Division of CBS Inc., by arrangement with
Doubleday and Company, Inc.

ISBN: 0-449-23784-2

Printed in the United States of America

22   21   20   19   18   17   16   15   14   13

CONTENTS

This isn't a book.

It's a group therapy session.

It is based on six predictable depression cycles that beset a woman during a twelve-month span.

These chapters will not tell you how to overcome these depression cycles.

They will not tell you how to cope with them.

They will have hit home if they, in some small way, help you to laugh your way through while hanging on to your sweet sanity.

January 2—March 4

*What's a nice girl like me
doing in a dump like this?*

It hits on a dull, overcast Monday morning. I awake realizing there is no party in sight for the weekend, I'm out of bread, and I've got a dry skin problem. So I say it aloud to myself, "What's a nice girl like me doing in a dump like this?"

The draperies are dirty (and will disintegrate if laundered), the arms of the sofa are coming through. There is Christmas tinsel growing out of the carpet. And some clown has written in the dust on the coffee table, YANKEE GO HOME.

It's those rotten kids. It's their fault I wake up feeling so depressed. If only they'd let me wake up in my own way. Why do they have to line up along my bed and stare at me like Moby Dick just washed up onto a beach somewhere?

"I think she hears us. Her eyelids fluttered."

"Wait till she turns over, then everybody cough."

"Why don't we just punch her and ask her what we want to know."

"*Get him out of here.*"

"She's pulling the covers over her ears. Start coughing."

I don't know how long it will be before one of them discovers that by taking my pulse they will be able to figure out by its rapid beat if I am faking or not, but it will come. When they were smaller, it was worse. They'd stick their wet fingers into the opening of my face and whisper, "You awake yet?" Or good old Daddy would simply heave a flannel-wrapped bundle at me and say, "Here's Mommy's little boy." (Any mother with half a skull knows that when Daddy's little boy becomes Mommy's little boy, the kid is so wet he's treading water!) Their imagination is straight from the pages of Edgar Allan Poe. Once they put a hamster on my chest and when I bolted upright (my throat muscles paralyzed with fright) they asked, "Do you have any alcohol for the chemistry set?"

I suppose that's better than having them kick the wall until Daddy becomes conscious, then ask, "Do you want the cardboards that the laundry puts in your shirts?" Any wrath beats waking Daddy. There has to be something wrong with a man who keeps resetting his alarm clock in the morning and each time it blasts off smacks it silent and yells, "No one tells me what to do, Buddy."

Personally I couldn't care less what little games my husband plays with his alarm clock, but when I am awakened at 5:30, 6:00, 6:15, and 6:30 every morning, I soon react to bells like a punchy fighter. That's what I get for marrying a nocturnal animal. In the daylight, he's nothing. He has to have help with his shoelaces. In all the years we've been married he only got up once of his own accord before 9:30. And then his mattress was on fire. He can't seem to cope with daytime noises like flies with noisy chest colds, the crash of marshmallows as they hit the hot chocolate, the earsplitting noises milk makes when you pour it over the cereal.

The truth of it is, he's just not geared to function in an eight-to-five society. Once he even fell out of his filing cabinet. Around eleven at night a transformation takes place. He stretches and yawns, then his eyes pop open and he kicks me in the foot and says, "What kind of a day did you have?"

"You mean we're still on the same one?" I yawn.

"You're not going to bed already, are you?"

"Yes."

"Would it bother you if I played the guitar?"

"Yes."

"Well, then maybe I'll read a little before I go to sleep."

"Why not? I have the only eyelids in the neighborhood with a tan."

No doubt about it, if I could arise in a graceful manner, I could cope.

It's starting to snow. Thanks a lot up there.

Before moving to the suburbs, I always thought an "Act of God" was a flash of lightning at Mt. Sinai or forty days and forty nights of rain. Out here, they call a snowfall an "Act of God" and they close the schools.

The first time it happened I experienced a warm, maternal glow, a feeling of confidence that I lived in a community which would put its children above inclement weather. The second time, that same week, I experienced a not-so-warm glow, but began to wonder if perhaps the kids could wear tennis rackets on their feet and a tow rope around their waists to guide them. On the third day school was canceled within a two-week period, I was organizing a dog-sled pool.

We racked up fifteen Acts of God that year and it became apparent to the women in our neighborhood that "somebody up there" was out to get us.

It got to be a winter morning ritual. We'd all sit around the radio like an underground movement in touch with the free world. When the announcer read the names of the schools closed, a rousing cheer would go up and the kids would scatter. I'd cry a little in the dishtowel, then announce sullenly, "All right, don't sweat in the school clothes. REPEAT. Don't sweat in the school clothes. Hang them up. Maybe tomorrow you'll visit school. And stay out of those lunch boxes. It's only eight-thirty." My words would fall on deaf ears. Within minutes they were in full snow gear ready to whip over to the school and play on the hill.

Little things began to bother me about these unscheduled closings. For example, we'd drive by the school and our second-grader would point and ask, "What's that building, Daddy?" Also, it was March and they hadn't had their Christmas exchange yet. Our ten-year-old had to be prompted with his alphabet. And the neighborhood "Love and Devotion to Child Study" group had to postpone their meetings three times because they couldn't get the rotten kids out from under foot.

"We might as well be living in Fort Apache," said one mother. "If this snow doesn't melt soon, my kid will outgrow his school desk."

We all agreed something had to be done.

This year, a curious thing happened. In the newspaper it was stated that snow was no longer to be considered an Act of God by the state board of education. Their concern was that the children spend a minimum number of hours in school each week and that the buses would roll come yells or high water.

Snow is a beautiful, graceful thing as it floats downward to the earth, and is enhanced greatly by the breathtaking indentation of school bus snow tires. Snow is now considered an Act of Nature in the suburbs. And everyone knows she's a Mother and understands these things.

"Whip it up, group. Everyone to the boots!"

"What do you mean you're a participle in the school play and you need a costume? You be careful in that attic, do you hear? If you fall through and break your neck, you're going to be late for school!"

A drudge. That's all I am. They'll all be sorry when I'm not around to run and fetch.

"So you swallowed the plastic dinosaur out of the cereal box. What do you want me to do, call a vet?"

Lunches. Better pack the lunches. Listen to

them bicker. What do they care what I pack? They'd trade their own grandmother for a cough drop and a Holy picture.

Of course, none of these things would bother me if I had an understanding husband. Mother was right. I should have married that little literature major who broke out in a rash every time he read Thoreau. But no, I had to pick the nut standing out in the driveway yelling at the top of his voice, "I am thirty-nine years old. I make fifteen thousand dollars a year. I will not carry a Donald Duck thermos to the office!" Boy, he wouldn't yell at me if my upper arms weren't flabby. He never used to yell at me like that. *He* should worry. He doesn't have to throw himself across the washer during "spin" to keep it from walking out of the utility room. He doesn't have to flirt with a hernia making bunk beds. He doesn't have to shuffle through encyclopedias before the school bus leaves to find out which United States president invented the folding chair.

It's probably the weather. "Everybody out!"

Look at 'em stumbling around the driveway like newborn field mice. It's the weather all right. No leaves on the trees. No flowers. No green grass. Just a big picture window with nothing to look at but . . . *a new bride moving into the cul-de-sac!* Well, there goes the neighborhood. Would you look at her standing at her husband's elbow as he stencils their marvy new name on their marvy new garbage cans? I suppose tomorrow she'll be out waxing her driveway. So give her a few years, and she'll be like the rest of us sifting through the coffee grounds looking for baby's pacifier.

What am I saying? Give her a few years of suburban living and she'll misplace the baby! What was it I was supposed to look for this morning? Maybe I'll think of it. I wonder how much time I waste each day looking for lost things. Let's see, I spent at least two hours yesterday looking for the bananas and enough straight pins to pin up a hem. Lucky the kids came up with the idea of walking across the floor in my bare feet or I'd be looking for pins yet. I suppose I could've uncovered the bananas by smelling breaths, but you have to trust someone sometime when they say no.

The day before that I misplaced the car keys. Of course, that's not my fault. That was the fault of the clown who left them in the ignition. You'd certainly never think to look there for them. Just say I spend about two hours a day looking for stuff. That amounts to 730 hours a year, not counting the entire months of November and December when I look for the Christmas cards I buy half price the preceding January.

I'd have a child growing up on the Pennsylvania Turnpike today if a group of picnickers hadn't noticed her sifting through trash barrels in the roadside park and become curious about how she got there. I wonder if other women piff away all that time looking for nail files and scotch tape.

I knew a woman once who always said, "Have a place for everything and everything in its place." I hated her. I wonder what she would say if she knew I rolled out of bed each morning and walked to the kitchen on my knees hoping to catch sight of a lost coin, a single sock, an overdue library book or a boot that would later inspire total recall.

I remember what I was going to look for . . . my glasses! But that was only if I wanted to see something during the day. So what do I have to see today that I couldn't put off until tomorrow? One of the kids said there was something strange in the oven. Probably a tray of hors d'oeuvres left over from the New Year's party. I'll look for the glasses tomorrow.

In the meantime, maybe I'll call Phyllis and tell her about the new bride. Better not chance it. Phyllis might be feeling great today and then I'd feel twice as crumby as I feel now.

This place will have to be cleaned before they can condemn it. Woudn't be at all surprised if I ended up like my Aunt Lydia. Funny, I haven't thought about her in years. Grandma always said she ran away with a vanilla salesman. Lay you odds she made her move right after the holidays. Her kids probably hid the Christmas candy in the bedroom closet and the ants were coming out of the woodwork like a Hessian drill team. One child was going through the dirty clothes hamper trying to retrieve her "favorite" underwear to wear to school.

Lydia spotted her nine-year-old dog (with the Christmas puppy plumbing) and ran after it with a piece of newspaper. The dog read a few of the comics, laughed out loud, then wet on the carpet.

Uncle Wally probably pecked her on the cheek with all the affection of a sex-starved cobra and said he wanted to talk about the Christmas bills when he came home.

She passed a mirror and noticed a permanent crease on her face where the brush roller had slipped. Her skirt felt tight. She sucked in her breath. Nothing moved. Her best friend called to tell her the sequin dress she bought for New Year's Eve had been reduced to half price.

Speculating on her future she could see only a long winter in a house with four blaring transistor radios, a spastic washer, and the ultimate desperation of trying to converse with the tropical fish.

You know something. The odds are Aunt Lydia didn't even know the vanilla salesman. When he knocked on the door, smiled and said, "Good morning, madam, I'm traveling through your territory on my way to Forked Tongue, Iowa," Aunt Lydia grabbed her satchel, her birdcage, and her nerve elixir, closed the door softly behind her and said quietly, "You'll do."

Each woman fights the doldrums in her own way. This illustrated guide, *What to Do Until the Therapist Arrives with the Volleyball*, is not unique. Its suggestions may, however, keep you from regressing into a corner in a foetal position with your hands over your ears.

A: KNIT.   Learning how to knit was a snap. It was learning how to stop that nearly destroyed me. Everyone in the house agreed I was tense and needed to unwind. So, I enrolled in an informal class in knitting.

The first week I turned out thirty-six pot holders. I was so intent on an afghan you'd have thought I was competing with an assembly line of back-scratcher makers from Hong Kong.

I couldn't seem to stop myself. By the end of the first month of knitting. I was sick from relaxation. There were deep, dark circles under my eyes. My upper lip twitched uncontrollably. There were calluses on both my thumbs and forefingers. I cried a lot from exhaustion. But I was driven by some mad, inner desire to knit fifteen toilet tissue covers shaped like little men's hats by the end of the week.

In the mornings I could hardly wait until the children were out of the house so I could haul out my knitting bag full of yarn and begin clicking away. "All right, group, let's snap it up," I'd yell. "Last one out of the house gets underwear for Christmas."

"It's only six-thirty," they'd yawn sleepily.

"So you're a little early," I snapped impatiently.

"BUT IT'S SATURDAY!" they chorused.

My husband was the first one to suggest I needed professional help. "You've gone beyond the social aspect of knitting," he said. "Let's face it. You have a problem and you're going to have to taper off. From here on in no more yarn." I promised, but I knew I wouldn't keep my word.

My addiction eventually led to dishonesty, lying, cheating, and selling various and sundry items to support my habit. I was always being discovered. The family unearthed a skein of mohair in a cereal box and an argyle kit hidden in the chandelier, and one afternoon I was found feverishly unraveling an old ski cap just to knit it over again. One night when the clicking of the needles in the darkness awakened my husband, he bolted up in bed, snapped on the light, and said quietly, "Tomorrow, I'm enrolling you in 'Knitters Anonymous.' Can't you see what's happening to you? To us? To the children? You can't do this by yourself."

He was right, of course. "Knitters Anonymous"

pointed out the foolishness of my compulsion to knit all the time. They eventually waned me off yarn and interested me in another hobby—painting.

Would you believe it? I did eight watercolors the first week, fifteen charcoal sketches the second and by the end of the month I will have racked up twenty-three oils . . . all on stretched canvasses!

B: DRINK. A while back some overzealous girl watcher noted a mass migration of the Red-Beaked Female Lush to split-levels in the suburbs.

That a total of 68 percent of the women today drink, there is no quarrel. But that they've all settled in the suburbs is questionable. Following this announcement, we in the suburbs called an emergency meeting of the "Help Stamp Out Ugly Suburban Rumors" committee. We decided to dispel the stigma once and for all by conducting a sobriety test among women at 8 A.M. Monday morning in the town hall.

We uncorked—rather, uncovered—only three sherry breaths, a cognac suspect, and one woman who wasn't sauced at all but who said she always shook that way after getting her four kids onto the school bus in the mornings.

A few of them admitted to nipping away at a bottle of vanilla in the broom closet or getting a little high sniffing laundry bleach, but most of them confessed drinking in the suburbs is not feasible. They cited the following reasons.

Privacy: "You show me a mother who slips into the bathroom to slug down a drink and I'll show you seven children hidden in the bathtub flashing a Popeye home movie on her chest."

Discretion: "To children, drinking means an occasion. When not given a satisfactory occasion to tout, they will spread it all over the neighborhood that Mama is toasting another 'No Baby Month.'"

Guilt: "With the entire block of my friends feeling trapped, bored, neurotic, and unfulfilled, why should I feel good and alienate myself?"

One woman did confess her system of rewarding herself with a drink had gotten a bit out of hand. At first she rewarded herself with a drink for washing down the kitchen walls or defrosting the refrigerator. Now she was treating herself to a drink for bringing in the milk or opening the can of asparagus at the right end.

Undoubtedly the girl watcher was tabulating

the many gourmet clubs that have sprouted up in the suburbs. They are the harmless little luncheons where a light wine is served before the luncheon and gourmet foods using brandies and wines are served to stimulate women's interest in cookery.

Some of these are held on a monthly basis to observe some special occasion such as a birthday or an anniversary of a member. In our group, we also observe Mao Tse-tung's backstroke victory, the anniversary of the escape of Winnie Ruth Judd, the January White Sale at Penguin's Department Store, the introduction of soy beans to Latin America, and the arrival and departure dates of the *Queen Mary*. Each month we present an award to the most unique dish served. Last month's prize was copped by my neighbor for a wonderful dessert which consisted of a peach seed floating recklessly in a snifter of brandy.

Frankly I think the girl watchers owe the women of the suburbs an apology for their accusations. Anyone here want to drink to that?

C: READ. One of the occupational hazards of housewifery and motherhood is that you never get the time to sit down and read an entire book from cover to cover.

A spot check of my most erudite friends revealed that the last books they read were: *Guadalcanal Diary*, *The Cat in the Hat Dictionary*, *The Picture of Dorian Gray*, and *First Aid*. (The fifth

fell asleep over her "Know Your Steam Iron War-
ranty and Manual," but we counted it anyway.)

This is a sad commentary on the women who
are going to be the mothers of all these scientists
and skilled technicians of tomorrow. As I always
say, "What doth it profiteth a woman to have
a clean house if she thinks anthropologist Mar-
garet Mead is a foot doctor!" (I recommended
her to three of my friends.)

First, to find the right book. When you live in a
small town you have to be pretty discreet about
the books you check out. I, for one, don't want to
be known behind the stalls as "Old Smutty
Tongue." On the other hand, I don't want to
spend my precious time plowing through *Little
Goodie Miss Two Shoes and Her Adventures on
Bass Island.*

"You know me pretty well, Miss Hathcock," I

said to the librarian. "What book would you suggest for me?"

"*Sex and the Senior Citizen* with a glossary in the front listing all the pages with the dirty parts in boldface type," she answered crisply.

"Now, now, Miss Hathcock. We will have our little humor, won't we? Keep in mind I have very little time for reading and I want a book I can talk about in mixed company."

"If I were you," she said slowly, "I'd check out *Come Speed Read with Me* by M. Fletcher. It guarantees that in three days it will increase your reading speed enormously. You will be literally digesting an entire newspaper in nineteen minutes, novels in thirty minutes, and anthologies in an hour."

I tested myself the minute I got home. It took me forty-five minutes to read one paragraph. Maybe it was possible I had lost my old power of concentration. According to the contents of the first chapter, my diagnosis was a simple one. My eyes jerked and stopped at every word. I read each word, not sentences or images. That would take work.

Whenever I got the chance I picked up my *Come Speed Read with Me* book and spent an hour or two in diligent application.

Yesterday I approached Miss Hathcock at the return desk.

"Well, how did your speed reading go?" she smiled. "Are you ready for the complete works of

Churchill? How about *Hawaii?* Or Ted Sorensen's *Kennedy?*"

"Actually," I giggled, "I kept drowsing over chapter two. That's the 'Lack of Attention' chapter. Once I hurdle that, I feel I can whip through the entire thing in no time at all. How about an additional twenty-one days renewal on it?"

"How about *Sex and the Senior Citizen?*" she sighed wearily. "And I'll wrap it in a plain piece of brown paper."

D: TELEPHONE. A noted heart specialist has openly attacked women's use of the extension phone. He has charged these convenient outlets

will (a) broaden hips, (b) cause sluggish circulation, and (c) eventually take away her lead over men in life expectancy.

Doctor, you are either naïve on the subject of telephone conditioning or you are pulling our fat, muscular legs.

At the first ring of the telephone, there is an immediate conditioned response that has every kid in the house galloping to the instrument to answer it. You show me a woman who is alert and who wears deep-tread sneakers and I'll show you a woman who gets to answer her own telephone.

Once Mama is settled comfortably on the phone, the children swing into action like a highly organized army on maneuvers, each marching to his favorite "No, No, Burn Burn" or whatever. Refrigerator doors pop open, cupboards bang back and forth, makeshift ropes carry kids sailing through the air, razor blades appear, strange children come filing through the doors and windows, the aromas of nail polish and gasoline permeate the air, and through it all one child will crawl up on the television set and take off his clothes! There is nothing like it to pep up tired blood.

Some mothers are clickers—that is, rather than interrupt a telephone conversation they will click fingers and point, pound on the table and point, whistle through their fingers and point, or pick up a club and point. So much for circulation.

Other mothers resort to muffled cries as they hold their hands over the receivers. They can't fake it. They've got to administer the whack, clean up the sugar, blow up a balloon, put out the fire, mop up the water *right now!* So much for hip exercises.

A few telephone exponents are a study in pantomime. I used to be mesmerized by a woman who formed the words, "I'm going to give you kids one in a minute," followed shortly by, "I'm going to give you kids two in a minute." She alone knew the magic number whereby she would stop and give them a belt.

Some mothers have even attempted to put a busy box, filled with toys, near their telephones. Of course, kids are too bright to fall for that. You could have Mary Poppins hanging by her umbrella whistling "Dixie" and kids would still roll the onions across the floor and gargle the laundry bleach.

I don't think women outlive men, Doctor. It only seems longer.

Shape Up Before You Ship Out

In the throes of a winter depression cycle, there is nothing that will set you off like a group of fashion authorities who want to know, "Is your figure ready for a bikini this summer?"

I got a flash for you, Charlie. My figure wasn't ready for a bikini last summer. Very frankly, I've hit a few snags.

You see, for years I have built my figure on the

premise that "fat people are jolly." I have eaten my way through: pleasant, cheery, sunny, smiling, gay, spirited, chipper, vivacious, sparkling, happy, and sportive and was well on my way to becoming hysterical. Now I find that a group of experts say this is a myth. "Fat people aren't jolly at all. They're just frustrated and fat." You'd have thought they would have said something while I was back on pleasant.

There was a time when I had a twenty-three-inch waist. I was ten years old at the time. As I recall, my measurements were 23-23-23. I'm no fool. Even at ten years, I knew I could never be too jolly with those figures so I started to eat.

In high school I used to reward myself with

after-school snacks for (a) not stepping on a crack in the sidewalk, (b) spelling Ohio backwards, (c) remembering my locker combination.

After marriage, I added thirty pounds in nine months, which seemed to indicate I was either pregnant or going a little heavy on the gravy. It was the former. I am listed in the medical records as the only woman who ever gained weight *during* delivery.

My husband, of course, tried to shame me by pasting a picture of Ann-Margret on the refrigerator door with a terse note, "Count Calories."

He hasn't tried that routine, however, since our trip to the shopping center last spring that coincided with a personal appearance by Mr. Universe.

"I thought we came here to look at a bedroom rug," he snapped. "You see one muscle, you've seen them all," he snorted.

"I've been married eighteen years and I've yet to see my first one," I said standing on my tiptoes. "Just let me see what he looks like."

Mr. Universe worked in a fitted black T-shirt and shorts. If muscles ever go out of style he could always get a job on the beach kicking sand in the faces of ninety-seven-pound weaklings and yelling, "Yea, skinny!" He thumped onto the platform and my jaw dropped.

"For crying out loud, close your mouth," whispered my husband. "You look like someone just dropped a bar bell on your foot."

"Did you ever see so many muscles in your life?" I gasped. "That T-shirt is living on borrowed time. And listen to that. He says it just takes a few minutes a day to build a body like his. Hey, now he's touching his ear to his knees. Can you touch your ear to your knee?"

"What in heaven's name for?" he sighed. "There's nothing to hear down there. Besides, I'd be embarrassed to look like that. My suits wouldn't fit right. And I couldn't bear having all those people staring."

"You're really sensitive about all this, aren't you?"

"I certainly am not," he said emphatically. "It's just that I'm not a beach boy."

"I'll say you're not a beach boy. Remember when that kid wanted to borrow your inner-tube last summer at the pool and you weren't wearing one?"

"Are we going to look at that bedroom rug or aren't we?" he growled.

"Not until you admit that you can't kick seven feet high, throw a football seventy-five yards and jump over an arrow you're holding in both hands."

"Okay, so I'm not Mr. Universe."

"Then you'll take that picture of Ann-Margret off my refrigerator door?"

"Yes. You know, in my day I used to have a set of pretty good arm muscles. Here, look at this. I'm flexing. Hurry up! See it? How's that for muscle?"

Personally I've seen bigger lumps in my cheese

sauce, but when you've won a war, why mess
around with a small skirmish?

I think the trouble with most women dieters is
that they can't get from Monday to Tuesday without becoming discouraged. I am a typical Monday
dieter. Motivated by some small incident that happens on a Sunday ("Mama's outgrown her seat
belt. We'll have to staple her to the seat covers,
won't we?") I start in earnest on a Monday morning to record my era of suffering.

Diary of a Monday Dieter

8:00 A.M.: This is it. Operation twenty pounds.
Called Edith and told her what I had
for breakfast. Reminded her to read
a story in this month's *Mother's Digest*, "How Mrs. M., St. Louis, ate
25 Hungarian Cabbage Rolls a Day
and Belched Her Way to a Size 10."

12:30 P.M.: Forced myself to drink a cup of bouil-
lon. Called Edith and told her I noticed a difference already. I don't have
that stuffed feeling around my waist.
I have more energy and my clothes fit
better. Promised her my gray suit.
After this week, it will probably hang
on me like a sack.

4:00 P.M.: An article in *Calorie* (the magazine
for people who devour everything in
sight) offers a series of wonderful din-

ner menus for weight-watchers. As I was telling Edith a few minutes ago, we mothers have an obligation to our families to feed them nutritious, slimming meals. Tonight we are having lean meat, fresh garden peas, Melba thins in a basket, and fresh fruit.

4:30 P.M.: Husband called to say he'd be late for dinner. Fresh garden peas looked a little nude, so added a few sauteed mushrooms and a dab of cream sauce. After all, why should the children be sick and suffer because they have a strong-willed mother?

4:45 P.M.: I ate the Melba toast—every dry, tasteless crumb of it! (Come to think of it the basket is missing.) Luckily I had a biscuit mix in the refrigerator and jazzed it up with a little shredded cheese and butter. The magazine said when you begin licking wax from the furniture you should supplement your diet with a snack.

5:00 P.M.: Well, maybe that lousy fruit in the bowl would look pretty good to Robinson Crusoe, but I put it under a pie crust where it belongs. In fifty minutes I'll have a warm cobbler, swimming in rich, thick cream. Who does my husband think he is? Paul Newman?

5:30 P.M.: The kids just asked what I am doing. I'm putting on a few potatoes to go with the gravy, that's what I'm doing. That's the trouble with kids today. Half of the world goes to bed hungry and they expect me to pour good meat drippings down the drain. Kids are rotten. They really are.

6:00 P.M.: Blood pressure has dropped. Stomach is beginning to bloat. Vision is impaired. I've added two more vegetables and a large pizza with everything to the menu. That fink Edith had the nerve to call and ask if she could have the blouse to the gray suit. Edith's a nice girl, but she's a pushy individual who drives you crazy phoning all the time. I told the kids to tell her I couldn't talk. I was listening to my Bonnie Prudden records.

6:30 P.M.: Husband arrived home. I met him at the door and let him have it. If it weren't for his rotten working hours, I could be the slip of the girl he married. He had the gall to act like he didn't know what I was talking about.

No, I don't think I'm ready for a bikini again this year. Heaven knows I try to bend to the dictates of fashion, but let's face it, I'm a loser. When I grew my own bustle, they went out of style. When my hips reached saddlebag proportions, the "long, lean look" came in. When I ultimately discovered a waistline, the straight skirt came into being. I had a few bright moments when they were exploiting the flat chest as denoting women with high I.Q.'s, but then someone revealed a certain clearly unflat movie star's 135 (I.Q. that is) and shot *that* theory down.

Here's my basic equipment, if you fashion moguls care to check it out, but frankly it doesn't look too encouraging.

Shoulders: Two of them. Unfortunately they don't match. One hooks up higher than the other, which they tell me is quite common among housewives who carry fat babies, heavy grocery bags, and car chains.

Midriff: If I can't tighten up the muscles in time for beach exposure perhaps I can use it for a snack tray.

Eyes: Some people with myopic vision look sexy. I look like I have myopic vision. Don't tell me what to do with my eyebrows. I tried several things and either look like Milton Berle or Bela Lugosi with a sick headache.

Waist: It's here somewhere. Probably misfiled.

Hips: Here. They weren't built in a day, friend, so don't expect miracles. Right now, they couldn't get a rise out of a factory whistle.

Knees: Let me put it this way. A poet at a neighborhood cocktail party once described them as "divining rods that could get water out of the Mojave Desert."

Legs: Ever wonder who got what Phyllis Diller discarded?

Guts: Hardly any.

Tell you what. If I don't "shape up" by June, go on to the beach without me. Stop on the way back and I'll serve you a dish of homemade short-cake, topped with fresh strawberries crusted in powdered sugar and wallowing in a soft mound of freshly whipped cream.

March 5—May 6

I want to be more than just another pretty face...

Talent is a big thing.

Most of us can't be like the optimist who was given a barn full of fertilizer and ran through it pell mell shouting, "I know there's a pony here somewhere." We wonder where we were when talent was passed out. Making Jockey shorts for Ken dolls? Fashioning angels out of toilet tissue rolls? Baking no-cal cupcakes for fat Girl Scouts?

Why do we feel so dumb? So out of touch with the world? So lacking in self-confidence? As you look at the reflection in the mirror, your brush rollers towering high above you, your cold sore shimmering from ointment, you mumble to yourself, "I want to be more than just another pretty face. I want to make some difference in this world. Just once I want to stand up at a PTA meeting and say, 'I entertain a motion that we adjourn until we have business more pressing than the cafeteria's surplus of canned tomatoes, and more entertaining than a film on *How Your Gas Company Works for You.*'" Just once I'd like to have a tall dark stranger look at me like I wasn't on the sixth day of a five-day deodorant pad. Just once I'd like to have a real fur coat that I could drag behind me on the floor. (Not those 218 hamsters with tranquilizers that I wear to club.)

But me? I couldn't even carry off a trip to Mr.

Miriam's Hair Palace. There I stood surrounded by elegance in my simple, peasant headscarf, my wrap-around skirt, my summer tennis shoes, and, my God! *Not Girl Scout socks!*

"Are you a standing?" asked the receptionist.

"A standing what?" I asked.

"Do you have a standing appointment?"

I shook my head.

"I say, you didn't cut your bangs at home with pinking shears or anything, did you?" she asked suspiciously. "Or turn your hair orange with bleach over bleach? Or fall asleep and forget to turn your home permanent off?"

"Oh no," I said. "I just want my hair done because I've been a little depressed since the baby was born."

"Oh," she said softly, "how old is your baby?"

"Twenty-four," I answered.

Because I was unknown to the shop, I drew Miss Lelanie, who had been out of beauty school three days—this time. (The lawsuit with the nasty bald woman is still pending.) With Miss Lelanie, I felt as relaxed as a cat in a roomful of rocking chairs. She didn't say anything, really. She just flipped through my hair like she was tossing a wilted salad. Finally she called in Mr. Miriam to show him what she had found. Both concurred that my ends were split, my scalp diseased, and I was too far over the hill to manufacture a decent supply of hair oil.

"It's all that dry?" I asked incredulously.

"I'd stay away from careless smokers," said

Miss Lelanie without smiling.

Miss Lelanie massaged, combed, conditioned, rolled, brushed, teased, and sprayed for the better part of two hours. The she whirled me around to look into the mirror. "Why fight it?" I said, pinching the reflection's cheek. "You're a sex symbol." Miss Lelanie closed her eyes as if asking for divine guidance.

I don't mind admitting I felt like a new woman as I walked across the plush carpet, my shoulders squared, my head held high. I could feel every pair of eyes in the room following me.

"Pardon me, honey," said Miss Lelanie, "you're dragging a piece of bathroom tissue on your heel. Want me to throw it away?"

I could have been a standing and I blew it. That's the way it is with me.

Even my own children know I'm a no-talent. There was a time when I could tell them anything and they would believe me. I had all the answers. "Mama, what does the tooth fairy do with all those teeth she collects?" I'd smile wisely and say, "Why she makes them into necklaces and sells them at Tiffany's for a bundle." "What's a bundle, Mama?" "Please, dear," I would say, feigning dizziness, "how much brilliance can Mommy pour into your small head in one day." And so it went. I was their authority on the solar system, the Bible, history, mathematics, languages, fine arts, the St. Lawrence Seaway, air brakes, and turbojets. I even had them believing the traffic lights changed colors when I blew hard and commanded them to "turn green." (So, my kids were a little slow.)

Then one day recently my daughter asked, "Do you know the capital of Mozambique?" "No, but hum a few bars and I'll fake it," I grinned. "Mother," she announced flatly, "you don't know anything!"

That was the beginning. Day by day they chipped away at my veneer of ignorance. I didn't know how to say in French, "Pardon me, sir, but you are standing on my alligator's paw." I didn't know how to find the expanding notation of a number in modern math. (I didn't even know it was missing.) I didn't know the make of the sports car parked across the street, or the exact height of Oscar Robertson. I had never read *Smokey, the Cow Horse*. I didn't even know General Stonewall Jackson always ate standing up so his food would digest better.

In desperatiton I wrote to Bennington College in Vermont, which, I understood, was offering a course just meant for me.

Sirs:

I read with great interest the possibility of a new course being added to your curriculum, "Boredom of Housewifery." Knowing there will be several million housewives who will invade your city riding trucks, tanks, cars, planes, trains, pogo sticks, rickshaws, bicycles, and skateboards, I hasten to be considered for enrollment.

My background would seem to qualify me. I have three children who are hostile and superior to me mentally, a husband who loves his work and plays the guitar, and a house that depresses me. I cry a lot.

I don't seem to know what to do with my time. I think I waste a lot of it. When I am in the car waiting for the children at school I have taken to writing down the car mileage, multiplying it by my age, subtracting the number of lost mittens behind the seat, and dividing it by my passengers. Whatever number I come up with, is the number of cookies I allow myself before dinner.

I am not stimulated by housework as are other women I know. They are always doing clever things with old nylon hose and egg cartons. Last month I stuck a four-inch nail into the wall above my sink to hold the unpaid bills. When I tried to share my idea with my friends they said I needed to get out more. Sometimes I think the winter has fifteen months in it.

I have also tried joining various organizations, but this does not seem to solve my problem. Last school year I was Sunshine Chairman of the PTA. It seems I spread more sunshine than the treasury was prepared to spread. They dismissed me with a polite note that read, "It is nice to make people happy, but you don't have to tickle them to death."

You stated that the program at Bennington would be designed to aid wives "whose vital intellectual capacity is sapped by what seems to them like endless hours during which they serve as combination caretakers, nurses, policewomen, and kitchen helpers." I like that.

The announcement did not deal specifically with any of the topics to be discussed, but I am hopeful they will cover "Lies and Other Provocative Sayings" for dinner parties, outings, and class reunions. I'd also like a class in "Conversational Hobbies." I passed up the chance to take "Auto Harp Lessons" because I thought I hadn't been driving long enough.

Sincerely,
Desperate

Needless to say the class was filled before they received my application and I continue to feel inadequate and unsure of myself. Why is this? I can see it in my husband's attitude toward me. The other night he took me to dinner. We were having a wonderful time when he remarked, "You can certainly tell the wives from the sweethearts."

I stopped licking the stream of butter dripping down my elbow and replied, "What kind of a crack is that?"

"Just look around you," he said. "See that sweet young thing staring into her young man's eyes? She's single. Now look at the table next to them. That woman has buttered six pieces of bread and is passing them clockwise around the table. Soon she will cut up everyone's meat within a six-table radius and begin collecting swizzle sticks to take home to the kids. She's obviously married. You can always tell. Married women rarely dance. They just sit there and throw appetizers down their throats like the main course just went out of style. Single women go out to 'dine.' Married women go out to 'eat.' "

All the way home, holding the doggy bag filled with tossed salad out the no-draft so it wouldn't drip through on my coat, I thought about what he said. It was true. Women were in a rut. At parties all the women retired to the living room to relive their birth pains and exchange tuna recipes while the men hovered around the kitchen and attacked the big stuff like strikes, racial differences, and wars.

"Why don't you ever talk with us about those things?" I asked.

"What things?"

"Like wars and economics and the UN?"

He grimaced. "Remember the last time at a party I mentioned Taylor was in Vietnam?" (I nodded.) "And you asked if Burton was there with her?" (I nodded.) "That's why."

"That's not fair," I shouted. "You know I'm nothing at parties. I'm just not large on small talk."

"I noticed that," he retorted; "you spring into the first chair you see like there are magnets in your garters and you never leave it. You just sit there and watch your feet swell."

"It all seems so ridiculous," I snapped. "The other night at that dreary party, one of your friends, whom I shall call Mr. Teeth for want of a better description, said to me, 'I've been looking for you all evening. What have you been reading lately?' "

"What's wrong with that?"

"Nothing. Only he wasn't even looking at me. His head was pivoting like a red light on a police cruiser all the while. I told him I had read 'The Causes and Effects of Diaper Rash' and he said, 'Good show! The critics in the East raved about it.' He hugged me and left."

"What about Larry Blagley. I saw him talking with you."

"You mean 'Mr. Sincere'?"

"I wish you'd stop tagging my friends those goofy names."

"I was enjoying a good, stiff drink when he said, 'Doesn't water pollution bother you at all?' I nearly choked to death. 'Am I drinking it?' I asked. He said, 'Why I have samples in my lab of that stinking, slimy glob of bilge and garbage that looks like so much sticky, clotted, ropey yuuuuuck. It infiltrates your drinking water and mine. If you saw it, it would make your hair stand on end.' 'Just hearing about it isn't doing much for the liver paste that's stuck in my throat either,' I told him."

"The trouble with you," said my husband, "is you're just too cute for words. Coming over and grabbing my sleeve and insisting we leave this deathly dull group!"

"So, I forgot we were the host and hostess. It's a perfectly natural mistake."

"You ought to get out more. Do something to make your day important. Give you something to talk about in the evening."

He had a point. What did I do all day? The only big thing that had happened was I used the wrong aerosol can for my deodorant and I didn't have to worry about clogged-up nasal passages in my armpits for twenty-four hours. No wonder he never talked to me. Out loud I said defensively, "Women would have more confidence if there were more Viktor Syomins in the world!"

"Who is Viktor Syomin?" he asked.

He was paying attention. "Viktor," I explained, "is a little-known Russian whose wife was attending Moscow University until one grim day her professor told her, 'In four years you have failed sixteen courses and you don't know anything.' Now any normal American husband would have looked at his wife and said, 'Face it, Luvie, you're a dum dum,' but not Viktor.

"Viktor stomped into the professor's office and demanded, 'You pass my wife or else.' The professor retorted, '*Chepuka*,' which I think means 'And-so's-your-amoeba-brained-wife.' At any rate, Viktor said, 'You have insulted my wife's intelligence,' and broke the professor's nose.

"It's not important that Viktor's assault and battery case comes up in three months," I concluded angrily. "What is important is that he regards his wife as more than a pretty face. He regards her as a mental equal. You hear that? A mental equal! Now, do you want to hear my hilarious story about the aerosol nasal spray I pffted away under my arms or not?"

After a moment's silence, he grinned. "You've got a big mouth."

It's not much of a talent to go on, but I think I just found a pony in my barn.

The Rocky Road to Self-Improvement

At some point in her life a woman will go the "self-improvement" route.

This could mean a $3.95 investment in a Bonnie Prudden exercise record, a short course in Conversational Hebrew, Contract Bridge for Blood and Revenge, Mau Mau Flower Arrangements, or a trip back through time to an ivy-covered university.

These courses do what they are supposed to do. They get a woman out of the house, give her a goal or a dream to hang onto, and focus a little attention on herself for a change. It gives her something to contribute to the conversation at dinner. ("You'll never guess who almost fell into the ceramic kiln and made an ashtray of herself!") In short, it gets her out of the proverbial rut.

You take my neighbor Marty. Marty is what we always called a "child-geared" woman. When her pediatrician recommended she use baby talk to communicate with her youngsters, Marty was the

first to crawl around on all fours slobbering uncontrollably and gurgling, "No, nee, now, noo,
noo." We wondered about it, but Marty said it
was a new theory, and she owed it to her kids to
try it. That was ten years ago. Today Marty's
children talk like Fulbright Scholarship winners. It's Marty who can't kick the baby-talk
habit. For example, the other night she said to her
husband, "I've laid out your jammies and your
bow wow. As soon as you drink your moo cow,
you can give Mama a sugar and go upsie-daisy to
beddie-bye." Sterling (Marty's husband) just
looked at her and said quietly, "I've been thinking, Marty, maybe you oughta have your tongue
fixed. I think you're regressing. Have you considered a self-improvement speech course to enlarge
your vocabulary?"

Marty was hurt and shocked. She hadn't
realized her speaking habits were that bad. Thus
was born Marty's "Word a Day" improvement
course. It worked very simply. Every morning
Marty would get down the large dictionary to her
encyclopedia set and flip through it at random.
With eyes closed she would point to a word on a
page. That was her word for the day. By her own
rules she would be compelled to use the word in
a sentence at least five times before the sun went
down.

We bled for poor Marty. We really did. Her
word-for-the-day was sometimes impossible to
work into everyday conversation. Like tse-tse fly.
At a woman's luncheon Marty threw it out. "Oh,

is that a tse-tse fly?" "No," said her hostess coldly, "that is a raisin and I'll thank you to keep your voice down while I am serving it." Or at a cocktail party when she was telling her husband's boss, "I was lying around 'supine' all morning until the mailman came." At his shocked reaction she added quickly, "That's not a dirty word. It's an adjective meaning lying down, lethargic."

Usually it wasn't too tricky to pick out her word-for-the-day by the number of times she used it. We recorded one sentence as follows: "My problems have been infinitesimal lately, but then I say to myself every morning, 'Marty, you are too young to let infinitesimal things bother you. At this rate you'll end up with infinitesimal flu!'" (Three down and two to go.)

As the pressures of home and family increased it became apparent that poor Marty often had no time to look up the meanings of her words. Thus, we would hear her lament, "I have always wanted to play the clavicle." Or, "I never win at Monotony. The kids buy up all the railroads and fertilities and where does that leave me?"

We heard her self-improvement route ended one night when she asked her husband, "Did Fred pass his civil service elimination or was he having one of those days?"

Marty told us her husband said to her, "Marty-kins, let's find our way back to snookums, horthies, and moo cows. I liked you better when I couldn't understand a word you were saying."

That's one of the hazards of self-improvement.

People overdo, and before you know it, they're taking themselves seriously.

We've often said that's what happened to poor Myrtle Flub. Myrtle was a real golf enthusiast. We met her in a six-week golf clinic at the YWCA. To the rest of us, golf was something to do with your hands while you talked. (Unless you smoked. Then, you never had to leave the clubhouse.) With Myrtle it was different. Whenever we got a foursome together, it was always Myrtle who insisted on keeping the scores in ink. Her clubs were never rusted or dulled by wads of bubble gum. (She was horrified the day I found a pair of child's training pants in my golf bag.)

She always played by the book. This was upsetting. We used to try to jazz up the game a bit. For example, if you forgot to say, "Mother, may I?" before you teed off, you had to add a stroke. If you clipped the duck on the pond and made him quack, you didn't have to play the sixteenth hole at all, and if you had more than fifteen strokes on one hole, you didn't have to putt out. This used to drive Myrtle crazy. She never understood why we allowed each other five "I didn't see you swings" in one game.

Then one day she arrived at the course, bubbling with excitement. "I've found a way to take points off my score," she said. (At last, we thought, she's going to cheat like the rest of us.)

"I have just read this article by a British obstetrician who says pregnant women play better golf than women who are not pregnant. He conducted this extensive survey and discovered golf scores were bettered by ten and fifteen strokes."

"But surely," we gasped, "you're not seriously considering . . ."

"If the road to motherhood is paved with birdies, pars, and eagles," she answered, "call me Mom."

The first few months of pregnancy, Myrtle wasn't too sensational on the golf course. She was nauseous. Her normally neat golf bag was a mass of soda cracker crumbs and once when I offered her a piece of cold pizza, she quit playing. Right there on the fifth hole, she quit.

During the early fall, she had a bit of trouble with swollen ankles, so her salt intake and her golf games were kept at a minimum. "Just wait until spring," she said. "I'll be the talk of the club." She was. When Myrtle tried to tee off it was like trying to land on an aircraft carrier without radar. She couldn't see her feet, let alone her ball. To be blunt, she was too pregnant to putt.

Last week we dropped by Myrtle's house en route to the golf course. (She'll resume play when the baby is older.) We talked about the good doctor's survey. "Who is this man?" asked one of the girls. "A medical doctor," Myrtle insisted, "who has done extensive research on women golfers. Here is the picture and the clipping."

We looked in disbelief. There was no doubt in our minds. He was the same man who played behind us the day we dodged the sprinkling system and made the rule that if you got wet, you had to drive the golf cart in reverse back to the club-house.

Boy, men sure are bad sports.

I have traveled the self-improvement route on a few occasions myself. A few years back, I found myself not only talking to a fishbowl of turtles, I started to quarrel and disagree with them.

As I told the registrar who was conducting some informal evening classes in the high school, "I want to acquire some skills and the self-confidence to go with them. I don't want to leave this world without some important contribution that will show I've been here. Is the '500 Ways with Hamburger' class filled yet?" It was.

She suggested a class called "Let's Paint." I explained to her I was a beginner. She assured me that "Let's Paint" was a class for amateur artists who had never before held a paintbrush in their hands. She should have added "between their toes or stuck in their ears," because they most certainly wielded them from every other point.

My first table partner was a slim blonde who sprung open her fishing-tackle box and ninety dollars worth of oil paints fell out. She hoisted her canvas on a board like a mast on a sailboat and in twenty minutes had sketched and shaded an impressionistic view of the Grand Canyon in eight shades of purple.

"What are you working on?" she asked, not taking her eyes from her work.

"It's nothing really," I said. "Just a little something I felt like doing today."

She grabbed my sketchbook. "You're tracing a snowman from a Christmas card?"

My next table partner was an elderly woman who confessed she hadn't had a canvas in front of her for years. I'm no fool. She had her own dirty smock and, I suspect, her own scaffold from which she retouched the ceiling of the Sistine Chapel on weekends.

"What have we here?" she bubbled, grabbing my sketch pad. "It's a kitchen window, isn't it? You don't have to label things, my dear. It detracts from the work. Of course, if you don't mind a suggestion, your curtains are a little stiff and stilted. Curtains billow softly."

"Well, ordinarily mine would too," I said, "but I put too much starch in them the last time. You can crack your shins on them."

My next table partner was a young wife awaiting the arrival of her first child. "Did you have any trouble with your still life of the fruit and the pitcher?" she asked shyly.

"Not really," I said, pulling out a sheet of sketch paper with only a few scattered dots on it.

"But the grapes, bananas, and apples?"

"My kids ate them."

"And the pitcher?"

"Dog knocked it off the table."

"And the little dots?"

"Fruit flies."

I like having a table to myself. Talking distracts me from my serious work.

Diseases I'd tell My Doctor About If It Weren't
Wednesday Afternoon

A: ACUTE POSSESSIONITIS. "I've got this problem, Doctor. Lately I've been experiencing a fierce
sense of possession. I want to have a closet all my
own, a dresser drawer that is all mine and no one
else's and personal things that belong only to me.
I want to share my life with my family, mind you,
but not my roll of scotch tape. Can you understand
that?"

He smiled. "I think so. Why don't you tell me
about it?"

"I guess I first noticed it one night at the dinner
table. I took a bite out of this fig newton and set

it down. When I went to pick it up again one of the children was popping it into his mouth. 'That's my fig newton,' I said, my lip beginning to quiver. 'You can get another one,' he grinned. 'I don't want another one,' I insisted. 'That was *my* fig newton and you had no right to take it!' He giggled, 'I knew it was your fig newton.' 'Then why did you take it?' I shouted. 'Because I'm nasty and maladjusted,' he shouted back.

"From then on, Doctor, I became terribly conscious of personal items of mine that were being used without my permission. I discovered the family was using my eyebrow pencils to write down messages by the telephone. My Sunday black earrings were the eyes of a snowman. My lace headscarf was the stole of a Barbie doll. My eyebrow tweezers were dissecting a frog. Even my chin strap was filled with buckshot and was on maneuvers in the back yard.

"I can't begin to describe the resentment that began to build. I finally bought a very large old desk that would house all my personal belongings. It was marvelous. It had forty-five pigeonholes, secret drawers, and sliding panels, and if you didn't hold the lid just right it would fall down and snap your arm off. I transferred all my valuables to the desk like a pack rat anticipating a long winter.

"For a while, things went well. Then things began to slip away from me. My paper clips one by one. My cotton balls. And my rubber bands. (I even disguised them in an old laxative box.)

But I'm tired, Doctor. I can't fight anymore."

He smiled. "You're suffering from an old 'return-to-your-single-status' psychosis where you enjoyed some rights and independence. It can happen in an eighteen-year-old marriage. Let me give you a prescription." He stood up, removed the pillow from his chair, unzipped the cover and removed the key. He proceeded to the sixth brick in the fireplace, where he extracted a small box and unlocked it. "My prescription blanks," he laughed nervously. "If I don't hide them from my nurse she uses them for scratch pads."

"I understand," I said.

B: DRAGGING POSTERIOR. "Doctor, according to national statistics, I make a dollar fifty-nine an hour. My fringe benefits are few. I get bed and board, a weekly trip to the discount house to listen to the piped-in music, and all the aspirin I can throw down.

"My problem is Sunday work. I am the only one in the house who works on Sundays. It's the same old saw. Everyone pads around all morning in pajamas, running through the comics in their bare feet, and lolling around on the beds like a group of tired Romans waiting for Yvonne De Carlo to appear with a trayful of tropical fruit."

"While you?"

"While I whip around the house getting meals, making beds, finding mates to white gloves, and keeping the fire exits clear of debris."

"And they do nothing?"

"Nothing is right. They eat and watch television. One morning I found them watching test patterns on television. They thought it was a golf show with a diagram pointing out the yardage to the cup."

"What happens when you sit down to relax?"

"One gets a bee caught in his nose. They rub poison oak into their pores. Sometimes they nip away at the paint thinner. Nine out of our last ten emergencies happened on Sunday. Once I almost got a nap. Then my husband said, 'You look bored. Let's clean the garage.' "

"What about the evenings?"

"Evenings are memory time. They remember they need an American flag out of the attic for a school play. One can't take a bath because his toenail is falling off, and somewhere along the line I must give birth to twenty-four pink cupcakes. It's my attitude that bothers me. Last Sunday I did a mean thing, Doctor. I flushed them out of their beds at 7 A.M. yelling, 'You're all going to be late for school.' They staggered around the driveway in the final stages of shock."

"There's no reason for you to have a guilt complex," he explained. "We all have our threshold of endurance. Just put it out of your mind."

"I can't, Doctor. You should hear what I've got planned for next Sunday!"

C: GLUE-BREATH. "It happened the other morning, Doctor. My cleaning woman approached me and said, 'You may fire me for this, but you've got glue-breath.'

" 'But I use a mouthwash,' I insisted. She backed up, weaving unsteadily and said, 'That soda pop isn't doing the job.' In my heart I knew she was right, but I can't help myself. Like most other housewives in America, I succumbed a few years ago to the lure of trading stamps. At first, it was innocent enough. We saved a couple of books and got a croquet set for the kids . . . then a few more books for a lawn trimmer for Dad . . . and finally eight or so books for a leg shaver for me . . . things we really needed.

"Then one day we read a story in the newspaper about a New York zoo that bought a gorilla for 5,400,000 trading stamps. Just reading about all those stamps gave our family a case of redemption fever. We gathered around the dining room table after dinner and began to speculate on what would happen if we upped our consumption of gasoline, oil, tires, windshield wipers, and sunglasses from Bernie's Service Station. 'In three years,' my husband shouted, 'we could buy the New York Mets!'

"Our son figured out if we could get doctors, lawyers, and the sanitary department to issue trading stamps we might even amass enough to earn a Rhino hunt weekend for two in scenic Kenya. We went half crazed with desire. One of the children vowed to start saving for Rhode Island, another for Richard Nixon's older daughter . . . another for a do-it-yourself missile site for the back yard. I personally wanted to visit the Senior Citizen

Center to which Cary Grant belonged. The possibilities were crazy and without limits.

"From that day on, our entire buying habits changed. We often ran out of gas looking for a station with our brand of stamps. We bought food we hated to get bonus stamps. In desperation, we even switched to a newly-formed church across town that gave one hundred and twenty trading stamps each time we attended. (We now worship a brown and white chicken with a sunburst on its chest.)

"I know it sounds ridiculous, but I have pasted stamps in 1563 books. I'll match that against J. Paul Getty's stamp books any day of the week! Someone in the family guards them twenty-four hours a day and we count them once a week. We stage mock fire drills from time to time so we can evacuate them quickly in case of fire. In the event of a nuclear attack, we have instructions to empty out the drinking water and save the stamp books. Trading stamps have possessed me, Doctor. What do you think?"

The doctor tapped his pencil slowly on the desk. "I personally think you are some kind of a nut with fuzzy breath, that's what I think. What in the world are you going to buy with 1563 books?"

"When I fill five more pages, Doctor," I said stiffly, "I will own this office building. And if I were you, I wouldn't have any more magazines sent to this address!"

D: CAR POOL ALLERGY. "You see, Doctor, chil-

dren see their mothers as symbols of some kind—hot apple pie, delicate perfume, a soft kiss to heal a scraped knee.

"My children see me as four wheels, a motor, and a drive shaft. I am Snow White with a set of car keys. Peter Pan off in a cloud of blue exhaust. Mary Poppins with fifteen gasoline credit cards.

"People are always talking about men who commute. I don't feel sorry for them. At least they drive on designated roads where their only annoyances are a few bad drivers and a few dozen police cars camouflaged as spirea bushes.

"But women in car pools! Women get cuffed with lunch boxes while they're driving. Women have to cut bubble gum out of their hair with scissors. Women have to charter new routes over barren fields and swamplands looking for the 'Blue Team on Diamond 12.'

"Frankly, Doctor, I've been involved in so many car pools I'm beginning to walk like Groucho

Marx. This business of chauffeuring really began to bother me about two weeks ago. I pulled up in front of a traffic light and five girls piled in. One said, 'Carol, tell your mother to turn right at the next street.' A girl called Carol said, 'She's not my mother. I thought she was your mother.' 'No,' said the other voice, 'My mother wears glasses. Or is it my father who wears glasses? Hey, gang, is this anyone's mother?'

" 'The back of the head does look familiar,' said one. 'Did you take a group of girls on school patrol on a tour of bus station restrooms recently?' I shook my head no.

" 'I got it,' said another. 'You brought the garbage home from Girl Scout Camp! I remember now. It was out-of-season so we couldn't bury it. When she came to pick up her group she got stuck with bringing the garbage home. Sorry, but I didn't recognize you without all those fruit flies.'

"I nodded affirmatively. How long ago was it when I begged for wheels of my own? A car was going to restore independence to my dreary life, open up lines of communication to a whole new world of culture and entertainment. It was going to free me from the bonds of my daily routine. What happened?

"When I left the girls off, I ended up with two small passengers, my Wednesday afternoon kindergarten drop-offs. 'I'm five years old,' one of them announced to the other. 'I wonder how old she is.' (Note: Small children always refer to the driver in the third person, never directly. This destroys the impersonal driver-passenger relationship.) 'I'm eight years old!' I yelled back impulsively.

" 'Do you think she's really eight years old?' asked the other one.

" 'I'm big for my age,' I added.

" 'My mother is that big and she's thirty-two,' said the first one.

" 'Big people act funny sometimes,' said the second child.

" 'Yeah,' said the first child, 'but it beats walkin'.' "

E: IDENTITY PAINS. "I might as well confess it before you hear it from someone else, Doctor. I've found my identity.

"You can't imagine what this means. People who have considered me a friend for years shout, 'Fraud, fake, and traitor.' Some of them have burned copies of *Hints from Heloise* on my front yard. I know I will be asked to turn in my Betty Friedan signet ring. Nevertheless it is true.

"I wasn't real took with the movement for women's equality in the first place. What with carying out the trash, changing fuses, cutting the grass, and fertilizing the shrubbery, any more equality would kill me. You have to know I'm the type if Carrie Nation had called and said, 'Would you like to make a contribution to your sex?' I'd probably have said, 'My husband gives at the office.'

"I don't know. I tried to have a real mystique going for me, but I didn't get too much mileage out of it. I used to shuffle through the house saying, 'Who am I? Where am I? Where am I going?' All I did was scare the Avon lady half to death. I even said to my husband one night, 'You know, I think I've lost my identity,' and without looking up he said, 'It's probably with your car keys . . . wherever they are.'

"When I told my mother about my 'Oedipus conflict and sibling rivalry that had embedded themselves into my personality,' she said, 'What kind of language is that for a mother?'

"Well, the first clue to my identity came one day when the phone rang and someone said, 'Hello, Erma.' I tell you my eyes misted up like Ben Cartwright on *Bonanza* when his horse goes lame. 'What did you call me?' I asked slowly. The voice repeated the name. That was it. That must be my identity. Feverishly I went through my billfold in my purse and emptied out a stack of credit cards, a YWCA membership, a library card, and a driver's license. They all bore the same name.

"I raced to the bedroom and began rummaging through drawers. There were old report cards signed by me, monogrammed handkerchiefs, and autographed copies of books scrawled, 'To Erma.' At last I knew my real identity.

"Then a card fell to the floor. It was addressed to Mrs. Erma Bombeck, Girl Scout captain. My first real breakthrough. I not only knew who I was but what I was. *I was a commissioned officer in the cookie corps!*

"I felt wonderful and proud, Doctor. My mystique had been solved. My problem now is I can't remember where I put the cookies."

Parting with Money is Taxing

There were really only two men I knew who ever got a laugh out of paying their income taxes. One was cheating the government and getting away with it. The other had a sick sense of humor and would probably have set up a concession stand at the Boston Tea Party and sold sugar cubes and lemon slices.

Sitting up with a sick taxpayer is no picnic. At best "How to live with your husband until his W-2 forms are filed" is pure agony. I have done it for years and these are the lessons I've reaped:

1. Never try to talk your husband out of his depression over his taxes. The last woman I heard who stood at her husband's elbow waving a flag and chanting, "Be thankful for Mom and apple pie," is now living with her mother and working in a bakery. This is no time to fool around.

2. Never suggest that he file his tax return early. There is nothing that will unsettle a man more than being jammed in a post office with a group of New Year's revelers who are filing early only because they are getting a refund. Better to have him in the cortege of cars that slowly inch their way to the mailbox at midnight of the April deadline, while a sullen group on the post office

steps chants, "We shall overcome."

3. Keep the children out of his path. From January through April they cease to have names. They become Deduction A, Deduction B, and Deduction C. Mentally he begins to add up what he has invested in their teeth, arches, sports program, fine arts, education, clothes, food, lodging, entertainment, vitamins, and social welfare. Once he has figured out that $600 wouldn't keep them in catsup and breakfast cereal, his resentment reaches a danger point.

4. Anticipate his low days. When he is virtually drowning in a sea of canceled checks, receipts, memos, and statements of interest and income, offer enthusiastically to have your gall bladder taken out next year to increase his medical deduction. Promise to adopt an orphan Parisian chorus girl, make a large donation to the indigent at the Polo Club, invest unwisely, lose heavily at Chinese checkers, buy an office building on credit.

Above all, be ready to produce explanations or at least to discuss any expenditure from a cold capsule to a major purchase like swimming lessons for your daughter.

"How in the name of all that is sane did you spend $175 for swimming lessons?" he shouted, the veins standing erect in his neck. "I could have gotten Flipper to tutor her in our own bathtub for $50."

"Actually the swimming lessons were only $4 for ten weeks at the 'Y,' but I encountered some extras."

"What extras?"

"Extras! There was 49 cents for a nose plug."

"That leaves $170.51."

"And the parking. I think that amounted to $35."

"$35?"

"I parked in a towaway zone. Then one night we stayed downtown and had dinner and went to a movie. That amounted to about $10."

"That narrows it down to $125.51."

"Of course, $12 or so went for bribes."

"Another towaway zone?"

"No, to keep our boys from playing with the paper towels in the restroom and skating on the lobby floors. I had to bribe them with food and things. After all, my pride is worth something."

"That's 'Pride: $12,' " he mused.

"Yes and don't forget the bedspreads. I get to town so rarely I felt I had to run over and look at the bedspreads on sale. I bought two. Take away $24.73."

"That leaves $88.78."

"Well, about $15 went for medication when she forgot to dry her hair and caught cold. If you're concerned about the waste of pills, I could pack them in her lunch."

"Don't be cute," he said. "What happened to the other $73.78?"

"My goodness, there were a lot of things. Name tapes for the towels, new swimming bag, new headlight for the mail truck I hit, and don't forget the nose plug."

"That was 49 cents, wasn't it?" he asked, unconsciously moistening his ballpoint pen on his tongue.

Laugh at income tax? My dear, I would sooner put out my foot and trip Tiny Tim.

Sick . . . Sick . . . Sick . . .

HER STORY:

Actually I was looking forward to Leonard's being home, even if he was recuperating from minor surgery. We were going to have leisure breakfasts, giddy coffee breaks, pore over old picture albums and maybe even harmonize on a few reckless choruses of "Mexicali Rose."

I don't know what went wrong. I ran trays like

I was working the dark corner of a drive-in. I fluffed pillows, rubbed his back, delivered papers, smoothed sheets, and was summoned from every room in the house. Of course, Leonard was never able to stand pain. When he suffered a paper cut in '59, I never left his bedside. The doctor said it was my strength that pulled him through.

"Did I tell you I was awake during the entire operation?" he yelled down the hallway.

"Yes!"

"Did I tell you about that herd of vampires who drew blood from me every hour of the day and night?"

"Yes!"

By the second week he had me looking up phone numbers of all his old Army buddies at Ft. Dix, digging out the ouija board, finding out how much insurance he had on his car (among other research projects), and nursing his pothus plant back to life. ("All right then, *you* tell Miss Cartwright her gift pothus died because it was potbound. Go ahead! Break an old woman's heart!")

"You hear me out there?" he'd shout. "While you're flitting around the countryside, stop off at the library and get us a book on playwriting. You hear? We could write a hit play together, you and I."

By the third week he was approaching full strength. He toured the house and discovered the kitchen cupboards were ill-planned, something strange had died in the utility room, and what this family really needed was a well-organized, well-planned duty roster.

His final week was probably his finest hour. He was in his "communications" syndrome, or as we called it, "Chopping Off at the Mouth."

"You tell Ed at the garage I said if he doesn't set that motor up he can jolly well push it all the way to Detroit with the broken nose I am going to give him when I get out of this bed. Got that? As for Clark at the office, you just tell him for me that I've dealt with his kind before and if he thinks he can pull this off while I am flat on my back he's got another thought coming. Remind him what happened in '48."

"What happened in '48?" I asked intently.

"Nothing, but Clark won't remember either. And another thing. You collar that grass cutter you hired and tell him for me to set that mower back where I had it. I don't want a putting green, just some front yard grass left."

I guess I know why the Good Lord had women bear the children. Men would have delegated the job!

HIS STORY:

Actually I was looking forward to staying home with Doris to help her over her bout with the flu. If a man can't pitch in and manage his own kids and his own house, I always say, what's he good for?

I don't know what went wrong. Lord knows I was doing the best I could under the circumstances. I tried to bring a little order to her kitchen, but when I flung open the cabinet doors and read the headlines on the shelf paper, DEWEY CONCEDES TO TRUMAN, I knew I was in for it. I lined up the kids and put them to work. Doris lets them get away with too much.

"Why in heaven's name does your mother keep the marshmallows in the oven?" I asked.

"She hides them," they said.

"Now you kids hike this turkey roaster up to the attic. She only uses it on state occasions. Give me those cocktail onions so I can put them on a lower shelf where they'll be within easy reach. Now, where's the coffee?"

"In the stove drawer, Daddy."

"What's wrong with keeping it in the canister marked C-O-F-F-E-E?"

"Because she hides the P-O-P-C-O-R-N there."

We were doing just fine, mind you, when she yells from the bedroom, "Why don't all of you go out and rotate the tires on the car or make lamps out of old bowling pins or something?" That's gratitude for you. Doris is a bit of Mama's girl. Faints when she has to remove a corn pad. I don't like to criticize her while she's flat on her back, but there was stuff in her refrigerator so old that a casserole actually attacked me and drew blood. "If you don't keep those left-overs moving," I warned her, "you're going to have to open a pharmaceutical house."

"Who was on the phone?" she yelled.

"Just the principal. Don't worry."

"What did he want?" she persisted.

"Nothing. He was just explaining the school's policy on bedroom slippers."

She groaned. "Why are the kids wearing bedroom slippers?"

"Because we can't find their shoes. They're probably on the washer, but we can't get to the washer until after seven. I figure the water from the washer should crest at that hour and then begin to recede."

"You mean the washer overflowed?"

How's that for innocence. If I've told her once, I've told her fifty times to put the little socks and underwear in a bag and then the pump wouldn't get stopped up, but she never listens. I didn't get so much as a "Thank you" for going door to door collecting for her "Research for Sweating Feet" drive, or for driving fifteen Cub Scouts on a tour of a frozen food locker.

If Doris only ran a home like men ran their offices, I wouldn't have to take up so much time in organization. All I did was slip a little note on her night stand asking her to fill in her reply on the following:

1. How do you turn on the garbage disposal?
2. How do you turn off the milkman?
3. How do you remove a Confederate flag tattooed in ink on the forehead of a small boy?
4. Where is the anise for the chili?
5. What is your mother's phone number?

That was certainly no reason for her to groan and start getting dressed. Sometimes I wonder why the Good Lord gave the job of having children to women, when men could organize the process and turn them out in triplicate in half the time.

May 7—July 9

**How do you get out of
this chicken outfit?**

"Pardon me," said the milkman politely tipping his hat, "but I think you put the wrong note in the bottle this morning. This one reads, 'HELP! I'm being held a prisoner by an idiot with a set of wrenches in a house that has been without running water for three days. How do you get out of this chicken outfit?' "

"You're new on the route, aren't you?" I asked.

"Yes, ma'am," he said, his eyes looking for an escape hatch through the taxus. "This sounds like a call for help," he hesitated. "I just take these bottles back to the plant to be sterilized and filled with milk again. I don't drop them in Lake Erie or anything."

"I know that!" I said irritably. "It's just that I'm married to this home-improvement drop-out and every once in a while I just have to try something!"

He didn't understand about modern marriages. I could tell that by the way he bolted to the truck. Some marriages are made in heaven with stardust in the eyes. Others are made in haste with piles of sawdust whipping around the feet.

Mine was the latter, which I discovered less than two weeks after I was married. My husband came home from the drugstore ecstatic with two cigar boxes under his arm. He rushed to the basement, nailed them together, painted them dark green and called them "shadow boxes."

Despite the fact they looked like two cigar boxes nailed together with "King Edward" bleeding through, I avowed they belonged in the Metropolitan. While showing guests through the apartment I would chin myself on them to prove their strength and exclaim that if I had known what a clever dog he was I would have married him in his playpen.

As usual, I overacted.

How was I to know that later he would saw an opening in our back door to let the dog *in*, then consider how to keep the snow *out*? How could I suspect that he would enclose our garbage cans with a fence so high you had to catapult the garbage and hope for the best? How could I imagine his fifth-grade practical arts course would become a way of life?

For a while he went through his built-in period. Everything in the house had to be contained, stacked, attached, enclosed and out of sight. The garage had shelf units to the ceiling that held all the dried-up cans of paint, old coffee cans, and discarded license plates. He enclosed the television set, the bookcases, the stereo, washer, dryer, bar, clothes, blankets, linens, sewing machine, and cleaning supplies. I climbed out of bed one morning and proceeded to stretch my arms and yawn. Before I could get my arms to my sides, I was supporting five shelves of cookbooks and a collection of glass elephants.

Later I was to discover he never went to bed
on a finished project. Fired with enthusiasm over
a plan for improvement, he would spread the
room with wall-to-wall ladders, open a myriad of
paint cans (ready for spilling), and roll up the
draperies into a ball on the sofa. Then he would
smile, climb into his coat, and say, "I am off to
study the blister beetle in South America. Don't
touch a thing until I get back."

On other occasions, he was not as inventive.
He'd simply pull the stove out from the wall,
remove the oven door, put the bathroom hardware to soak in a kitchen sink full of vinegar,
then announce, "I don't have tools like the rest

of the fellas. I do the best I can with a Boy Scout ax and crude tools I've been able to fashion out of boulders and buffalo hide. But when you don't have the right tool for the right job, you can't turn out the work of a craftsman."

Eventually the news that I was supporting a home-improvement drop-out was no secret. We were the couple with the screens in all winter and the storm windows in all summer. We spread grass seed in the snow and put up our TV antennae in an electrical storm.

Even the simple jobs, he attacked with all the grace of a herd of buffalo under fire.

"I was wondering if you could reach behind the washer and put that simple plug into that simple outlet?" I inquired one evening.

"Let's see now," he said surveying the situation. "First, I'll need my Home Workshop Encyclopedia, Volume VIII. Dig that out for me, will you? Get the chapter on 'Outlets: Electrical.' Now, get my utility belt, my insulated gloves, and hard safety hat with the light attachment. They make these utility rooms for pygmies, you know. And with a running jump I'll hoist myself to the top of the washing machine where I'll—"

"Break the washer cycle dial with your big foot," I said dryly. "Look, maybe I'd better do it," I said. "I'm smaller than you and I can just reach over and—"

"This is man's work," he said firmly. "You go finish shoveling the snow off your driveway and leave me to my job at hand."

"No, I'll just stick around in case your eyeballs flash for help."

He lowered himself behind the appliance and inserted the plug—halfway—blowing out all the power on the kitchen circuit. Shocked (but literally), he backed into the dryer vent, disconnecting it. Simultaneously he dropped his flashlight from his helmet into an opening between the walls. For his "big finish" he rapped his head on the utility shelf and opened a hissing valve on the hot water heater with his belt buckle.

I folded my hands and closed my eyes in prayer. "May he never retire."

Ironically, most women envy me my do-it-yourself husband. "At least he does *something!*" said our new neighbor. "You should be thankful for that."

I smiled. "Would you mind sitting in this chair? I wouldn't ask you to move but my husband's leg is coming through the living room ceiling and I wouldn't want him to fall in your lap. Basically he's shy."

She looked rather alarmed as he yelled down through the opening, "Erma! Put an X on what's left of the ceiling so the next time I'll know there's no stud here!"

"I still think it's wonderful," the neighbor persisted, "how you two tackle all kinds of home projects together. I see you out there cutting grass while he trims the hedge and washing the car while he's cleaning out the glove compartment.

It's just wonderful."

I was silent a moment, then I pulled my chair closer. "Let me tell you a secret. I have always resented the helpless female. I resent her because I am secretly jealous of her ability to train grown men to 'heel' and sick and tired of having her feel my flexed muscles at parties.

"If I had it to do all over again, I would be one of those helpless females who faints at the sight of antifreeze. But I was the big mouth who, early in marriage, watched my husband try to start the power mower and said, 'If you are trying to start that power mower, Duckey, you had better attach the spark plug, open the gas line so you can get fuel to the distributor, and pull the choke all the way over. Also, if you don't stand on the other side of the mower, you'd better lean against that tree for balance because you are going to lose your right foot.' "

"How masterful," she said, dabbing her forehead with a lace handkerchief.

"Not so masterful," I said. "From that day forward I was awarded custody of the mower. I also had to repair spoutings, clean out the dryer vent, repair the clothesline, build the rock garden, drain and store the antifreeze, and wash the car."

"My goodness," she whispered, "I'm so addlebrained about cars I scarcely know how to turn on those little globes in the front . . . the . . ."

"Lights," I prompted. "Incidentally, what's that pet name your husband calls you?"

"You mean, 'Satin Pussy Cat'?"

"That's the one. My husband calls me 'Army,' after a pack mule he had in Korea. You're the one who's got it made. I'll bet you never fertilized a lawn, changed a fuse, plunged a sink, hosed out a garbage can, or hung curtain brackets."

She threw back her head, revealing her slim, white throat, and laughed. "Why I get light-headed whenever I step up on a curb."

"Take today. I've got this clogged-up washer. I can either ring for Rube Goldberg and his wonder-wrenches, or I can try to fix the thing myself."

She smiled slyly. "I'll bet it's your turbo pump that's clogged. All you have to do is remove the back panel, take out the pulsator, disconnect the thermoschnook, and use a spreckentube to force out the glunk. Then put on a new cyclocylinder, using a No. four pneusonic wrench, and you're back in the laundry business."

"Why you helpless little broad—er fraud! You could run General Motors from a phone booth. You're faking it, aren't you? That helpless routine is all show. And what does it get you? Nothing but dinner rings, vacations out of season, small fur jackets, and a husband standing breathless at your elbow. Do you know the last time my husband stood breathless at my elbow I had a chicken bone caught in my throat? Is it too late for me? Do you suppose a woman over thirty-five could learn to be helpless?"

She smiled. "Of course. And you can start by asking that nice milkman if he'd be a dear and drop your note in the bottle into Lake Erie, if it isn't too much trouble . . ."

The Outdoor Nut

I have always been led to believe a good marriage was based on things a couple had in common.

A while back I read where Liz Taylor, commenting on one of her earlier marriages, said the common bond between her and her husband was that they wore the same sweater size. The obvious conclusion must be: They just don't make sweaters anymore like they used to. In reality, it's what you *don't* have in common that holds a marriage together.

Early in my marriage (my honeymoon, to be exact) I discovered I was married to an outdoor nut. As I sat there in a cabin on Rainbow Trout Lake fingering my nosegay, I said, "What do you want? Me? Or a great northern pike?" Friends have since told me I would have fared better in the competition had I picked a smaller fish. I was pushing.

Through the years the condition has only worsened. All winter long my husband has what is commonly referred to in fishing circles as the fever. He sharpens his hooks, teases the feathers on his lures, reads articles on "Backlash Lake" and "Angler's Paradise," and follows me around the kitchen inviting me to watch his wrist action.

His wading boots (boots that extend up to the armpits so that when the water pours in, you are assured of drowning instantly) hang on a hook in the garage with all the readiness of a fireman's hat. Whenever a fellow fisherman gives the hysterical cry "The white bass are running!" he grabs his boots and does the same.

Actually I have never known the white bass to do anything but run. They certainly never stop long enough to nibble at the bait. Theoretically the bass are always on a "hot lake." Now a "hot lake," I discovered, is where all the "hot liars" hang out. The reasons they give for the fish not biting are enough to stagger the imagination.

1. The fish aren't biting because the water is too cold.

2. The water is too hot.

3. The fish are too deep.

4. It is too early.

5. It is too late.

6. They haven't stocked it yet.

7. They're up the river spawning.

8. The water skiers and motorboats have them stirred up.

9. They've been poisoned by pollution.

10. They just lowered the lake level.

11. They're only biting on bubble gum and bent nails.

12. Some novice has just dumped his bait into the water and they're stuffed to the gills and can't eat another bite.

13. They haven't been biting since the Democrats have been in power.

When outdoor camping became the symbol of togetherness, I knew my husband wouldn't rest until he had me reeking of insect repellent and zipped into a sleeping bag out where the deer and the antelope play.

I've relived that first camping trip in my mind a thousand times. (They tell me only shock treatments could erase it permanently.) I've tried to analyze why we failed. First, I think we had seen too many Walt Disney films and expected more help from the animals than we got. Second, unlike other families, our family does not have the necessary primitive instincts for survival. We are lucky to get the car windows rolled down to keep from suffocating.

I personally opposed erecting our tent in a

driving rain. I thought it would put us all in a bad humor. As it was, no sooner had we driven the last peg when a passerby remarked to his companion, "Look at that, Lucille. It's listing worse than the *Titanic* just before she went down." Then my husband poked his head out of the flap and retaliated, "Same to you, fella," and I don't mind telling you it took two stanzas of "Nearer My God to Thee" to quiet them down. From that moment on, the bathhouse set referred to us as "Old Crazy Tent."

The rain presented a bit of a problem—all fifteen days of it. This took a lot of ingenuity. "I don't like to mention it," I said one afternoon, "but I think this weather and this tent are beginning to get on my nerves."

"Why do you say that?" asked my husband.

"Because I spent an entire morning counting the grains of sand in the butter."

"The kids keep busy enough," he said.

He was right. They examined their hair follicles under a flashlight, clipped toenails, ate crackers in someone else's sleeping bag, took the labels off the canned goods, kept a rather complete log of frequent visitors to the bathhouse, and wrote postcards home telling everyone what a "blast" they were having.

On the sixteenth day good fortune struck. A hysterical woman from the next tent heard via her transistor that we were in for a tornado. I combed my hair and put on a trace of lipstick. It was the first time I'd been out of the tent in two weeks.

Sitting in the car, with the thorny feet of one of the kids in my ribs, I heard someone from the back seat say, "We'll survive all right." He had thought to grab two cans without labels on his way out. One was a small tin of cocktail weiners, the other was a can of cleanser.

On the eighteenth day it became apparent we had three choices to make: (a) Fix the tent so we could stand up in it, (b) Have our legs fixed so they would measure no more than one-fourth the length of our bodies, (c) Get into the car and make a side trip.

The children voted for a visit to a deer farm about twenty miles from the campsite. It was one of those commercial little ventures where you pay a price and enter the compound and the deer are roaming free among the visitors. There's also a souvenir shop that sells mother-of-pearl ashtrays, a rocking plane ride that costs a dime and makes the kids throw up, and a popcorn stand. We each bought a box of popcorn and set out to spend a quiet afternoon among these gentle animals with the large trusting eyes.

When I first felt a sharp pinch on my backside, I whispered to my husband, "You devil you." The second time it happened I became quite irritated and turned sharply to face a pair of large, brown trusting eyes and two hoofs on my coat lapels. It seemed popcorn drove the deer half out of their skulls with mad desire. The entire herd charged us, pushing, shoving, nipping. They had one child cornered, another one sobbing in the dirt, and my husband pirouetting on his toes like a ballet dancer. We agreed the tent wasn't much, but it was safe from a deer stampede.

The end of three weeks of camping found all of us "adjusting." Slapping the laundry against a flat rock, walking around with sand in our underwear, and taking a bath in a one-quart saucepan had become a way of life.

Sometimes at night when the campfire glowed and you sipped your coffee in the stillness of the night, you felt you might be present at the creation. The kids intent on listening to animals rustling in the bushes and watching the flickering patterns in the fire forgot to argue with one another. No telephones. No Avon ladies. No television. No lawn mowers. No committee meetings. No vacuum sweepers. Just peace.

Then one night, there was peace no more. A twenty-two-foot trailer slithered into the clearing next to us. We could hear their voices crack through the silence of the lazy morning.

"I swear, Clifford, I don't mind roughing it, but with no electricity to hook up to, this is ridiculous. What am I supposed to do about my electric coffee pot and my blanket and my heater?"

"Don't tell me your problems," he shouted. "What about my shaver and my electric martini stirrer?"

"Well, I hope they have a laundromat and a shower house with hot water . . ."

"And a boat dock," he added, "and a swimming pool for the kids. They'll be sick if there's no swimming pool. You know how cold the lakes are."

"Did you check on whether or not they picked up the garbage every day? I don't want a lot of animals around the trailer. I didn't come out here in the wilderness to fight off animals. What in the world is that infernal noise?"

"I think we're near the beach. That water lapping and rolling in all night long is going to drive me crazy. Did you bring my pills, Arlene?"

"Of course, dear. Why don't you set up your screened cabana and listen to the radio? I'll try to rustle you up a drink. I don't suppose that little shopkeeper who looks like Gabby Hayes has ever heard of ice cubes before."

I turned to my husband. "Let's knock the other prop out from under our tent tomorrow and head up toward Blue Water Cove. I hear it's a 'hot lake' and 'the bass are running' like dishonest congressmen."

He grinned. "I think you've got 'the fever.'"

It's summertime and once again our daughter, the Midwest's answer to Tokyo Rose, has been circulating daily bulletins of our vacation plans.

I had one phone call from a woman two blocks over to look up her sister in San Juan, a request from a retired couple for a bushel of grapefruit from Orlando, and just yesterday a carry-out boy winked and said, "Are you really going to Berkeley to burn your library card?"

Actually I'm an advocate of separate vacations: the children's and ours. Or as comedienne Joan Rivers said, "They hated the children and would have separated years ago, but they're staying together for the sake of each other."

There is something about packing five people into a car with nothing to do but tolerate each other that leads to rough-housing, name-calling, eye-gouging, and eventually recoiling next to the spare tire in the trunk. Each individual pursues his or her own antagonistic topic.

The children, for example, will ramble on for miles about the last restroom they visited, describing in intricate details the messages written in lipstick on the walls. Then they will amuse themselves by the hour playing "auto roulette." This is a precarious game of trampling, jostling, and hurling of bodies to see which one gets a seat nearest the window.

Despite the enthusiastic reports from parents that their children broke out in hives from the excitement of viewing the Grand Canyon, we have noted ours couldn't care less. Their interests run toward amusement parks, souvenir shops, miniature golf ranges, zoos with souvenir shops, parks with swings and slides, restaurants with souvenir shops, pony rides, and national monuments with souvenir shops. I get the feeling if we drove the car to Lincoln's Memorial, climbed his leg and spread out a picnic lunch on his lap, one of the kids would observe, "Keep your eyes open for a motel with a heated swimming pool and a nearby souvenir shop."

The compulsive desire to buy a carful of souvenirs before we got to the city limits became so bad, we had to set down some explicit rules for souvenir buying:

Know your history. Don't be lured into buying a genuine replica of a ballpoint pen used by Stephen Foster when he wrote, "I Dream of Jeanie with the Light Brown Hair." (We paid a few dollars more and bought the typewriter used by Thomas Jefferson when he wrote the Declaration of Independence.)

Learn to be crafty. Beware of Indians selling electric blankets, authentic Japanese kimonas made in West Virginia, and President and First Lady T-shirts. (The barbecue sauce we bought, but T-shirts!)

Select a souvenir that will remind you of your visit. This is especially difficult with children who insist on buying a sweat shirt that proclaims, "I'M AN ALCOHOLIC. IN CASE OF EMER-

GENCY, BUY ME A BEER," from scenic Bar Harbor.

Don't pay exorbitant prices for souvenir items you can buy at home. Take that small Frankenstein toy we bought in Tennessee—the one where you pull a switch and his pants fall down and his face turns red—$3.95, batteries not included. With what I would have saved buying it out of a catalogue, I could have bought that beautiful satin pillow in the Smokies that read, "There's No Salt Like a Mother's Tears."

Lastly, consider how good a traveler your souvenir will be. Once when we bought a bushel of peaches from Georgia, we had to drive steadily with no stops for forty-eight hours to avoid being eaten alive by fruit flies.

On another occasion, all five of us had to ride together in the front seat to avoid conflict of interest with a small alligator in the back seat.

Next to children on a trip, there is nothing more trying than their father. He doesn't go on a trip to enjoy the scenery and relax. He's on a virtual test run to prove his car's performance in a grinding show of speed and endurance equaled only on the salt flats testing grounds.

First, there's the graphic charts he insists be kept listing the mileage, gasoline and oil consumption, and itemized expenses encountered during the trip. Three things usually happen to these charts: (a) They are used to wrap up a half-eaten Popcicle and discarded along the way, (b) They are grabbed in an emergency to squash bugs on the windshield, (c) They are committed to memory and used as a mild sedation on neighbors and friends upon your return.

Next, he will insist you read and interpret road maps. To do this you must consider that you are dealing primarily with a maniac, a driver who wants to arrive at his destination three hours before he leaves home. He abhors heavy traffic, detours, toll stations, construction, and large cities with a population of fifty or more. He is depending upon you to anticipate these discomforts and avoid them at all costs. In short, he is hostile. You will find your road map, folded incorrectly in the glove compartment. Usually it will be a little out of date (listing only the original thirteen colonies). Once when I told my husband we measured but a hairpin and a mint away from our destination, he beat his head on the steering wheel and openly accused me of moving the Mississippi River over two states.

Another challenge is getting the driver of the car to stop for food. Rationalizing that even at the '500" they have pit stops, our driver invariably feeds us on promises of what lies ahead at Futility City.

With bloated stomachs and sharp teeth from gnawing on our safety belts we hit Futility City only to discover one filling station, a hound dog in the middle of the road, and a brightly lighted stand where they sell shaved-ice cones. The hound dog looks interesting.

Since this is to be an honest account of the behavior patterns of the average vacationer, I can't leave out "Mother." Mother climbs into the car and, like an evangelist who just had the tent collapse on her flock, can't resist a captive audience. She goes the discipline route.

I have been known to go across an entire state, ignoring national monuments, freaks of nature, postcard countrysides, faces carved in mountains and herds of wild buffalo, while my long-playing mouth recites misdemeanors the kids made when they were on Pablum. My sermon on "All right now, which one of you clowns turned on the car heater?" extended over three states.

Sometimes mothers are permitted to drive, but only under the following conditions: (1) city traffic at 5 P.M. when the population is 250,000 or over, (2) unmarked dirt roads at midnight, (3) highways under construction with detour signs that have blown over, (4) in a tornado on an eight-lane highway where the minimum speed is 65 mph.

The irony of all this is that we don't know what a madcap time we're having until we see our vacation on our home movies. In the flickers, we hide our heads in our armpits, dance a jig, act like we're fighting Dempsey for the title, and pull down limbs of trees and point to them like we've just discovered a cure for arthritis.

We've got some wonderful footage on my husband where he is standing on his head removing a

fishhook from his underside and mouthing ob-
scenities into the camera. All the rest of us are
holding our sides laughing fit to die. There's
another classic where my Wallie the Whale water-
wings spring a leak and I disappear beneath some
lily pads and never surface again. Oh, and there's
a thrilling shot of one of the kids being sick on a
small fishing boat off the coast of Florida and we
are hovering over him offering him salami and
mayonnaise sandwiches. That one really breaks
us up.

Another vacation this year? You bet. We're firm
believers that at least once a year a family ought to
get away from it all so they can appreciate good
food, plush lodgings, convenient stores, and
breathtaking scenery—upon their return home
after two grim weeks of togetherness.

Must try to remember to send in the boys' camp
applications early. You see, I *do* remember last
year's disappointment:

Mr. Grim Gruber, Director
Camp Discouragement for Boys
City
Dear Mr. Gruber:
   The afternoon mail brought me your fine bro-
chure on Camp Discouragement for Boys. You
may or may not remember me. My son attended
your camp last summer for two weeks. (He was the
blond boy whose soiled socks stuck to the light
bulb in the mess hall.)

We were so pleased with the peace and tranquility we enjoyed in his absence, Mr. Bombeck suggested I rush down before Thanksgiving to make sure you have enrollment space. (He also wanted me to remind you he fought for your freedom in World War II, but I don't like to bring pressure.)

Your camp originally came to our attention as it was the only one we could spell. The previous summer we sent him to Camp Mini-something-or-other and discovered we were obviously misspelling the name of the camp. We kept getting letters from a chieftain in the Blackfoot reservation in North Dakota who thanked us profusely for the cookies and clean socks.

I do hope your fine counselor, Mr. Bley, is well enough to return this summer. I was surprised to hear of his "health problem" as he looked so well when I met him on the opening day of my son's camping period. Winning that flag for keeping the latrine clean seemed to mean so much to him. What a pity he had to relinquish it the following week. He will just have to get used to spirited boys, won't he?

I've been meaning to share with you some of my son's hilarious reports of your camp. He wrote us that when a boy talked after lights out, the boys got to slug him, and when he continued to talk, the counselor slugged him. I ask you, where would we be without a boy's imagination?

Incidentally, this is probably an oversight, but he has never received his camp award for throwing

*a frozen pancake thirty-two feet high. I under-
stand from him this is some kind of a camp record.
(Even if he was aiming it at a senior leader during
evening meditation.) Although we are not "showy"
people, we do have a spot for it in the trophy
case in the hallway, alongside his birth certificate
and a note saying he passed his eye test at school
—his two accomplishments to date.*

*Did you ever solve the mystery of the missing
bathing suits from camp? My son was terribly upset about the nude swimming as he is a sensitive
boy.*

*Do write me your confirmation of my son's
registration.*

> *Sincerely*

Dear Mrs. Bombeck:

We do remember your son.

*Mr. Bley continues to improve and now is per-
mitted a limited number of visitors on Sundays.
We are enclosing your son's camp award and are
sorry for the oversight.*

*The mystery of the missing bathing suits was
solved soon after we searched your son's foot
locker.*

*Registrations have been filled since just before
Thanksgiving.*

> *Sincerely,*
> *Grim Gruber, Director*
> *Camp Discouragement for Boys*

Nagging—American Style

As the bride in the newspaper account told the
police the other day after she shot her new husband at their wedding reception, "No marriage is
perfect."

After I had read the story and had gone beyond
the point of wondering why she was wearing a
gun to her wedding, I got to wondering why she
had shot him so soon. Surely they didn't have the
time to approach the big problems that psychologists are always warning us about like: communications, consideration, honesty, thoughtfulness,
in-laws, money, and children. It had to be then a
perfect "case" for what I have always contended.
The biggest problems in a marriage are all those
little pesky differences that drive you behind a
locked door in the bathroom, to the sofa to spend
the night, to Mother's studio couch, to the lake
with the boys, to the nearest bar, or straight into
the arms of the Avon lady. Nagging one another
about the most inane things you can think of then
becomes one of the few ways you can give vent to
these differences.

I have always said half of the arguments in this
country are caused by a simple little thing like a
mosquito in the bedroom. It's true. The trouble
festers when it becomes evident two opposites
have married: (a) those who don't mind mosquitoes in the bedroom and (b) those who find
it impossible to exist with mosquitoes in their
bedroom.

Usually this discovery is not made until the first summer after marriage. When it happens, it's enough to make World War II sound like a wet cap pistol.

Generally, but not always, it's the woman who can't stand the sharp, whining buzz about her head. Promptly she will throw back the covers, illuminate the bedroom with light, stand in the middle of the bed and announce, "Clyde, we can't sleep with that mosquito in this bedroom. Clyde! Clyde! I say, we can't sleep with that mosquito in this bedroom."

Now, Clyde comes out of his unconscious state mumbling, "Hold him, Tom, while I get the net. You don't want to lose him at the boat. He looks like a three-pounder."

"Wake up," he is ordered. "You're not fishing. We're chasing a mosquito. Here, take this paper and don't miss!"

"Look," he pleads sleepily, "why don't you just ignore him and go to sleep. What's a small mosquito?"

"They're noisy and they carry malaria," she states flatly.

He groans, "With malaria I can stay home from work and get paid. Exhaustion, they won't buy."

"Wait a minute," she says excitedly. "I think he's in the bathroom. Quick, shut the door."

"Now, can I go back to bed?" he asks.

"No, I think there's a pair of them. This dizzy wallpaper. You can't see anything on it at night. I hate this wallpaper. Be still. He was on my pillow a while back. There he is . . . get him! You missed! For a man who can hit a baseball, a golf ball, and can fly cast into a circle, you're lousy at hitting mosquitoes."

"It's *your* mosquito, Great White Hunter, you kill it!" he says.

"And how did we get mosquitoes?" she retaliates. "I'll tell you how. They slip through your homemade screens."

"Well, they had to go on a diet to do it," he yells back.

"And another thing," she shouts. "Your mother had no right to wear navy blue to our wedding."

"You always bring that up," he informs her. "It has nothing to do with mosquitoes."

"How would you like to sleep in this disease-ridden jungle all by yourself?"

"I'd sleep in a crocodile's stomach to get that bright light out of my eyes," he blusters.

"Okay, Clyde," she storms. "That tore it. I'm going to the sofa for a decent night's sleep. If you want to chase mosquitoes all night, that's your business!"

Second only to the mosquito is the problem of the electric blanket. When electric blankets came out, some simple-minded designer hung a single control box on it and hoped for a miracle.

I defy you to put any blissfully happy married couple under a blanket with a single control and have them speaking to one another in the cold light of morning. Quite frankly, I haven't seen such a home wrecker since they legalized the Watusi.

Why only last week, a pair of my dearest friends, Wanda and Lester Blissful, separated over a single-control electric blanket. Naturally the card club doesn't have the full details yet, but the way we understand it, Wanda was readying for bed one night when Lester said gruffly, "Are you wearing that little sleeveless gown to bed?"

"I don't usually wear a snowsuit," she smiled stiffly. (Wanda's a real corker.)

"If you're planning on hiking that blanket up to a seven again tonight, forget it," he said firmly. "Last night, I slept like the FBI was trying to wring a confession out of me."

She smiled. "You exaggerate. I had the control

on five. The night before you had it on two and I nearly froze. You know, Lester, if I had known you were a No. two on the electric blanket, I would never have married you. There's something wrong with a man who would let his veins freeze over."

This is all hearsay, mind you, but we heard they sniped at each other all night long. Lester said, "I feel a Mau Mau is having me for lunch . . . literally!" Wanda said, "That's better than feeling like a prime beef in a food locker!" Lester retaliated with "Toasted marshmallows, anyone?" Wanda shot back, "Welcome to Ski Valley."

After a sleepless night for both of them, they decided things weren't working out between them and they made an appointment with their lawyer.

Their properties, holdings, and children were divided with cold efficiency. There was no problem here. Then Lester spoke, "Who gets custody of the electric blanket?"

"What do you need it for?" yelled Wanda. "You could get the same cold feet by hanging them out of the window."

"And you could get equally warm by wetting your finger and sticking it into an electrical outlet!" he charged.

At this point the lawyer interceded and suggested they buy an electric blanket with dual controls. He said he and his wife would assume custody of the blanket with the single control.

Their case comes up next month, so they say at card club.

Very frankly, two things have nearly wrecked our marriage: a home freezer and the checking account. Now, I know what you're going to say. Right away, you're going to jump to the conclusion that I bought an expensive home freezer without telling my husband and that I abuse the checking account by spending too much money. You are wrong. They are just small things to "nag" about.

For example, we've been arguing about that home freezer for three years now. It's been paid for since a year ago last August. (In fact, I heard there was a Conga line at the credit office that snaked out to the elevator and that the manager treated the staff to cranberry juice out of paper cups, but that could be a rumor.)

At any rate, I insisted we buy the freezer because I couldn't live through another "harvest" without it. I wanted to preserve some of that fresh corn on the cob, green beans, melon balls, peaches, and strawberries. So, my husband agreed to the freezer.

The first week, I snapped and broke thirty pounds of green beans. I blanched them, cooled them, put them into plastic bags, then into boxes where I duly marked the date: June 5. By June 28 we had consumed thirty pounds of green beans. I went the same route with corn and carrots. No matter what quantities I put into the freezer, we had it eaten clean by the end of the week.

In the fall I bought a bushel of apples. I peeled, cored, blanched, cooled, bagged, boxed, and labeled. The yield was eight quarts which someone figured cost me $2.33 a quart, counting labor. (On a rice-paddy minimum wage scale.)

One day my husband decided to check out the freezer. I held my breath. "Well, now, what do we have on this shelf?" he asked quizzically.

"Snowballs," I said softly. "The kids made them up when it snowed and then when it's summer, we've got this wonderful, rich supply of snowballs that we couldn't possibly begin to have if we just had the freezing compartment in the refrigerator."

"And what are all those brown paper bags filled with? Steaks? Rump roasts? Chops?"

"You're warm," I said, slamming the door shut.

"How warm?" he asked, opening it again.

"Chicken innards," I said.

"*Chicken innards!*"

"That's right,' I explained. "You always said I wasn't to put them into the garbage can until the day of pick-up and I thought I could store them in the freezer until garbage day. I guess I forgot to put a few of them out."

"Is this what I think it is?" he asked tiredly.

"It is, I believe, a transistor battery. Someone said if you put them in a freezer, they'd recharge themselves."

"So, this is what I gave up cigarettes for," he whimpered. "This is why I painted my heels black so no one would know I was wearing socks with holes in them. This is why I didn't buy a library card . . . just to save money. All for a frozen patch of snowballs, batteries, and chicken necks!"

"Aren't you being a little dramatic?"

"You are some kind of a nut," he accused. "It's a good thing they don't try to match you up in some computer, or you'd be married to Bert Lahr and living on a Funny Farm."

I'd like to say I filled the freezer to capacity with a hind quarter of whatever it is you freeze and we lived happily ever after. I'd like to say it, but I can't. I figured if we didn't argue about all those chicken innards, we might argue about something serious.

As for the checking account, it's simply a little thing about being "neat." The first year we were married, we opened our first checking account. My first entries looked like the work of a monastery monk. They were bold and black, lettered evenly, and stood out in complete legibility.

As the months wore on I began to scribble, abbreviate, and write notes in the margin. Then I would rearrange deposits and dates with bent arrows. Finally, my husband said one day, "I am going to start you in a nice new bank tomorrow. Would you like that? Your checks will start with No. one again and your ledger will be spanking clean."

The next bank was the same story, only they had no sense of humor for my notes attached to the checks. ("Luvie, hang on to this one until Monday. Our new money isn't dry yet.") We pushed on to another bank and another account.

In time, I began to shop for banks like a new home owner. I can tell you in a flash which banks have dry inkwells, which ones sell bookends, and which ones flaunt lollipop trees and pastel checks. At one establishment I received a nasty note advising me to sign my name the way I signed it on the records. My husband was visibly annoyed with me. "How did you sign your name originally?" he queried.

"Alf Landon," I said.

He collapsed in a chair and it served him right for doubting me.

Another time they became quite oral about the omission of my account number. There followed another inquisition. "Well, what number *did* you use?" I tried to remember. "I think it was my social security number . . . or my oil company number . . . or my swimming club number . . . or was it my record club?"

Things did go a little better when my husband figured out my checkbook abbreviations. For example, NS beside an entry meant "No Stamp" to mail the check. Thus that check would be reentered as a deposit and added on to the total. An OOB meant "Out Of Balance" and was the amount the bank and I differed. Thus, a subtraction and we began even again.

FB was entered when the item was so frivolous and ridiculous I knew he'd raise the roof if he knew. It stood for "Fringe Benefits." Others took some explanation. "What's this entry for Nursery —seventy-one dollars? We haven't had a baby in eight years," he growled.

"Geraniums," I said.

"Seventy-one dollars worth of geraniums!"

"Oh, of course not, ninny, that bill was for seventeen dollars. I made a mistake and transposed the numbers and I had to record the check like I wrote it. I only subtracted seventeen dollars though because the nursery wouldn't cash a check for seventy-one dollars. No one buys that many geraniums." We were overdrawn and moved on to another bank.

To date, I have been in more banks than Jesse James. But I figure if my husband wanted a financial giant, he should have shopped a little longer and not snatched the first skirt to come down the pike.

I suppose I should condemn marital nagging, but I'm not going to.

The American Institute of Family Relations observed a while back there are three times during a day when wifely nagging is the most dangerous: at breakfast, before dinner, and again at bedtime.

So what's left? A spontaneous argument can be rather stimulating after a morning playing "Red Goose Run" with Captain Kangaroo. It picks up tired blood, clears the old sinuses, sharpens the reflexes, and gives you a chance to use words like: insidious, subversive, ostentatious, incarceration, ambiguous, partisan, incumbent, and other words which you don't know the meaning of either, but which you're reasonably sure are fit for children to hear.

Besides, it's a challenge. There's a sameness to nagging that occurs after you've been married awhile. The routines became as familiar as the dialogue of two vaudevillians. My husband has one called "Where's the table salt?" or as the kids call it, "The Great American Tragedy." I could serve eagle eyeballs under glass, wearing a topless bathing suit, and he'd shout, "What does a man have to do to get salt to his table!"

I have some old standards that I replay from time to time. There're "This house is a penal institution," "I didn't know you were allergic to grass when I married you," and "Why is it other men look like a page out of a Sears catalogue and you drag around in baggy pants like Hans Brinker?"

A little nagging is a healthy thing in a marriage. The way I figure it, you can either nag your way through fifty or sixty years or wear a gun to your wedding.

July 10—September 5

What's a mother for but to suffer?

Of all the emotions enjoyed by a mother, none makes her feel as wonderfully ignoble as her "What's a Mother For But to Suffer?" period.

It doesn't happen in a day, of course. She has to build up to it through a series of self-inflicted tongue wounds. She observes, for example, "I could be St. Joan of Arc with the flames licking around my ankles, and Harlow would roast marshmallows." Or, "If I were on the *Titanic* and there was only one seat left in the lifeboat, Merrill would race me for it." Finally, at the peak of her distress, she will sum up her plight thusly, "I could be lying dead in the street and Evelyn would eat a peanut butter sandwich over me."

The image of her own sacrifice and thankless devotion to motherhood grows and grows until finally she is personified in every little old lady who scrubs floors at night to send a son through law school to every snaggle-toothed hag who sells violets in the snow.

Outwardly most women are ashamed of this emotion. They are loathe to admit that a small child, born of love, weaned on innocence, and nurtured with such gentleness could frustrate them to such cornball theatrics. They blame society, the educational system, the government, their mother, their obstetrician, their husband, and

110

Ethel Kennedy for not telling them what mother-hood was all about. They weren't prepared and they're probably bungling the whole process of child-rearing.

They just took a few of "what Mother always saids" and stirred in a generous portion of "what Daddy always dids" and said a fervent prayer that the kids didn't steal hubcaps while they were trying to figure out what they were going to do.

I've always blamed my shortcomings as a mother on the fact that I studied Child Psychology and Discipline under an unmarried professor whose only experience was in raising a dog. He obviously saw little difference.

At the age of two, my children could fetch and I'd reward them with a biscuit. At the age of four, they could sit, heel, or stay just by listening to the inflection in my voice. They were paper trained by the age of five. It was then that I noted a differ-ence between their aims and goals and mine. So I put away my Child Psychology and Discipline volume and substituted a dog-eared copy of *Crime and Punishment*. I am now the only mother in our block who reaches out to kiss her children and has them flinch and threaten to call their attorneys if I so much as lay a finger on them.

Then a friend of mine told me she had a solu-tion that worked pretty well. It was "Wait until your father gets home." This seemed to be work-ing for me, too. It certainly took away the "acid stomach condition" that had been so bothersome. But one afternoon I heard the children making plans to either give Daddy up for Lent or lend him to a needy boy at Christmas and I felt a twinge of conscience.

We talked it over—their father and I—and finally conceded child-raising was a two-headed job, literally speaking. We would have to share the responsibilities. We have a list of blunders that span Diana Dors twice, not the least being our stab at sex education.

The sex education of a child is a delicate thing. None of us wants to "blow it." I always had a horror of ending up like the woman in the old joke who was asked by her child where he came from and after she explained the technical process in a well-chosen medical vocabulary, he looked at her intently and said, "I just wondered. Mike came from Hartford, Connecticut."

My husband and I talked about it and we figured what better way to explain the beautiful reproduction cycle of life than through the animal kingdom. We bought two pairs of guppies and a small aquarium. We should have bought two pairs of guppies and a small reservoir. Our breakfast conversation eventually assumed a pattern.

"What's new at Peyton Place by the Sea?" my husband would inquire.

"Mrs. Guppy is e-n-c-e-i-n-t-e again," I'd say.

"Put a little salt in the water. That'll cure anything," he mumbled.

"Daddy," said our son. "That means she's pregnant!"

"Again!" Daddy choked. "Can't we organize an

intramural volleyball team in there or something?"

The first aquarium begat a second aquarium with no relief in sight.

"Are you getting anything out of your experience with guppies?" I asked my son delicately one afternoon. "Oh yeah," he said, "they're neat."

"I mean, have you watched the male and the female? Do you understand the processes that go into the offspring? The role of the mother in all this?"

"Oh sure," he said. "Listen, how did you know which one of your babies to eat when they were born?"

We added a third aquarium which was promptly filled with salt water and three pairs of sea horses.

"Now, I want you to pay special attention to the female," I instructed. "The chances are it won't take her long to be with child and perhaps you can see her actually give birth."

"The female doesn't give birth, Mom," said my son peeling a banana. (I felt myself smiling, anticipating a trend.) "Ridiculous," I said. "Females always give birth." The male began to take on weight. I thought I saw his ankles swell. He became a mother on the twenty-third of the month.

"That's pretty interesting," observed my son. "I hope when I become a mother, it's on land. I can't tread water that long."

We blew it. We figured we would.

If you want to know the truth, we haven't made out too well in the problem of sibling rivalry either. I think the rumor is that more parents have been driven out of their skulls by sibling rivalry than any other behavior phase. I started the rumor.

In infancy, it's a series of small things. Big sister will stuff a whole banana in the mouth of baby brother with the threat, "Shut your mouth, baby, or out you go." Or big brother will slap his toddler sister off her hobby horse with the reprimand, "Keep that squeak on your side of the room." It eventually reaches a point where they are measuring their cut of meat with a micrometer to see they are getting their fair share as set down by the Geneva Convention, and being represented by legal counsel to see who gets the fruit cocktail with the lone cherry on top.

The rivalry of each day, however, seems to culminate at the dinner table.

SON: She's doing it again.

FATHER: Doing what?

SON: Humming.

DAUGHTER: I am not humming.

SON: You are so. There, she did it again, Dad. Watch her neck. She's humming so no one can hear her but me. She does it all the time just to make fun of me.

FATHER: I can't hear anything. Eat your dinner.

SON: How come *he* got the bone?

FATHER: What difference does it make? There's

no meat on the bone, anyway.

OTHER SON: Then how come *he* got the meat? I got stuck with the bone the last time.

DAUGHTER: I got dibs on the last black olive. *You* got the ice cube in your water after school and *you* got the bike for your birthday, so I get the black olive.

FATHER: What kind of logic is that! I swear it's like eating with the mafia. (*Turning to Mother*) How can you sit there and listen to all this drivel?

MOTHER: I'm under sedation.

This seemed to be the answer until recently, when some dear friends of ours confided in us that they had all but solved their sibling rivalry problems at the dinner table. We listened to them talk of peace, love, and tranquility throughout the meal by engaging in a new game called Category. It worked very simply. Each member of the family was allowed one night at the table where he alone named the Category and led that particular discussion. Hence, everyone had a chance to speak and sooner or later each child could talk about something that interested him.

I had to admit, Category sounded like a better game than we were playing at present called Trials at Nuremberg. This also worked rather simply. We would wait until we were all assembled at the table, then right after the prayer we'd confront the children with crimes they had committed in their playpens up to the present day. We'd touch upon bad manners, bicycles in the driveway, socks

under the bed, goofing around with the garbage
detail, throwing away their allowances on paraffin
teeth and anything else we could document. By the
time we reached dessert, we usually had a couple
of them sobbing uncontrollably into their mashed
potatoes, begging to be sent to an orphanage. We
decided to give Category a try.

"Tonight, I'm going to talk about 'Friends,'"
said our older son.

"Don't talk with food in your mouth," amended
his father.

He swallowed and continued, "My very best,
first choice, A-1 top of the list, first class, Cadillac
of a friend is Charlie."

"Charlie who?" someone interrupted.

"I don't know his last name," he shrugged. "Just Charlie."

"Well, good grief," I sighed. "You'd certainly think if you had a big, fat Damon and Pythias relationship with a real, live friend you'd get around to last names."

"Who's Damon and Pythias?" asked a small voice.

"Aw, come on," said the speaker. "It's not your turn until tomorrow night. Anyway, today my best friend, Charlie, threw up in school—"

"*Mother!*" screamed a voice. "Do I have to sit here and listen to stories about Charlie up-chucking?"

"Tell us about another friend, son," pleaded his father.

He continued. "Well, my second best B-2, second from the top of the list, Oldsmobile of a friend is Scott. Today, Scott went after the janitor to bring the bucket when Charlie threw up and—"

"Please!" the entire table groaned.

"Well, it's my category," he insisted, "and they're my friends. If I have to sit and listen to you talk about your junk, you can listen to me."

"I wish Charlie were here to eat these cold mashed potatoes."

"Yeh, well, when it's your turn to talk, I'm going to hum."

"All right, kids," interrupted their father. "While we're on the subject of cold mashed potatoes, who left the red bicycle right in the middle of the driveway tonight? And, as long as we're all together, which one of you lost the nozzle off the garden hose? (*Aside*) Hold up the dessert, Mother, I've got a few things to discuss. Now, about the telephone. I'm getting a little sick and tired of having to shinny up the pole every time I want to call out . . ."

Very frankly, I don't feel the problem of sibling rivalry will ever be worked out in our time. Especially after reading a recent survey taken among brothers and sisters as to what they liked or disliked about one another. These were some of the reasons for their contempt of one another. "He's my brother." "She says hello to me in front of my friends." "She's a girl." "He's always hanging around the house when I'm there." "She acts big and uppity." "She's a sloppy beast." "He knows everything." Only one brother said something nice about his sister. He wrote, "Sometimes when she takes a bath, she uses a neat deodorant." I ask you, how are you going to build a quiet meal around that!

The second-largest problem to parents is status. It changes from year to year, beginning with "I'm five years old and *my* mama lets me stay up to watch the late, late show," to "I'm in the sixth grade too and I'm listed in the phone book under my own name."

It gets pretty ridiculous, of course, but it's just another hair-shirt in a mother's wardrobe. Another challenge for a mother who must make a decision not to measure her own children's happiness with another mother's yardstick. Just last month,

I heard that the latest status symbol around the bridge table is children's dental work. Wild? Not really. The more fillings, the more space maintainers, the more braces, the more status. If the orthodontist says your kid has a bite problem, lady, you're in.

Here's a conversation I overheard illustrating the point.

"You talk about dental work," said a small blonde. "Come here, George. Open your mouth, George." The lights danced on George's metal-filled mouth like Ali Baba's cave. "That," she said emphatically, "is my mink stole. A mother's sacrifice. And is he grateful? He is not."

"Think nothing of it," said her companion. "Come over here, Marcia. Let the lady look at your braces." Marcia mechanically threw back her head and opened wide. The inside of her mouth looked like it was set to go off. "That," she said, "is my trip to Europe. What do you think of that?"

"I think we worry too much about them," said the first one. "Always nagging. 'Brush your teeth, don't eat sweets.' I mean we can't run around after them like those hags on television, can we?"

"Wait till you see what I'm buying George for his mouth this month," the blonde confided. "You'll be dumbfounded. It's very new and expensive and I understand there aren't a half dozen people who have them in their mouths yet. George and I will be one of the first."

"What is it?" asked the first one breathlessly.

"Promise you won't tell anyone?" (*Hushed tone*) "It's a telltale tooth."

"A telltale tooth?"

"Right. They cram six miniature transmitters, twenty-eight other electrical components, and two rechargeable batteries into what looks like an ordinary 'bridge' of a first molar. Then, as they chew, the telltale tooth broadcasts a stream of information to the dentist that tells what the child has eaten and what is causing the breakdown of his teeth."

"A fink tooth! Well, I'll be. I think I'll get one of those for Marcia. Maybe we could hook up her transistor to it and do away with that wire coming out of her ear. Then the music could come from her teeth. Wouldn't that give the kids in her class a jolt!"

"Well, I thought I'd get an antenna for George's. Then maybe he could hook up to that Early Bird channel from Telestar and draw in something from overseas."

"There goes that patio cover you were saving for—but then, what's a mother for, but to sweat in the hot sun."

A mother's suffering—a privilege or a put-upon. Who knows? I only know that when you can no longer evoke any empathy from your children with it, then you must take a firm stance, throw back your head, look determined, and as my old Child Psychology professor advised, "Pull up hard on the leash!"

Color Me Naïve

Boy, maybe I'm naïve or something, but what's with these women who waddle into the hospital complaining of a bad case of indigestion and deliver twins two hours later? When presented with their case of indigestion swathed in pink blankets, they express shock and say, "I didn't even know I was pregnant!"

I'm the suspicious type. I think when they got to the stage where they couldn't see their feet over their stomachs, couldn't fit behind a car

steering wheel, couldn't wear anything but a tent with a drawstring neckline, they suspected, all right.

Granted, some women show less than others during pregnancy, but the only women I know who actually carry babies "concave" are magazine models and television actresses. And I never saw one of them I didn't hate! What they do is they nail these fashion models in the second week of their pregnancy, pour them into a Paris original and try to convince Mrs. Housewife that even models have babies and they don't look like Humpty Dumpty with a grouch.

Television is worse. On soap operas, for example, the actress rarely gets out of her street clothes. Oh, she may complain of a backache, tiredness, nausea, and swollen ankles, but the straight skirts and severe sheaths continue. I have also noted the length of pregnancies on a soap opera is no more than eight or nine weeks, a decided improvement over the standard nine months. Finally, in the ninth week (when they have padded her with a cotton swab) she complains of labor. She is fresh from the beauty shop and is ready to deliver. The baby is never seen. She (a) loses it, (b) puts it up for adoption, or (c) never wants to see it again. This creates fewer problems for casting.

You can expect such an unrealistic approach from medias that deal in make-believe, but in real life it would sound like an old William Powell-Myrna Loy movie.

MYRNA: William, I should have told you before, but we're going to have a baby.

WILLIAM: (*The match he is holding burns his fingers.*) A baby, but when?

MYRNA: Tomorrow.

WILLIAM: But why didn't you tell me, my dear?

MYRNA: I was afraid you'd be cross with me. Are you surprised?

WILLIAM: I can't believe it. So that's why there's a baby crib in our bedroom . . . and I've been cooking all the meals . . . and your suitcase is packed . . . it's all beginning to make sense now. But how was I to know? Day after day I'd find you just sitting in that chair.

MYRNA: I can't get out of it.

WILLIAM: Could I get you something? A glass of water? An obstetrician?

MYRNA: Just a helping hand out of this chair. (*She stands up, forty-five pounds heavier than she was nine months ago, shoulders flung back, feet apart.*) There now, be honest, didn't you suspect something?

WILLIAM: Nonsense. You still look like the bride I married.

I recently became very interested in the story of a London housewife who was at odds with English automobile manufacturers over the low position of steering wheels for expectant mothers who have to drive a car. The automobile manufacturers retaliated with "Why should pregnant women have to drive at all?" which is the type of answer you'd expect from a bachelor engineer whose mommy told him she got him with green stamps!

Actually, pregnant women don't have to drive cars. They could ride motorcycles sidesaddle, strap their feet to two skateboards, or raise their umbrellas and think Mary Poppins, but the fact remains automobiles are an intricate part of a woman's life and to give them up for six months or so is like going back to nesting in a rocking chair for nine months.

I know of what I speak. Before American cars were equipped with tilt-away steering wheels, I had a traumatic experience that I have not been able to relate to more than thirty or forty thousand of my most intimate friends.

I was going into my eleventh month of pregnancy (the doctor and I disagreed on this point) and had gone to the store to purchase a half gallon of ice cream and a loaf of bread. The car seat was back as far as it would go, which created a small problem. My feet no longer reached the brake pedal or the accelerator, so I had to crouch. When I crouched, my vision was impaired and I had to hang my head out of the no-draft. When I did this, I hit things.

No matter. I got to the store and parked the car, nose in, and made my exit without incident. However, on my return I noticed I had been hemmed in on both sides by parked cars.

I eased open the door a crack and proceeded to stuff myself into the car, stomach first. However, I became wedged between the arm rest of the door and the steering wheel. I could not go forward or backward. Now, try that on for laughs. My stomach was stuck and my ice cream was melting.

People began to stand around in curious mobs. Quickly I pulled backward, releasing me from the front seat. To save face, I nonchalantly opened the back door of the car and slid in like a guest. Now, to get to the front seat. Bent from the waist, I faced the rear of the car and tried rolling over the top of the front seat. The ashtray tore a hole in my bread wrapper.

Humiliated, I plopped down on the seat to think. What do you do when you go to the supermarket manager and ask him to announce over his microphone that the black station wagon bearing license plates —— is blocking a *stomach?* I licked the sticky ice cream off my fingers and decided to give it one more try. I'd back into the front seat. I was doing fine until another fat part of me made contact with the horn. A small child pointed and said, "Mommy, is that woman sitting on her horn going to have a baby?"

Tears welled in my eyes. "Don't be ridiculous, kid! I'm carrying it for a dear friend."

Whenever I'd get really depressed over my plight, I'd think about a footnote I read once in a Population Study Patterns report. (I picked that up in a doctor's office. It beat reading *Gall Bladder Digest.*) It said an Austrian woman had set an "apparent world population record" by bearing sixty-nine offspring. What's more, she did it the government way: in carbons and triplicates. Here's her tally.

BIRTHS	SETS	TOTALS
Quadruplets	4	16
Triplets	7	21
Twins	16	32
	TOTAL:	69

I used to think about her a lot. Without ever having set eyes on her, you can tell many things from these figures. Obviously this is a woman who hates the pesky details of packing a suitcase. You'll note she made only twenty-seven trips to the maternity ward. Likewise, she's a woman who doesn't waste time in repetition. If she had felt a single birth coming, she would probably haved phoned it in.

She's a person used to looking upward, not having seen her feet in twenty-seven years. Heartburn to her is a way of life, while a knit suit is as unreal as Santa Claus. In all probability, her sense of humor has been dulled. When she and her husband planned their marriage in the first full bloom of courtship, and he proposed, "We'll have thirty-one boys for me and thirty-eight girls for you," she probably blushed and said, "You're a regular card, Stanley."

As she tallied up the twenty-ninth, thirtieth, and thirty-first births, undoubtedly "Tell Mother we're expecting again" became a rather dreary chore. After arrivals forty-three, forty-four, and forty-five, she probably had reached the yellow pages of the phone book for names and was re-

duced to calling number forty-six the Aufder-
heiden Bottling Company. Upon the birth of
fifty-one and fifty-two, the problem of how to get
to thirty-seven PTA Open Houses likely threw
them. When the children reached the sixties, it
was undoubtedly a strain to remember not whose
birthday was Saturday, but how many.

I can visualize many problems with sixty-nine
children in the house. Taking numbers to get into
the bathroom, getting your clothes issued from
a quartermaster, substituting the word "invasion"
for "visit" and tactfully suggesting to two red-
heads they've been sleeping with the wrong family
for three years.

The story goes on to reveal that the average
woman has a potential capability of producing
something like twenty offspring, discounting the
possibility of multiple births. (If that doesn't
make your day, it's beyond help.) So, if you stand
now at the national average, which is 2.7 children
per family, you and your husband are going to
have to go some to make a footnote out of yourself!

No story on motherhood these days is complete
without mention of two static words, "The Pill."
I'm inclined to go along with the sign on a diaper
service truck I saw last week. As it whizzed
through town at a law-breaking speed, I caught
the sign painted on its rear doors, "What Pill?"

Actually, there are two things in this country
directly opposing The Pill, both birds.

First, Europeans are staging an all-out effort to

increase the population of the storks. To keep
them from becoming extinct, sympathetic French
citizens are keeping them in their kitchens to
protect them from cold snaps, an emergency stork
committee has been named to make sure the birds
survive the hazards of high-tension wires and television antennae, and at one point an airlift was
staged to transport young birds from Algeria to
France. And how do you think these grateful birds
will repay the French citizens for their hospitality? By moving on to Chicago, Los Angeles, New
York, Denver, and Philadelphia, what else?

Frankly I'm pretty jittery about the whole deal.
I get panicky when I see a dove fly in Clara's
window.

The other bird who is blocking the breakthrough of The Pill to American women is the
pigeon. With the projected people population
running into the billions, overcrowded schools,
limited housing, lack of food and threat of unem-
ployment, the birth control pill was awarded by
the government to the pigeons so that they could
control their numbers.

I suppose if you're a pedestrian who walks
under high window ledges, this might have some
meaning for you, but I don't think the pigeons
were even seeking assistance from the government.

Crawling out on a rather narrow ledge of the
courthouse, I talked recently with a spokesman—
the only bird who knew pigeon English—about
the talked-about Pill.

"Well, if people don't want us around, why

don't they say so?" he cooed. "I'm sick of this shilly-shallying. When we first moved from the suburbs into the cities, the natives took potshots at us. Of course, they were severely criticized by the ASPCA—not the barbershop harmony group, dear, the Society for the Prevention of Cruelty to Animals.

"Next, they tried a variety of insecticides to make us leave our perches. Finally, they put electrical charges on the buildings where we walk. And if you think that doesn't give you a jolt when you set down for a landing, you haven't changed radio stations while you were in the bathtub lately.

"No, I think they've gone too far. Oh, I suppose we do produce at a rather astounding rate. But there's nothing else to do up here all day long but fly over parked cars and mess around the statues in the parks."

I asked him how the women of this country should go about getting The Pill.

"All I can offer is some advice on how we got to be a menace. We just made our numbers felt in the downtown area."

"I'll tell them," I said.

The more I think of it, however, the more I'm convinced that fertility, or the lack of it, doesn't depend on a pill, a chart, or a clinic. It rests solely with the predisposition of women.

For example, go buy a new bathing suit, go on a diet, invest twenty dollars in a pair of stretch pants so tight you can trace your lunch and *voilà!* Pregnancy! Or more drastic measures: Let your

Blue Cross lapse, buy a small sports car with two bucket seats, or adopt a baby. You asked for it. Instant parenthood.

If you're really serious about limiting your family, you should follow the following advice:

1. Young mothers are urged to hang on to maternity clothes, sterilizers, bottle warmers, beds, baby tenders, sheet blankets, pads, and reusable pacifiers. If storage space is needed, dig a hole under the house if necessary.

2. Don't make vacation plans in September for the next summer at Lake Erie or in New York. Clinical records have indicated women who planned to scale the inside of the Statue of Liberty were so pregnant by vacation time they were lucky the ferryboat didn't capsize.

3. Resist the impulse to sign up for self-improvement courses in the daytime or academic study at the university in the evening. This is a sure way to get back to testing strained liver with the tip of your tongue.

4. Do not be tempted by the job markets until you are beyond sixty. Remember. Roads to fertility begin at the employment office—especially for those who make a big deal inquiring about vacations and retirement benefits.

5. Keep a keen eye on budget spending. Deferred accounts, long-term credit buying is like waving a red flag before the odds.

6. Don't become too enamored with water sports such as expensive boats, water skiing, and

scuba diving. This could be awkward and limiting later on.

7. Don't make any public speeches over bridge tables on topics such as, "I named my last one Caboose. And that's it!" or "Did you hear about Fanny and she's forty-two!"

I may be naïve, but I'm no fool!

The Disenchanted

Some woman once nailed me in a restroom in Detroit and said, "I can hardly wait until your children are a little older. You will have such fun writing about them during that stage." The woman, an obvious sadist who hangs around restrooms and stirs up trouble, never mentioned the precise age at which child-rearing got to be a fun thing. I am still waiting.

When the children were quite young, I used to envision a time when they would gather at my feet and say, "Now don't you lift an arthritic finger, Mother. I know exactly where your pinking shears are. Let me run and get them for you." Frankly I cannot remember a time when our popularity as parents has been at such an all-time low.

Our children barricade themselves behind locked bedroom doors, emerging only when the telephone rings. The "phonomania" is probably our doing. We noted long ago that some of our friends had a real phone problem with their children. (One couple had the run of the phone from 4 to 6:30 A.M. weekdays only, during the months with R in them.) So we decided that when our children were old enough to point to the telephone and say, "Mommy, what is that?" we'd answer, "It's a cavity machine to check the cavities in your teeth." (We also told them steak made little children sick, but that is another story.) Our yarn about the cavity machine began to leak holes when our daughter discovered by lifting the handle of the cavity machine and dialing a few numbers she could be in touch with thousands of cavity machines throughout the world. She has had a Princess phone stuck in her ear ever since.

The key word with growing children—are there any other kind?—seems to be communication. If you're a lip-reader of any repute whatsoever, you have no problem. However, if you must compete with local disc jockeys which feed hourly through their earplugs this could get pretty sticky. We have solved this problem by buying time on the local station and reporting personal messages: "We moved last week." "Daddy's birthday is in September." "Do you still lisp?"

Naturally you can't live among all those decibels and not be affected by it. I didn't know how noise could become a way of life until the other day when I answered the door and a young man said, "Pardon me, madam, I'm doing a survey among mothers to see whether or not they agree with an acoustical engineer from Arizona that rock 'n' roll may cause teenagers to go deaf."

"No, I don't need any rolls or bread today. If you've got any of those little buns with the jelly inside, though—"

"No, madam," he said, raising his voice, "you don't understand. I'm not a bakery man. I'd like to get your opinion on what hearing experts are saying about rock 'n' roll music and whether or not you think excessive—"

"*Oh, Excedrin!* You want me to do a commercial? My yes, I have headaches all the time. It's this loud music. You see, we've got four radios in the house. Along about four o'clock it sounds like the U. N. General Assembly singing a serenade in four languages to Red China. I simply crawl under the sink with a shaker full of Excedrin and—"

"Madam," he said facing me squarely, "we're not doing a commercial. We're doing a survey. Do you have a teenager in your home?"

"You're going to have to keep your lips in full view of my eyes at all times," I explained. "And talk a little slower."

"I'm sorry," he said. "Do you have a teenager in your home?"

"I think that's what it is," I said hesitantly. "The bangs are two inches above the hemline and there's a small lump on the hip shaped like a small transistor, two button eyes, and a long cord that connects the hip to the ear."

"That's a teenager," he added impersonally. "Now, have you noticed any impairment in her hearing since she started listening to rock 'n' roll music?"

I pondered. "Nothing unusual. She still doesn't respond to simple commands like 'Clean your room,' 'Change your clothes,' 'Get the door.' On the other hand she picks up phrases like 'Have you heard the story about . . .' 'The bank balance is down to . . .' and 'Let's feed the kids early and slip out to dinner . . .' like she was standing in the middle of the Capitol rotunda in Washington."

"Then you have noticed that increased decibels have made a change in your teenager?"

"Pardon me while I get the phone."

"I didn't hear anything," he said.

"It's always like that after I've listened to three hours of Maurice and His Electric Fuse Boxes. Did you know that group once recorded the guitar player's hiccups and sold two million records? Are you saying something, young man? I told you you'd have to keep your lips in full view of my eyes at all times. *And speak a little slower!*"

Other than noise, possibly nothing is more perplexing to parents than the current hair styles. In our family it all began when our daughter said she was going to let her hair grow. Like a fool I thought she meant down her back! Little did I dream it would cascade over her face and that only a slight part in the middle would stand between her and asphyxiation.

Quite frankly the whole thing got on my nerves. "Are you awake under there?" I'd ask, my eyes squinting for a peek of flesh. "If you are, just rap twice on the table." Sometimes when the hair wouldnt' move for a while, I'd get panicky and take her pulse. Then a voice would come out of the hair, "Mother! Please! I'm on the phone." For all I knew she could have had a ouija board and another friend in there with her. Occasionally she would style her hair in such a way that a single eye would be exposed. The eye would follow me about the room, not moving and rarely blinking. I often found myself addressing remarks to it.

One day when I came to the conclusion that she looked more like a troll than a human, I ventured a wild suggestion, "Why don't you cut your hair?"

I saw the hair part and a pair of lips emerge and say, "You've got to be kidding! I'd be the laughingstock of the school. No one cuts their hair anymore."

I saw my chance and took it. "That's it. Be a pace setter. Dare to be different. There is absolutely nothing more fresh and feminine in this world than short-cropped, clean hair with a little curl in the end and a little side bang. I tell you, you'd stand out like a pom pom girl in St. Petersburg, Florida. For the first time in your life, dare to look like a girl."

She pondered it for three weeks. Then her eyes glistening with sentiment, she was sheared and was once again able to distinguish light from darkness. I admit I was pretty proud of myself. "You really look the way a young lady should look. I wouldn't be surprised if all the girls in your school followed your lead. It's so girlish . . . so ladylike . . . so feminine."

We were both standing in line at the local hamburger emporium when we heard it. An elderly couple quite frankly stared at my daughter's tapered slacks, boots, short jacket, and cropped hair for a full three minutes. Then they clucked, "Look at that boy! It's disgusting! What kind of a mother would let him dress like that!"

I will be glad when the hair grows back in again. Then I will only have one sad eye to follow me about.

Truly I wish I could collar that woman in Detroit and ask her when I get to laugh. Maybe it was the other night when the kids were talking with one another at the dinner table and they began to spell in front of us. Maybe it was when I overheard one of them asking their father if he wasn't a little old for a button-down collar. Or maybe it was when one of them shot me down for saying hello to them on the playground in front of their friends.

A parent gets a lot of theories these days on how they should raise their children. Treat them as children. Treat them as adults. Treat them as equals. Treat them as pals. Okay, when my children stop telling me Doris Day is three years older than I am and looks ten years younger, I'll consider them as associates. Until then, when do I get to laugh?

Reflections at Summer's End

The end of summer is to me like New Year's Eve. I sense an end to something carefree and uninhibited, sandy and warm, cold and melting, barefoot and tanned. And yet I look forward with great expectation to a beginning of schedules and appointments, bookbinders with little tabs, freshly sharpened pencils, crisp winds, efficiency, and routine.

I am sadly aware of a great rushing of time as I lengthen skirts and discard sweaters that hit above the wristbones. Time is moving and I want to stop it for just a while so that I may snatch a quiet moment and tell my children what it is I want for them and what all the shouting has been about.

The moment never comes, of course. I must compete with Captain Kangaroo, a baseball game, a Monkee record, a playmate, a cartoon or a new bike in the next block. So, I must keep these thoughts inside . . .

Too fast . . . you're moving too fast. Don't be in such a hurry to trade formulas for formals. You're going to own your own sports car before you've tried to build one out of orange crates and four baby buggy wheels. You're going to explore the world before you've explored the wonders of your own back yard. You're going to pad with cotton what the Good Lord will provide if you are just patient.

Don't shed your childhood like a good coat

that's gotten a little small for you. A full-term childhood is necessary as is all phases of your growth. Childhood is a time for pretending and trying on maturity to see if it fits or hangs baggy, tastes good or bitter, smells nice or fills your lungs with smoke that makes you cough. It's sharing licks on the same sucker with your best friend before you discover germs. It's not knowing how much a house cost, and caring less. It's going to bed in the summer with dirty feet on clean sheets. It's thinking anyone over fifteen is "ancient." It's absorbing ideas, knowledge, and people like a giant sponge. Childhood is where "competition" is a baseball game and "responsibility" is a paper route.

I want to teach you so much that you must know to find happiness within yourself. Yet, I don't know where to begin or how.

I want you to be a square. That's right, a square! I want you to kiss your grandmother when you walk into a room even if you're with friends. I want you to be able to talk openly of God and your love for Him. I want you to lend dignity to the things you believe in and respect for the things you don't believe in. I want you to be a human being who needs friends, and in turn deserves them. I want you to be a square who polishes his shoes, buttons the top button of his shirt occasionally, and stands straight and looks people in the eye when they are talking to you. There is a time to laugh and a time to cry. I want you to know the difference.

I want you to be a cornball, a real, honest-to-God, flag-waving cornball, who, if you must march, will tell people what you are for, not what you are against. I'm so afraid in your ultimate sophistication of growing up, you'll look upon Betsy Ross as a chairman who needed a service project, upon Barbara Frietchie as a senile who should have been committed to an institution by her son, upon the little old man who doffed his hat as the flag went by as the town drunk who never missed a parade.

Please cry when school children sing "The Battle Hymn of the Republic," when you see a picture of the Berlin Wall, when you see the American flag on the silver suit of an astronaut. Maybe I'm in a panic for nothing. It just seems that during the last few years the flag has become less symbolic to people. I think all of last year I only read two stories concerning a flag: one was about a flag being burned in front of a foreign embassy, the other involved an undergarment manufacturer who was under fire from the DAR for daring to make panties out of the Stars and Stripes. Have some feeling for it and for what it stands for. Wear it on you as big as a conventioneer's badge.

Please remember to have compassion. It's funny, a mother rarely forgets the first time her child leaves his small, self-centered world and thinks of someone other than himself. I remember when our youngest was six years old he came home from school one afternoon and demanded, "I need an old toothbrush and a toy truck."

"Don't tell me," I said laughing, "you're making a Thanksgiving centerpiece for the dining room table."

"Nope," he said proudly. "We're winning the war in Vietnam."

"With a toothbrush and a toy truck?"

"Mom," he said patiently, "you don't understand. Let me explain it to you. You see, we're fighting a war in a place called Vietnam and there are people over there who have nothing to brush their teeth with or anything. They don't need money. They just need toothbrushes. Can I have yours?"

"Well, don't you think we ought to send them a new one?"

"That's okay," he reasoned. "Now I have to

pick out a truck . . . not one that's all beat up, but something a soldier would want to play with."

My eyes fairly popped out of my head. "*A soldier wants to play with!* You mean the Vietnamese children, don't you?"

Now his eyes widened. "You mean there are children in Vietnam? In the war?"

"Right in the middle of it," I explained. "Now go back and pick out a truck."

I found him sitting in the middle of the floor with a truck on his lap, preoccupied with his own thoughts. "I never thought there would be children in a war," he said.

"Few people do," I answered.

"Well, what do the children do all day while the soldiers fight?"

"Try to act like the war's not there."

"Do they play in another language?"

"No, it's a universal one."

"Will I be a soldier when I grow up?" he asked solemnly.

"I hope not. Why?"

"Because it's a crumby trick sending a neat package to a kid and having him open it and finding a silly toothbrush and someone's secondhand birthday truck. It's a rotten trick on a kid."

If I could only be sure all the lessons are sinking in and are being understood. How can I tell you about disappointments? You'll have them, you know. And they'll be painful, they'll hurt, they'll shatter your ego, lay your confidence in yourself bare, and sometimes cripple your initiative. But people don't die from them. They just emerge stronger. I want you to hear the thunder, so you can appreciate the calm. I want you to fall on your face in the dirt once in a while, so you will know the pride of being able to stand tall. Learn to live with the words "No! You can't! You're out! You blew it! I don't know." And "I made a mistake."

Adults are always telling young people, "These are the best years of your life." Are they? I don't know. Sometimes when adults say this to children I look into their faces. They look like someone on the top seat of the Ferris wheel who has had too much cotton candy and barbecue. They'd like to get off and be sick but everyone keeps telling them what a good time they're having.

Do not imagine for a moment that I don't feel your fears and anxieties. Youth does not have an immunity from disappointments and heartbreaks. No one does.

Fears begin the day you were born: fear of baths, bed wetting, the dark, falling off the sink where you are being bathed, strangers throwing you into the air and not catching you, going hungry, noises, open pins.

Later, it's monsters, parents leaving and not coming back, death, hurts, and bad dreams. School only adds to anxieties. Fear of not having friends, being called upon and not knowing the answers, telling the truth when you're going to be punished, not getting to the bathroom in time, not being liked by a baby sitter, not loved by your parents when a new baby arrives in the house. As you mature, they continue to multiply. Fear of not achieving, not having friends, or not being accepted, not getting the car, worrying about war, marriage, career, making money, being attractive to the opposite sex and making the grades to graduate.

Fears are normal. We all have them. Parents have the greatest fears of all. For we are responsible for this life which we have brought to this world. There is so much to teach and the time goes so fast . . .

Was that brisk draft of air a prelude to another fall, or did someone just rush by me in a hurry to turn on Captain Kangaroo?

Out of the Nest

We call him "the baby."

He weighs forty pounds, stands stove-high and can kick a football higher than the house. Somehow, I have the feeling we will call him "the baby" when he is forty, has children of his own, and a hairline like the coast of Florida.

This day, in particular, is special. It's the day when "the baby" goes to school for the first time. I don't know why I feel so irritable. One minute I'm yelling at him, "You slam that door once more, fella, and I'll mail you to a school in Nebraska with no return address."

The next I'm scooping him to my bosom and saying, "Let's run away to Never-Never land, you and I, where little boys never grow up and I could get the job of Mother that Mary Martin gave up."

This should be a happy morning. I remember all those promises I made to myself while sloshing over diaper pails and shaking boiling hot milk over my wrists at 2 A.M. just six short years ago.

"Just wait," I told myself. "When this whole mess is behind me I'll go back to bed in the mornings, have lunch with someone who doesn't eat his meat with a spoon, shed fifteen pounds, do my nails, learn how to play bridge, and blow this firetrap called home that has held me a virtual prisoner."

I nurtured this dream through measles, fractures, tensions, traumas, Dr. Spock, and nursery school. And now that I am so close to realization, I feel guilty. What am I doing? Sending this "baby" off to learn calculus before the cord is healed. How can I possibly think of my own comforts when he is harboring all those insecurities? Indeed, how does the State of Ohio know my son is ready for the first grade? They look at him and what do they see? A birth certificate and a record of immunizations.

I look at him and I see a smile . . . like Halloween. I see two short legs that won't get him a drink of water without a stool under them. I see two pudgy hands that can't work together to hold a slippery bar of soap. I see a shock of red hair that doesn't come up to his father's belt buckle. I see a little boy who never went to the restroom all during nursery school because he didn't want to admit he couldn't spell the difference between B-O-Y-S from G-I-R-L-S on the door.

I should have prepared him more. I piffed away all that time on Santa Claus, Easter Bunny, Tooth Fairy, and Mary Poppins. I should've dealt with the basic realities like tolerance, forgiveness, compassion, and honesty. For from this day forward his world can only widen. An existence that began in a crib, grew to a house, and extends over a two-block bicycle ride will now go even beyond that. I will share him with another woman, other adults, other children, other opinions, other points of view. I am no longer leading. I am standing behind him ready to guide from a new position.

Who is this woman who will spend more daylight hours with him than I? Please, Miss Chalkdust or whatever, give him the patience and gentleness he needs. Please have a soft lap and a warm smile. Please don't be too pretty or too smart, lest I suffer from the comparison.

A note. Maybe I should pin a note on his sweater to make sure she understands you. I could say, "Dear Miss Chalkdust or whatever: I submit to your tender, loving care my son who is a little shy and a lot stubborn. Who can't cope yet with zippers that stick or buttons on sweaters that don't come out even. One who makes his 5's sideways but works seriously and in earnest. I may sue you for alienation of affection, but for the moment, God Bless You!"

Note. There is no time for a note. The bus is here. It's such a big bus. Why would they send their largest bus for someone so small? He is gone. He didn't even look back to wave.

Why was I so rotten to him all summer? I had five summers to be rotten to him and I had to concentrate all my rottenness into this one. It's funny when you think about it. You give six years of your life readying a child for school and all of a sudden you find you're being replaced by a stranger and a thirty-five-cent plate lunch.

The house is so quiet. It's what I've always wanted, isn't it? A quiet house. I wonder who my tears are really for. I hate to admit it, but I think they're for myself.

I think I'm afraid. What kind of a woman am I? Am I going to be the woman who wanders through the house, unfulfilled and bored, who occasionally plucks a pair of sticky socks off the ceiling and sobs into them, "My baby, my baby!"? Will I dust and vacuum the house every day and be tidied up by ten-thirty only to sit and drink coffee and watch for the big, yellow bus to deposit my brood at the curb that I may once again run and fetch like a robot that has been programmed for service?

Will my children go on being my crutch? My excuse for not stirring from this house? Will I dedicate my entire life to their comforts?

Or could I be like that robin in our spouting

last spring? What a time to be thinking about robins in the spouting. I watched that little feathered mother-to-be all spring as she and her mate built the nest and she perched on her eggs to wait. Then, day of days, the babies were born and both she and the father scratched and carried to fill the demands of those ever-open mouths in the nest.

Finally the day came when they lined them up and one by one the babies flew. At first they hesitated and hung back until they were nudged out of the nest. Then, they swooped up and down like an early prop plane gone out of control. They exhausted themselves flapping their wings. Some set down in makeshift landings that were unbelievable. Others perched precariously near the danger of cats and barking dogs, but the mother never budged. She just watched and observed, her snappy, black eyes never missing a move. Day by day the birds flew more, flew better, and flew further until the day came when they were all ready to take their place in the sky with the parents.

I thought of my friends and I remembered the ones who were as wise as the robin. They too nudged their youngsters out of the nest, and then the youngsters sprouted their own wings and led the way. They emerged from a cocoon existence of peanut butter and naps into great beautiful butterflies. The sound of the school bell was like V-E Day to them. They assumed leadership, developed, and grew into active citizens in the community, unearthed talents that surprised everyone (including themselves), and set about restoring order to their lives and rejuvenating their own appearance.

The bus? It's here so soon. Before I've scarcely had time to get my bearings. There he comes hopping off the step and yelling excitedly, "I passed!" It's such a small bus. Why would they send such a small bus for such a group of big, boisterous boys? Or could it be . . . the same bus they sent this morning and my son just grew a lot?

Maybe we've all done some growing today.

grandma (grand'ma), *n.* The mother of one's father or mother.

The role of a grandmother has never been really defined. Some sit in rockers, some sky dive, some have careers. Others clean ovens. Some have white hair. Others wear wigs. Some see their grandchildren once a day (and it's not enough). Others, once a year (and that's too much).

Once I conducted an interesting survey among a group of eight-year-olds on grandmas. I asked them three questions. One, what is a grandmother? Two, what does she do? And three, what is the difference between a grandmother and a mother?

To the first question, the answers were rather predictable. "She's old (about eighty), helps around the house, is nice and kind, and is Mother's mother or Father's mother, depending on the one who is around the most."

To the second question, the answers again were rather obvious. Most of them noted grandmothers knit, do dishes, clean the bathroom, make good pies; and a goodly number reveled in the fact that Grandma polished their shoes for them.

It was the third question that stimulated the most reaction from them. Here is their composite of the differences between a mother and a grandmother. "Grandma has gray hair, lives alone, takes me places and lets me go into her attic. She can't swim. Grandma doesn't spank you and stops Mother when she does. Mothers scold better and more. Mothers are married. Grandmas aren't.

"Grandma goes to work and my mother doesn't do anything. Mom gives me shots, but Grandma gives me frogs. Grandma lives faraway. A mother you're born from. A grandmother gets married to a grandfather first, a mother to a father last.

"Grandma always says, 'Stay in, it's cold outside,' and my mother says, 'Go out, it's good for you.' "

And here's the clincher. Out of thirty-nine children queried, a total of thirty-three associated the word "love" with Grandma. One summed up the total very well with, "Grandma loves me all the time."

Actually this doesn't surprise me one small bit. On rare occasions when I have had my mother baby-sit for me, it often takes a snake whip and a chair to restore discipline when I get them home.

"Grandma sure is a neat sitter," they yawn openly at the breakfast table. "We had pizza and cola and caramel popcorn. Then we watched Lola Brooklynbridgida on the late show. After that we played Monopoly till you came home. She said when you were a kid you never went to bed. One night you even heard them play 'The Star-Spangled Banner' before the station went off."

"Did Grandma tell you I was twenty-eight at the time?" I snapped.

"Grandma said twenty-five cents a week isn't very much money for an allowance. She said we could make more by running away and joining the

Peace Corps. She said you used to blow that much a week on jawbreakers."

"Well, actually," I said grimacing, "Grandma's memory isn't as good as it used to be. She was quite strict and as I recall my income was more like ten cents a week and I bought all my own school clothes with it."

"Grandma sure is neat all right. She told us you hid our skateboard behind the hats in your closet. She said that was dirty pool. What's dirty pool, Mama?"

"It's Grandma telling her grandchildren where their mother hid the skateboard."

"Mama, did you really give a live chicken to one of your teachers on class day? And did you really play barbershop once and cut off Aunt Thelma's hair for real? Boy, you're neat!" They looked at me in a way I had never seen before.

Naturally I brought Mother to task for her indiscretion. "Grandma," I said, "you have a forked tongue and a rotten memory. You've got my kids believing I'm 'neat.' Now I ask you, what kind of an image is that for a Mother?"

"The same image your grandmother gave me," she said.

Then I remembered Grandma. What a character.

In fact, I never see a Japanese war picture depicting Kamikaze pilots standing erect in their helmets and goggles, their white scarfs flying behind them, toasting their last hour on earth with a glass of sake, that I don't think of riding to town with my grandma on Saturdays.

We would climb into her red and yellow Chevy coupe and jerk in first gear over to the streetcar loop where Grandma would take her place in line between the trolley cars. Due to the rigorous concentration it took to stay on the tracks and the innumerable stops we had to make, conversation was kept to a minimum. A few times a rattled shopper would tap on the window for entrance, to which Grandma would shout angrily, "If I wanted passengers, I'd dingle a bell!"

Once, when I dared to ask why we didn't travel in the same flow of traffic as the other cars, Grandma shot back, "Laws, child, you could get killed out there." Our first stop in town was always a tire center. I could never figure this out. We'd park in the "For Customers Only" lot and Grandma would walk through the cool building. She'd kick a few tires, but she never purchased one. One day she explained, "The day I gain a new tire is the day I lose the best free parking spot a woman ever had."

I don't have Grandma's guts in the traffic or her cunning. But I thought about her the other day as I sat bumper to bumper in the hot downtown traffic. "Hey, lady," yelled a voice from the next car, "wanta get in our pool? Only cost a quarter. We're putting odds on the exact minute your radiator is going to blow. You can have your choice of two minutes or fifteen seconds." Boy, Grandma would have shut his sassy mouth in a hurry.

We had an understanding, Grandma and I. She didn't treat me like a child and I didn't treat her like a mother. We played the game by rules. If I didn't slam her doors and sass, then she didn't spank and lecture me. Grandma treated me like a person already grown up.

She let me bake cookies with dirty hands . . . pound on the piano just because I wanted to . . . pick the tomatoes when they were green . . . use her clothespins to dig in the yard . . . pick her flowers to make a necklace chain. Grandma lived in a "fun" house. The rooms were so big you could skate in them. There were a hundred thousand steps to play upon, a big eave that invited cool summer breezes and where you could remain "lost" for hours. And around it all was a black, iron fence.

I liked Grandma the best, though, when she told me about my mama, because it was a part of Mama I had never seen or been close to. I didn't know that when Mama was a little girl a photographer came one day to take a picture of her and her sister in a pony cart. I couldn't imagine they had to bribe them into good behavior by giving them each a coin. In the picture Mama is crying and biting her coin in half. It was a dime and she wanted the bigger coin—the nickel— given to her sister. Somehow, I thought Mama was born knowing the difference between a nickel and a dime.

Grandma told me Mama was once caught by

the principal for writing in the front of her book, "In Case of Fire, Throw This in First." I had never had so much respect for Mama as the day I heard this.

From Grandma I learned that Mama had been a child and had traveled the same route I was traveling now. I thought Mom was "neat." (And what kind of an image is that for a mother?)

If I had it to do all over again, I would never return to Grandma's house after she had left it. No one should. For that grand, spacious house tended to shrink with the years. Those wonderful steps that I played upon for hours were broken down and rather pathetic. There was a sadness to the tangled vines, the peeling paint, and the iron fence that listed under the burden of time. The big eave was an architectural "elephant" and would mercifully crumble under the ax of urban renewal.

Grandmas defy description. They really do. They occupy such a unique place in the life of a child. They can shed the yoke of responsibility, relax, and enjoy their grandchildren in a way that was not possible when they were raising their own children. And they can glow in the realization that here is their seed of life that will harvest generations to come.

scuba diving. This could be awkward and limiting later on.

September 6—November 2

Don't sweat the small stuff

Several years ago I adopted an expression to live by. I don't know where I picked it up, probably from some immortal bard on a restroom wall, but it has worked like therapy for me.

To begin with, I used to be a worrier. I worried about whether or not our patio doors were covered by insurance if they were hit by a polo ball. I worried about that poor devil on television who flunked his nasalgraph test. I worried about Carol Channing going bald. I worried about who would return our library books if my husband and I both "went to that great split-level in the sky" together.

When the children were babies, it was worse. I used to get up at night and hold mirrors under their nostrils to make sure they were still breathing. I worried about their spitting out more food than went into their stomachs. I developed a "thing" about germs. When I changed diapers, I washed *their* hands. When we went bye-bye in the car, it was like moving the circus. I had a fetish about the kids drinking their moo-moo from any cup that didn't have their name on it.

Then, along came the thought-provoking slogan, "Don't Sweat the Small Stuff," and my entire life changed.

The things I couldn't do anything about I

ignored. The things I could I numbered and filed them in their respective places. I stopped worrying and started relaxing. I quit scaring the kids half to death at night with the mirror routine. I discovered I could pack baby's entire needs for the weekend in a handbag and they could drink out of animal skins if they had to. As for germs, I conducted an experiment one night and found to my delight that a pacifier recovered from a package of coffee grounds in the garbage can rinsed well under hot water and jammed quickly into baby's mouth, actually enjoyed improved flavor.

I quit worrying about Mao Tse-tung, the population of India, litterbugs filling up Grand Canyon, and our wading pool becoming polluted. I quit worrying about what would happen to me if I wore white shoes after Labor Day. Before, I rather imagined Saks would fly their flag at half mast. Maybe *Life* magazine would send a reporter-photographer team to follow me about and record the shock of the man-on-the-street. Or maybe Brinkley would use me in one of those amusing little sign-off stories that Huntley pretends he doesn't hear.

It used to be that getting the jump on fashions each season was like running through your lifetime after a train and never catching it, or waking up each morning and discovering it is always yesterday.

It's true. If you want to buy a spring suit, the choice selection occurs in February: a bathing suit, March: back-to-school clothes, July: a fur coat, August. Did I tell you about the week I gave in to a mad-Mitty desire to buy a bathing suit in August?

The clerk, swathed in a long-sleeved woolen dress which made her look for the world like Teddy Snowcrop, was aghast. "Surely, you are putting me on," she said. "A bathing suit! In August!"

"That's right," I said firmly, "and I am not leaving this store until you show me one."

She shrugged helplessly. "But surely you are aware of the fact that we haven't had a bathing suit in stock since the first of June. Our—no offense—White Elephant sale was June third and we unload—rather, disposed of all of our suits at that time."

"Are you going to show me a bathing suit," I demanded, "or do I tell everyone that you buy your fitting-room mirrors from an amusement park fun house?"

"Please, madam, keep your voice down. I'll call our manager, Mr. Wheelock, on the phone. (*Lowers voice*) Mr. Wheelock, we've got this crazy woman on the floor who insists upon buying a bathing suit. You heard me right. A bathing suit. I told her that. What dose she look like? W-E-I-R-D. She's wearing a pink, sleeveless dress, carrying a white handbag and has (ugh) white shoes. I agree, Mr. Wheelock, but what should I tell her? Very well. (*Louder*) Madam, Mr. Wheelock says since you are obviously a woman of fine taste, we will call you in February when we unpack our first shipment of swim suits. Would you like that?"

Now, normally, I would have jumped up and down pounding my head with my handbag and become quite physical about it. Instead, I simply smiled and said, "Of course I'll return in February when I will personally release a pregnant moth in Mr. Wheelock's fur vault!" I didn't, of course, but with a crazy woman who wears white shoes in August, the salesperson couldn't really be sure, could she?

I quit worrying about removing upholstery labels that said, DO NOT REMOVE LABEL UNDER PENALTY. I quit worrying about the goonie birds becoming extinct and the communists infiltrating Cub Pack 947.

I stopped taking seriously all this nonsense about hand-me-down clothes having a traumatic effect on your children.

I mean, any mother with half a brain knows that children's apparel comes in three sizes: "A little large, but you'll grow," "Just right—so enjoy," and "A little small, so stoop a little."

I think it was last year when we had a rare phenomenon at our house. All the coats were "Just right—so enjoy." By my rough calculations, this event will not occur again in my life span. Now, did the children appreciate the aesthetic beauty of a sleeve that hit smack between the wristbone and the hand, and hems that neither hit midthigh nor dragged behind them like a train? They did not.

"I'll be the only boy in the sixth grade wearing white go-go boots with tassels." "What are you complaining about? I'll be the only patrol boy wearing Cinderella mittens." "You're kidding with this hat. I know I'll grow, but how big can a head get?"

I just rationalized that I was supplying them with a lifetime of laughs. It's a curious tradition, this passing down of clothes within a family. It's the American way, you know. If you're the oldest in the family, you wear new, but you learn early, "Don't tear it, stain it, sweat in it, or drag it across the floor. It's got a long way to go." If you are somewhere in the middle, the attire is a little lighter from constant washings, a little frayed around the buttonholes, and a little smoother in the seat. If you're "the baby," heaven help you. When style was passed out, you weren't born yet. You're in line for the dingy diapers, the sweaters that were washed by mistake in hot water, the pajama bottoms that don't match the tops and the snowsuit that "cost a pretty penny in its day." (No one seems to remember the day *or* the year.)

Traumas! Hogwash! I have never seen people enjoy such unrestrained belly laughs as when they're reminiscing about the hand-me-downs of their childhood. The long underwear tucked inside the shoes so people would think you were wearing your Sunday-best white hose to school. Wearing your mother's boots—the skinny pointed heels—and stuffing the heels with paper. The first snow when kids emerged like patchwork refugees who had just climbed out of a ship's hold.

No, I rather think kids will have to look back kindly on their days of hand-me-downs, for they'll just have to remember with warm, wonderful nostalgia, the year the coats were "Just right—so enjoy."

I don't worry anymore about whether or not my light bulb goes off in the refrigerator when I shut the door . . . or what my dog thinks about when he sees me coming out of the shower . . . or whether or not de Gaulle wants the Statue of Liberty back.

I even adjusted to the family's nonconformer, the child who is a rebel, a loner, a renegade—the one I'm convinced the hospital gave me by mistake.

Every family has at least one. He's the preschooler with the active thyroid who gets locked in restrooms because he stayed behind to find out where the water went after you pushed down the handle. He's the one who wanders away from home and gets his arm stuck in a piece of construction pipe. He's the one who rejects storebought toys in favor of taking the registers out and making tunnels out of old oatmeal boxes. He gets more lickings than all the other kids in the family put together.

In school he gets checkmarks for daydreaming, for not being neat, for not working to capacity. It doesn't seem to bother him. In his preoccupation for other things he is unaware that he drives his family crazy, arriving late for dinner every night, wearing his socks and underwear to bed to save time in the mornings, cutting the grass only when he needs money.

I used to worry about him a lot. Had he been a genius I'd have been properly awed by it. Had he been a slow learner, I'd have shown due compassion. But to be neither of these things only confused, puzzled, and tried my patience.

I feared for this unpredictable child who was not only out-of-step with the world but whose feet rarely touched the ground. With his insatiable curiosity and hardheaded drive would he beat paths of greatness and discovery, the likes of Winston Churchill or Michelangelo? I wanted to believe that. Or would he find his measure of happiness drifting in and out of this world, living solely off his enthusiasm, imagination, and penchant for living life to its fullest?

Then one day I saw him clearly in the lines of Henry David Thoreau. He wrote, "If a man does not keep pace with his companions, perhaps it is because he hears a different drummer. Let him step to the music which he hears."

I quit beating my drum for conformity and listened to his beat for a while. His pace was a bit more relaxed, the order of his schedule a bit different. For example, watching a caterpillar cross the driveway took precedent over taking a bath. Finishing a pair of homemade stilts preceded dinner. The awe of discovering newborn robins in the spouting beat reading about Columbus discovering America.

I was not aware of how "far out" I had traveled with his drums until the other day. I was in the process of interviewing a woman to spend a few days with the children while my husband and I went out of town.

As we talked, my nonconformer entered the room. Now, had he been a usual child he would have been holding a conventional water tumbler filled with water. As it was he had seen fit to fill an old-fashioned glass with two ice cubes and float a cherry and a slice of orange on top of it. Did I panic? I did not. I took a deep breath, smiled at my horrified visitor, and said, "I don't sweat the small stuff anymore."

To which she gasped, "You mean with a kid drinking in the afternoon the stuff gets bigger?" and bolted for her car.

Oh well, she wouldn't have lasted around here two days.

A Man and His Car

I shook my husband awake out of a sound sleep. "I've had that bad dream again," I said.

He yawned, "What bad dream?"

"The one where Lady Bird Johnson comes knocking at our door and asks us to get rid of those junk cars in our driveway."

"Didn't you tell her we're still driving them?" he asks sleepily.

"Yes. Then she looked very concerned and said we should apply for federal funds. She said those rusty heaps in front of our house have set her beautification program back ten years and that no matter what our politics we should care about our country. Then she just faded away."

"That sounds like a nice idea."

"Wake up. We've got to talk about those cars. They're eyesores. We should replace one and I think it ought to be yours."

"Nonsense," he grumbled, "I just spent an entire Saturday touching up the rust spots with black paint."

"On a mouse-gray body, that's hardly a secret," I snarled. "It looks so garish with all those stickers on the rear window, SEE ROCK CITY, BUY LIBERTY BONDS, NRA. Why don't you scrape some of them off?"

"Because they're holding in the rear window." He yawned again.

"I'll bet it was that rusty tailpipe that caught her attention. We could wire it up off the ground."

"Okay, tomorrow take a little wire off the door handles and wire up the tailpipe. You can reinforce the running boards if you want to."

"Yeah, and I might shine up the chrome around the headlights and get a new set of wicks for them. That'll spruce things up a bit."

"While you're at it, why don't you spend a little time on *your* car? It's not exactly a Grand Prix entry, you know."

"Well, I haul twenty or thirty kids a week around in it. What do you expect?"

"All I know is, the insurance company wouldn't insure it. They just sent us a survival kit. Those springs in the seats are exposed so badly if you weren't buckled in with seat belts, you'd be driving from the roof. There's no door on the glove compartment, the rear window won't go up or down, and you have to turn on the radio with a pair of pliers. And who in heaven's name scratched 'Official 500 Pace Car' on the door? You know the best thing we could do for Lady Bird would be to erect a billboard in front of both of them."

"She suggested that," I said quietly.

"Then it's settled," he sighed, pulling up the

covers. "Now will you turn off the light and let me go to sleep?"

I ignored him and reached in the headboard bookcase for something to put me to sleep. I thought I had made a wise choice. It was one of those books that lists surveys and studies conducted by industries and researchers to find out what motivates people to buy as they do. For example, I discovered that people buy home freezers because they are emotionally insecure and need more food than they can eat. Then I bolted upright. There in front of me was a chapter on what motivates men to buy the cars they do. It said researchers found when dealers put a convertible in their show windows men flocked to look at it. But they invariably bought a sedan. Why?

Psychologists who studied the problem came up with the fact that convertibles were symbolic mistresses. They were flashy. They brought out the eyeballs. They attracted attention. Men looked at them longingly, dreamed a little, lusted a lot. But, in the end, man's common sense, his practical side, his down-to-earth rationalization, told him it was not for him and he bought the sedan. The sedan represented the symbolic wife, the plain, safe girl who would be a substantial mother to his children.

As one "practical sedan" to another, I don't mind telling you this bothered me. Especially, when I began thinking back to the women—er, cars my husband had picked out in the past.

Our first car—which he obviously identified

with me—was a secondhand, plain, drab-looking, black you-know-what with a broken window—on my side—and a glove compartment door that sprung out in your lap every time the motor turned over, plus a small printed note on the fender that read, "Please, Don't Kick the Tires."

It was good, clean transportation despite the fact it was an obvious alcoholic and couldn't pass a service station without stopping for a slug of gas with an oil chaser. It was hot in the summer and cold in the winter and asthmatic all year round.

Our first new car, in 1951, indicated I still had not changed. It was as proper as a hearse—no chrome, no extras, and no nonsense. I don't think any self-respecting tiger would have been caught dead climbing into its tank!

We bought another new car in 1955. Only the

color and the mortgage balance changed.

I slipped out of bed and peered through the window. Suppose men really picked cars like they picked wives. Was this a car to have an affair with? Was this the jaunty sports cap, silk scarf flying crazily in the wind type of car? Was this a mistress, or a mother in sturdy, sensible sneakers?

In the driveway was our small cheapie foreign car that boasted it never changed body styles year after year. The pitiful bit of chrome on the bumper was rusted from the salt on the streets in winter, and a paper towel was stuffed around the windshield because the thermostat was broken and the heat was intense. The color was mouse gray.

I shook my husband awake. "Let's go out and buy a new car tomorrow. Something impractical. Something wild. It's important to me."

"Are you crazy?" he groaned sleepily. "Why I've got too much money tied up in that old heap to let her go. She's good till the fuel pump goes. Besides, she's comfortable."

"That's a rotten thing to say to anyone," I sobbed and went to sleep.

I suppose I'd still have that mouse-gray image in the driveway today if it hadn't been for the garbage truck that plowed into me. As I told my husband when I returned his car minus two fenders, two headlights, and a trunk lid, "That tears it. This car is Hitler's Revenge and it must be replaced. I can't drive a car I can't communicate with."

"If I've told you once I've told you a hundred

times," he said, "the car doesn't understand a word of English. It responds only to German commands."

"I tried that," I said. "I saw this garbage truck begin to back up and I said, 'Das ist ein garbage truck, lunkhead, let's get out of here.'"

"What happened?"

"Nothing happened. It just sat there like a stick until the truck hit us. I tried blasting the horn and it peep-peeped like it was apologizing. Incidentally, the horn broke off in my hand. It's in the glove compartment."

"Then what happened?"

"I ran out of German, that's what happened. The truck still didn't know I was back there and started at me again. I tried every German word I knew: glockenspiel, pumpernickel, Marlene Dietrich. I even sang two choruses of 'O Tannenbaum.' That's when the second impact hit. That did it. I whacked it on the instrument panel and said, 'Du bist ein cheapie, that's what you are. One more hit and we're going to look like a crock of sauerkraut.' Just about that time the driver got out of his truck and said, very surprised, 'I thought I hit a bump in the road.' How's that for humiliation!"

"Don't worry. I think we can fix her up," said my husband.

"Fix her!" I shouted. "You wouldn't dare. Not after what she's put me through. Just think of the merits of a big car. No more shinnying into the seat like a snake into a sleeping bag. No more mud goggles on rainy days. No more massaging your cold feet and shifting gears at the same time.

"Think what it would be to pass cars on a hill. And to ride with your legs outstretched, instead of in a foetal position. Just imagine. We could talk to a car in English. No more having to say, 'By the way, what is it you say when you want the car to go in reverse?' "

"Mutter, bitte," he said.

"Which means?" I sighed wearily.

"Mother, may I?"

"It figures. Tomorrow, we buy a new car."

I never realized it before, but there's an umbilical cord connecting a man to his car. It is perhaps the most possessive, protective, paternal relationship you'll ever encounter. Bound together by a thirty-month loan contract, their hearts beat as one until the car goes back on the lot and is exchanged for a new model to which he transfers his love and affection.

The book was right, of course. He eased onto the seat of the sports car in the show window, his arm slipping ever so slyly over the back of the seat. He caressed the steering wheel and the visor with a gentleness I had never seen before. (I thought I saw him pinch the directional lights.) Then he took a deep breath of resignation, walked over to the conventional model and sighed, "We've got the children to consider."

I was pleased to note my image had improved considerably. It had a radio that didn't take ten minutes to heat up. It had power steering and power brakes. And the color was a deep purple. (Which my husband noted matched the veins in my nose.)

Then I went too far. One night I asked to borrow his car. You'd have thought I wanted to borrow his dental plates to eat caramels.

"Isn't there any other way you can get to card club?" he asked.

"Yes," I replied. "I could tape peanuts to my arms and maybe attract enough pigeons to fly me there, but I'd rather drive the car."

Reluctantly he walked me to the door. "You have your license? Your key ring? Extra money? Witnesses?"

I grinned. "I don't want to marry it, just drive it to card club."

"You have to understand about this model," he explained patiently. "She starts cold. Now some cars need pumping. Don't pump her. *She hates to be pumped!* Get that? All you do is ease the choke out about a quarter of an inch. Then push the accelerator all the way to the floor and just ease up on it a bit. Okay? Not too fast. At the same time, turn the key and gently now, slide the choke back in."

Given the least kind of encouragement—like keeping awake—he also delves into "baby's sluggish crankcase, her puny pistons, her fouled plugs, and her dulling points."

As I slid into the seat, he let fly his last arrow. "Don't gun it and you'll make it."

I turned off the motor. "Don't gun what and I'll make it where?"

"Don't gun the motor and you'll make it to the gas station. The tank says empty, but I know there's enough to coast you in, especially if you make the light on the corner and roll the last fifty feet. Oh, and if it keeps dying on you there are emergency flares in the trunk."

A man and his car—he loves and cherishes it from the first day forward, for richer for poorer, for better or for worse, in sickness and in health, and if Detroit ever turns out a model that sews on buttons and laughs at his jokes, ladies, we're in trouble!

The Watercress and Girdle Group

The name of the game is clubwork.

It's played from September through May by thousands of women who spend billions of volunteer hours every year deciding whether to put kidney beans or whole tomatoes in the Circle Meeting chili, or whether to spray-paint the pipe cleaners for the PTA Easter luncheon pink or purple.

Some women readily recognize the overorganization, the tedious details, the long drawn-out devotion to three-hour meetings. But they rationalize that the real cause is worth it. Other women become impatient with sloppy leadership, dull monologues, and that "why-do-today-what-you-can-talk-about-for-three-more-hours-next-Wednesday" syndrome.

Clubwork is therapy for a lot of women. It gets them into their girdles and out among people. It gives them something else to think about besides how to disguise leftovers and how to get crayon stains out of a shirt pocket that has gone through the dryer. Let's face it. The government couldn't afford to buy the services that come out of women's groups if it cashed in the President and all his holdings.

I like clubwomen. Some of my best friends are clubwomen. I even took one to lunch last week. Some I like better than others. Program chairmen, for example. I have always had a soft spot in my heart for them. Those of us in the business of giving speeches have concurred unanimously that program chairmen rate a special place in heaven, where the sun always shines, birthdays cease to show after the age of thirty-three, and John Mason Brown sits at their right hand.

Of all the offices on the duty roster, possibly none is more underrated than the woman who must entertain the membership during an entire club year. For audience variety, she has the elder pillars of the club who attend once a year on Founder's Day and who are too proud to wear their hearing devices. ("The speaker was a sweet little thing, but she mouthed her words.") She has the strait-laced group who objected vigorously when a speaker reviewed *The Scarlet Letter.* ("That hussy! She treated it like a piece of costume jewelry!") She has the new bloods who are pressuring her into arranging a "wine tasting" program. ("Preferably *before* the business meeting, honey.")

While the rest of the membership and the officers spend a quiet summer, the program chairman never sleeps. Oh, the president spends a few anxious evenings rolling and tossing and making plans to have her appendix taken out early in September so she can relinquish the gavel to the vice president.

There's the vice president looking suspiciously at the president whom she suspects is not above having her appendix out to get out of the job of president.

There's the recording secretary in a state of

numbness, as she has only attended one meeting as a guest before they elected her to the office. There's the corresponding secretary, who is three years behind in a letter to her mother, wondering how all this is going to work out. And there's the bewildered treasurer, who is setting her husband up as a pigeon for the club's books in the fall.

Not the program chairman. She is haggling with a department store to stage a free fashion show for women with large thighs. She is buzzing the "hot line" to her president every two days with cries of "I can't get Arlene Francis for twenty dollars . . . shall I try for Betsy Palmer?" She is fighting the battle of personages on vacations, unlisted phone numbers, and speakers who won't commit themselves beyond next weekend.

And she is probably anticipating a scene typical of the one I was involved in recently when the program chairman said brightly, "Marcia, you haven't been to one of our meetings in a long time. I'm sure it's due to the popularity of our speaker, Mrs. Bombeck." To which Marcia looked annoyed and snarled, *"Bombeck!* Good Lord, I thought someone said *Steinbeck* was coming!"

Another clubwoman for whom I have great empathy is the perennial Chairman of the Bazaar. Here is a small lump of helplessness who couldn't say no. Molded by flattery and strengthened by self-confidence, she is put adrift in a sea of home-baked bread and knitted toilet tissue covers.

I know of what I speak. Several years ago I was

a bazaar chairman. The doctor tells me in time I may be able to hear a telephone ring without becoming incoherent. I wish I could be sure.

One of the first things a bazaar chairman must adjust to is what happened to all the well-wishers who, only a week ago, hoisted you to their shoulders, marched you around the gym, and sang, "For She's a Jolly Good Pigeon." Their generous offers of "I'll donate thirty quarts of my famous calf's-foot jelly" and "Leave the raffle tickets to me" now sounds like, "Are you kidding? This has been a nothing year for calves' feet" and "Honey, I couldn't sell an inner tube to a drowning man."

In desperation, a bazaar chairman will eventually take on the guise of a Mafia moll, stopping at nothing to "firm up" her committees. I've heard ruthless threats behind the coffee urn that would make your hair stand on end. "All right, Eloise, you take that White Elephant chairmanship or the entire world will know you've got a thing going with your son's orthodontist. I'm not bluffing either. And you just never mind why Jeannie Crabitz took the fish pond. That's between the two of us."

The families of bazaar chairman are also affected by this new-found diversion. Plaintive pleas of "Daddy, when is Mommy coming home for a visit?" are often answered with a sour, "She has to come home on Wednesday—it's the night she defrosts our dinners for the week."

As the bazaar draws near, the fever increases while the house takes on all the physical properties of urban renewal. "I can't sleep," complains her husband, staggering into the living room. "My bed is full of plastic cigarette holders and Hawaiian leis."

"Well, stack them in the closet," she says tiredly.

"What!" he snaps, "and disturb the goldfish that are stacked on top of the stuffed poodles and the Japanese fans?"

The last two days before the bazaar are the wildest. With a lot of luck, the raffle prizes will have been delivered to another state . . . the kitchen committee resigns en masse, resolving only to speak to one another in church on Sundays . . . and there's a strong possibility Santa Claus may not "dry out" in time to make the scene for the kiddies.

Each phone call brings a new trauma: "She insists on donating a size forty-eight angora pullover and I refuse to have it in my booth" . . . "My pickles were solicited for the Country Store booth and if the kitchen wants some, let them do their own telephoning" . . . "I will not have my pitch and throw game in the schoolroom. Last year we broke the blackboard and I had a migraine for a week."

When the last bit of popcorn is swept from the gym and the blackboard repaired and the angora pullover en route to the "missions," some poor, unsuspecting newcomer is bound to remark, "It was a lovely bazaar."

She doesn't know it yet, but that lump of innocence is next year's bazaar chairman.

One of the most overzealous groups of club-women I know are the Garden Clubbers. They cannot comprehend that some of us are born into this world to plant glad bulbs upside down. Some of us are resigned to a life without manure and mulch. And that when some of us have a green thumb, it's a skin condition.

Don't misunderstand me. I have nothing but respect for Garden Club women. Especially after the episode my mother and I endured with the dried weeds project. We just couldn't imagine there being much skill to throwing clumps of fall foliage into a pot!

"Why, they must think we're a couple of rubes who just blew into town with the egg money," Mother said. "Imagine! Paying $7.95 for a pot of dried milk pods, a few pine cones, and a couple of sticks with berries on them. We could fill a bathtub with this stuff for forty-nine cents of spray paint."

Maybe it was the vision of a floral-filled bathtub that prompted us to do it. Looking back, we like to think one of the kids left the cap off the glue and we inhaled enough to make us fly. At any rate, the next weekend found Mother and me hacking our way through the woods like Jon Hall and Sabu.

Cattails, we discovered, flourished only in swamps where the bog was knee-high. The pret-tiest leafy specimens were always at the top of the trees. The most unique pods were always situated in the middle of a livestock relief station.

And the most graceful Queen Anne's lace was always over the next hill.

I have no intention of humiliating my mother by relating that grim scene of her up to her knees in jungle rot, clutching a bundle of poison sumac to her chest and shouting hysterically at a snake slithering over her gym shoes. (Only to report that she shouted to the heavens, "Oh please! I'm Evangelical and I tithe!")

I think our little excursion can best be told by a tabulation we compiled of the expenses incurred in the pursuit of dried stock for floral arrangements.

Expenses

1 can gold spray paint	$ .69
1 can silver spray paint	.69
1 gallon paint thinner	1.25
(Used to remove spray paint from patio floor)	
1 ironing board cover	2.00
(Note to amateurs: put the leaves *between* wax paper before pressing)	
1 pair gym shoes	4.00
1 sweater (Abandoned at snake pit)	5.95
1 car wash and vacuuming	2.00
1 doctor (for sumac)	5.00
1 prescription (for sumac)	3.57
1 overdue book on *Dried Flowers for Fun and Profit*	.62
Personal Aggravation	500.00
TOTAL	$525.77

It's not that I don't appreciate Garden Club-bers' talents, it's just that they are always trying to convert you to Gardenism. One enthusiast, in particular, bugs me all the time. She's always pinching my brown leaves off my indoor plants and feeling the soil around my pots to see if they've been watered lately. She makes me nervous.

"What did you do with that slip of creeping phlox I gave you?" she asked the other day.

"It crept into the soil and died," I said.

"If I've told you once," she sighed, "I've told you a thousand times plants are like little people. You simply have to give them a little water, a little love, and a lot of understanding. Now, this is lovely and green. What do you call this?"

"I call that a rotten onion that has been around for nine weeks and is pithy and mushy on the inside, but has bright green sprouts on the outside."

"You're terrible. You really are," she chided. "You should belong to a Garden Club. Then you could exchange ideas and learn from the other members."

"I belong to the 'Wilt and Kill,'" I offered.

"The 'Wilt and Kill'?" she asked her eyes widening. "I don't think I know it."

"We're a group of Garden Club rejects . . . meet the first rainy Monday of the month . . . answer roll call with our current houseplant failure."

"You're putting me on."

"No, I'm not. It's not too easy to qualify. One girl used a nine-foot sunflower plant as a border.

She got in. Another padded her beds with plastic flowers from the dime store . . . in the winter. She qualified. I call every flower Semper Fidelis. It's the only Latin I know. I'm an officer."

"Incredible. I've never heard of it."

"We have a wonderful time. At the last meeting Maybelle Mahonia set up the projector and showed home movies of her garden. It was as barren as a missile site. We got a prize for every weed we could identify. Would you like to hear our slogan?"

"I don't think so," she said, feigning dizziness.

"It's 'From Futility to Fertility We Stand Together.' "

"Oh dear. I must be going. Incidentally, how is your sweet potato vine?"

I smiled. "It was delicious."

Ah clubwork . . . the escape hatch from the land of peanut butter and the babblings of children. If it bothers you that so much leadership ability is dormant somewhere, not because of apathy, but because these women don't want to pay the price of boredom to do the job, you could lure them back into the meeting halls easier than you think.

1. Pick a leader because she's a leader, not because she owns the punchbowl and the folding chairs.

2. Frisk all grandmothers and new mothers at the door for snapshots of children. (Check knitting bags, bras, garters, and umbrellas.)

3. Forget the democracy bit. Run the meeting

like a railroad or you'll never get home in time
to thaw the hamburger.

4. When ankles swell and handbag handles
cause red marks to streak up the arm, adjourn
the meeting.

5. Plan brief, meaningful meetings and get
something done. I wouldn't be surprised if capable women beat a path to your mousetrap!

While You're Down in the Dumps . . .

When my husband and I appear at an antique
show there is a scurrying of feet while one dealer
whispers to another, "Stick a geranium in that
slop jar, Irving, here comes a couple of live ones."

This is partly our fault. We stand there open-
mouthed and bug-eyed, clutching green cash like
we just hit town long enough to buy the fertilizer.
On at least one occasion I have rushed over to a
large hulk of metal and shrieked, "Is this a 1900
milk separator?" "No," someone replies patiently,
"that's a 1962 drinking fountain."

We have maintained a rule of thumb. If you
can sleep on it, plant flowers in it, frame it, play it,
eat it, stuff it with magazines, records or blankets,
ring it or open a conversation with it, we'll buy it.

Then we have an open category of things we're
going to do something with some day. This takes
in a cast-iron angel with a broken foot, a hand-
driven child's washing machine, a Civil War grave

marker, and a collection of "Go with Willkie" campaign buttons.

In Maine one summer we picked up a faded, musty chessboard for two dollars. It hung in our garage like a conscience for two years before my husband painted it bright red, mounted it on a turntable, and called it a "lazy susan for gracious eating." "This is going to revolutionize our eating habits," he said. "No more bloated stomachs from waiting for the kids to pass the food. No more flesh wounds from knife cuts and fork pricks. No more unnecessary conversation at the dinner table." He put the lazy susan on the table, placed our food on it, and whirled it. It looked like a fattening roulette wheel. "The success of this device," he went on, "can be summed up in two words: *keep alert.* When the turntable stops at your plate, take whatever is in front of you. You will have eight seconds to spear or spoon the food to your plate. We cannot make exceptions. I'll blow a whistle and the turntable will move again. This way in thirty-two to forty seconds we will all have our plates loaded with hot food and ready to eat. Get it?"

We got it. The first night the food was not placed in its proper order and we had whipped potatoes *over* gravy and strawberries *under* shortcake. The "whistler" promised us this would be remedied at the next meal. Then, we had the problem of overhang. That is, a coffee pot handle, a large plate or an onion ring strategically placed could conceivably clip the glasses or cups and

throw the entire timetable off schedule by as much
as four or five seconds.

It was time for another lecture. "All right,
group, I've noticed this time your performance
was a little ragged. You spoon drippers and bowl
clangers all know who you are. No need to mention names. Now, let's put our shoulders to the
wheel and shape up!"

Within two weeks, I noticed some drastic
changes. I was five pounds lighter and—due to the
centrifugal force whirling around before my eyes
at mealtime—I was hopelessly hooked on Drama-
mine.

I did what any mother would do—I stole his
lousy whistle!

Other antiques we bought were equally popular. A dear little 1809 collapsible rocker attacked
the baby when he tried to sit in it and he's avoided

it like a penicillin shot ever since.

The pump organ that was to bring togetherness to our brood also brought disharmony to the family circle. But how do you tell this to a man who has just displaced a disc and two old friends lugging it into the hallway?

Add to that a bill for $140 to replace the reeds and keep its bellows from becoming asthmatic and you've got a pretty good argument for sentiment.

"Where are we going to put it?" I asked.

"Think of it," he said, "a bowl of popcorn, a basket of juicy apples, and all of us locked arm in arm singing, 'Kentucky Babe.' Doesn't that just make your flesh crawl?"

"I'll say. Where are we going to put it?"

"I still remember a chorus or two of 'There's a Fairy in the Bottom of My Teacup.' If you promise me not to drown me out, I might let you read poetry in the background on Sundays."

"We can't leave it here in the hallway. It's on my foot."

"And home weddings," he rambled. "Think of it, with a vase of . . . what are those flowers at weddings?"

"Orange blossoms, and get this thing off my foot!"

The organ, with all its scrolls, ornate panels, carpeted pedals, and elevated candle holders, was christened "The Heap" and was placed in the living room. Its stay here was a short one. Guests complained the organ, the candles, and the flowers were a little much and gave them a creepy feeling.

(The fact that the only song my husband knew with two hands was "The Old Rugged Cross" didn't help things either.) "The Heap" was reassigned to our bedroom. Here, it became a living tabernacle for unpaid bills, unanswered letters, ties that needed cleaning, old road maps, car keys, and odd bits of change. Occasionally we'd crack our shinbones on it, which prompted us to move it to the family room. It lasted there two days. A cry of dissension went up among the young television viewers who were forced to read lips over the roar of the foot pedals and the gasps of the bellows. The next stop was the porch solarium where "The Heap" developed a decided wheeze in her bellows from the moisture. She came to rest in the kitchen.

Our problem is twofold. Serving five people seated around a pump organ and living in constant fear of a spontaneous chorus of "There's a Fairy in the Bottom of My Teacup."

Very frankly, it is next to impossible to instill respect in small children for antique furniture. Cries of "Get your feet off that distressed table!" or "Don't sit on that woodbox, it could go any minute," leaves them confused and mumbling, "She's got to be kidding."

At roadside shops on Sundays, they make snide remarks about "all this junk" and end up buying a bag of hoarhound candy which they immediately discover they hate and spit out in my hand.

Those of us who don't have Early Grandmothers with attics, or an "in" with a dealer who reads the obituaries daily, must come by antiques the hard way, via the dump.

My affinity for dumps dates back further than my affinity for antiques. As a child, I lived three blocks from a Discount Dump. It was outside the high-rent district and it was every man for himself. I could canvass that dump in fifteen minutes in my bare feet, taking in every seatless wicker chair, canning jar carton, and soiled lampshade.

When we were married, the dump seemed a logical place to accessorize our home. Of course, I'm not attracted to all dumps. Certainly not the status dumps. They have their own curator. They're no fun at all. The curator lives in a small shack and spends his days cleaning and stacking old bricks, boxing sundry tools for easy inspecting, putting cast-offs in some kind of order and reading *House Beautiful*.

He usually greets you at the car with a brisk "May I help you?" When you say, "No, I'm just browsing," he follows along closely at your elbow, pointing out how that rusty auto crankcase would make an adorable planter for a solarium or how that little bamboo birdcage was owned by one bird in East Brunswick who slept a lot.

Other dumps are literally for the birds. Last summer in New England, for example, our garbage was becoming a conversation piece. Also, a health hazard. It was packaged and laid wall to wall throughout the kitchen, dining room, and half of the living room. When I asked a neighbor about it, she said, "You mean you haven't seen the dump? You have to go there yourself to believe it. Also to get rid of your garbage."

"*To the dump!*" I shouted wild with excitement.

"What are we going to buy?" asked one of the kids.

I ignored him. Why hadn't I thought of going to a dump in New England? It was probably lousy with Americana—Revolutionary troops marching over the wasteland dropping sabers by the dozens, pewter cups, personal letters to General Washington, signet rings—I could hardly contain myself.

We drove around a long, dusty road until finally we saw more seagulls than we had seen in the travel folders. So this was where they hung out! No sabers, no pewter cups, no antique goodies at all, just garbage. We backed up the car and started to unload. "What are we going to buy?" a small voice persisted. "I saw a rat," said another. "Of all the parents in the world, we had to get the funny ones," snarled the other one.

No matter. I will go on sewing my heirloom quilts on hot summer days and collecting old hatpins. They're lethal-looking, but they're marvelous for releasing the lock on the bathroom door when someone gets locked in. How the kids will divide all those Willkie buttons when they grow up is their problem.

"Mums the Word for Dad"

The news that the television networks are telecasting a record number of football games again this season is being met with some violent reactions from housewives across the country.

A few women in the Peaceful Acres development in Connecticut smashed television screens with broom handles. A group of California housewives focused national attention on the problem with their "Psychiatric Drive-Ins" open twenty-four hours a day during the football season. The most notable effort was a group from Virginia who heaved a football through Lady Bird Johnson's window with a terse message, "Would you want your daughter to spend a weekend with one?"

I talked briefly with a group of Ohio women. "It isn't the several hundred games we object to," said the spokesman. "This is only the beginning. Add to that the state and the local games and you've got ten or twelve football games being aired each day of the weekend. Roughly this amounts to one husband propped up in a chair like a dead sponge surrounded by bottle caps."

Heaven knows, men aren't the more talkative of the species. In fact, I have just come by some statistics that claim men average no more than six words a day in their own homes. Furthermore, their only hope of increasing this total is through conscientious massage of the throat muscles.

Even out of football season, men approach their

homes in the evening with all the detachment of a census taker. He garages the car, feels the stove to see if there's anything going for him, changes his clothes, eats, and retires to the living room where he reads the newspaper and engages in his nightly practice of finer isometrics—turning the television dial. He remains in a state of inertia until the sound of his deep, labored breathing puts the cork on another confetti-filled evening.

The frustration of wives who want to talk with someone who isn't teething is pitiful. While some accept the silent evenings as a way of life, others try desperately to change it. When one woman attempted to apologize at the dinner table for the children—who were performing a native tribal dance through the mashed potatoes—her husband looked up sharply from his plate, glanced at the children, and shrieked, "You mean they're all ours?" (five words)

One of the most disappointing attempts at starting a conversation is, "What kind of a day did you have, dear?" One husband reportedly answered by kicking the dog, another went pale and couldn't form words, another bit his necktie in half. Some just stared blankly as if they hadn't heard the question. Only one man formed a verbal reply. It was "Shut up, Clara."

Other women work constantly to raise the odds.

WIFE: Know what we're having for dinner? Braised cue tips with sumac topping, onion balls in sour cream, and a bird of paradise nesting in a floating sea of chicken fat.

HUSBAND: I had it for lunch. (5 words)

WIFE: There's another man, Lester. We're civilized people. Let's talk about it.

HUSBAND: Wait till the commercial. (4 words)

WIFE: I broke my leg last week, Wesley. I was waiting for you to notice. See how well I'm doing on crutches?

HUSBAND: Get me a cold one while you're up. (8 words, but he was stoned)

"With the football season it's worse," said a small blonde. "My husband sits down at eight o'clock on a Friday night and never takes his eyes off the screen. I say to him, 'You wanta eat now, Ed?' and he just sits there. I say to him, 'You comin' to bed now, Ed?' and he just sits there. I said to him the other night, 'The woman is here to buy the kids, Ed,' and he didn't move a muscle. I finally took his pulse. It was weird."

"I know what you mean, honey," said a small brunette. "My Fred says to me, 'We need a color TV set. The networks have eighty-three games in color this year.' I said to him, 'If you like to see all that red plasma and those blue bruises, it's okay with me. Frankly, I like to see a man with his front teeth.' He gets real sore. Plugs the high school game into his ear, puts one eyeball on the state game and the other on the National Football League and yells, 'Keep those kids quiet.' We don't have kids."

"If you're thinking of joining them, forget it!" said another voice. "I used to watch football games at college and loved 'em. But on TV! First, I sat through shots of last week's game, then a preview of this week's line-up. When the game finally started, we saw it in live action, then slow motion, then stop action and instant replay. After that we switched to another camera to see if he got a better 'side' of the ball carrier. At the half we had highlights of the first half, followed by interviews of people who chewed over the way they played the first half and predicted what they were going to do the second half. Finally, the game over, we had a recap of the game by the announcer topped off by fifteen minutes of Scoreboard."

"Then what's the answer?" someone asked.

"We fight back with *Peyton Place*," said a newly-wed snapping her fingers with inspiration.

"Here's the deal. We get the network to bring on *Peyton Place* thirty minutes early and watch exciting shots from last week's show, followed by previews of this week's action. Then we have Betty Furness interview Old Man Peyton and his grandson just for a little flavor.

"When the action starts, the camera will replay in slow motion all the scenes, then stop-action all the dirty parts and have an instant replay of all the violent parts. After that, we'd switch to another camera for another view of Betty Cord in her negligee. At the 'break' they'd show action from the first half followed by an interview by Ann Landers, who would chew over the first half and offer advice on how it should be played the second half.

"When the show is over, Dr. Joyce Brothers

would tally up the marriages for each, the divorces, the surgery, and their standing in the league."

"It's just got to work," said a quiet brunette. "I'm so desperate, I'm beginning to talk to my kids."

November 3—January 1

Eat your heart out, Heloise!

It happens every November. I don't know why. I suffer an attack of domesticity. I want to bustle about in a starched apron, bake bread, iron sheets, and make my own soap. I want to beat mattresses, mend cleaning rags, wax the driveway, and can green beans. I want to dust the coffee table and arrange it with a vase of flowers and a copy of Norman Vincent Peale. In short, I am nauseating.

I call it my "Eat Your Heart Out, Heloise" syndrome. It's like a strange power that overcomes me and lasts no longer than two days. During that span I can hardly remember what I have done or why I have done it. All I know is when I return to my old self, I usually have a pot of ox tail soup brewing and am sitting in my rocker reading, "How to Remove Kite String Marks from the Spouting," and wondering what I am doing here.

Last November's seizure was a doozie. When I returned to my slovenly ways I discovered I had rearranged the furniture, giving it all the personality of a bus station restroom. Ignoring the advice of experts, I washed the draperies, causing the lining to sag like a toddler's underwear.

I discovered I had gone to town and returned home with twenty yards of red corduroy for bedspreads. Heaven knows what I would have purchased if I owned a sewing machine. They tell me I alerted the entire household, lined them up on the front lawn and insisted we begin fertilizing early for spring, putting in the screens and beating the rugs. I have never viewed such sickening efficiency in my life. The woodwork glistened. The windows sparkled. I had even taken the paper clips out of the tea canister and replaced them with tea.

I have talked with other women about this strange phenomenon and they assure me it is normal. This return to order is sparked by cool weather, an anticipation of the holidays and a large guilt complex that I shouldn't be enjoying myself so much with the children in school.

I have found that a cold shower shocks me back to my slovenly ways. I know I am slovenly because I gave myself one of those magazine quizzes once to find out if I was "children-geared," "husband-geared," or "house-geared."

The "child-geared" mother often referred to her husband as what's-his-name and took a tape recorder to the labor room to record her suffering so she could play it at her children's weddings. I wasn't that. A "husband-geared" woman fed her husband steak and the kids hamburger. I wasn't that. A "home-geared" woman fixed up the basement for the family to live in and cried whenever someone splashed water on her kitchen tiles. I wasn't that.

According to my score, I wasn't crazy about any one of the three. In fact, in homemaking I only scored five out of a possible hundred points. (I changed the paper in my birdcage with some kind of regularity.)

What makes this confession so incongruous is that fifteen years ago, I did a three-times-a-week newspaper column on housecleaning. As I remember it, one day I slipped out of my office for just a moment to go to the coffee machine. When I returned I had been elected by the department as its next homemaking editor. (Incidentally, newspapering is the only profession in the world so full of finks you have to have your own food taster.) In short, I had been had.

I called it "Operation Dustrag" and set about advising the housewives of the city how to develop a positive attitude toward cleaning so they wouldn't become cranky and irritable with their family. I assured them if they stuck with me and my thrice-weekly household cleaning schedule, we could restore order to their houses and literally tap-dance our way to House Beautiful. (I think I promised them prosperity, an end to World War II, and a cure for the common dustball, but no one got legal about it.)

What really amazed me was how seriously women took their housekeeping chores. To some, it was a way of life. Their plaintive pleas rolled in daily: "How do I clean my alabaster?" (Madam, I didn't know birds got dirty.) "How can I prevent scrub water from running down my arms to my elbows?" (Hang by your feet when you wash the walls.) "Is there a formula for removing chocolate from overstuffed furniture?" (No, but there's one for beating the stuffings out of the little boy who ate the chocolate on the overstuffed furniture.)

After several irate calls from women who had tried my little balls of paraffin in their rinse water to make the chintz look chintzier—one woman said if her curtains had wicks they'd burn right through Advent—I promised my editor I would try these things at home first. My home began to take on all the excitement of a missile at countdown.

I concocted a mixture of wall cleaner that nearly blew our house off the foundation. I tried samples from manufacturers that took the coin dots right out of the kitchen tile. I had so many sample-type gloves, I wore them for everything from cleaning out the dryer lint trap to shaking hands with my husband.

My succinct advice went on day after day.

To make a towel for the children's bath, simply take two towels and monogram each with an F. One F will represent face, the other, feet. Then, simply toss both towels into a corner on the floor. This sounds primitive, but after three days they won't even want to know which F they're using, and at least the towels will always be where they belong, on the floor.

For mildew or musty odor on the shower curtain, simply take a sharp pair of scissors and whack it off. Actually, the more mildew, the more interesting the shower curtains become.

To clean piano keys, try having your children

wear chamois gloves moistened with clear water. I daresay their practice sessions won't sound any different and you'll have a clean keyboard.

To remove gum stains, pick off as much gum as possible, then soften by applying egg whites. An egg white stain is better to live with than chewing gum.

A sterilizer that has boiled dry will make an interesting conversation piece on the ceiling over your stove. Small rolls of dust under the bed will entertain small children for hours. (Likewise in-laws, malicious neighbors, and the Board of Health.)

The end of "Operation Dustrag" came as a shock to no one. It was entered in statewide competition under the category "columns." As I sat at the banquet table listening to the names of winners, I was numb. If I won something it was another year of "Help Stamp Out Dirt." If I didn't, I couldn't trust myself to go to the watercooler without drawing some other dreary chore.

Needless to say, the column went unnoticed. By Wednesday of the following week, I had been assigned to Society where "the bride walks to the altar on the arm of her father" and other funny things happen.

Several years later when I retired to actually keep house, I discovered the real keyword to housecleaning was incentive. I was a fool not to have realized it before. There had to be a reason for cleaning house. At our place, the motivation seems to center about one word: *party*.

When we can no longer "dig out," we simply announce to twenty or thirty of our most intimate friends, we are going to entertain. Then we swing into action. My husband knocks out a wall or two, gives the baseboards that long-promised second coat, changes the furnace filter, replaces light bulbs where there has been no light for five years, squirts glazing compound into holes and wall cracks, and hot-mops the driveway.

The children are in charge of scouting the sandbox and toy chests for good silverware, hauling away the debris under their beds, disposing of a garbage full of bottles and returning the library books.

I have my own busy work. I discard all the jelly glasses and replace them with "matched" crystal, exchange all the dead houseplants for new ones from the nursery, and of course plan the menu and the guest list.

Our parties have always been memorable. We always have the wet picture frames that someone invariably leans against and has to be cut out of with sharp scissors. We always have the freshly laid fire in the sparkling clean grate and the closed draft that sends our guests coughing into the dark streets. We always have one guest who is rude enough to inquire why our living room wall is sagging and suggests perhaps our attic is a little overloaded.

The "day after party day" then is always designated "Clean the attic day." Now let me offer this bit of advice. If your marriage is already a little unstable to begin with, forget the attic. We never do, but then we've been written up several times in the *Ladies' Home Journal* feature, "Can This Marriage Be Saved?"

Usually we let down the attic stairs—which the Good Lord knows is enough of a physical strain the day after a party—and we scale the heights together. After considerable effort, my husband speaks, "Let me begin by saying that you can't be illogical or sentimental about this stuff."

"Well, that's pretty pompous coming from a man who still has his Jack Armstrong signet ring, a book of shoe stamps from World War II, and his first bow wow!"

"Those are collector's items," he explains. "That's different. I'm talking about junk. Right now, we are going to establish a rule of thumb for saving things."

We sit down on a carton marked RAIN-SOAKED HALLOWEEN MASKS. "Now," he continues, "if we can't wear it, frame it, sell it, or hang it on the Christmas tree, out it goes! Understand?"

At the end of two hours we haul four pitiful items to the curb: a broken hula hoop, an airline calendar showing Wiley Post spinning a propeller, an empty varnish can, and one tire chain.

"This is ridiculous," he growls, crawling back into the attic. "Let's take this stuff one by one. What's this?"

"That's our summer cabin inventory."

"What summer cabin?"

"The one we're going to buy someday. So far, we have a studio couch, a lamp with a bowling pin base, six Shirley Temple cereal bowls, two venetian blinds, and a chair with a rope seat."

"And this?" he sighs.

"That's my motherhood insurance. They're all my old maternity clothes, bottle sterilizer, potty chair, layettes, baby bed, and car seat. You lay a hand on this stuff and we'll both live to regret it."

"And all this trash?"

"That belongs to you. Consecutive license plates from 1937, old fertilizer bags, a rusted sickle, a picture of the Cincinnati Reds, autographed by Bucky Walters, the medical dictionary wrapped in a plain, brown wrapper, cartons of English quizzes from the class of 1953, eighteen empty antifreeze cans, a box marked 'Old Furnace Filters' and a bait box that is trying to tell us something."

"Okay," he sighs, "I won't raise a finger. Put it out at the curb and call the junk man."

I grinned. *"The junk man.* You've got to be kidding. Gone is the simple, little peddler who used to beat a path to your curb in search of a bushel basket of cast-offs. Gone are the agency trucks who used to be in your driveway before you got the receiver back on the hook. Hustling junk is a real art nowadays."

And I meant it. It had been my experience that if you're stuck with an old swing and gym set, it is easier to start a second family than to try to unload it. If you're saddled with an extension ladder with a couple of rungs missing, hire an

adventurous painter with no dependents. As for
having a car in the driveway that won't run, fella,
that's about as thrilling to move as a dead horse!

On the day the agency trucks go by, I find myself running around the garage like a frustrated
auctioneer, spreading my wares out attractively in
the driveway and adjusting spots to highlight the
plastics. "Boy, have I got goodies for you today,"
I yell. "I've got a set of corn holders, a size-twelve
wedding gown worn only once, a box of Mason
jars that will drive antique collectors mad, and a
carton of coat hangers that are still in their pro-
ductive years. That is, if you'll take this bed.

"You don't want the bed? Tell you what I'm

gonna do. I'll throw in two pairs of ice skates, a garden hose, and a pressure cooker. No deal? All right, sir, you seem like a man of some discernment. As a special offer this week, I am offering your truck first choice on a nearly new beer cooler, thirty-five back issues of *Boy's Life*, and a hand-painted Nativity scene. If you'll take the bed off my hands.

"Really, sir, you do drive a hard bargain. To show faith, I'll tempt fate by giving away my layettes. That is positively my final offer. After all, this bed is a real find. It was only used by a little old lady from Pasadena who had insomnia. What do you mean, who told me that ridiculous story? You did when I bought the bed at your outlet store for ten dollars."

"Your story is touching," said my husband, "but what are we going to do with all this trash?"

I shrugged. "Bring it downstairs and we'll plan our next party."

"One More 'Ho Ho Ho' and I'll Paste You in the Mouth"

"Who cares if it fits? She takes everything back anyway. Billie Joe, if you get hit by a truck, the next time I'll leave you at home! Why did I wear these boots? It never fails. I wear boots and the sun comes out! Will you please stop pulling at me. I did buy my Christmas cards last January. I just can't find them. Cheap stuff. They always put out cheap stuff at Christmas. Did you see that man shove me? Same to you, fella!

"Don't dilly-dally to look at store windows. I've got all my baking to do, the house to decorate, presents to wrap, the cards to mail . . . mailman! I forgot to get something for the mailman. Boy, everyone's got their hand out at Christmas, haven't they. Well, did you see that? I was here first and she hopped in right in front of me. We oughta get numbers like they do at the butcher counter. That would take care of those pushy ones. Same to you, fella!

"I don't care if the box fits, just any box will do. So don't send it. Let me occupy a whole bus with it. You tell the policeman when I occupy a whole seat that your truck driver couldn't deliver it. Lines . . . lines . . . I'll have to get in line to die . . . Billie Joe, you're too old for the Santa Claus bit. Don't think I don't know why you want to stand in line . . . for a lousy candy cane. You'd stand in line if they were handing out free headaches.

"What music? I don't hear any music. I think I'll just give Uncle Walter the money. He's always liked money. In fact, he's never happy with anything else you give him. And that gift exchange. Wish we could get out of that. I always get something cheap back. My feet hurt. You'd think some man would get off his duff and give a woman a seat. No one cares about anyone anymore. I don't hear any music.

"My headache's back. Wish I could take off

these boots. I think we're ready to . . . wait a minute, Billie Joe. I forgot Linda's birthday. Doesn't that beat all. It's what she gets for being born on Christmas Day. Now, I've got to run up to the fourth floor and fight those crowds all over again. You wait here with the shopping bags and don't wander, do you hear? No sense running you all over the place. Boy, some people have a fat nerve having a birthday on Christmas Day. I don't know of anyone who has the gall to be born on Christmas Day. What did you say, Billie Joe?"

"I said, 'I know SomeOne.' "

"Deck the Halls with Boughs of Holly . . ."

My idea of decorating the house for Christmas is to light up the rooftop with bright strings of bulbs, drape garlands of greenery from pillar to post, flash spots on bauble-studded trees, garnish the garage door with a life-sized Santa Claus, and perch a small elf on the mailbox that says "Y-U-L-E" where his teeth should be.

My husband's idea of decorating for Christmas is to replace the forty-watt bulb in the porch light with a sixty-watter.

"You act like I'm against Christmas or something," he said defensively. "Why, no one gets any more excited about the holidays than I do."

"Yeah, we've noticed how emotional you get when all those cars line up and breathless little children point to our house and say, 'Wowie, that's some sixty-watt porch light bulb!' "

"The trouble with you," he continued, "is that you overdo. If you'd just keep it simple. But no! You can't rest until you have me shinnying over the rooftops in a snowstorm with a shorted string of light bulbs in my teeth."

"I don't want to talk about it. You've been crabby ever since you dropped your GI insurance. Heaven knows, it isn't the children's fault."

"What do you want to say dumb things like that for? And where are you going with those bulbs?"

"I am going to hang them on the bare branches of the tree in the front yard."

"I hope they're weatherproof. Remember the year you hung those little silver birds from the branches? I don't think I shall ever forget looking up from my breakfast and seeing those little feathered devils disintegrating before my eyes. It was like watching their intestines unravel."

"You've told that story a thousand times. These bulbs are waterproof."

"Junk . . . nothing but junk!" he said, pawing through the boxes. "I wouldn't be caught dead standing out there in the snow draping this wretched stuff over the trees."

"I know. You're the type who would buy roller skates for Tiny Tim!"

"Do you have a ladder?"

"I don't need one. I'm going to balance a bar stool on the milk box."

"I knew it," he said, "you just couldn't stand to

see me sit in here where it's warm. You've got to involve me in your Disneyland extravaganza. All right, we might just as well do the job right. First, I'll make a sketch of the tree and we'll figure out mathematically how many blue, gold, and red bulbs it will take to make it look right."

"You ruin everything," I grumbled. "You and your planning. Did anyone ever tell you you're about as much fun as a fever blister under the mistletoe?"

"I tell you what," he shouted, jumping out of his chair. "Let's keep it simple this year. I'll put a sixty-watt light bulb in the porch light and we'll all stand around and sing, 'Good King Wenceslaus.' You know, I bet I'm the only one here who knows the second stanza by heart . . ."

"Up On the Housetop Reindeers Pause . . . Out Jumps Good Old Santa Claus . . ."

If there is one man singularly responsible for the children of this country, it's Doctor Spock. (That reads strange, but I don't know how to fix it.)

What I'm getting at is, this man is the great white father of every parent who has bungled his way through a vaporizer tent or a two-year-old's tantrum. Why, there was a time when, if Doctor Spock had told me to use one-legged diapers, I would have done so without question.

Now he has shaken me up. He has said there is

no Santa Claus and urges us to tell our children the truth.

"Kids, brace yourselves," I said. "Doctor Spock says there is no Santa Claus and that I should never have taken you to see a live one in the first place because his behavior is noisy and his clothes are strange. Also, he inspires greed."

They looked at each other, obviously stunned.

"That's just not true," one said. "You know there's a Santa Claus, just as you believe there are fairies dancing on our lawn."

"Knock it off with the 'Yes, Virginia' bit. I told you that. Now I'm telling you Santa Claus is an upsetting experience. There can't be a Santa Claus."

"There can be if you want him to be," they said cautiously.

"I don't know," I hesitated. "He does have a certain magic that makes people happy and kind toward one another. He does keep the work economy steady for elves and gives seasonal employment to reindeer. Heaven knows, he has your father spending more money than he earns and all of us crawling around on the rooftops with strings of lights in our teeth. I don't know what to believe anymore. I've always had such faith in Dr. Spock!"

"Have you ever seen Dr. Spock?" asked one.

"No, but . . . *now cut that out!* I know he exists. The point is how can I go on believing in a Santa Claus who parachutes from a helicopter over a shopping center parking lot, breaks his leg and ends up in a hospital?"

"Well, where else would you go with a broken leg?" asked another.

"The point is, kids, he's merely a mortal man, and mortal men don't go around pushing their fat stomachs down skinny chimneys."

"Of course he's mortal," they explained. "Otherwise, how could he have eaten all those cookies you put out for him last year?"

"That's right," I said excitedly, "he really did come, didn't he, and left me that dreamy black jacket that I *know* your father wouldn't have bought. You know something? I believe in Yogi Bear, and his behavior is noisy. I believe in Phyllis Diller and her clothes are strange. I believe in the Bureau of Internal Revenue and they're not exactly philanthropic. Kids, there is a Santa Claus!"

As the curtain closed on this domestic scene, the seven-year-old leaned over to whisper in his father's ear, "Boy, Dad, she gets harder to convince every year!"

Memo to: Mr. Kravitz, principal
From: Katherine Courageous
Re: Christmas Pageant

The Christmas Pageant will be a little late this year. Possibly January 23 if that date is agreeable with you.

Although an enthusiastic Pageant Committee has been at work since October, we have had some problems. To begin with, there were several on the committee who insisted on making a musical out of the Nativity story. At one point, we had the precision drill team making a "B" for Bethlehem in the background while a trio of baton twirlers marched around the stable. This idea was scratched when someone remembered batons hadn't been invented yet.

Remember how excited we were about the donation of a "live" donkey? Our custodian, Mr. Webber, does not share our excitement. Although his phrasing was a little less delicate, he intimated that if the animal was not "gym-floor trained" by January 23, we could jolly well go back to papier-mâché. He also said (this is quoted out of context) that the smell of the beast wouldn't be out of the auditorium in time for the Lions' annual Chili Supper next May.

We have had a few casting problems to plague us. I had to award the Mary, Mother of Jesus, role to Michael Pushy. (His parents donated the donkey.) Michael refused to wear a wig, which might be a little confusing to the audience, but I'll make a special note on the program. I've had great pressure from Mrs. Reumschusser. It seems her son, Kevin, is a Ted Mack loser who plays "Rudolph the Red-Nosed Reindeer" on the spoons. I am using him at intermission.

The costumes didn't arrive until three days ago from the Beelzebub Costume Company of New Jersey. There was obviously an error. Instead of thirty Roman soldier uniforms, there were thirty pink suede bunny leotards with matching ears. It was quite apparent to me that after I had tried a few on our "little people," this was not our order. Miss Heinzie and myself couldn't help but speculate that somewhere there is a tired businessman with a Roman soldier sitting on his lap.

The shop department is not yet finished with the special scaffold for parents wishing to take pictures and tape-record the program. We felt this necessary after Mr. Happenstance's accident last year when he panned in too closely and fell into the manger.

I hate to ask, but could you please do something diplomatic with Mrs. Ringading? She has threatened the refreshments committee with her traditional whiskey balls and rum cookies. You know what a fire hazard they created last year.

In view of the fact that two of our shepherds have diarrhea, we respectfully request the Pageant be postponed until January 23 or after.

"God Rest Ye Merry Gentlemen . . ."

That clicking sound you hear about this time is the result of fourteen million husbands pushing the panic button. They are pushing it because they are hours away from Christmas and still have no gift for what's-her-name, mother of his four children.

One of the more conscientious husbands can always be counted upon to come up with the item

mentioned last July when his wife snarled, "What I need around this house is a decent plunger!" Inspired by his power of retention he will sprint out and have a plunger wrapped as a gift. No one will be more surprised than he when his wife cups it over his mouth!

Others will seek out the advice of young secretaries who have read all the magazines and know that happiness is an immoral nightgown. Depending upon the type of wife she will (a) return the nightgown and buy a sandwich grill, or (b) smile gratefully and wear it to bed under a coat, or (c) check out the secretary.

For the most part husbands are cast adrift in a sea of confusion and bewilderment, sniffing perfumes, fingering sequins, and being ever on the lookout for a woman who looks like his wife's size.

Don't ask me why my heart goes out to these

desperate men. Maybe it's that time of year. Maybe it's the den mother in me. Maybe I have really forgotten the rotten gift I found in my stocking last year: a gift certificate for a flu shot! At any rate, some of my women friends have asked me to pass along to men some guideposts to shopping.

First, women are never what they seem to be. There is the woman you see and there is the woman who is hidden. Buy the gift for the woman who is hidden.

Outwardly, women are a lot of things. They're frugal souls who save old bread wrappers and store antifreeze during the summer in the utility room. They're practical souls who buy all black accessories and cut their own hair. They're conservative souls who catch rainwater in a saucepan, and take their own popcorn to the drive-in. They're modest souls who clutch at sofa pillows to cover their exposed knees. Some still won't smoke in front of their mothers. So, they're dependable, brave, trusting, loyal, and true? Gentlemen, take another look.

Hidden is the woman who sings duets with Barbra Streisand and pretends Robert Goulet is singing to her. Who hides out in the bathroom and experiments with her eyes. Who would wear a pair of hostess pajamas if everyone wouldn't fall down laughing. Who reads burlesque ads when she thinks no one is watching. Who would like to feed the kids early without feeling guilty.

Who thinks about making ceramics, writing a play and earning a paycheck.

That's all the help I'm going to give you birds. You've got just a few hours to get to know your wife. If you still think she rates a monogrammed chain saw, that's up to you!

There is a wonderful story of Christmas, about a great cathedral whose chimes would not ring until, as the legend goes, the real gift of love had been placed on its altar.

Year after year, great kings would offer up the riches of their land, but the chimes would not ring.

One year, a small waif in a shabby coat entered the great cathedral and proceeded down the long aisle. He was stopped and asked what he could possibly give that kings had not already offered. The small boy looked down and hopelessly examined his possessions. Finally, he took off his coat and laid it gently at the foot of the altar.

The chimes rang.

To receive a gift, molded from love and sacrifice, selected with care and tied up with all the excitement the giver has to offer, is indeed rare. They don't come along often, but when they do, cherish them.

I remember the year I received my first "Crumb Scraper." It was fashioned from half a paper plate and a lace doily. I have never seen such shining pride from the little four-year-old girl who asked, "You don't have one already, do you?"

The crumb scraper defied description. When

you used one part of the cardboard to guide the crumbs into the plate, they bounced and scattered through the air like dancing snowflakes. But it didn't matter.

I remember a bookmark created from a piece of cardboard with a picture of Jesus crayoned on the front. It was one of those one-of-a-kind collector's items that depicted Jesus as a blond with a crew cut. Crayoned underneath the picture were words to live by, *OH COME HOLY SPURT*.

My favorite, though, was a small picture framed with construction paper, and reinforced with colored toothpicks. Staring out at me was a picture of Robbie Wagner. "Do you like it?" asked the small giver excitedly. "I used a hundred gallons of paste on it. Don't put it near heat or the toothpicks will fall off."

I could only admit it was beautiful, but why Robbie instead of his own picture? "The scissors slipped and I goofed my picture up," he explained. "Robbie had an extra one."

There were other gifts—the year of the bent coat hanger adorned with twisted nose tissues and the year of the matchbox covered with sewing scraps and fake pearls—and then the small home-made gifts were no more.

I still receive gifts at Christmas. They are thoughtful. They are wrapped with care. They are what I need.

But oh, how I wish I could bend low and receive a gift of cardboard and library paste so that I

218 *AT WIT'S END*

could hear the chimes ring at Christmas just once
more.

Let Faith Be Your Guide

I waited until the end of the book to tell you why
I wrote it.

I figured if you got this far, you might need an
answer. If you didn't get this far, it wouldn't
make any difference.

It goes back to the first time I saw authoress
Faith Baldwin in a full-page magazine ad admon-
ishing, "It's a shame more women don't take up
writing." I said aloud, "Ain't it the truth, Faith."

She looked directly at me and said, "If you're a
woman who wants to get more out of life, don't
bury your talents under a mountain of dishes.
Writing will provide a wonderful means of emotional release and self-expression, to say nothing
of the extra income. You don't have to go to an
office with half your mind on your household,
wondering if it rains, did you close the windows.
(I liked that.) Even though you are tied down to
your home, you can still experience fulfillment."

Faith, you had me pegged, all right. I had been
a little bored at home. (A *little* bored. Who am I
kidding? I was picking lint off the refrigerator.)
So, I began to write about what I knew best: the
American Housewife. Very frankly, I couldn't
think of anyone in the world who rated a better
press.

On television she is depicted as a woman consumed with her own bad breath, rotten coffee, underarm perspiration, and irregularity problems. In slick magazines, she is forever being brought to task for not trying to "look chi chi on her way to the labor room," for not nibbling on her husband's ear by candlelight, and for not giving enough of those marvy little intimate dinner parties for thirty or so.

In cartoons, she is a joke. In erudite groups, an exception. In the movies, the housewife is always the one with the dark hair and the no-bust. Songwriters virtually ignore her. She's the perennial bad driver, the traditional joiner, the target of men who visualize her in a pushbutton world. (All of which are contingent on service repairmen whose promises are as good as the word of Judas.)

If she complains, she's neurotic. If she doesn't, she's stupid. If she stays home with the children, she is a boring clod who is overprotective and will cling to her children till they are forty-eight years old. If she leaves her home to work, she is selfish, ambitious, and her children will write dirty words in nice places.

Faith didn't tell me about the secondhand typewriter that tightened up when it rained or had a "7", an "s", and an "o" that stuck. She didn't tell me how I'd have to set up a table at the end of my bed and how my files would spill over into the bathroom. (The Internal Revenue Service didn't buy it either. They're still questioning my expenditure for a new shower curtain for my office.)

She didn't tell me about the kids reading over my shoulder and saying, "What's so funny about that?" or interrupting one of my rare literary spasms to tell me that if you filled a washcloth full of water and squeezed it, it would take fourteen drops to fill your navel.

She didn't tell me about the constancy of a column that makes no allowances for holidays, vacations, literary droughts, or kidney infections.

She just said, "Write about home situations, kids—things that only a woman who stayed at home could write about."

At first, I began writing for one woman. I visualized her as a moderately young woman, overkidsed and underpatienced with four years of college and chapped hands all year around. None of the popular images seemed to fit her. She never had a moment alone, yet she was lonely most of the time. She worried more about toilet training her fourteen-month-old than Premier Chou En-lai. And the BOW (Big Outside World) was almost a fable to her.

After a while I began to visualize other women as I wrote. The woman with no children who made a career out of going to baby showers, the teenagers with wires coming out of their ears, hair cascading over their eyes and looking for the world like hairy toasters, the older woman who gagged every time someone called her a senior citizen, and the career girl who panicked when she saw the return of the dress with waistlines and belts. ("God only knows what I've grown under these shifts for four years.")

Through the columns and through the mails, we shared some common ground together. It was—in essence—group therapy. They'd write, "Honey, do something about your picture. You look like a fifty-year-old woman who has just been told by her obstetrician that she's pregnant!" Or they'd say, "You had to tell the world about my urban renewal living room, didn't you? Are you sure you don't live next door to me?" Sometimes their loyalty knew no bounds. "Erma, you're the only woman I let my husband take to bed with him. (Via the Sunday Section) He says you're like an old friend."

Other readers were not so enamored. "Who do you fancy career girls think you are, sitting in a plush office telling us housewives what it's like?" Or the note from an obvious health faddist, "Lady, you make me sick!"

These women and many more make up this book. They represent a myriad of moods, situations, frustrations, and humor that make up a housewife.

When my son learned that I was writing a book his first reaction was, "It isn't going to be dirty, is it?" I turned to him and said, "Kid, I couldn't get this thing banned in a Christian Science reading room." Then, that began to worry me a bit. Other than a small portion dealing with the sex education of our son in the fourth chapter, I have acted like Sex and the Married Housewife do not live in co-existence with one another.

To be perfectly honest, I didn't know how to handle it. I grew up in an era when sex education was a dirty word. I didn't read *Little Orphan Annie* until I was twelve because Mother thought Daddy Warbucks was a dirty old man. I didn't even know *National Geographic* ran pictures until after I was married. Daddy always cut them out.

I can remember, of course, slipping a book by Kathleen Norris off the shelf and putting it between the pages of *Girl's Life*. The heroine, usually named Hiliary, was "pouty, wild, untamed, spoiled, breathless and rich." She always had sensuous lips. (I thought that meant a fever blister until I was fourteen.) The hero was usually Brad who was stubborn, tough, square-jawed, and who spoke huskily when he made love. My eyeballs fairly popped as I got to the meaty parts where Brad and Hiliary met to embrace. Then, it was always the same. "The fire in the fireplace flickered and died." I don't know how many books I plowed through where "The fire in the fireplace flickered and died," leaving me in a world of ignorance and speculation. I hadn't the foggiest notion what was going on while the fire was going out. So you can blame my omission on Kathleen Norris!

I have purposely not let my husband read the manuscript. With a book without sex in it, I can use all the lawsuits I can get to publicize it.

I could be terribly heroic and say I wrote the

book because the American Housewife deserved a new, honest image.

I could be terribly sentimental and say I wrote the book because four men have always told me I could do it when I knew I couldn't. There is James W. Harris, my high school journalism teacher, who first had the kindness to "laugh when I sat down at the typewriter." There is Glenn Thompson, editor of the Dayton *Journal Herald*, who took me out of a utility room and is responsible for any measure of success I enjoy. There is Tom Dorsey, director of Newsday Specials, who took a "flyer" on an unknown writer whose credits consisted of bad checks and grocery lists. And not the least my husband, Bill, who when I cling to his knees and beg for criticism of my work, has the wisdom not to give it to me.

To be honest, however, I will have to admit that I wrote the book for the original model—the one who was overkidsed, underpatienced, with four years of college and chapped hands all year around. I knew if I didn't follow Faith's advice and laugh a little at myself, then I would surely cry.

BESTSELLERS

☐	BEGGAR ON HORSEBACK—Thorpe	23091-0	1.50
☐	THE TURQUOISE—Seton	23088-0	1.95
☐	STRANGER AT WILDINGS—Brent	23085-6	1.95
	(Pub. in England as Kirkby's Changeling)		
☐	MAKING ENDS MEET—Howar	23084-8	1.95
☐	THE LYNMARA LEGACY—Gaskin	23060-0	1.95
☐	THE TIME OF THE DRAGON—Eden	23059-7	1.95
☐	THE GOLDEN RENDEZVOUS—MacLean	23055-4	1.75
☐	TESTAMENT—Morrell	23033-3	1.95
☐	CAN YOU WAIT TIL FRIDAY?—	23022-8	1.75
	Olson, M.D.		
☐	HARRY'S GAME—Seymour	23019-8	1.95
☐	TRADING UP—Lea	23014-7	1.95
☐	CAPTAINS AND THE KINGS—Caldwell	23069-4	2.25
☐	"I AIN'T WELL—BUT I SURE AM	23007-4	1.75
	BETTER"—Lair		
☐	THE GOLDEN PANTHER—Thorpe	23006-6	1.50
☐	IN THE BEGINNING—Potok	22980-7	1.95
☐	DRUM—Onstott	22920-3	1.95
☐	LORD OF THE FAR ISLAND—Holt	22874-6	1.95
☐	DEVIL WATER—Seton	23633-1	2.25
☐	CSARDAS—Pearson	22885-1	1.95
☐	CIRCUS—MacLean	22875-4	1.95
☐	WINNING THROUGH INTIMIDATION—	23589-0	2.25
	Ringer		
☐	THE POWER OF POSITIVE	23499-1	1.95
	THINKING—Peale		
☐	VOYAGE OF THE DAMNED—	22449-X	1.75
	Thomas & Witts		
☐	THINK AND GROW RICH—Hill	23504-1	1.95
☐	EDEN—Ellis	23543-2	1.95

Buy them at your local bookstores or use this handy coupon for ordering: